American Landscape

Heartland Books

ISBN: 0-6157-6090-2
ISBN-13: 9780615760902 (Heartland Books–Imprint)

Copyright Registration: TX 1-737-118

While the author has made every effort to provide accurate telephone numbers and Internet addresses at the time of publication, neither the publisher nor the author assumes any responsibility for errors, or for changes that occur after publication. Further, the publisher does not have any control over and does not assume any responsibility for author or third party websites or their content.

PUBLISHER'S NOTE

American Landscape is a work of fiction. Names, characters, places, and incidents either are the product of the author's imagination or are used fictionally, and any resemblance to actual persons living or dead, or locales is entirely coincidental.

American Landscape

A Novel
By

Robert M Tucker

Heartland Books
2013

Contents

There is a mysterious cycle in human events. To some generations much is given.
Of other generations much is expected.
This generation of Americans has a rendezvous with destiny.

(Franklin Delano Roosevelt, 1936)

American Landscape is a sweeping generational saga of loyalty and betrayal at the beginning of J. Edgar Hoover's reign of surveillance and blackmail of innocent people in 1920.

Hoover and his deputy henchman, Clyde Tolson, have assigned young FBI recruit Howard Gimble to stop the union organization work of Yelena Ivanov, whom Howard has known and loved since their childhood years together.

Within the scope of world shattering events, the lives of Howard and Yelena, Ev Carmody, a Federal Marshal, and Randolph Logan, a young newspaper reporter, converge in the small desert town of Mesa, New Mexico.

Ev Carmody, a man of honor, is obsessed in his battles against corporate greed and the exploitation of American citizens and natural resources. Yelena and Howard enter into his landscape, a microcosm of immigrants, frontier drifters, and Navajo Indians.

In a final clash of cultures and future hopes and destinies, Howard, Yelena, and Ev and Randolph Logan unite together to fight tyranny and injustice in the American Dream under the shadow of the impending Second World War.

Randolph Logan's stories of the New Mexico incident about Yelena Ivanov and the FBI published in The Mesa Independent had caught the attention of the Albuquerque Journal editor in chief who republished and distributed the series in the United Press throughout the country. The unauthorized news stories incurred the wrath of J. Edgar Hoover, Director of the FBI, whose mission was to destroy the lives of those who were involved.

I
LANDSCAPE

Chapter 1
DECEPTION

Howard's first glimpse of Yelena Ivanov was through the window of his moving Pullman railcar. Although he recognized her in an instant, she did not resemble the teenage girl he carried in his memory from childhood. The image of her standing on the station platform flashed by as though she did not actually exist in that time and place.

When the train finally screeched and clashed and ground to a halt expelling great clouds of hissing steam and filling the air with an elongated squeal of metal on metal, his car was thirty yards beyond the platform. He would have to wander back through the passenger compartments and discover her in a different reality.

During Howard's briefing back in Washington, Assistant FBI Director Clyde Tolson had given him information as to the car Yelena would be in. Although she was berthed in a Pullman, her fare was as a passenger in regular seating. So Howard would have to do a little roaming to locate her. He left his berth and went out into the lounge area of his car which was filling with passengers coming on board. He took a sofa chair off to one side that allowed him a partial view of the platform back down the track, but not sufficient to see all the passengers.

He would give her time to settle into her seat. To suddenly appear or discover her would be likely to raise her suspicion. As it were, he was not comfortable with the deceit he had been ordered to perform. He was basically a good-hearted man with integrity. Lying and dishonesty did not come naturally to him as it did his superiors and he could not conceive of Yelena Ivanov being a political criminal. He would have to proceed carefully. For reasons other than his job, he did not want to lose her again. He hoped he could rekindle their childhood friendship in a legitimate way. Just as she had introduced him to a world of music and beauty, he had no inclination or impulse to betray her and he had never forgotten his love for her.

He remembered her asking him when they were children, "What do you what to be when you grow up?"

"I don't know, but I want to wear a suit and a hat."

Yelena had burst out laughing, causing Howard to flush with embarrassment. Now, he was about to confront her years later wearing the notorious suit and a hat.

At least I don't smoke cigars, he thought.

After some time, he heard the whistle blow and the conductor's distant fading call of "All aboard!" Even after the cranking of the pistons driving the wheels forward and slow repetitive chugs of the engine, Howard hesitated to move. He waited until the train was rolling free of the urban setting and picking up speed headed toward Chicago. Balancing against the swaying rhythm of the train and the creaking undercarriage, he rose from his chair and walked toward the rear.

At one point, in crossing the vestibule opening from one car to another, he surprised a hobo who scrambled up the ladder quick as a cat and disappeared over the edge of the roof. Howard wondered how he could hang on up there at the speed the train was racing along.

The coal-burning engine sent a steady cloud of black smoke over the length of the train. The odor of its sulphurous residue drove Howard into the next car.

Given the direction he was moving, Yelena was not seated as to be facing him. Reflective sunlight periodically exploded through the windows slashing across the murky interior of the regular seats interfering with clear visibility. Unable to recognize her from the back of her head, he did not want to be obvious in turning to scan the faces of the passengers in search of her. So he continued on to the end of the train without having found her. He decided it would be best to wait for a while before making the trek forward. He took an empty seat near the rear of the last passenger car and rode impatiently for thirty minutes with frequent glances at his watch. Enroute back, he stepped into the commode to relieve himself and buy a little more time.

When he finally saw her seated in the third car from the end of the train, he hesitated, unsure if he recognized her while he made the transition in his mind from the image of the teenage girl he had known to the woman whose features resembled Yelena's.

She wore a full-sleeved white blouse high buttoned at the neck and tucked in at the waist of a long gray skirt. Black lace and grommet medium heeled shoes encased her slightly exposed ankles. Her dark hawkish eyes watched him coming toward her along the aisle. He glanced away out the windows at the countryside flashing past, then tried to appear to casually refocus his attention on her and discovered her challenging unwavering stare locked on him. She remembered that he had gone by in the opposite direction not long before. This time, he continued to look at her.

Her brown hair was pulled back into a twist. She wore no makeup. Taut pale skin stretched over her cheeks and jaw belied her age. Howard knew she could be no older than twenty-eight or twenty-nine, but now appeared to be closer to forty. He saw pain and stress and suspicion in her eyes that he remembered had once expressed mischievous humor and a piercing intellectual curiosity.

Wondering if she now in some way recognized him, he continued along the aisle toward her and stopped with an acceptable social distance between them.

"Excuse me," his facial expression conveyed a respectable warmth and interest , "are you by chance Yelena Ivanov?"

At first, she did not answer, nor did she look downward or away. "Are you by chance Howard Gimbel?"

His face broke into a smile of relief. "Yes, yes, I am. Then you remember me."

Her stern expression did not change. "In a manner of sorts."

"I never thought I would see you again. May I—- May I sit down?"

She shifted a full length black wool coat nestled around a lumpish soft bag on the bench next to her and slid across. He carefully lowered himself onto the opposite facing bench so that they could relate to each other in a diagonal direction without violating personal leg space. Physical contact would not be appropriate, especially the touching of knees.

She offered nothing by way of a conversational opening which caused Howard to feel flustered and anxious, but he recalled that he had always felt that way around her because of her supreme composure, sense of superiority, and self-possession. She did not look away. As always, she was still in charge.

Feeling as awkward as a young boy, he stupidly asked, "Do you still play the viola?"

Her eyes rolled over him with a moment of condescending amusement. She would forever be an adult to his child. His innocence and unconditional adoration had endeared him to her during their youth. Now, youth was a fading moment of a distant and painful past. Howard's sudden reappearance in her life rekindled memories that she thought she had buried forever, but could no longer ignore.

She struggled with her resentment that his presence catalyzed and the conflicting necessity to at least respond to him in a civil manner. He had done nothing personally to wrong her and her family. The irony that his father had destroyed their lives recalled her anguish with a sudden rush that clutched at her heart and prevented her from speaking.

Finally, she said, "Is that what you remember about me?"

"Yes, oh yes, I have never forgotten the music you and Lilya played."

She looked away from him out the window. He misread her compressed silence. "I'm sorry if I said something I shouldn't have. So much has happened since then. Are you all right?"

She nodded once firmly. He restrained himself from reaching out a hand in emotional support and concern and fought down the sudden flood of affection for her that had lain dormant for seventeen years.

She wondered how he could still believe in her, in a past that was dead and could never again be revived. But he knew nothing about her and what had happened since then. How could he? She hoped that by remaining silent, he might just get up and leave her alone, walk out of her life again.

Do not cling to the illusion you hold of me, she wanted to tell him. *Do not believe in me as you knew me, because I no longer participate in the realm of beauty, art, and creation. That was destroyed by ignorance, prejudice and politics. I dwell in darkness. The light I knew was in another life. Do not rekindle those memories of me. I am no longer the Yelena Ivanov of your childhood.*

She wished him to vanish as a ghost of the past, but he prevailed, remained seated there, pulling her forward despite her resistance.

"And Lilya, how is she?"

Yelena continued to stare out the window. She would not look at him, only respond to his disembodied voice. "Lilya is dead."

It was Howard's turn to resort to silence and sift through his emotions. He wanted to know how and when she died, but did not dare to ask and further open the wounds of memory. He forgot his purpose, his deception and only cared deeply for this woman he had never ceased to love.

"She was fifteen," Yelena spoke, startling Howard who did not expect to learn anything further about her sister.

"I'm so sorry," he breathed.

"Save your regrets," she said. "They mean nothing."

"I greatly admired her."

"It doesn't matter."

Howard hesitated at her rebuff. "It matters to me," he said softly. "Knowing you and Lilya was the best thing that ever happened in my life."

Yelena slowly swung her gaze back to look at him. "A gang of men broke into our house in the middle of the night and dragged us from our beds. They smashed and destroyed everything."

At the image of his father among the mob, an overwhelming weakness and despair inwardly clamped down on Howard. "They didn't kill her, did they?"

"No, not then. Not in that way, but another way."

"When I went to your house, I saw what they had done," said Howard.

"Did you know your father was with the men who came to the house?"

Howard was repulsed by his own necessary lie. He shook his head.

"They called themselves Palmer Men," said Yelena. "They weren't the law. They were instigators of violence and mayhem and hysteria . Nothing more than vigilantes."

"I always wondered what became of you and your family. I tried to find you."

"You would never have found us. My mother and father were deported to Russia. We never saw them again. Some years later, I went to look for them through musicians we had known. There was no information. They had disappeared."

"When I went to your house, it wasn't just your family. It was all of the Russian sector."

"That's what comes from having the wrong last name in a time of war."

"What was wrong with your name? Many families have Russian names."

"My father was a member of the Socialist Party. We were victims of a communist witch hunt."

"Well, things are different now," Howard's false words echoed in his head.

Yelena shook her head. "No, they are not—- not here and not in Russia."

"I suppose not," he quietly acquiesced.

After several moments, to divert his questions away from herself, she said, "You look like some sort of businessman."

"Actually, I work for the Government."

Yelena's expression hardened.

"I'm involved with one of the President's new programs in New Mexico with the Civilian Conservation Corps and the Bureau of Indian Affairs."

"And what do you know about Indians?"

"Not much I admit."

"Typical of the Government."

"I'll be working with people who do."

"That's good for the Indians. What other qualifications do you have? People get jobs like yours because of who you know. How did you get to know highly placed people in the Government?"

"No one that high up. After I graduated from law school, I applied for a position with the General Services Administration." Howard knew that from this point onward he had better be consistent with his story and accept the lie he was living.

"So, little Howard Gimbel grew up to become a lawyer."

"I never really practiced law."

"Does that mean you aren't tainted by it?"

"In a manner of speaking."

"I have no respect for lawyers or politicians. They live in the same cesspool of corruption."

"I'm not one of them."

"You are when you work for the Government."

Knowing full well he was their pawn, Howard shrugged. "I never thought of myself that way."

Yelena returned her gaze to a lowered crossing guard, flashing red lights, and a dinging bell gone in a moment.

"What about you," Howard asked. "Did you ever get married?"

She shook her head, intending that a sufficient commentary on what she thought of marriage.

"How far are you traveling?"

"A long distance."

"Do you have employment?"

She looked at him. "Why are you interested? Why do you care?"

"We were friends."

"We are no longer friends."

Howard thought it wise not to press further for information. "I'm terribly sorry to have bothered you, Yelena," he said with a quiet sincere apology and rose. "I hope you have a good trip." He walked away and she did not look at him.

Upon returning to his own Pullman car, he ordered a double scotch neat and went to his private compartment. Hearing of Lilya's death filled him with a deep sadness. *He remembered early on a summer morning when Yelena and Lilya had taken them to their secret place in a*

*secluded woods beyond the city. They had followed a narrow winding path
through tall elms and sycamores, then among dense stands of blackberries to
an open meadow where they had seen a doe and her fawn and a large bushy
tailed red fox who had stared boldly at them before loping away. Numerous
squirrels gamboled about and rabbits scattered and quail thundered into the
air at their approach.*

*The children's talk was as whimsical and elusive as the dandelion silk
they blew from the heads of plucked flowers into the warm breeze. Sitting
next to a river inlet, they ate sausage sandwiches and apples and cookies prepared for them by Frau Ivanov.*

*Afterwards, they had shed their clothes and gone swimming in a shal-
low part of the river where the current was not strong. Howard had to continually avert his eyes from staring at the girls' nakedness, as they laughed and
splashed about without embarrassment.*

*Noticing that Howard did not know how to stay afloat, Yelena assisted
him. The closeness of her body electrified him and she allowed her hand to
deliberately brush against his penis, causing an instant erection that persisted
when he exited the water and quickly concealed with his clothes.*

Howard longed for that simplicity of life, the warmth and love
instead of being ensnared in a web of prejudice, hate, and deception.
People were starving. They were without homes. They were trying
desperately to survive and Yelena's purpose was to help them. And
here he was placed in the position of working against them. *Not my
idea of a hero,* he thought. *Not at all.*

Staring out her window as the shifting images of night drifted
and smashed by the swiftly moving train, Yelena's early memories
of Howard Gimbel, the boy who had adored her, clashed with who
he had become and what his purpose was in being on this train. She
knew his sudden appearance was not a coincidence. She lived in constant dread of the law, the life of a fugitive fueled by her rage against
injustice.

Even if Howard were sincere in wanting to renew their acquaintance, she could not allow that to happen. The risk was too great.
She sensed that he was the bait the U.S. Government was using to
lure her in. Howard had always been a caring loving person. Anyone
could use him to further their own ends. She could almost smell FBI

in the way he had presented himself. She had already encountered many undercover agents during her career as an organizer. Howard was transparent.

She half-surmised what life would have been like if the Palmer Raids had never happened. Certainly, Lilya would not have died. Their friendship with Howard might have even grown into something greater. She enjoyed the thought of Howard being in love with her then and wondered if he had ever gotten married. She had not glimpsed a wedding band on his finger, but she had been too distraught at his suddenly being there to notice such a detail. She had immediately been on the defensive and only wanted him to leave her alone. Her life had taken a different turn.

Howard had been devastated at Yelena's sudden disappearance from his life, and especially learning of the violence perpetrated against the Ivanov family. He had tried desperately to find the two sisters. He would have sheltered and taken care of them. He would have learned to play the clarinet or guitar and they would have toured from town to town and given musical recitals to earn their keep. They might have even joined the Chautauqua and traveled the circuit. And eventually, he would have asked Yelena to marry him and they might have settled on a farm out on the prairie or in a small town and raised many children. Now, here they were on opposite sides of the law, on a train in the middle of the night bound for the Southwest.

Howard did not want to think about what lay ahead, what he was being forced to do by an authority beyond his control. He had rather hoped that Yelena might discover him eating alone in the dining car and change her mind and join him. After waiting an hour, he ordered a meal, dawdling over his steak and potatoes. She never did appear.

He had so much he wanted to tell her, especially after she and her sister, Lilya, disappeared. To hear that Lilya had died brought tears to his eyes. He thought of her as a sister and Yelena as the woman he truly loved.

How could these things happen, he thought. What was it about society that brought lives crashing down.

Chapter 2
MUSIC

Yelena Ivanov had told Howard that music captured fleeting moments of life and feeling. She said that people were ticking away their lives like a metronome that would eventually wind down and stop. She said what was important were relationships that people had with each other. Relationships were the only thing that endured. "They become our memories and music tells us how we feel about those memories of events that occurred in the past, the present, and how we will live and perceive the future. Events are like themes in a symphony. Life is a symphony."

Howard Gimbel thought these were very wise words for a young Russian girl to be telling him. But he did not question how or where she had gained such wisdom, because he was deeply in love with her.

Although he had heard a symphony when her parents once took him to see their daughters play a violin duet in a concert, he didn't understand what Yelena meant by her reference to life being a symphony.

Yelena and her younger sister, Lilya, were child prodigies. They had given violin recitals and had played with three major orchestras in Cleveland, Pittsburgh, and Philadephia. They had also been Howard's closest friends since he was eight, until the entire Ivanov family disappeared on the night of January 2nd, 1920. He had never heard from nor seen them since.

What first impressed young Howard about the Ivanovs was the world of aromas in which they lived. The smell of fresh wood and varnish from the neighboring workshop competed with Mother Ivanov's old world culinary creations that swirled in clouds of tantalizing vapors from large brass pots and pans in her kitchen, which was the social center of the family. The adjacent eating room shared the predominant space of the music and practice room, which in other homes would be the living room. It contained a piano, a couch, four lamps, and several straight-backed chairs. The majority of Yelena and Lilya Ivanov's time at home was spent in the music room.

Howard's first invitation into the Ivanov home was the afternoon he was noticed by the girls, then eight and ten years old, peering in the side window to hear and see them playing the viola and violin. Eight years old himself, he had been walking to the open market on an errand for his mother when he was drawn to the sound of their music.

Yelena ceased playing, went to the door and ordered him to stop spying on them. "Come inside if you want to listen. You can be the audience."

Blushing with embarrassment, Howard had quickly and quietly entered and seated himself on the straight-backed cane chair that Yelena pointed to with her bow. He remained perfectly still, afraid to move and disturb the girls' concentration. He observed their rapid fingers like white long-legged spiders traversing the narrow necks of their graceful instruments, the fluid motion of their thin girlish arms manipulating their bows.

He noticed that the younger sister, Lilya, played with her luminescent blue eyes wide open. She appeared porcelain and frail next to Yelena, whose hard stringy body moved and swayed with the dynamic syncopated rhythm of the music. Yelena played with her eyes closed.

Although their sculpted balanced features were similar enough that Howard could identify them as sisters, he noted distinctive differences. Lilya projected an aura of highly controlled energy in her cool pristine stance and style. Yelena appeared to have sprung from a different mold. Tight dark brown curls crowned her perfect head, that made Howard feel he would like to ruffle it with his fingers, where Lilya's silky blonde tresses rolled halfway down her back. Yelena's skin tone was a permanent natural tan in contrast to the paleness of her younger sister.

The Mozart sonata for violin and viola they were playing seemed extraordinarily long to young Howard, who was unaccustomed to hearing any kind of music, let alone classical compositions. He marveled at how they could retain all that music in their memories. It flowed from their fingers and bows as an extension of their existence and with no greater difficulty than their natural breathing. He sat unmoving in awe of their achievement that set them apart as gifted and special from other children he knew. To his way of thinking, the Ivanov sisters were magical, from some other world.

When they finished, Howard clapped vigorously, his face a wide smile of appreciation until Yelena's intense brown eyes silenced, but did not dampen his enthusiasm.

"You did not sustain the legato in section four and your allegretto in section six was quite lacking," she spoke to Lilya. "Also, you accelerando where it is supposed to be played andante and you rush us so it is difficult to maintain synchronisity."

"Interpretation does not supersede progression when playing Mozart. We have to include both, but we do not sacrifice one for the other."

Howard stared at the girls as though they were speaking a foreign language, as the language of music was, indeed, foreign to him. "They don't even talk like other kids," he thought. Their slight Russian accent added to the impression.

"We will take this up tomorrow with Herr Richter," said Yelena, referring to their Austrian violin teacher. She carried her viola and bow to a blue felt-lined case among stacks of sheet music on a nearby side table. "Anyway, we have practiced enough for today. We must give some attention to our curious visitor." She turned to Howard, restoring his smile.

"What's that sound that makes the violin shiver?" he asked.

"It's called shivering," said Yelena.

"No it isn't. She's just joking" said Lilya. "It's a technique called *tremolo*."

Aromatic baking smells of ginger and cinnamon suffused the air from the kitchen into the practice room initiating hunger impulses in Howard and the girls. They timed the conclusion of their practice sessions according to what delights their mother drew from the oven. As if on cue, Mother Ivanov appeared at the door carrying a tray filled with warm cookies and three perspiring porcelain mugs of cold milk.

А сейчас, мои дорогие, время перекусить и поговорить с гостем.

"Time for a snack, my dears, and also for your guest."

Вы говорите по-русски или по-немецки?
"Do you speak either Russian or German?"

"Essen zeit, meine leibchen und fur gast," she reverted to German, the language of the girls' childhood.

"You're supposed to have a snack with us," said Yelena.

Howard wobbled up from his chair and joined the girls gathered around their mother as they helped themselves to the offered treat. Out of politeness, Howard took only two to the girls five.

"Danke, Mama," said the girls.

"Danke," said Howard, speaking one of the few words he knew in German from hearing the language spoken in the open street market. He also knew *guten tag* and *bitte*, but would be instantly lost in any further conversation. He also knew *ya*, yes, and *nein*, no, and *nicht*, not.

"Sprecken Sie Deutsch?" Mother Ivanov inquired.

"Nein, sprecken Deutsch nicht."

"Perhaps you will learn some from Yelena and Lilya," she said in slightly broken English. "They also know some words of Russian."

Howard nodded and looked over at the girls contentedly munching their cookies and slurping milk and clearly ignoring any additional imposed obligation on their lives.

From what he remembered, they always spoke to him in English and spoke German with their parents. Yet later, he overheard the girls' mother and father speaking Russian. He had heard Russians being called *Bolsheviki*, in a tone of distain, but didn't know what that meant.

Upon finishing her cookie, Lilya encased her instrument, then crowded in next to Yelena, who was inspecting this boy who had come to their window as if he were a special prize. Howard blushed at their intense scrutiny. Because of the girls' demanding practice schedule, they had only a few acquaintances from school and no real friends. Now this boy had been drawn in by their music.

"Do you play an instrument?" Lilya asked.

"No, I don't play anything." Howard squirmed slightly on the hard seat. He wanted desperately to return to a standing position and relieve the burning sensation in his buttocks, but did not wish to offend his two admirers. They took in every detail of his worn black shoes, brown knee socks and knickers and his dark green sweater with three small holes in the fabric of the right sleeve, which had since passed through the digestive system of a moth.

"What do you think about when you play?" Howard asked.

"Herr Richter says that music is the purest form of expression," said Yelena. "When you play, nothing else matters. You live in the moment of the sound you are creating. I think about nothing. I feel the music. It comes from somewhere inside. I don't know where. It is my being."

"To me it is like clear flowing water that has no beginning and no end," said Lilya.

That Mother Ivanov adored her gifted daughters was clear to young Howard. Her eyes held love and tenderness with each glance, a profound appreciation for their unique, but fleeting existence. They were growing rapidly and soon would be young women, their accomplishment as musicians taking on an emerging maturity of interpretation and style.

Their teacher, Herr Franz Richter, had once commented to her the early appearance of adult understanding and expression in playing Beethoven and Schumann. The light youthful energy and enthusiasm suited the girls perfectly at their current ages and they would often play the energetic dynamic works of Mozart and Paganini at their concerts.

Frederick and his wife considered their daughters to have been born as ethereal creatures of music. From the moment of their respective births, almost two years apart, the parents believed they were guardians of a shared spiritual treasure. Frederick and Gladys were both moderately accomplished violinists themselves. Frederick had also specialized in the cello. They had filled the infants' formative years with hours of classical music that determined their first impressions of the world.

Mother Ivanov's dimpled cheeks were like two rosy plums. Her sky blue eyes glowed with an inner happiness under a crown of tousled blonde hair. Her face seemed to Howard to be uplifted in a perpetual smile that exhibited perfect gleaming white teeth. If Howard possessed in his young life the image of a beautiful woman, he would have chosen Mother Ivanov.

She was as different as sunlight from shadow in comparison to his own mother, who was weary and worn at the age of twenty-eight. Howard rarely saw his mother smile. Gravity tugged downward at her sallow features and her straggled brown hair that hung stringy and unwashed to her shoulders. Howard knew she wasn't old, but her glimmer of youth and promise had been snuffed out by the impoverished conditions of her life. She had been the seventh child of a Catholic family of eleven children. There had been no encouragement to improve her options beyond six years of elementary education. Her parents had needed all of their children to work to supplement the meager family income just to be able to feed them all.

There had been no beauty during her childhood, only wishing for something better. The illusion of that something quickly faded with her marriage to Clement Gimbel, a young shy factory worker at the steel mill. They lived in the same block of the tenement and he had seen and approached her while she was selecting fruit from a stall in the open market.

Physically small in stature and lacking self-confidence, he appealed to Grace's need for a non-abusive relationship as she, her mother, and her sisters had endured at the hands of her father. Not long after she and Clement were married, she came to resent that he did not have the personality to dominate her. Even as a small child, Howard could see that she was the stronger of the two, with an eloquence of speech and a profane vocabulary learned from her own father. In contrast, Clement struggled with language, suffering embarrassing hesitations in his search for words to adequately express himself. Howard grew to love and respect his mother more than his father, whom he perceived as being weak and ineffective.

The memory of the night his father became a "Palmer Man" returned to Howard. Clement's brown eyes flashed with an intensity the boy had not witnessed before. His father was among the nondescript gray pieces that broke off from the impersonal mass of laborers from which he took his identity.

Every four weeks, Grace gave him a bowl haircut with her sewing shears that rendered him the ascetic bony features of a Benedictine monk. What Clement could not be he admired from afar–public heroes of any kind. He included any man who was successful, who could stand out from the crowd and speak his mind in a manner that caused others to listen and become aroused by his vision. Such men were leaders, especially captains of industry and politicians.

He had once seen Attorney General Mitchell Palmer speak at a recent political rally in Pittsburgh promoting a communist witch hunt as his path to the White House. Clement remembered and admired the flow and power and imagery of his words.

"Out of the sly and crafty eyes of these Bolsheviks leap cupidity, cruelty, insanity, and crime. From their lopsided Slavic faces, sloping brow and misshapen features may be recognized the unmistakable criminal type."

Howard never imagined how the words and actions of this man and his assistant, a clerk by the name of John Edgar Hoover, would influence his life because of Howard's childhood friendship with Yelena Ivanov and his father's role as a Palmer Man.

The irony of the distant forces of Washington politics recruiting the participation of such a lowly laborer as his father did not go unnoticed by Howard. But his realization did not occur until many years later when Howard was a young newly minted agent being given his assignment in the FBI office of Clyde Tolson, Director Hoover's second in command. Only then did the coincidental pieces come together with a heart rending crash at his entrapment.

Intellectually, Howard perceived himself ensnared in a political web as an extension of his father who had acted out of prejudice and ignorance, whereas he was fully cognizant of what he was being forced to do against his own sense of ethics and morality. The removal of Yelena Ivanov would complete the eradication of her family and her existence and everything in which Howard believed as his reasons for joining the FBI.

In retrospect, Howard saw the Ivanov family as innocent victims of social repression and the political ambition of John Hoover. At the age of 24, on August 1, 1919, Hoover's administrative assignment to Attorney General Mitchell Palmer in the Department of Justice was only a step on his climb to creating a personal empire of fear and repression within the Federal Government. Being in charge of the new division of the Justice Department's Bureau of Investigation masked his low esteem and secret of his origin as a mulatto who passed for white while nurturing his ascendancy to power.

As a newcomer to the Bureau, Howard heard the circulation of rumors by other agents that Hoover had arranged the destruction of records of his birth, and was the only member of the Bureau who did not have a record of his ancestry in the files. The Director's dishonesty and corruption of justice set off a warning bell in Howard's mind to beware of coming to his attention. When Tolson called him to his office, remaining unobserved was no longer an option.

Pushed by a Senate resolution to persecute aliens and orchestrated by his young protégé, Attorney Mitchell fanned the flames of paranoia against radical and anarchist groups following the end of the First World War. They targeted members of the Union of Russian Workers, a social organization that established reading libraries and provided instruction in the English language to Russian immigrants, as well as helping them adjust to the new culture.

In a Congressional hearing, Hoover pronounced, "Their publication of books and pamphlets on anarchism and socialism and the rights of labor against the economic ruling class are propaganda to spread Bolshevism in America and promote armed insurrection. The proclamation by the left wing of the socialist party of the need for social change by the majority of citizens is nothing less than a call to revolution against the United States Government."

Hoover seized the opportunity to expand his attack against the Communist Party. He diverted the law by the Department of Labor to inform arrested suspects of their right to an attorney and targeted members of the Communist Labor Party.

As witnessed by reporters:

"The indiscriminate raids were conducted with extreme brutality against people innocent of any crime. Faces and clothing smeared with blood, Russian men and women tried to escape from the policemen wielding clubs and blackjacks and were driven back inside the 'Peoples Building', headquarters of the Union of Russian Workers, where their agonized screams rose over the thud of descending blows against heads and flesh.

After being interrogated, wearing blood-soaked bandages, they were violently thrown out into the street amidst jeers from onlookers and dragged and loaded into waiting patrol wagons that clanged away with their battered human cargo."

The raids continued for six weeks resulting in the arrests and seizures without warrants of three thousand citizens and their detention in overcrowded temporary holding facilities with unsanitary conditions that added to their suffering.

To create the illusion of a nationwide uprising, Hoover conducted raids in more than thirty cities and towns in twenty-three states. Two-hundred forty nine members of the Union of Russian Workers were finally deported on December 21, 1919.

As a boy, Howard remembered his father telling him about heroes and being heroic. He pointed out that Howard should aspire to become a man just like them. At the time, Howard didn't fully comprehend what his father meant other than those men wore suits and bowler hats, smoked cigars and waved them about in the air while they talked in loud domineering voices.

There were two exceptions to his limited understanding. Howard had seen pictures in the newspaper of Lindbergh, the pilot who made a record breaking solo flight across the Atlantic Ocean, and Babe Ruth, who had also set a record for hitting the most home runs in a single season. So Howard equated the more significant heroes with the setting of records that caused other men and women to admire them.

But what happened on that night of January 2nd, 1920, predated the likes of Lindbergh and Ruth. The hero at that time was of the bowler-hatted cigar smoking variety.

"Would you like to see Papa's workshop?" Lilya touched Howard's arm.

"Sure. What does he work on?"

"Papa is a *luthier*," said Yelena. "He makes violins. He also makes violas, and cellos, and mandolins."

"I know what a violin looks like and sounds like," said Howard. "I don't know what those other ones are."

"We'll show you," Lilya took his hand and led him into a large neighboring room the size of a second house.

Again, Howard's senses were assaulted by odors, this time stain and resins. The man he saw stooped over a work bench was not much older than his own father, yet he somehow appeared to be older and wiser. Howard thought the manner in which he moved might be an indication of age. Frederick Ivanov appeared to be slow and patient.

Howard was amazed at the large number of tools that were required to make a violin. At one point, he silently counted sixty eight. Most were tools to carve and form the wood, such as knives, planes, saws, shavers, borers, rasps, reamers, and planes. Others were templates, calipers, and clamps. There were also numerous cylindrical containers filled with strong smelling stains, varnish and wood preservatives.

"Papa, this is our friend, Howard Gimbel," Lilya introduced him. "He came to hear us play and he wanted to see how you make violins."

"You are most welcome, my boy, most welcome. My daughters play well, don't they?"

"I have never heard such beautiful music, sir."

Frederick nodded and smiled. He was glad that Lilya and Yelena had found an American friend. Since their arrival one year ago, their primary association had been with musicians and conductors from the old country. There had been few opportunities to assimilate.

"The proportions of the violin are the key to its sound," he said, gently lifting the section he was carving. These proportions, especially decreasing the thickness toward the sides give the instrument its strength and sweetness of tone."

"The making of a violin requires a great deal of time and precision," He explained. "Even the preparation of the glue. Only the finest glue can be used. It is called Cologne glue."

Howard watched him apply glue of a thick oily consistency from a gluepot with a tiny brush that would fit the narrow areas of wood. He could see instruments about the workshop in the various stages of their creation from the walnut wood mold, the spruce wood top and bottom, and the ribs or sides. Corresponding necks and bridges lay near their other component parts waiting to become attached and to be born as a whole and complete instrument. The smells of glue, varnish, vinegar and alcohol used to create the color of the wood remained with Howard as the primary association by which he recognized and remembered Herr Ivanov.

Frederick had learned his trade beginning as a young boy in Ingelfingin, Wurtemberg, Germany, the original home of August Martin Ludwig Gemunder, among the most prominent German *luthiers* or violin makers. His creations were of the highest quality and considered to be the equal of Stradivarius and Guarnerius instruments. August Gemunder, the son, had learned the art of violin making from his father. In 1905, August, the son, had created a scientific model of his own design which became endorsed by musicians of the highest reputation. Frederick had sought out August, who had established himself in New York, while the reputed violin maker was visiting Germany. It was with the assistance of Gemunder that Fredereick with his wife and two daughters arranged to come to America in 1918.

"Sounds in themselves alone no more make music than words alone make language. Those are the words of Charles Gounod, who wrote the famous German opera, *Faust*."

American Landscape

Howard remembered running home and with great enthusiasm telling his mother and father about his new friends who played the viola and violin. Grace and Clement had stared at him without comprehending a word he said. But over the next few weeks, Howard's mother noticed how much time he spent away from home and decided to walk by the Ivanov house and see what was drawing her son away from her.

Approaching along the cobblestone street, she noticed the explosion of red and purple and golden blooms in Mother Ivanov's window flower boxes against the backdrop of airy white curtains that allowed sunlight to penetrate the interior of the house. The splashes of color struck Grace as being incongruous with the neighboring ghetto in which she lived where there were no flowers, except at the flower stalls in the open market. Flowers were an extravagance. No one that she knew could afford such decoration when putting food on the table from day to day was a priority.

She envied those who led a decent life. She understood what drew her son to prefer the company of the Ivanovs over his own parents, but understanding did not lessen her pain. They provided him light and color and the beauty of musical sound and composition in contrast to the drabness and drudgery of what she and her husband could offer. Music did not exist in their family, only the strident noise of abuse and complaints and the wails of small children and the periodic screams and sobs of Alice Chatham, in the tenement next door, when her husband came home from work drunk and beat her.

Chapter 3
THE END OF MUSIC

Yelena heard the voices and heavy tread of the approaching mob in the street below. Burrowed deep within her blankets, her subliminal consciousness intensified and erupted fully awake at the snapping and cracking of wood as the front door was smashed open by a wielded sledge hammer and iron bars.

She looked at her sister, Lilya, sitting bolt upright in the neighboring bed, at their mother's piercing scream from the next room down the hall.

They heard their father's shouts as, downstairs, furniture and glass cabinets splintered and exploded into a shower of fragments and Frederick's cellos, violas, and violins created with such loving care were pounded into kindling. Clumping footfalls on the stairs preceded the surging charge of the invaders who burst into the girls' and their parents' rooms and dragged them from their beds.

Умоляю, умоляю вас, не бейте нас. Мы ничего не сделали.
"Please, Please do not harm us. We have done nothing.

Я делаю музыкальные инструменты, не бомбы.
I make musical instruments, not bombs.

Мы не большевики.
We are not Bolsheviki.
"Fuckin' Bolshis! Go back to fuckin' mother Russia!"
The blow from a steel bar crushed the fingers of Frederick Ivanov's right hand and caught the side of his wife's head on the upswing opening a bloody swath on her scalp and turning her screams to moans as the attackers dragged her and her husband from their bed, bodies thumping down the stairs and out into the street where

uniformed police and their crazed raggedly dressed recruits from the crowd kicked and prodded them into a waiting patrol wagon.

The girls' cries were drowned by the curses and shouts of sweating bearded drunken men who wrested them from their beds and carried them screaming and urinating with terror out into the street where they struggled and broke free and ran off into the night down a dark ghetto alley. Yelena grabbed Lilya's hand and they stumbled on blindly deeper within the labyrinthine tenements until they collapsed from exhaustion against the side foundation of a boarding house.

Yelena wrapped her arms around Lilya and held her and caressed her head until her sister's sobs lessened long after Yelena's tears had ceased.

"What happened?" Lilya gasped. "Who were those men?"

"I don't know. I don't know," Yelena whispered.

"What of *mutter* and papa? Where did they take them? Why? They have done nothing."

"I don't know. I don't know."

"Can we find them tomorrow?"

"We will try."

"Can we go back?"

"Not tonight. We will see tomorrow."

"What if we can't find them?"

"We will see tomorrow."

Stained and filthy and throwing off a putrescent odor from urine soaked shifts clinging to their skin, the sisters were discovered sleeping side by side the next morning by the proprietress who came out onto the porch and started around the back to empty a slop bucket.

"Girls," she said, nudging them with her foot. "Girls, what are you doing here. Wake up. You cannot stay out here. Wake up."

Yelena's eyelids fluttered open and she looked up into the concerned kindly features of a stout Slovenian woman wearing a freshly laundered blue apron over her plain linen dress. Her wide face broadened into an even wider smile that, with blonde hair sprouting at an angle from her head, gave her the appearance of a scarecrow.

"Where are you from?" she asked in broken English.

Yelena staggered to her feet and helped Lilya to stand. "We are Russian."

"Ach, Russian. There was trouble over there last night. What is your name?"

"Yelena Ivanov. This is my sister, Lilya."

"Ivanov. Russian, yes."

"Our house was raided last night by a mob, we don't know who."

"Palmer men."

"Palmer men?"

"My boarders have talked about them. It is not safe for you to go back to your home."

"They took our mother and father. They would have taken us, but we ran from them."

"You had better come inside with me. Get clean and some fresh clothes. I am Maria Dudek. This is my boarding house. Come now. You come with me." She lead them up the wooden steps onto the porch and, with some trepidation, they followed her inside. They were ensconced in the odors of frying pork, the sweet yeasty smell of freshly baked bread, and the sharp aroma of coffee.

Another woman, short and thin with dark tight hair and a beaked nose, was cooking with several pots and pans at the open kitchen range next to counters and cupboards along an entire wall that faced out into a large open room occupied by ten men, immigrant steel workers who were just arising from their cots and in various states of undress. They paused at the sight of the two girls clothed only in their shifts. Maria quickly escorted them along the aisle between the cots and up the stairs at the far end of the house.

"They are good men," she said, "good boarders, all of them, or I would not allow them to stay. You do not have to fear them. They will go to work soon and some men from the night shift will come. We feed them and then they sleep."

Maria ushered the girls onto a second floor containing several cots lined against the walls. Women's stockings and undergarments hung on clotheslines strung across the room like layers of a tattered curtain. Several women moved about dressing themselves and preparing to go to work at a textile mill or a glass factory or a rubber tire plant. A few were seamstresses employed at a clothing factory. The girls caught snatches of other European languages among them, Swedish, German, Italian, Slovak, Slav, and Rumanian, but no Russians.

"These women can help you find jobs," said Maria. "There is work. You can stay here. This will be your room, but after two weeks, you will have to pay your board. You will have clean beds and the food is good. Jovina is my cook. All my boarders are pleased with the food. The men use the water closet and bath downstairs. The women have their own up here, but it is crowded and you must take your turn and be quick. I will bring you some dresses and shoes and underclothing. Anything too large you can alter. If you do not know how to sew, you will learn."

"Mutter taught us how to sew," said Yelena.

"And another thing, you must not speak Russian here. I do not want the Palmer men coming in here and breaking up my house. You must also change your name. What is your surname?"

"Ivanov."

"You cannot be Ivanov no more. Call yourselves Botchko. It is easy to remember. Do you speak any Czech?

Yelena shook her head.

"I will teach you some words. The bosses at the factories want to hear English anyway. I will bring you some breakfast and coffee. When the other women are done at the *wasser kloset*, then go and wash."

Understanding the significance of Maria's kindness, Yelena touched her arm. "Thank you, Maria, for helping us."

"No Russki. Remember, no Russki."

The girls nodded.

Antonia Mazarek was twenty-three years old, a brunette with a brooding, glamorous face, heavy arched eyebrows and large dark dramatic eyes with a slight upward slant at the outer edges accentuating the lines of uplifted rosebud cheeks. An expressive mouth fully accentuated her words, making the mundane sound important and causing the listener to focus on what she said. When she first met the girls, her sensuous lips slipped up in a slow provocative smile revealing perfect gleaming white teeth. She reminded Yelena of a panther, her long legs and arched feet moving in a sleek rhythm when she crossed the room.

Antonia was unlike any other woman that Yelena had known. She envisioned her stepping out of an epic story of gods and goddesses and becoming entrapped in the mundane affairs of humans groveling to survive. Her beauty prompted immediate respect and caused onlookers to project their imaginations as to her identity, even though the clothing she wore was of the lower working class. They wondered if she were a princess or a duchess who had fallen upon misfortune.

During their first week at the boarding house, Yelena and Lilya grew aware of the inner strength and fierce independence of the women with whom they shared the room. They were of various shapes and sizes, three dark-complexioned peasant women short and stout, two thin anemic women with red-orange hair who appeared to be related, five other northern Europeans who ranged from average weight and height with varying shades of blonde and brown hair and either blue or hazel eyes and clear attractive faces to one whose rough features and a large chin mole gave her a tough unapproachable countenance.

They all had hopes for better conditions in their lives, but realized that changing their status depended upon marriage. With the exception of two of the Scandinavians who were being courted by workers from a steel mill, the others remained wary of encouraging romantic attention, given the reality and daily reminder of poverty around them.

The women treated each other in a friendly respectful manner and included the girls as equals. They were impressed, as well as sympathetic, when Antonia related Yelena's and Lilya's musical background. The women, by and large, had no music in their lives other than remembered folk tunes and dances from their native countries. Their current existence consisted of long days of dull repetitive labor. Their laughter was harsh, borne of stress and suffering. The drudgery of their lives left them no opportunity for enjoyment other than occasional biting sarcasm against a boss or a coworker.

Antonia took an instant liking to Yelena and Lilya. To her, they had come from a special world, the world of artists and musicians, people with talent and vision whose performances elevated audiences, even momentarily, from the mundane realities of their lives and gave them hope of something greater in experience.

"I heard a concert once back in my home country," she said. "The orchestra played Dvorak."

"We have played works by Dvorak," said Yelena. "Lilya played his violin concerto in A minor."

Antonia confided in them her own dream. "I have always had this feeling I was meant to become important, to do something special with my life, to become a great person, but I do not know what or how. I have only a little education. From the way you talk, you girls seem to be well educated."

"Most of our education is in music," explained Yelena. "But we attended a private gymnasium."

"What has happened to you is a tragedy. I came to this country with nothing but the clothes on my back. The two of you have a gift and you are still young."

"Our gift is of no use."

"There must be a way."

"We dare not show our faces in a public concert hall. We would be arrested and deported. Our instruments have been destroyed."

"But there are other violas and violins."

Yelena shrugged. "For now, we need to find work like everybody else."

"I can help you with that. I can take you to the person who hires at the factory where I work. The conditions are not good and the pay is barely enough to keep us alive, but it is better than living in the streets."

When Antonia departed from the boarding house with the girls, the eyes of every man followed her. She was the embodiment of ideal beauty. She was aware of the stares of men and seemed to Yelena to expect their admiration of her natural physical gifts while the two girls accompanied her along the street toward the factory.

A sickly gray-green haze continuously clung to the colliding gabeled rooftops and drifted erratically through the winding tenement canyons cluttered with hanging clothes like drab moss.

People existed in small apartment cells along miles of deteriorating buildings that provided shelter from the elements, but little else. Just as the dilapidated stairs and walls creaked and groaned against each other, the lives of the occupants were heaped upon one another and their noise and emotions of the moment resounded any time of the day or night. Their behavior was influenced by the sordid conditions of the pressing rooms that reeked with the odors of unwashed existence and reverberated with anger, beatings, and howls of abuse..

Crawling with vermin, underfed children with scabrous skin and drooling noses and wearing ragged clothing clotted the hallways and wooden stairwells, dodging and scattering like rodents with the arrival home of cursing drunken fathers to avoid their predictable cuffs and kicks.

The factory was a series of gray soot-encrusted buildings that stretched on for a few city blocks. An ever present pall of smoke stained the paned windows and blocked the access of sunlight struggling to penetrate and touch the moving life within. Handlers and expeditors brought and staged materials on handcarts from the warehouse. Others unreeled or unraveled yarn, hemp, wool, and cotton, weaving it on enormous looms into broadcloth for shipment to manufacturers of furniture, carpets, and clothing.

Watching the mob of women in uniform white and blue dresses, the girls waited in a long line to apply for work. The man who hired them was unconcerned about their ages and turned them over to a thin severe looking woman supervisor with a crooked nose that reminded the girls of a witch. After rendering them the demanding rules of the twelve hour work day, she assigned them to their tasks initially with an experienced person to train them. At a wage of five dollars a week, they began as scrap gatherers, pushing carts up and down the aisles of weavers and seamstresses and scooping up cloth remnants that were then either burned in a large furnace or recycled for padding in quilts, furniture and mattresses.

Within a month, the girls' expressions took on the dull weariness of their coworkers at the long hours of regimentation, a fifteen minute break for a noon meal of bread and cheese. They feared to ask permission to relieve themselves and their discomfort increased as the day wore on. Several women had been fired for taking too long in the women's facility. Only by combining the paltry sum they were each paid at the end of the week, were the girls able to keep their beds at the boarding house.

Yelena was awakened one night by her sister's uncontrollable weeping. They had pushed their cots together so they could be close to each other during the night.

"Lilya, Lilya, I'm here," she whispered. "It's okay. I'm here."

"I miss *Mutter* und Fater," she stuttered in mixed German. "I miss her cooking. I miss the smell of Fater's workshop. I miss playing the violin."

Yelena sat up and held her and rocked her in her arms. "I know. I know. I feel the same way. I miss them too. I miss them and love them."

"Will we ever see them again?"

"I cannot say. All we can do is hope that something will change for us. For now, we must survive."

"I don't think I can stand another day at the mill. It is so horrible there. *Shrecklich.*"

"Shh, Shh, Our music is here inside us. We hold it in memory. We can hear it even if it is not there. We will play again one day."

"Will we?"

"I am sure of it."

"I love you, Yelena."

"I love you too."

"Without you I would die."

"Shh...Shh."

For Yelena and Lilya, the weeks tumbled over each other until six months had passed. They had grown accustomed to the grinding routine of work at the factory and hastily eaten meals and snatched a few hours sleep each day at the boarding house.

Lilya continually complained of the need to return to their earlier life and became increasingly delusional, which worried Yelena that her sister was slipping away from reality. Other workers commented to Yelena that Lilya muttered and talked to herself as she pushed her cart and gathered scraps from the factory floor.

Late one afternoon, a guard escorted Lilya down from the ninth floor, out across the compound, and through the gate. With a thirst and dryness in her mouth, she stared vacantly down the length of the tall chain link fence topped with coils of barbed wire and began walking with a shuffling step into town.

She found her way to the street and to the house where she and Yelena had lived with their parents and went to the door. Her knock was answered by a stranger, a haggard middle-aged woman with two small boys clinging to her dress and staring up at her with curiosity.

Lilya uttered something in Russian, then tried German. Not understanding, the woman shook her head and closed the door. Lilya sat down on the doorstep and watched the passing vehicles and pedestrians. Then she rose and walked aimlessly toward the river that divided the city.

Word reached Yelena that her sister had been removed, but Yelena could not leave her job and go to Lilya until the whistle blew signifying the end of the shift. When she rushed out through the gate among a throng of women, she found no sign of her sister. Yelena ran back through the tenements to the boarding house. Maria Dudek told her that Lilya had not returned. Frantic that Lilya had lost her sanity, Yelena walked the narrow streets until long after dark in search of her. By the following morning, Lilya had still not returned. Yelena had to go to the factory to keep her own job.

Three more days passed with no sign of her. On the fourth, Yelena heard a group of older boys gathered on a street corner talking about the body of a girl who had been pulled from the river. Fearing the worst, Yelena went directly to the city morgue and was subjected to viewing the cadavers of seventeen young women before she recognized the bloated body and face of her sister disfigured by fish and turtles that had fed on her.

American Landscape

Yelena doubled over retching on the floor and staggered out of the morgue. Sobbing, she ran through the winding streets to the boarding house, slammed through the door past the men and women at supper, and clattered up the stairs to the second floor room.

A while later, Antonia found her lying curled in a tight ball on her cot and staring with an expression of horror and hate at a spot on the wall. She gently placed a hand on the girl's shoulder and let it rest there.

Chapter 4
THE ORGANIZER

Yelena's first glimpse of Damon Roikos was his dark hair lifting and tossing in the wind above the throng of women who swirled past him like a human current escaping the unlocked dam of the factory in which they had been confined for the day. She saw leaflets flying about in the air as though he were magically releasing doves from his hands. The women were grasping the fluttering pages and hurrying on.

As she maneuvered through the crowd to approach him, she noticed a cadre of uniformed company guards shoving women aside, knocking them to the ground in their thrusting charge to get to the agitator. He glanced up and saw they were coming for him waving their leaded batons with elation and demonic cruelty flashing in their eyes.

Too late, the tall young man began to run. The lead guard caught him in his first sprinting stride and swung the baton in a wild wide arc that nicked his left ear and raised the scalp of his dodging dark head. The blow leant speed to the victim, who quickly outdistanced his pursuers shouting curses in his wake.

Yelena scooped up one of the loose flyers scuttled by the wind and trampling feet and ran after the man. She caught up with him a few hundred yards later kneeling at the side of the road. His hand clutched the side of his head dripping blood.

She stared at his face, a distinctive nose recessed at the bridge and slightly extended and upturned at the tip. An unruly lock of hair draped over his oval brown eyes fluid with pain. His generous mouth grimaced into a quick grin. She saw a flash of white teeth.

Yelena glanced at the flyer in her hand announcing a local chapter meeting of a labor union." "Do you need help?" she asked, wanting to reach out and touch his beautiful face, sooth his wound.

"All I can get," he winced as a light laugh escaped him.

"You're badly hurt," she said.

"Mostly my pride that I wasn't fast enough to outrun the bastard. They've never caught up with me before."

"Perhaps you waited too long to run. What would they do if they caught you?"

"Beat me to an inch of my life and throw me in jail."

"But why? What law have you broken? All you're doing is handing these out." She raised her flyer.

"It's not what's written there. And I'm not the one breakin' the law. I'm helpin' people stand up for their rights. It's them that's breakin' the law. They call us Reds. We aren't. We stand for human rights. The Feds and capitalists try to make it look like we want to bring down the Government. We just want a fair share for the workers."

He stood up a little too quickly, took a weaving step and stumbled. Yelena steadied him, then hooked her right arm through his left. He glanced down at her. The top of her head came to his shoulder. "Still woozy, I guess."

"Where do you live?" she asked.

He gestured with his other hand in the direction of the city.

"Let me help you." They walked in a stumbling fashion toward the edge of town.

"Someone is to meet me here," he said. "I thought they would be waiting."

"You're still bleeding?"

"It could have been worse. They put lead cores in their clubs."

"I still don't understand why they would want to kill you?"

"Have you read the flyer? The company owners don't want a union. They'll do anything to keep us out."

"Who are you with?"

"Here he comes now."

A cloud of dust stirred up from the spoke wheels of a Ford moving rapidly in their direction. The bare-headed driver stopped the vehicle a few feet from where they stood.

"Your head don't look good," he said. "Busted you open. Who's this?"

Robert M Tucker

"She helped me. Don't know her name."

"Yelena," she said. "My name's Yelena."

"Well, Yelena, on behalf of the Socialist Labor Party, we thank you."

As Damon opened the rear passenger door to step inside, Yelena moved to follow. He hesitated and looked back at her. "What are you doing?"

"I want to come with you."

"We can't take you. We're on union business."

"Aren't there any women?"

"Not with our group."

"Then I'll be the first."

"What can you do?" demanded the driver.

"I can get inside the factories. I can talk to the workers."

"You know, she's right," he said to Damon.

Damon stepped aboard and Yelena slipped in on the seat beside him and pulled the door shut. "Let's go," he said. "I need something to stop the bleeding."

As he put the car in gear and made a wide turn at the center of road so they were headed back into town, the burly mustached driver cast a glance over his shoulder at Yelena and said, "Name's Dennison, Andrew Dennison. Damon and me, we're friends."

Yelena nodded and held onto Damon's arm. He slouched forward with his eyes closed in pain. Drops of his blood stained Yelena's dress.

They drove to a warehouse located near the railroad yards.

Peter Brezna, a veteran of the union wars, came out to greet them and to assist Damon inside. He was 40 years old, of medium height with challenging intense blue eyes that peered at her out of a round face. His broad chest de-emphasized a slight paunch. Thick dark hair parted on one side swept across his head in a straight cut wave. From apparent experience, he quickly and expertly attended to Damon's head wound.

" Working as a union subversive is a dangerous business," said Peter. "If they discover you, you could be arrested or even murdered by company goons."

"I don't want to leave. This is something I want to do," she explained earnestly. My parents were exiled by the Government because of their name."

"The Palmer raids?"

"Yes. My sister did not have the strength to survive. She killed herself. I am left with nobody."

"Where do you live?"

"A boarding house."

"What about your room?"

"I have nothing there worth going back for."

"She sounds committed," said Brezna. "We can use her inside. She can talk to the other women. Get them to cross-over."

"Just tell me what to say and I will say it," said Yelena.

"You have to be careful who you talk to," warned Damon. "The mill owner has spies among the workers. One word to the wrong person and you can end up in jail with a beating along the way."

"I'm thinking it would be a good idea for you to come to a meeting," said Peter. "There are others you should know about and how we work."

"How did you become part of all this, this movement?"

"When you come to the meeting, I will tell you."

The opening line of Peter Brezna's speech to the gathering of several hundred women garment and mill workers inspired Yelena. A number of men scattered throughout the crowd were considered to be company spies, but their presence did not deter Peter.

"There is a conflict between the working class and the capitalist class and the working class must defend itself, if necessary, by force."

"As most of you know," Brezna continued in a deep sonorous voice that echoed from the warehouse rafters, "several of our officers have been indicted and convicted on charges of treason under the pretense of the Espionage Act, a convenient ploy that the FBI and the Federal court hide behind to deprive us of our constitutional rights. Our most honored labor organizer Eugene Debs was recently arrested for giving a speech in Canton, Ohio that criticized the war. He has been sentenced to ten years in prison. We are not currently living under a Government of the people, by the people and for the people. The United States Government is against its own people." His speech went on to characterize the corruption of economic power.

"As collective members of the union, you too have power that is equal to and greater than theirs. The conflict of which I speak is not only how much or how little you are paid, but having a share in the results of your labor and ownership of the means to your livelihood.

"You are all prisoners and victims of their greed and corruption.

To improve your working conditions and the scale of pay, you must stand firm together against your employer. The only way you will have change is to be stronger than your opposition."

"I am the eldest son of a rural Kansas family of ten children. I was forced to leave home when the bank foreclosed the mortgage on our farm after driving us into debt. While my parents and brothers followed the mass of similarly dispossessed farmers into the immigrant ghettoes and slavery of Chicago factory workers, I hopped a freight in search of employment with the Phelps Dodge Mining Company in Arizona.

"Two weeks after being hired, I joined the Western Federation of Miners and became an activist with the International Workers of the World, the IWW, that pitted the working class against its employers. My commitment to the cause of working people was cemented when armed vigilantes hired by the mining company owners, forced over one-thousand miners at gunpoint into railroad cattle cars. When the train finally stopped miles out in the New Mexico desert, we were abandoned without food and water. A few died of exposure during the long trek back.

"Nation-wide strikes held by mine workers have been perceived as a threat against the Capitalist system by subversive Socialist groups. We are not a threat to the Government and the Constitution on which it is founded. We are only a threat to those few who rule the economy of our country."

A series of bombings fueled the panic spreading through American society and increased the controversy with the Socialists. Attorney General Mitchell Palmer was among the targeted victims.

On the night of June 2, 1919, a handmade bomb exploded at Palmer's home. The blast was powerful enough to shatter windows of several other homes in the neighborhood. Copies of an anarchist flier were found scattered about the street.

Within an hour of the blast, bombs were set off in eight other cities at the homes of prominent officials. Prior to these incidents, explosive devices had been mailed to thirty-six of the most prominent political and financial leaders in the country, including J.P. Morgan and John D. Rockefeller.

The New York Times headlines screamed that the Russian Bolsheviks were responsible and caused mass hysteria in the cities. Any member of a socialist organization was branded a Red, accused of having ties to communism and the Russian Revolution. Palmer put the country in a state of national emergency that he said justified aborting The Bill of Rights.

"The blaze of revolution is sweeping over every institution of law and order," he thundered at a press conference. "It's eating its way into the homes of the American workman. Its sharp tongues of revolutionary heat are licking the altars of the churches, leaping into the belfry of the school bell, crawling into the sacred corners of American homes, seeking to replace marriage vows with libertine laws, burning up the foundations of society."

Palmer's strategy to rid the country of the Red menace was the mass deportation of radicals. But first they had to be rounded up, which required an army of vigilantes in all the major cities. Anyone belonging to an organization advocating violence was to be arrested and deported.

He petitioned Congress for appropriations and received the response that all foreign radicals were to be deported.

Palmer appointed J. Edgar Hoover to lead his newly created intelligence department in spying on and ridding the country of anarchists. Their first field assignment was to raid the Union of Russian Workers in New York. On January 2nd, 1920, Justice Department agents assaulted the communist headquarters and private residences of Russian American citizens that led to the arrests and deportation of thousands of innocent people throughout major cities. The Ivanov family was among them.

As Yelena listened to Brezna's speech, the ideas and strategies he envisioned caught her imagination and she realized there was a means she could retaliate for the injustice done to her family and to her people. She learned in subsequent meetings the methods for interfering with the production process, the efficiency of tasks and quality and quantity of products. Sabotage undermined the boss and his profits on which his entire life was centered, the core of his moral and economic system. During the ensuing years, she would coordinate strikes and dismantling of production equipment and establish the administrative foundation for local unions to prevail with support from the national level.

For the first two years, she lived and worked closely with Damon, learning the skills of persuasion, understanding how to appeal to workers with a means to improve their lives. During the strike at a garment factory in New York, she was arrested while speaking from a platform and jailed for ninety days.

She began attending meetings of the Communist Party, whose ideology Damon did not agree with and which eventually caused them to drift apart

The persecution of people who held socialist views consumed J. Edgar Hoover. His obsession with spying on both private and public citizens and archiving information that he could use against them, especially their sexual behavior, placed him in a position of being able to extort and to bring them under his sway. He could destroy political careers and depose government officials with whom he disagreed simply by leaking his information to the press or having them discover a compromising photograph upon opening their desk drawer. No one had to question who sent the photograph.

When the Attorney General appointed Hoover Director of the Bureau of Investigation, Hoover set out to expand the jurisdiction of his organization which was limited to violations of federal law and providing assistance to police and other criminal investigation agencies. To change the authority of the Bureau, he devoted time, effort, and appropriations to upgrade the recruiting and training of agents. Howard Gimble was among the fifth wave of recruits.

Law enforcement being a state activity, not a federal one, Hoover's power was limited. His agents were not allowed to carry guns and they did not have the right to arrest suspects.

"Ladies and gentlemen," he said, appearing before a Congressional committee, "we live in dangerous times. We are threatened in our own cities by heavily armed thieves and racketeers and foreign insurrectionists who will not hesitate to shoot our men down. For us to be an effective law enforcement agency, our men must have the right to bear arms and to make arrests for the protection of the citizens of America and for their own defense. I am asking you to give them what they need to be able to do the job the United States Government has hired them for. They are not sacrificial lambs sent out to be slaughtered by the criminal element. Our men are highly trained and they deserve the best we can offer. I expect that every one of you will pass this legislation for the good of the people and the good of the country. Thank you, ladies and gentlemen."

After he petitioned Congress, they agreed to establish the Federal Bureau of Investigation (FBI). Now that his agents were armed and could act against crimes of violence, Hoover set about establishing what he called a world-class crime fighting organization. He formed a scientific crime-detention laboratory and the FBI National Academy, from which Howard Gimbel graduated in 1936. Two years later, Agent Gimbel was summoned to the office of Clyde Tolson, Assistant Director of the FBI and briefed on his assignment to terminate the activities of the union organizer, Yelena Ivanov.

Yelena's public and private activism caught the notice of J. Edgar Hoover, whose agents tapped her phone and spied on her at all hours of the day and night. Armed with the new law in support of unions, during the summer of 1939, Yelena was on a train bound for New Mexico where she would organize a unionization of the miners. It was a time when she would come face to face again with Howard Gimbel, a young agent with the Federal Bureau of Investigation.

Chapter 5
HERO WORSHIP

"You need to git yerself work." Howard's father stumbled drunkenly through the door one evening shortly after the disappearance of Yelena and Lily. Ya need to help feed the family now. They kicked me out of the mill, and not 'cause I didn't do my job. They gave it to a young shit, younger 'n me."

"You'll have to go find another job," his wife ordered. "You can't just lie around here all day."

"It's time the boy pulled his weight and did his share." Clement screamed at her. "If they want to hire the young ones, they can hire him."

"If you don't find other work and bring home money we need to buy food and pay for this rat trap we live in, I will leave you."

"Ha! That'll be the day. You ain't goin' nowhere, bitch!"

He floundered about their flat in rage and frustration. He raised his hand and threatened her, but he never struck her. She increased the hours she worked in sewing sweat shops and he saw less of her and his son. Other than to sleep, young Howard avoided going home.

Within a month after he began working at Dominick and Lucy Moscone's bakery, Howard became aware that the childless couple regarded and treated him in a special way.

He showed up promptly at four o'clock in the morning to help them mix dough, fire up the oven and open the store before he went to school. He returned promptly at three in the afternoon to assist Dominick with restocking inventory sacks of yeast and flour and tending to walk-in customers at the front counter.

In the morning, Lucy always had a plate of warm pastries and a large bowl-size cup of hot milk in coffee. After school, he would discover freshly baked cookies and a glass of cold milk set out timed for his arrival.

Howard associated the pungent smells of the bakery with its owners. Coming through the front door, he walked into a warm yeasty aroma that wafted out from the large cast iron oven in the back. The sweet scent of sugar and butter commingled with the yeast to transform the air into a heady perfume that soothingly overtook the senses and precipitated an intense hunger that could only be satisfied by sampling the source.

The Moscones did not have to advertise to promote their business. The tantalizing smells drifted out the open door and down the street, lifted on upward currents of air that carried wisps of scent into adjacent neighborhoods and stimulated the imagination.

Dominick and Lucy reminded Howard of loaves of their own bread. Although not obese, they were both smooth and rounded. Their skin was the complexion of light brown crust and a perpetual rosiness glowed from their faces from the heat of the oven. Their rich chocolate eyes exuded kindness and good heartedness.

Howard had happened upon the bakery while seeking work to supplement his parents meager income. His father could not rise above the foundry's low wage, had been fired from his job, and his mother worked as a seamstress in a sweat shop.

Italian words and phrases smattered the Moscones' broken English that, at first, escaped Howard's understanding. As the months passed, he began to grasp their vocabulary and grammar to the point he could carry on brief functional conversations, which benefited him when waiting on the mothers and grandmothers from the surrounding neighborhood ghetto populated largely by Italian immigrants.

Howard learned to conceal his embarrassment during moments Lucy bestowed an adoring gesture of motherly love, as though claiming him as her son. After Dominick privately exclaimed to him that Lucy was barren, despite continual prayer and the blessings of their priest, Howard submitted to her emotional need, following Dominick's example of calling her *Mama*.

The acknowledgment so pleased Lucy that she would embrace him upon his arrival and departure. Her hand occasionally caressed his cheek in passing behind the counter. When he was seated eating one of her pastries, she planted a spontaneous kiss on the top of his head. Although self-consciously at first, he would pat her hand in return and give her a greeting and departing kiss on the cheek.

Not having children placed Dominick and Lucy at a disadvantage in the family economy of immigrant society. They had no means to contain their costs and grow their business. All around them were families with extended kinships to the homeland. Although they knew friends from Genoa, their city of origin in Southern Italy, they did not have any ties of blood.

From experience within his own family and from reading newspapers and listening to discussions among men in barbershops and saloons and by women who came into the bakery, Howard realized that immigrant families relied on their children to contribute to the family economy. He knew boys and girls whose parents had forced them to stop attending school and take unskilled jobs in factories and textile mills.

Howard's father constantly pressured him to quit school and learn a trade or skills or apprentice in a business. The coaxing had sent the young man of fifteen out into the streets in search of a job.

Howard did not benefit the Moscones as a family member, but fulfilled their emotional need. Once he started working at the bakery and brought home his small weekly wage which he gave to his mother, the insistent demands from his father ceased.

Regardless of the family taking priority over his personal dreams and aspirations, Howard continued with his schooling. He had the choice of working in the foundry like his father, but the symbolic image of capitalists wearing bowler hats stuck in his mind along with the inequality of distributed wealth and power. His intelligent observance of urban business and local customs brought into focus the limitations of being consigned to the laboring class.

Despite the inadequacy of a ghetto education., he loved to learn. Although schools were barely funded and teachers often went unpaid, Howard responded to their dedication. He studied diligently and asked where he could find more books to read. Most he received on loan from his teachers and the school library. Local libraries had been shut down for lack of funds. Newspapers were another source of his reading. He followed the sagas of public figures as ongoing stories.

Mob leaders and politicians dominated the news features. The most prominent among them was Al Capone, who created a criminal empire by violating the 18th Constitutional Amendment banning the sale, transportation, and manufacture of alcohol. The vast market for this illegal commodity gave rise to gangsters who controlled entire cities.

Capone had the distinction of being "Public Enemy Number 1". He generated $60 million a year from alcohol sales and an extra $45 million a year from other rackets. He bribed the Chicago police and politicians of Chicago and through their support, opened thousands of speakeasies.

Among the first movies Howard saw for a nickel was *Public Enemy*, starring Tom Powers as a self-made man who realized the American dream by rising above his ethnic working class origins to become a major crime figure. Edward G. Robinson as *Little Ceasar* was based on the widespread breaking of the Volstead Act, the law to enforce Prohibition and Paul Muni in *Scarface* also depicted ethnic gangsters breaking their cultural chains and going head to head with the American Anglo-Saxon ruling class.

Howard questioned Hollywood glamorizing lawless mobsters and their ruthless killings and murders. He also wondered why audiences were drawn to gangster films as popular entertainment until it dawned on him that they represented the hopes of immigrants coming to America and living imprisoned in urban slums. Wealth and fame could be achieved most expeditiously by breaking the law.

Howard was alternately influence by reading the novels of Dashiell Hammett whose detective heroes confronted the treachery, greed, and violence of the criminal element. But fictional heroes had no effect on real-life conditions. A fact that caught Howard's attention was that Hammett was a member of the communist party. The Director of the FBI, J. Edgar Hoover, was frequently in the news with his diatribe, accusations, and investigations of communists.

The name of J. Edgar Hoover, kept the memory alive of Howard's friends, Yelena and Lilya Ivanov. He struggled with the conflicting perception of Hoover as a Federal law enforcer and Hoover's repressive persecution of innocent people. Even at his young age, Howard could detect Hoover's hypocrisy, that he was "protecting the American way of life from filthy radicals, communists, perverts, and cream-puff liberals."

Hoover's fixation with Reds to the exclusion of mobsters, labor racketeers, and corrupt politicians puzzled Howard, especially following the day Howard was sworn in as an agent of the FBI. Within a year, Howard realized he had joined the Bureau to support the values of law and order it represented, not the man who was its leader. Hoover barely acknowledged the existence of organized crime, but assigned the majority of his agents to investigate suspected communists.

Two events stimulated Howard's imagination to become a crime fighter. The first was the day he met Franco Pasarelli. The second was reading in the newspaper and hearing Walter Winchell on the radio news describe the heroic exploits of the prohibition agent Eliott Ness in bringing Al Capone to justice. A distinction between Ness and Hoover stood out in Howard's mind. Ness was a champion of the law and not an agent in the FBI. Hoover's primary focus was not fighting crime, but his personal political agenda against communists.

When Franco first sauntered into the bakery, Howard took him to be about his own age. His blue eyes crinkled with amusement that matched his winning smile. Howard caught a flash of perfect white teeth revealed by a sultry curl of the boy's lips, as Franco sniffed the air.

"Smells good," he said in perfect English with a slight tinge of Italian accent. "You the baker?"

"I help out," Howard smiled back.

"If I lived in Philly, I'd come in here every day just to buy bread."

"Where are you from?"

"New York."

"I've never been there."

"New York is great. Lot's goin' on."

"Are you visiting someone?"

"You could say that." He strode to the counter. "Can you keep a secret?"

"Sure, I don't know anyone to tell a secret to anyway."

"You mean you ain't got no friends?"

"Well, Lucy and Dominick, they own the bakery."

"It's good to have friends and to have secrets, especially about other people. It gives you power over 'em."

Howard sharply disagreed, but kept his opinion to himself. "What's yours?"

"You could say I'm stayin' with my aunt and uncle, but I'm really hidin' out. Gotta lay low for a while."

"Why?" Howard thought Franco looked and talked like a character in a gangster movie.

"I helped do a job in Brooklyn."

"Are you a gangster?"

Franco burst out laughing. "Am I a gangster? Do I look like one to you?"

"No, you look like any other kid, but you talk like a gangster, in the movies."

"Yeah, I seen them movies. Don't let how I look fool ya. I'm a gangsta, just like them guys."

"The pictures I've seen, all the gangsters wear suits and ties and Fedoras."

"I have 'em back home. Can't wear 'em now or I could be recognized. This is my disguise."

"Are the police looking for you?"

"Most certain. That's why I ducked in here and glad I did. That smell."

"What did you do? What crime did you commit?"

"Helped pull a bank job."

"You robbed a bank?"

"Sure, do it whenever I need spendin' money. Like havin' my own personal account, just like rich people."

"But if you're caught and they arrest you, you'll go to prison."

"Won't get caught. Ain't a copper alive smart enough to catch me." Franco laughed. "Besides, most a them are on the take."

"Sounds dangerous. You could get shot."

"I dodge the bullets."

"You've been shot at before?"

"Sure, lots of times."

Howard stared at him in disbelief which further inflated Franco's sizeable ego.

"Hey, I need a pal here in Philly and it sounds like you need a pal. When do you get off work?"

Howard was certain he didn't want to be Franco's pal. The thought of fraternizing with gangsters and committing criminal acts and being shot at did not appeal to him. Someday, he hoped to arrest people like Franco.

"Well, we close at five. Then I have to clean the mixers for tomorrow morning."

"You have to work on Saturday?"

Howard nodded. "I also have my studies."

"Aw, I figured I don't need school no more so I quit. I got a job lined up. We all got jobs in our family."

"Robbing banks?"

Franco guffawed. "Naw, there's other kinds of business. But I sure had you goin' there, didn't I. No, I don't rob banks. I came to Philly to run numbers for my Uncle Angelo."

"I don't know anything about that."

"It's easy. I can teach you how."

"Well, I have a job."

"Yeah, you do."

"Did you want to buy some bread or something?"

"Sure, I'll take one a those." Franco pointed to a fat brown loaf lightly dusted with flour. "Listen, you got an alley out back?"

"Yes, we get deliveries there."

"Mind if I see?"

"I guess it's okay. You have to go through the kitchen."

"Ah, get me even closer to those great smells. Whatta place to work in, a bakery like this."

"You want to take your bread?"

"Sure, how much? Don't matter. Keep the change. Plenty where that come from." Franco tucked the loaf under his arm as he came around the end of the counter. "Name's Franco—- Franco Pasarelli. What's yours?" He extended his hand.

"Howard Gimbel."

"Pleased to make your acquaintance."

Howard nodded with a small grin. "Me too."

"So, where's the door? I'll just go out the back. Learnin' my way around town so to speak."

"Straight through there."

"See you again soon, Howard."

Howard raised his hand in a less than enthusiastic wave.

Howard discovered his role model in the prohibition officer, Eliott Ness. Ness battering down the doors of breweries became legend, as well as his refusal to take bribes, which garnered him and his men the name "The Untouchables."

What Howard admired about Ness was his absolute integrity and willingness to risk his life to fight crime. Al Capone tried three times to have him assassinated. The news carried the story of how Ness's body guard was gunned down and how Eliot narrowly averted getting into his car rigged with a car bomb.

Howard followed the news of the trial proceedings against Al Capone, who was convicted on charges of tax evasion, rather than his illegal empire that The Untouchables had smashed.

In wondering how to become such a guardian, Howard discovered that Eliott Ness had a college degree and had taken graduate studies in law and criminology from the University of Chicago. Howard did not forsee ever having the financial resources to go to college. He wondered if he might start off being a policeman, then becoming a detective. But his relationship with the Moscones moved him in a different direction.

One day, Howard was convinced that he spotted Yelena walking quickly along with a mob of workers streaming from the factory into the ghetto at the end of the day. As the men and women jostled along like jetsam, the crowd broke into smaller segments seeking escape to their individual abodes, their faces and identities becoming more distinct.

She was too far away to hear him. So he did not call out. He rushed after her departing figure, but lost sight of her in the maze of narrow streets.

Having caught a glimpse of Yelena, he was determined to find her. He hoped that if he waited at the same location, she might pass along the street at the same time. He would push his way into the crowd and touch her on the shoulder and she would turn in surprise at the sight of him.

The next evening, as he walked home along the usual route, he wondered if they had unknowingly passed many times and just never noticed each other. At that hour, the setting sun splayed out in a bruised maroon diffusion across the dust gray polluted sky. The ghetto occupants maneuvered along in numb unfocused reality.

Although he watched carefully, to his profound disappointment, he did not see her again. He positioned himself at strategic locations on other streets leading from the factory to no avail. When she did not come across his sight again, he went to the factory itself, but the guards would not let him enter and they would not give out or acknowledge any names of the workers.

He believed she must live somewhere in one of the ethnic ghettos, but there was little possibility he would ever find her.

Time worked against him. He had to attend school. He had to be at work. He had to be at home. He tried to retain in his memory any of the violin and viola pieces he had heard Yelena and Lilya play, but they were just as elusive as the players. He did not possess the ear or mind of a musician.

Because he grasped only brief conversational snatches of the gossip exchanged between the Italian women who came into the bakery and Lucy, he never fully understood the context of what they were saying. But often, he knew they were talking about him when they glanced in his direction and nodded and smiled. Howard figured that Lucy was probably saying something nice about him, or else he was being overly self-conscious.

Early one morning as he and Lucy were kneading and pulling and shaping dough together, she commented in her doting motherly way, "You don'ta look happy, bambino. Always your eyes dark and your mouth a frown. Why is this? A younga man like you. You shoulda laugh and smile alla time."

"Sometimes when I hear you sing, I remember two friends I had." He referred to Lucy's occasional humming and bursts of song from Italian arias. Although she did not have a trained voice, she was a natural soprano and had sung in church choirs as a child and as a young woman."

"My singing makea you sad? Oh, then I will stop. I sing to celebrate life. I should take you to hear good singing at the opera in New York."

"It's not that, Lucy. I love your singing. You can sing all you want. I can't sing and I can't play music, but I had two friends, girls, who played the viola and violin. They played in concerts. I saw them once and I also watched them practice."

"Are they not still your friends?"

Howard shook his head.

"Ah, now I know why you are sad."

"They were thrown out of their home by the Palmer men. Their parents were deported and the girls disappeared."

"I don't know about these Palmer men."

"It happened two years ago. There wasn't any news about the girls. They weren't communists."

"Ah, this thing about communists. It is not good."

Chapter 6
ON THE BICYCLE

According to Howard Gimbel, no one ever came away from a meeting with J. Edgar Hoover feeling good about himself. If they did, Hoover would have believed that he had failed to dominate and control them during the interaction with fear of his position and power. His intent was that the citizens of America, especially politicians, and his own agents, should live in a constant state of paranoia.

Howard believed the reason why he had been summoned was far different than what the FBI Director had in store for him. Rumors were always leaked by Hoover through one or more of his underlings to ensure that the target recipient felt the full sting of his intent before they actually stepped before him, or more commonly before his assistant director, Clyde Tolson, to receive their assignment or punishment, as the case might be.

Howard had heard through one of J. Edgar's "leaked" rumors that the director was displeased about something he had done, but there was no indication of what. That was how the boss worked, kept his G-Men off balance. He used informants even among his own agents. Hoover's network of spies extended to every field office. No one escaped his scrutiny and you never knew what you had done to offend his lordship. You became concerned when you received one of his famous memos written in graceful language that notified you that you had been relieved of your duties.

Some agents who had gone by the way had been caught in flagrant violation of J. Edgar Hoover's standards. Howard Gimbel would never forget the day he graduated from FBI training. He and his fellow graduates had expected to hear an inspiring commencement address from their famous director. But when the pudgy short man with the rapid quirky gait sped out onto the raised speaker's platform, as though he were trying to contain an imminent bowel movement, and, on tip toes, was barely able to peer down at them over the top of the podium, he spoke only two sentences in his stuffy autocratic accent as if the words were being strained with concise difficulty through his nasal passages.

"If any one of you drinks alcoholic spirits on the job or off, you're out," he raised a fist and jerked his thumb in a quick backwards motion, as though hitching a ride. "If you violate any rule of conduct of this organization, you're out," he repeated the gesture. Then just as abruptly as he had stepped on-stage, he turned on his heel and exited without another glance or care at his audience.

There was no applause, only dead silence, followed by an uncomfortable shuffling of the gray-suited men. No one dared to venture a word of criticism or approbation out of fear that the over-zealous, new G-man seated next to him might report his comments to the boss.

This first impression of Hoover caused Howard to question his choice of careers, but he was determined to live up to the heroic example of Elliot Ness and the Untouchables in their fight against crime. What his partner, Tim Landon, knew about Howard was that he did not believe crime was limited to the lower classes. He himself questioned whether he shouldn't have become a politician crusading for social reform, rather than an FBI agent with limited authority and no influence whatsoever. Only the Director had influence, and of a negative kind.

Howard was accustomed to waiting. Waiting was a competency required for his line of work. To fill the time, he would alternately focus on his inner thoughts as they were precipitated by the details of his immediate surroundings.

Not wanting his eyes to wander endlessly around the room, he surreptitiously watched Hoover's secretary, Helen Gandy, working at her desk. After she had signed him in with a stodgy uninviting acknowledgement of his entrance, she had returned to her interrupted typing. The steady metallic clicking of the keys on the tall Underwood was the only sound in the oak wood paneled office.

Helen Gandy recalled the many immigrant *haus fraus* he had either seen or known as a boy. Her heavy brow creased inward with a scowl of concentration that bore down over a thick nose and accentuated the wrinkles under her dark probing eyes. Gravity pulled at her from the frowning corners of her severe mouth, to a drooping chin, and a squarish dark dress that denied it concealed the body of a woman.

Gimbel had heard it discreetly mentioned by a fellow agent, that Hoover had hired Helen Gandy as his secretary, because she reminded him of his mother. At the age of 35, Hoover still lived with his mother in the same house in which he'd been raised as a child. His curious relationship raised speculation among Washington politicians. Hoover's manufactured public image, however, overcompensated for any aspersions cast against his virility. In his paranoiac quest to root out communists and eradicate crime, he exploited every opportunity to perpetrate the myth that he was a fearless strongman.

The stark unassuming office occupied by Helen Gandy and the closed back office where Hoover secluded himself left Gimbel wondering how so much influence and power could emanate from this alcove on a side street of the nation's Capitol. Gimbel suspected he had been drawn in much as a spider reels in its struggling prey and wraps it in a food cache cocoon for future consumption. He could not shake the intuition that he had been hired to play a key role in Hoover's master plan to expose and eliminate communists from American society, because Hoover himself had recruited him. Although he had earned a law degree, Howard had never thought of becoming a G-Man until two of them called at his home a week after his graduation from Pennsylvania State University.

His immediate reaction when he opened the door and they introduced themselves by showing their badges was that he was being investigated as a potential witness for a trial. But when he invited them in, they put him at his ease by congratulating him and explaining they were seeking qualified men to join *The Bureau*. They had checked his academic record, which was superb, and his family background, which demonstrated a high level of morality and support of American values. They described the training he would undergo and the elite group of peers with whom he would work to enforce the laws of the Federal Government.

The student was both impressed and pleased by their interest and apparently genuine praise. They invited him to visit the local FBI office where he would meet the SAC or Special Agent in Charge and could learn more about a career with the Justice Department. The two agents were at Howard's door promptly at eight o'clock the next morning to drive him downtown.

Much had happened during the ensuing six years, particularly the crash of the world economy in 1929 and the onset of The Great Depression and the Presidential election of Franklin Delano Roosevelt.

Howard's summons to J. Edgar Hoover's office in June of 1939 was the first time he stepped through and out of Hoover's hallowed doors, even though he worked in the same building. He had passed the feared little man in the hall from time to time and seen him with his ever present companion, Clyde Tolson, coming from their favorite local restaurant at lunchtime.

Hoover's rise to prominence in the Federal Government on the strength of his personal agendas left Howard feeling uncertain and ambivalent as to what constituted true law enforcement. Hoover had transformed what had been a bureau of corruption into a highly efficient investigative agency with the technologies of a crime laboratory and fingerprinting.

He had also established the National Police Academy. Yet President Roosevelt had authorized him to spy on opposing politicians and wire tap the phones of John L. Lewis and other union officials in the CIO. With the few exceptions of the arrests of John Dillinger, Pretty Boy Floyd, and Baby Face Nelson, Howard perceived that Hoover was more intent on violating and suppressing human and civil rights in his world of extreme conservatism, bigotry, and racism. He was a tyrant and a Czar in an imperfect democracy. How he managed to circumvent the Constitution astounded Howard.

"Good Morning, Agent Gimbel," Clyde Tolson, the associate director, suddenly emerged from a side office and strode across the waiting room to greet him.

Howard quickly stood, grabbing his snap brim hat before it could slip from his lap to the floor and cause him a moment of embarrassment in addition to his mounting anxiety. "Good morning, sir." His extended hand met Tolson's with a firm grip. This occasion was the first time he had a close-up look at Tolson.

A number of rumors and impressions circulated around the Bureau offices regarding Tolson, Hoover's second in command. Howard was impressed by his athletic features and friendly business-like manner. He was every inch the model of a G-man, handsome in a nondescript way with the thin stringy physique of a tennis athlete. He bore an uncanny resemblance to Hoover in that he copied how Hoover dressed and walked and his mannerisms. Taken side by side, they could be mistaken for brothers, Tolson a slender version of his pudgy pugnacious boss.

Carefully concealed rumors were uttered that Hoover and Tolson were homosexual lovers. Neither maintained a female relationship and they took numerous vacations together to play the horses in Miami and in California. Their enjoyment of New York nightlife exempted them from Hoover's short speech at Howard's graduation from the academy, "If any one of you drinks alcoholic spirits on the job or off, you're out. If you violate any rule of conduct of this organization, you're out."

Howard and his associate FBI agents shared a common perception about Hoover's lieutenant. Tolson was politically savvy and acted as Hoover's shadow. He looked after his interests to protect the image and reputation of his Boss whenever criticism was directed at the Bureau. John Edgar Hoover was the Bureau. He had hand-picked Tolson, who, as a former clerk and confidential secretary in the war department, could maneuver through Washington's bureaucracy. Agents knew Tolson was Hoover's mouthpiece when a career change or the termination of a career was being conducted.

The coined phrase that Hoover was putting an agent "on the bicycle" meant he was being demoted and given an undesirable assignment, usually in a distant location, to pressure the man into quitting the Bureau. Due to lack of objective evidence, terminations were not always a clean straightforward affair. They were often premised on Hoover's personal prejudices and opinions about a man. If he didn't like someone, he would get rid of him.

Although Tolson was outwardly friendly and gregarious, he was distrusted by most agents in The Bureau, because he was the Director's yes-man.

"Please accompany me to my office," Tolson invited in a cordial, yet businesslike manner.

Howard followed barely a step behind. Once they were inside, Tolson closed the door and walked around to the leather chair behind his desk. "Be seated, Agent Gimbel," he gestured to one of two straight-backed wooden chairs facing him. Howard complied, feeling like a school boy confronted by the principal. He lightly clutched the brim of his hat centered on his lap.

Tolson slightly raised, then dropped a file on his desk top. "We've been looking over your record. Since you joined the Bureau, you've been steady and consistent in your duties. No blemishes or deficiencies and you've complied and lived up to the personal standards established by our esteemed Director."

"Thank you, sir. I endeavor to do my best."

"Which is why we've called you here."

Howard wondered at the plural reference, since no one else was in the room, unless Hoover were going to make an appearance. But then Howard intuitively understood that Tolson always spoke in the plural in deference to his boss who ruled his political empire with an iron fist. Even Tolson operated under the shadow of Hoover's will.

"You've kept a low profile during assignments and investigations," Tolson continued.

"That's right. I have never sought any special recognition. I consider myself a member of a team that is mutually supportive."

"We know that about you. However, you have not significantly distinguished yourself in the line of duty."

"I'm not certain I understand, sir." Howard's immediate thought was that Tolson referred to Howard's first assignment with

Tim Landon. They were supposed to tap the phone of a Senator that Hoover didn't like because "he has communist sympathies." In fact, the Senator was a social democrat and promoted bills and voted reforms for oppressed labor and for agrarian populists. Hoover considered him to be "un-American." The two neophyte agents were also to shadow the Senator for thirty days,

Tim was an experienced electrician. So he handled the installation of the device in the Senator's office and home phones. They gained entry by posing as phone repair line technicians. They monitored the Senator's conversations from a nearby office bearing the name of a fictitious company on the door.

They discreetly followed the Senator and noted with whom he dined and who visited him at his office and private residence, a large town home a few blocks from the Capitol building.

When Tolson presented Howard's and Tim's report to Hoover, the Director had expressed disappointment in the lack of evidence regarding the Senator's "questionable political and moral values." He said he knew that the man collaborated with communist organizations and engaged in "scxual philandering," which he claimed was a common practice among the rank and file of senators, congressmen, lobbyists, Presidents, and their amoral staffs. "Only the FBI is clean," he stated, "because I keep it that way."

Tolson explained that The Boss wanted the two G-men to "prove yourselves. Go out and be more thorough in your investigation. This is, after all, a matter of national security. You haven't given The Director anything more than he already knows or could learn if he attended cocktail parties. But, of course he doesn't drink alcohol. He wants you to probe deeper, find out the Senator's secrets and bring them in. Is that clear?"

Tim and Howard had nodded in agreement. What Hoover wanted was very clear, but they didn't discuss the matter until they left the building and were walking down Pennsylvania Avenue where they could talk freely, since Hoover bugged the offices of his staff.

"He wants us to dig up dirt," said Tim.

"But we already know there isn't any." Howard jammed his fists into the pockets of his gray flannel trousers. "Welch doesn't cheat on his wife."

"It's pretty clear we have to invent something to please The Boss."

"Come on, Tim. We can't do that. We're talking about the man's life and career. He hasn't done anything immoral or illegal."

"In this town, it happens all the time."

"What about our ethics, the ethics of the FBI?"

"J. Edgar just wants to hold sway over everybody in Washington. He's a blackmailer. That's where he gets his power. Callahan got invited once down into the vault. Hoover collects some real spicy stuff on film, some of our prominent leaders and movie stars goin' at it like rabbits. The files he has on everybody, so he says, is to keep the Government running on the straight and narrow. Presidents and senators come and go, but Hoover doesn't."

Howard shunted away the memory of his discussion with Tim Landon and focused on what Tolson was saying.

"Don't get me wrong, Agent Gimbel. Your comportment is very acceptable. But the results of your work are, shall we say, mundane."

"I try to blend in. It has never been a priority with me to distinguish myself." Howard and other agents well knew the danger of seeking the limelight. Hoover himself was compulsive about personal recognition and publicity. If any name or photograph appeared in the press regarding a Bureau achievement, it had better be Hoover's, or the unsuspecting agent would find himself out of a job the following day.

Hoover's private agency publicity mill, Crime Record, maintained a steady stream of editorials to favored journalists and publishers in support of his image and Bureau operations. The department also rained rebuttals, with the occasional use of blackmail, against attempts to discredit Hoover's illegal methods.

"We're putting you on a special covert assignment," said Tolson.

"Thank you, sir. I'm honored to be considered."

"We're putting you under cover."

"I'm prepared for any contingency, sir."

"I'm certain you are. Do you recall the name Yelena Ivanov?"

Wondering, but half-knowing, where the question would lead, Howard did not immediately respond, as buried painful childhood memories erupted from the past. He nodded. "Yes, I know who she is."

"You were childhood friends."

"Yes, we knew each other."

"Did you know that during the Palmer investigations, it was your father who apprehended the Ivanovs and arranged for their deportation from the United States?"

Howard tried to contain how stunned he was at this sudden revelation. "I remember he came home one night and told us he had become a Palmer man, but I didn't know what that was except he was protecting America."

"That's exactly what he was doing. Do you know what was going on in this country at that time."

"I know there was some unrest. I was a young boy then. I don't really have a sense of it. All I remember is that the two Ivanov girls were gifted musicians, child prodigies, and their father made violins."

"Frederick Ivanov and his wife were Russian socialists who had migrated to Germany years before the revolution. That made them communists in our country. 1920 was a turning point for the FBI, which didn't exist as you know of it today. It was The Director's steppingstone to the formation of this agency of which you have become a proud and valued member."

As a boy, Howard did not understand the political implications of what was happening in the world; but as a college student, he had read the history.

The Espionage Act had expired at the end of the First World War. No federal law existed that forbade a United States citizen from being a socialist, IWW union member, or an anarchist. Ignoring this fact, the Attorney General, Mitchell Palmer, had forged ahead with his plan by appointing a young file clerk who, fifteen years later would be Howard Gimbel's boss, J. Edgar Hoover, the Director of the FBI.

The upheaval of society through revolution was linked to race riots in Washington and Chicago and labor unrest in industries. The cost of living had risen beyond what most Americans could afford and wages had dropped to a bare subsistence level. With massive unemployment came cheap labor and by the end of 1919, more than four million workers were on strike.

J. Edgar Hoover and his staff gathered information on anyone who had "any connection with an ultra radical body or movement." From mailing lists and the Bureau of Investigation's extensive files, Hoover's staff compiled and assembled thousands of profiles on individuals identified as radicals, communist sympathizers, Reds.

In addition, he encouraged local police departments to recruit honest and patriotic men to join "Red Squads," to become "Palmer Men."

Howard remembered his father flushed, brimming with self-importance, bigotry and emotion bursting through their tenement door into the kitchen and proclaiming in a loud drunken bray, "Look at me! I'm a Palmer Man now! I'm a Palmer man!" He brandished his badge that had been given to him by the police sergeant at Clement's swearing in. "Do you see this?" He waved the badge in their faces. "Do ya see this! This makes me important. This makes me somebody to reckon with! Do you know who we are, the Palmer Men? We're gonna find every goddamn communist and anarchist and kick their Red asses out of the country!" He staggered and attempted to strut his skinny frame around them sitting at the spindle legged wooden table. His father's hawkish emaciated features reminded Howard of a bird of prey. "And we're gonna start tomorrow night. Tomorrow night. Get 'em when they don't expect it. Get 'em when they're asleep so they can't run away and hide."

Clement Gimbel lived in a world of envy and labored in the pictorial depiction of hell's furnaces. He worked in a factory that melted raw scrap metal into molten alloys that were converted to "pigs" and shipped to manufacturers of metal products.

Six hours ago, he had stood on the bridge overlooking the lava of molten metal streaming into giant cauldrons that spumed explosive flames and steam from the popping bubbling liquefaction that would disintegrate a worker should he have the misfortune to fall into one of the vats.

His job was to unload scrap metal from freight cars onto large hand carts which he pushed on rails to the staging areas of ten gigantic forges. The position that he aspired to was at the other end of the process where the molten metal was poured into molds to be formed into pig iron and steel bars and rails.

Every worker wore protective leather aprons and gloves made from asbestos, The handlers were the strongest men. They had the toughest job. Using large metal tongs, they hefted the iron pigs as they dropped out of the forge onto a conveyor. They worked in teams, lifting and stacking. They were steady, rippling with muscles, priding themselves in maintaining a steady rhythm and not letting the conveyor overrun and jam the flow of iron.

Not being of their physical caliber, Clement was pleased that the handlers would include him in their evening stop at the pub enroute home from the mill. He was especially pleased that Aubrey Killian knew his name and would raise a glass with him. It was from Aubrey that he heard about the police recruiting men to join the Red Guard. Aubrey's brother was a policeman.

After shedding leather aprons, gloves, and hardhats in the dressing room, the workers would rush out in a mob through the guarded chain link gate topped with glistening deadly concertina wire. Clement always experienced the sensation that when the guards opened the gate, he was being released from prison. Once you were inside the factory fence, you could not leave until the whistle blew at the end of the day.

Clement bobbed and jostled along in the sea of immigrant faces, listening to the bitter laughter, swearing at the sweat and grime and harshness of their working conditions. The men swarmed along the narrow tenement streets like water released from a dam.

Once inside the pub amidst whirling smoke and deafening noise, only a word or phrase could be snatched from the fetid air reeking of garlic and whiskey and beer.

"...And the bastard says to me..."

"...Here's to the fucking Irish..."

"Watch your fuckin' tongue! I'm fuckin' Irish!"

A roar of laughter.

"...Like he just got off the boat..."

"...Keep the bitch knocked up I say..."

" Got a real set of melons on 'er you ain't never seen the likes of..."

"...The foreman he says to me..."

"...It was different in the old country..."

"...He got no right..."

"...Hear what I tell you..."

"...Face like a goat..."

"...Ain't no beauty yerself..."

"...Bust his head open..."

"...He can't get away with it..."

"...Throwed 'im in the clink..."

"...Just come out myself a week ago..."

"...Got it comin' to 'im."

"...Brain of a piss ant..."

A pint of warm beer was shoved into Clement's hand. He touched the edge to his lips and liquid amber flowed down his throat and warmed his stomach. The instant surge of alcohol mixed with raucous laughter at obscene jokes caused Clement to feel that he truly belonged among them. He reveled at being in the womb of the manliness surrounding him. Another long swallow precipitated an initial euphoria that left him glowing and secure that he was a man among men, that he belonged. He raised his voice and joined in the laughter and his eyes rolled cockeyed with tension and delirium.

This was the memory Howard held of his father and how it had determined the direction of his life, to provide redemption for people he loved and fight for the rights of others like them. His personal journey had now placed him in direct conflict with the woman whose values and ideals he believed in, to help the victims of a society founded on greed and the exploitation of its people.

The image of the smashed and splintered instruments strewn about the room returned to Howard. The entire Ivanov household had been gutted during the Palmer raid in which Howard's father had participated. Clothing and furniture had been dragged out into the street. Plates and crockery and paintings had been smashed. Shards littered the floor. The silver and candlesticks had been stolen.

"Yelena Ivanov has never changed her name since then," said Tolson. "We find that odd, almost as though she's flagrantly thumbing her nose at us. Today, she is an influential union organizer working with the CIO," said Tolson. "She is the only woman who has the political ear of John L. Lewis and she's an avowed communist. Of course, Lewis is only using her like he does everybody else. And being that the goal of the Bureau is to stamp out communism wherever it rears its ugly head, we want to terminate her activity."

Howard struggled with the implication that had just been presented to him. Were Hoover and Tolson expecting him to assassinate his childhood friend, Yelena Ivanov? He had never killed anyone in self-defense, let alone murdered another human being in cold blood. He had not heard the exact words, but the innuendo hung in the air.

Until the passage of the National Industrial Recovery Act, union membership had been considered un-American. Although the President, Franklin Delano Roosevelt, had signed the bill into law, big business interests and right wing conservatives would not recognize unions. They hired armed gangs and planted spies among the work force to curb union activity by using fear and violence to intimidate and coerce anyone who might be inclined to join a union.

"We want you to get close to Yelena Ivanov and learn more about who she works with and where they are. We know for a fact that she spearheads a network of communists in this country. We want to find them and eliminate them. We suspect John Collier is one of them. He's the Commissioner of Indian Affairs and is in charge of the Federal Recovery Program in New Mexico. You will be working closely with him to establish a law and order program on the reservation. Of course, you will not let it be known that you are from the FBI. We have kept a file on Collier ever since his days organizing cooperatives and praising Russian communism."

Tolson handed him a plain manila envelope bulging with documents it contained.

"You will find this information helpful that we have compiled on Collier and also on how to establish a law and order program according to Government policies and standards. These relate to policies of the Bureau of Indian Affairs and Government management of tribes on reservations. It is important that you become familiar with this information."

Howard accepted the package with a nod.

What Tolson didn't convey, but that Howard later learned, was that the Dawes Act had removed the protection of Indian lands and opened the way for big business interests along with lawyers and bankers to steal and convert the land to white title. Howard had no knowledge he was being thrust right into the middle of the conflict and was expected to help the exploiters in another instance of a long history of treaty violations.

"We want to ensure that the interests of the United States Government are not compromised in any way," Tolson emphasized the Bureau's position. "We've also acquired recent intelligence that Yelena Ivanov is planning to travel to the Southwest for the express purpose of organizing strikes at the mines. We want you to renew your relationship with her. As the Law and Order Director, you are more likely to be perceived by her as being sympathetic with the Indians, since you are conspicuously there to help them. You will keep the Special Agent in Charge in Santa Fe briefed of her activities. His name is Halen Braun. He will contact you when you arrive in New Mexico."

"How long am I to be there?"

"Until you get the job done. We anticipate your assignment will be for the duration of two years, possibly three."

"I understand. When does the assignment begin?"

"You are booked on a train leaving Washington the day after tomorrow. Miss Gandy will provide you with your ticket on your way out."

"That doesn't leave me much time to prepare for being away for such an extended period."

"We understand the hardship, but your readiness and flexibility are essential to the success of this operation. Yelena Ivanov will be boarding that same train when it stops in Wabash, Indiana, where she currently is staying with accomplices. We have had other agents shadowing her and using wire taps on her phone and in her room. She has purchased a ticket and will be traveling coach. You will coincidentally happen upon her and engage her in conversation. Remember old times when you were children together and were close friends. Rekindle that friendship. Become her traveling partner and confidant."

Tolson paused before dismissing him. "If there is any doubt in your mind that you can carry out this assignment, then this is the time to express it."

Howard knew that was the cue as to whether he would continue his career with the FBI or not. If he wavered in the least, Tolson would terminate his employment on the spot. Hoover had demoted him, put him on the bicycle. They wanted to see how long he could ride it before he fell.

Howard was appalled at what Tolson knew about his childhood friendship with Yelena Ivanov. Tolson could only have acquired that information from Howard's father, a probability that left Howard feeling even more disgusted and ambivalent about him.

"There is no doubt in my mind that I can fulfill this assignment," Howard lied convincingly. He would do everything in his power to protect Yelena, not destroy her.

"Good. Oh, and by the way, you don't have to be concerned with finishing out your current duties. We're moving a new man into your position to work with Tim Landon."

Howard nodded, attempting to conceal a sudden wave of depression with a limp smile. He and Tim had met while attending The Academy and had been friends ever since. This sudden move on Howard would cause Tim to become paranoid about his own position. But they both knew there were no guarantees when you worked for the Bureau.

"Do you have any questions?" Tolson indicated he wished to end the discussion.

Howard shook his head. "No, sir."

"We appreciate your steadfastness, Agent Gimbel, and we expect to hear great things from you. Just keep your SAC, Halen Braun, informed. He'll be your channel of communication with this office." Tolson rose and reached a hand across his desk. Howard followed his example. As he walked to the door to let himself out, he noticed that Tolson immediately busied himself with some other documents as though the change he had forced into Howard's life were of no consequence.

Helen Gandy wordlessly held out Howard's train ticket packet. He approached her desk. He did not thank her and she did not bother to look up from her work.

Chapter 7
INTO THE LANDSCAPE

Howard gazed out the train window that framed an ever shifting panorama of woods and farms and lowered gates at clanging small town rail crossings.

The image of his friends, Tim and Lucy Landon, waving from the platform had fallen to the rear of his line of vision as the iron wheels engaged and the green and gold liveried chain of 81 feet long 80 ton cars lurched forward. The sweating monstrous black steel engine released explosive clouds of billowing steam that swept up and over the station platform erasing them and their final frantic gestures with a long blast of its hoarse bellowing whistle.

Howard settled back into the upholstered comfort of his chair in the lounge. The journey would be long, several days by train with various short and longer stops in cities and towns along the way. But he felt he could grow accustomed to this manner of travel. He had complete freedom of movement and his choice of seating on sofas and chairs reminiscent of an upscale home in the city. Deep plush carpeting covered the floor. Highly polished brass light fixtures cast their illumination over mahogany tables and fine panel woodwork. Along the aisle toward the other end of the lounge were two sets of tables where gourmet meals were served.

The white-jacketed Negro porter had carried Howard's baggage on ahead of him to his private bedroom at the middle of the car. Both a sofa and an upper berth converted to beds with spring mattresses at night. Howard was surprised to discover he had a private toilet, although a shower was farther down the hall. The berth also had a porter call, a reading lamp and a fold down writing desk. He felt like he was riding in a hotel on wheels.

American Landscape

Only people who still had money rode in the Pullman. Howard felt somewhat out of his element at their apparent vestige of wealth even in these hard times. The men and women were elegantly dressed and did not invite social interaction. Although he made a few restless trips to the lounge for cocktails and meals, he did not engage other passengers in conversation. After reading a copy of the New York Times and thumbing through a *Saturday Evening Post* magazine, he retired to his private room where he had a view of the scenery through his own spacious window.

The singular beauty of the rural towns and countryside would be periodically interrupted by images of destitution and squalor. Occasionally he glimpsed a hobo camp or jungle down an embankment near a stream, a gathering of outcasts, ragged homeless men living in tarpaper and cardboard shacks called "Hoovervilles," so named after the outgoing President, Herbert Hoover, who citizens blamed for The Depression. They called it the "Hoover Depression." Pulled-out empty trouser pockets were satirically referred to as "Hoover flags." These angry dispossessed citizens sat about small fires and ate whatever food they could beg or steal. Seeing them and their suffering from the comfort of his Pullman window raised Howard's sympathy. Without his job, he could easily be cast among them. He conjectured that they would probably kill for the steak dinner he would enjoy that evening and the whiskey cocktails. But he had no realization or understanding of their social code and mutual support of each other.

Sharing was the common rule. Each man contributed by collecting fuel for the fire used to brew coffee or cook a Mulligan stew, or he foraged in the area for food, either stealing from local hen houses or gardens or begging for handouts or *lumps*. Mutual respect for the belongings of others prevailed with the exception of occasionally hi-jacking or robbing men while they slept.

As the train slowed in approaching a town, Howard saw several such men leap from different sections of the train and scurry away into the woods and brush like insects frantically deserting a rotten log that had been disturbed. Railroad police patrolled the train while it discharged and took on new passengers and mail. He saw one of the dark uniformed *cinder bulls* waving a bat during a brief chase after a high-stepping transient who quickly outdistanced him.

The hobo jungles were establishd for quick access to and from train yards or rail lines, but far enough at the outskirts of a town to avoid attracting the attention of irate local citizens and the law. The train was their primary method of transport as they journeyed across the country in search of work. They were knowledgable about trains and the workings of the railroad.

Some camps were of a temporary nature and others permanent, where trains were scheduled for frequent stops at water towers. The jungle camps offered a few conveniences, utensils and pots and kettles, a rope on which to hang clothes. A user of such a camp would dry the cooking and coffee cans and turn them upside down so they would not rust or fill with rain water. A migrant with integrity would leave it in the condition he found it for the next man who happened along.

As Howard read in the NewYork Times about FDR's plans for economic recovery, it became clear that industrial leaders had created and nurtured this transient workforce. They could conveniently hire from this source of temporary labor and get rid of workers with no ties or obligations, no pensions or other benefits. Workers were a disposable commodity.

They were simultaneously a cornerstone of industrial society and also among its greatest victims. They were welcomed in areas of underemployment or whenever their labor was required, cutting timber in the Northwest, following wheat harvests across the plains, and laboring in mines and factories. They were often seen as champions of the general populace for their unwillingness and financial inability to live conventional lives . Conversely, they were also viewed as a menace by those who possessed wealth or even a modicum of economic security.

Howard knew that unemployment could be a breeding ground for lawlessness. When the hoboes' labor was no longer needed, they were driven out of town on the "Hobo Express." Local police and vigilantes would meet incoming freight trains, arrest, and ship out the hoboes in trucks to the county or state line. Anti-tramp laws were enacted across the country. Lacing a handout of meat with strychnine or arsenic to discourage "dangerous," "vicious," "thieving" beggars from coming to the door was a proposed solution. The word would spread among them so they would avoid spending time in such a town.

Traveling across West Virginia, Howard sensed by the train's marked slowing that it was beginning to move upward in elevation. The ponds and meadows and farms appeared less frequently across his window on the world until they were replaced altogether by a continuous wall of thickening fir and pine and deciduous hardwood forests of maples, oaks and white blooming service berry trees interspersed with occasional meadows of brilliant red and gold flame azaleas and mountain laurel and pink clusters of rhododendron.

As they bore deeper and deeper into the Appalachian wilderness, Howard experienced the sensation of the slowly crawling train being swallowed and absorbed into the bowels of a great green land beast. The once awesome smoke-belching roaring black engine with clashing piston driven wheels and chain of cars were rendered diminutive in scale by the massive spreading mountains and, from a distance, appeared no bigger than a child's toy.

This impression was the first of a growing perception by Howard, as he journeyed across the country, that Americans existed in a vast changing landscape to which they attached themselves and adapted in different ways from rural agrarian societies to urban industrial centers. What he witnessed was the scrambling disarray of a people drawn by the social forces and demands of industry from the fields and farms of Europe and the United States into the coalition of a massive immigrant society.

The economic depression had cut them loose and set them adrift, floundering to restore security and balance in their lives in the absence of employment while surviving at a subsistence level.

The Appalachians extended in three divisions from Quebec in Canada and paralleled the eastern coast into the Southeastern states. The train meandered through the densely forested hills and river valleys of the central ranges, the Catskill, Allegheny, and Blue Ridge Mountains, caused by the principle geologic uplift when crustal tectonic plates collided during their formation 500 million years before.

Beginning in Pennsylvania, the Blue Ridge chain extended south-west in progressively greater heights through Virginia and western North Carolina where it divided into Georgia to become the Great Smokey Mountains.

In passing through the Appalachian Mountains and coming into the coal fields of eastern Pennsylvania, the stations were established in the proximity of mining operations of coal towns where long haul freight trains would attach cars loaded with bituminous and anthracite bound for the steel mills of Pittsburgh, Cleveland and cities in Indiana.

In nearly every city and town where the train stopped to refuel coal and take on water, the image that stuck in Howard's mind was the regimented impoverished conditions under which people were living. He would take these opportunities to stretch his legs and walk about within the proximity of the railroad stations. He also noticed commonalities from one *patch* to the next of the society and community values of coal towns that were the result of their operational and economic infrastructure.

Most families lived in low rent identical housing furnished by the companies. The houses were constructed either of wood frame or of shingle siding and were squarish and functional. Smaller homes consisted of a kitchen-living room and one or two bedrooms. Outhouses were located in the backyards.

Immigrants from many parts of Europe including French, Italian, Polish, Czech, Ukrainian and Slovakian filled the ranks of men who earned their living from mining.

Mining engineers occupied a row of red brick houses with wide large porches facing the main road that ran through the center of town. The mine superintendent's impressive white house and well-maintained grounds marked the beginning of First Street. Adjacent neatly occupied brick houses belonged to the company physicians and hospital staff.

Beyond these areas, miners and their families lived in three bedroom shingle houses lining each side of the street called Nine Row. Across the railroad tracks, smaller cheaper houses clustered to form a shanty town.

The remainder of the town both to the left and right of the main road followed the pattern of four to six room, tall, narrow, rectangular houses, most without bathrooms.

A large boarding hotel, offices, a saloon, a post office, and a mercantile store dominated the center of town near a company bank, a company-regulated newspaper, churches and sometimes a movie theatre. A multi-storied school constructed of brick or stone provided education through eighth grade.

Among the men he saw on the street going to and from work, Howard thought they were a tough breed of necessity to work in the physically dangerous conditions of the mines. They would use their safety lamps to check for explosive methane gas that might have accumulated and for black damp which signified an oxygen deficiency. They also had to watch that the ribs of coal or the coal face did not roll on them and they often worked lying on their backs in cold ground water.

Explosions and fatal accidents were common. A scorching fireball could fill a cavern, choking the miners' lungs, bursting their veins, and striking them to earth in writhing tortuous death.

Miners were paid an average of two dollars a day, or thirty-five cents a ton. The company then took out deductions for rent, coal, electricity, and medical care. What was left paid for a meager diet of soup made from left-over bones when a family did have meat, bread and old country variations of pasta stuffed with potatoes, cheese, or fruit. Some families maintained vegetable gardens and canned and stored their produce in cellars as a winter supplement.

Howard grew aware that he was leaving the Appalachian's behind as the terrain gradually changed to low rolling wooded hills and level cultivated farmlands with occasional herds of pastured dairy cattle.

Among his tasks, Howard had been assigned by J. Edgar Hoover to oversee and monitor the activities of John Collier, a known communist, on the Civilian Conservation Corps Indian reservation land projects in New Mexico. Howard began to sense the FBI Director's behind the scenes disapproval and resistance to the President. Tim Landon had told him that Hoover had agents spy on FDR and his family and opened files on their personal lives, taking a special interest in Eleanor Roosevelt, whom he held under great suspicion and despised for her independent progressive thinking and behavior.

The route of the train followed a succession of cities enshrouded by polluting clouds of black smoke continuously belching from the coal-burning steel mills into the atmosphere and descending as fine soot over the buildings and vehicles and people—- Pittsburgh, Cleveland, Gary—- cities populated with Italians, Poles, Hungarians, Slovenians, Ukrainians, and other eastern Europeans who came to the region to work in the mills and transplant their cultures to the neighborhoods.

The location of raw materials, coal in Pennsylvania and iron in upper Michigan and Minnesota with transportation by freighters on The Great Lakes affected the movement of disaffected Europeans to seek a better life working in the mines and steel mills. The impoverished conditions under which they were forced to exist caused them to further pursue the reality of that sought after better life, a political and social force that now had Howard Gimbel on a train to prevent Yelena Ivanov from helping the working class to accomplish their dream, a unifying aspect of the different cultures that came together.

First generation immigrants tended to maintain their separation from others. Their children, by contrast, assimilated and integrated as a result of being exposed to new cultures at an early age. Young children had less experience with their native society than their parents, and were less attached to related beliefs, values, and customs. Their parents settled where they would not be isolated from the background and social contacts that provided a familiar environment. They clustered in urban villages adjacent to those of other European neighbors. Networks evolved of people who helped each other and maintained their original languages and religions in churches, schools, hospitals, and social organizations.

As the train approached the outskirts of Wabash, Indiana, Howard tried to reconcile his conflicting feelings of anxiety and anticipation at meeting Yelena Ivanov again after seventeen years. He wondered if she had changed much and if he would have trouble recognizing her.

***

Chapter 8
BARRICADES

Yet a mile from the crossing, against the horizon of the vast rolling plain, the three sons could see the approaching train under the full moon. At that distance, it appeared as a moving string of connected tiny yellow lanterns, no larger than gold beads. This necklace was lead with deceptive swiftness by an arcing light, a searching blinding eye that slashed the darkness of the sweeping prairie night.

As the young men watched, there was no physical reference by which to gauge the speed of the train. Its movement tricked the eye as it seemed to thrust along in fits and bursts so that it was never at any single moment where the eye registered it had seen it. Its voice was a distant haunting wail, drifting to them like that of a coyote on the desert scented wind. The voice curled gently around Norm's mind, lulled and caressed him, drawing him on. He was in a stupor, near dozing at the wheel. His brothers were unaware of anything beyond the glow of their own headlights out there somewhere in the shifting shadows of brush. The wail was only a coyote.

Their effort to follow the constantly shimmering lights failed them. The train was only a tiny crawling creature somewhere out there ahead of them, elusive as a firefly, no longer at the front nor to the side of them. It was consumed in the swarmy insect glow of their own dim lights and existed only as a rapid pulsation that could not be fixed in time and space. The flashing eye swept toward them, caught them in its brief flash and was gone. Still three hundred yards out, it moved on steadily inevitability toward the crossing.

Norm was certain he saw and heard the train rush past. He perceived the minute string of lanterns moving away beyond, distant, tiny, diminishing. Warmth and drowsiness consumed him. The voice brushed him, a soft feather in his mind, a distortion of dreams where there existed no up and down nor left from right. He floated secure in the golden wash of light, did not hear his brothers' screams nor sense that other hands frantically clawed at the wheel.

For an instant, a growing threatening buzz descended over them like an approaching yellow jacket or carpenter bee as if they dozed in a flower-scented field on a hot summer afternoon. The tiny creature exploded rearing above them, an iron horse with clashing tons of snorting black metal, a roaring black Cyclops of hissing steam.

An acrid scorching of the air seized away their breath and seared their lungs. The moving wall of death instantly numbed their minds and spat them into oblivion with such impact that their limbs separated from them flailing the night in a disembodied limbo. They were no more than the smashed insects that fluttered out of the darkness into their headlights and splattered their windshield.

In the small desert town of Mesa, the Liggets were considered curiosities of a sort indigenous to the Southwest. Too coarse and removed from any but the most functional amenities, they were shunned by the local civilized citizenry, including ranchers, miners, and railroaders. Most would rather raise a glass with an Indian than a Ligget. Some fatal blood had been spilled over such social discrimination, not Ligget blood. Even Carmody had to back off on one occasion.

Jerome Ligget had bought a saloon patron a drink in an attempt to be friendly. The man had committed the unpardonable sin of refusing it. With great indignation, Jerome had tried to force it down the man's throat. The man had pulled a knife. Jerome had easily taken away the knife and planted it squarely in the man's stomach. When Sheriff Carmody arrived, witnesses said the stabbing was done in self defense. The man survived but avoided saloons when the Liggets happened to be in town.

Thereafter, whenever Jerome offered to buy a man a drink, it was never refused. His message had gotten through. Although the drink would be accepted with reluctance and fear, Jerome's social status and self-importance remained secure in his own mind.

Sheriff Carmody knew of the Liggets running operation and illegal sale of bootleg liquor on the Navajo reservation. He couldn't blame the three sons of Jerome Liggett, because they lived under the thumb of the old man.

Jerome deeply loved his sons. He gloried in them, their tawny strength, their thick blunt noses like his own, their granite faces, their rough voices, the different expressions seen in their eyes reflecting three distinct personalities. Norm was arrogant and overconfident. Elmo was a sullen malcontent. Roger, the youngest, was innocent. Jerome believed their flesh and bone, their souls were extensions of his own being. They were his creations. His sons comprised his world and gave his life meaning.

The old man would have been against it even though the bitch had been drunk on her ass and willing as axel grease. "Sell 'em the corn," he would say, "but keep your god damn meat in your pants," he told his sons.

"Blossom's different," they justified among themselves. "Everyone knows what she is. We didn't just come along and rape her. She asked us. She was willing. We didn't break any law. The Injuns don't have any rights nohow. And what the hell does an Injun whore know about the law or even care worth a shit. Her own family knows what she is and what she does and they don't turn down the money she brings home. They sure as hell ain't gonna come after us. It'd be different if we forced her, but we didn't. She asked us."

Between the three brothers, they had sampled a good quart of their own corn whiskey. Now, careening along the rutted wagon track, they wondered if it might not have been advisable to make Blossom their last stop. Reckless jolts snapped their buzzing heads. The two boys in the back seat lurched and crushed against each other. They growled their discomfort at Norm, the eldest, who was driving, but their curses did not penetrate his drunken senses. Trying to focus on the rutted desert road took his full concentration.

Cases of whiskey in the rear slammed against the side panels with a threatening rattle of glass, as the 1930 Ford pickup swung sliding into the loose sand on a sharp curve then bucked over a series of potholes that set the brothers to a fresh stream of cursing.

From the sage and mesquite in the surrounding night, the dull yellow beams drew clouds of insects whose wind-wracked bodies plastered the windshield and headlamps in a gooey past of tiny guts. Norm had to periodically stop the truck and wait while his youngest brother, Roger, fourteen, got out and scraped them off. The process tended to smudge the windshield and did not much enhance visibility until Norm's middle brother, Elmo, sixteen, suggested they apply a little whiskey as a window cleaner.

The kid grabbed a bottle from the rear and liberally splashed some coursing down over the smeary mess. Norm leaned out and admonished him to go easy on the product. They'd have to partially re-fill that bottle with water to sell at a full price. The concoction was so rot gut strong that diluting it wouldn't be noticed. It was a practice he thought he might suggest to the old man. "A little water won't make a difference. Might even add to the taste. Reservation bucks can't tell horse piss from booze anyhow." To them, whiskey was whiskey. Their craving gave the Liggets a way to make a living.

The kid clambered back in and they drove on. Running was a lucrative trade in spite of the rarely enforced Federal law that prohibited liquor on the reservations. Indians couldn't buy it in the town bars either. They were considered wards of the Government.

Norm had heard it said that the blood chemistry of Indians caused them to easily succumb to alcoholism. That generic weakness of their race was effective to the whiskey trade.

The Liggets kept their still hidden in a deep cavern up a blind canyon on their land. No one had ever discovered it, not even Carmody the time he had driven out there sniffing around. Pushing his badge, he was looking into the deaths of three young Navajo men from alcohol poisoning.

Bootlegging had proven to be so profitable after seven years that they kept only goats and a few head of scrawny cattle as a front for their activity. They also cultivated a large field of corn and squash and beans. Some of the corn they consumed in the traditional manner. The majority of the crop was converted to alcohol.

Jerome Ligget told his sons that after another few years, he planned to pull up roots and move to California. They would say goodbye to those miserable high desert New Mexico winters forever.

Norm cut to the right where the wagon road split north and south and headed toward Red Rock Crossing. He would occasionally vary their route to avoid any setup Carmody might take it into his head to try on them.

Once, Carmody had almost caught them in the act. But their Navajo contact had warned them. They had made the mistake of going over the same run week after week for three months. The first law of a bootlegger was to never create a pattern. They had violated their own principle. They had grown so secure in their invulnerability they had even dropped the precaution of night cover and had taken to running in broad daylight.

Elmo began to half sing, muttering and croaking under his drunken breath, as the three brothers rocked and swayed in unison. The stink of Blossom, the Navajo girl, still clung to them. Elmo was singing to dispel her from his mind. He also wanted to rid his thoughts of the sour odor of the still over which they labored day and night back in the cave, and that worthless plot of rock hard desert ground they called a ranch.

"Three more years," the old man had said. "Three more years and we'll pack up and go to California." Elmo had decided that three years was just too damn long to wait. He could hardly stand it for another three months. *"Don't say anything to the old man though, not by a fucking long shot, never. Just be on that train when it passes through Mesa and don't look back."*

"Christ," he thought, *"if the old man ever gets wind of my plan, and he might ... "*

Jerome could read his sons, smell their moves and what they were up to just like a bear. He'd chain Elmo to the wall of that god damn whiskey piss smelling cave and treat him like a prisoner for the next three years.

Elmo had determined he'd be damned if he was going to spend the rest of his life expected to be like his cracker father. *"We're all crackers. That's just what we are when you get to the bottom line. Moving to*

California won't make a damn bit of difference. If you're a cracker in New Mexico, you're still a cracker in California." He wanted to get away from his father permanently and improve himself. He wanted to change his life, maybe even get an education of sorts.

He had secretly taught himself to read and do figures. His old man had burned any book Elmo ever brought home, until Elmo had taken to hiding them. No reading was allowed, no thinking for yourself. *"I'll tell you and teach you everything you need to know,"* he thundered. Christ, they were prisoners of the old fart. It was time to get away from these unyielding mesas and wind blasted prairies that baked you in silence and stretched on endlessly. *"Maybe I'll even change my name. Elmo Ligget sure don't turn any heads."*

"Hell, you want to do something with your life, you have to go where there's somethin' worth doin'. I'm gonna be seventeen and I sure ain't gettin' any younger. If the country goes to war, I'll be cherry pickin' ripe for the army. And there are sure signs of a war coming on, what with Mussolini and Hitler in Europe. America can't stay out of it forever. Any fool can see that. Shit, in a few years, there won't be an able bodied man in this country left out of uniform. By then, I don't want my ass anywhere near New Mexico.

"The U.S. Army might be the way for some boys to run off and get their feet wet, dip their rods in a little of that Texas poontang. Not this one, hell no. What sense is there in trading my old man for another drill sergeant and the chance of getting my head shot off in a foreign country. My old man would hide us back up in the canyons anyway or the mountains of California. He would have us live like Indians if he had to just to keep us out of the service.

"I figure I done my time anyway, sixteen years of it, ever since I turned five. That's another reason to change my name, stay out of the Army. But I can't even tell my kid brother about it."

He could barely control the thoughts he had. They swam in his head. No wonder the old man accused him of keeping to himself.

"If I told them my ideas about the great things I want to do, to travel around the world on a tramp steamer like I read about in that book by Jack London ... Maybe I could write a book like him and get in the movies."

He had talked to the movie people when they were out there on the desert a year ago. They had paid him ten dollars to film him driving his truck down the road right past a woman who was a star in the movie. He didn't remember her name. But he did remember seeing William Boyd who was Hopalong Cassidy and had been given a photo with Boyd's autograph by a member of the crew. He kept the photograph hidden along with his small collection of books in a private cave.

If what he did was called working in Hollywood, then he wanted it.

He loved his brothers. It was just the old man he couldn't stomach. He felt genuine affection for the kid. Roger looked up to him even more than to Norm, who being the oldest, considered himself the wisest in all matters the old man didn't horn in on that pertained to the three of them.

Recently, the old man had even taken to seeking Norm's advice, which added fuel to Norm's filial fire. He lorded his importance as being the favored son over his two younger brothers. Since there wasn't anyone else he could influence in a radius of a few thousand miles, he dominated his brothers with his personal failings.

Norm studied his father. He tried to mirror him in every way which pleased the old man no end. Jerome Liggit made no attempt to hide his preference for this number one son and never had, even during the boys' youth when they were close upon the heels of one another in age and lack of aspiration. Jerome did not possess a sense of proportion nor perceptiveness about himself, his family, or anyone, except at a basic level. Whatever he felt in his guts was the center of the universe. He was an infantile man. His physical and emotional abuse of his wife had killed her shortly after the birth of Roger.

Jerome had wept copious tears, not of pity, but that he had lost a good cook and house slave. Subsequent hired help had usually not lasted more than a day. Women did not cope well with an after dinner rape by a drunken sweating bear-like man of a Neanderthal mentality. They were discovered gone by morning.

The giant gears of the iron wheels locked in a long screeching grind, showering sparks and white heat that nearly welded them to the rails. Sporadic small brush fires flared and died in the wake of the train.

Only the constant pressure of his full weight thrown hard against the brake quelled the engineer's retching horror. The sliding of metal and violent clanging mesh of jungles of steel rang high-pitched in his head.

Gresham, the fireman, struggled up from where he had been flung to his knees on the corrugated metal floor and finally the train came to a stop. The two men stared at each other stupefied, fearing to climb down from their compact highly contained mobile inferno, afraid of what they would find and see on the desert floor in the night. The engineer, O'Hagen swiped at his red beefy face and cried out in a hoarse whisper, "I'll go."

Grabbing a lantern, he swung down from the cab and stood swaying, bloodshot eyes staring back down the length of the train. He heard shouts and screams and curses and saw figures flitting erratically inside the Pullman car windows. A few were suddenly slammed open and heads thrust out with rolling wild-eyed searching of the darkness.

"What is it? What the hell happened? My God, my arm's broken!"

They saw O'Hagen's light. Walking past, he made no reply as he swung the beam in a slow arc over the mottled brush. And there it was, a man's scorched leg, a little further on, part of a boy's face pressed into a piece of the steel frame of a truck door. He had seen enough. He snapped off the light and returned raggedly out of breath to the engine.

As he climbed up into the cab, Gresham asked him, "How many?"

O'Hagen shook his head. "They'll have to come out from Mesa in the morning and piece 'em together, whatever they can find. He shuddered at the thought of the men whose task it would be to derive identities from unrecognizable burned and twisted flesh and bone. How many were there? He didn't know and couldn't tell. He didn't want to know.

Rushing headlong through the desert night had always been a pleasant dream until now. His mind was peopled with visions of a gaping nightmare. He had noticed the slowly moving headlights miles before the train arrived at Red Rock Crossing. He could not fathom why the truck had not stopped to wait for them to pass. Despite his steady warning whistle, they chose to ignore what it was telling them and had deliberately driven in front of the engine. He clutched the controls to still his shaking hands as the iron beast gained momentum and thundered on through the night.

In her Pullman car, Yelena rubbed the wrenching pain in her right shoulder. She had caught the brunt of the seat in front of her, as she was hurled out of a sound sleep by the screeching terrorizing halt of the train. She only half-listened to the explosive babble of surrounding passengers and sudden speculation that the train had collided with some large object, perhaps a cow.

Continuing to rub her shoulder, she closed her eyes and leaned back. It would be good to get to a hotel, soak in a hot tub, crawl between clean sheets and stay there for two full days. "I need to rest up," she thought. "Prepare for what lies ahead."

She had found it difficult to sleep soundly on the train. The rocking and swaying and incessant telegraphic clacking of the wheels invaded her scattered dreams and kept her consciousness at the surface. Who else might be on the train also concerned her. She avoided making eye contact with the men who passed along the aisle and when she went to eat in the dining car. To her relief, she did not encounter Howard Gimbel again.

She thought his sudden re-appearance in her life an odd coincidence, almost surreal like the fragments of her dreams. She had completely forgotten about him over the years. The painful memories of her family's oppression remained an impulse, like a tumor hovering in the back of her mind, a driving force for her work, what she considered now as her calling.

She lived in constant fear that she was being watched. She had been followed many times and did not want to be caught off guard. Gimbel looked like a government man, but he hadn't talked like one. Despite her unwillingness to acknowledge him, she had sensed his genuine emotion in meeting her again. She trusted no one. The prospect of being roughly hand-cuffed and imprisoned in the baggage car was not on her agenda.

She had to run, to keep moving, to travel, stay one jump ahead of the Feds until she reached her destination and could go into hiding. They could be on the train behind her and maybe even waiting for her arrival. They had the means of tracking her that were invisible to her.

She had taken a chance appearing at a union rally back in Wabash, Indiana. She had attempted to be unobtrusive working in the background talking to the local leaders and motivating them to call their people to action. Arguing that she would inspire the workers, they had insisted she take the platform. Once they saw her and listened to her speak, they would be convinced to strike.

There were spies in the crowd. She could spot the company goons armed with billy clubs. With the arrival of two police cars, she left the platform in mid-sentence. Hiking up her skirts, she clattered down the wooden steps. A group of union members encircled her and helped her to move quickly out of the area while members of the crowd surged to block the passage of the police and absorb the goons' heavy blows.

After that incident, there had been no need to even take a vote. The workers would stage a strike.

Wabash had been a stopover for only a few days. She had begun her westward journey in New York where she had met John L. Lewis, President of the Congress of Industrial Organization, the CIO, and heard him speak. Lewis was recruiting labor leaders and organizers of every sort .

Just as owners hired club-wielding goons, snitches, and spies, the union leaders did not sever their radical ties, but recruited communist agitators and gangsters as the occasion required. The familiar inspiring words that Biblically thundered forth from the ogre-like dark glowering countenance of John L. Lewis still rang in Yelena's ears. The thoughts and images he conveyed echoed the speech she had heard at her first union meeting with Damon Roikos.

After two weeks of rallies and travel, Yelena was not in a mitigating mood to deal with the welcoming committee she knew would be awaiting her arrival. She would have to beg off the immediate organizational activities they would surely press on her to undertake. Given their suffering and zeal for change, they always did. They overlooked the fact she was human. Sometimes even she lost that perspective about herself. They would have to give her a little time and allow her to rest, although time and age were not yet slowing her down.

Her twenty-ninth birthday had come and gone uncelebrated and unnoticed. She could not bother to think of her youth, of love and personal fulfillment. She had experienced a few fleeting romantic months with Damon Roikos until he accused her of being more dedicated to the cause of her revenge than she was to him. In fact, it was Damon's projection of his own personal ambition to rise in union politics and lack of commitment to her that had caused the rift. They had ceased to speak to each other, even during an occasional encounter at a rally or convention.

Through her curtain of weariness, she smiled inwardly at the thought of the power and influence she wielded that found its source in the needs of the people. She had recreated her appearance so that she was almost innocuous in stature. She did not exude any warmth and femininity. When she worked a crowd, a different energy pervaded her eyes and demeanor. Her words and manner of speaking from the platform could weave persuasive magic and transform a mob of men, sway them to do her bidding, and rush to her call for action.

She was a leader in her own way, shrewd, calculating, dynamic, and in control. She knew how to appeal to their wants and needs with an economy of speech. She painted graphic word pictures of what their lives and working conditions could and should be if only they would unite. She was widely sought and respected among the labor ranks. Businessmen and certain politicians feared and despised her for her potential to topple their empires founded on greed and corruption.

But after all, she was only a woman. A woman could easily be crushed. She had no voice and no power in a man's world. And once she disappeared, she had no influence.

Chapter 9
THE WELCOMING COMMITTEE

Randolph Logan was at the station waiting for the arrival of the union organizer, Yelena Ivanov, on the night train. His intent was to get a short interview with her for a story in the Mesa Independent. The mood and tension between the sheriff, Everett Carmody, and Halen Braun, a Federal agent from Santa Fe, led him to believe that speaking to Yelena Ivanov might not be possible. He recognized that some other agenda was afoot and not of the welcoming kind. It piqued his curiosity that this woman could cause so much concern among a few politically powerful men in New Mexico.

Mesa was a desert prairie stop for freight and passenger trains enroute to California and back again to Chicago and points east. For Logan, these trains that brought people to his town and took others away became the mainstream of his life. As a young boy, he would run from his adobe house where he and his mother lived down the dusty street to the station when he heard the distant whistle of an approaching train still miles away and unseen through the dense sage brush and low growing pinion pines that dotted the landscape like shaggy buffalo frozen in time.

Living in isolation had raised his curiosity about the world beyond his narrow confines stuck in the vastness of the arid plains, which was the reason he had chosen the career of journalism. He had always been a seeker of news. The coming and going of roaring, clanging, plunging trains symbolized for him the movement and industry of life and forces from afar that were outside his immediate realm of experience.

He was a voracious reader of any publication he could lay his hands on. Although the local newspaper was limited, it did give him an occasional glimpse of the country beyond the desert sunrise and sunset. What it did not give him was understanding. He soon learned that was gained through life experience which he could not acquire by watching strangers momentarily disembark from the train to stretch their legs and walk about on the station platform. Few of them remained behind when the whistle to depart called them aboard and those who did never talked to him.

Eventually, he began writing down his impressions and observations and created the stories of those who touched his life, people whose circumstances had planted them in his desolate little town or who were just passing through. What he observed was the view of a microcosm amid the sweep of the American Landscape.

***

Everett Carmody's dark eyes ranged from the wall clock to the dirt-filled creases of his worn boots planted on the gouged wooden desk, then stared out the latticed window at the railroad signal glowing back at him. A group of seven men in long black coats huddled just beyond the circle of yellow light that thrust from the dispatcher's office onto the station platform. Two of the men shifted impatiently like waiting horses. A match flared, went out. A trace of smoke rose above their heads white against the night sky.

He knew who they were and so did Randolph Logan. They knew their faces from Saturday nights in town, miners from the Wooten Coal Company. Three had occupied the jail twice in the past month for brawling in a local cantina. They didn't hold their arrest against Sheriff Carmody. That was his job. They half feared and respected him for what he had to do. In the long run, they realized he protected them more from themselves than anybody else, since unbridled violence encouraged more of the same and someone could end up dead.

Although avoidance of the law was common among mine owners, ranchers, politicians, and was incessant among the working class and Indian populations, the men and families from the mine generally held Carmody in high regard. But lately, he had noticed a change in the way they looked at him when he approached.

In turn, Carmody perceived the men standing out there on the platform as perpetrators of chaos, anarchists. They would not have agreed with him. That they did not view themselves or their motives as anarchy, but basic human rights, had no influence on Carmody. The forces that had placed him there in the night were too complex for any of them to comprehend.

Perhaps understanding would come to him. For now, he had no recourse but to go with the surging tide of social and economic depression that swept the country and consumed all of them. His job was to not be concerned with the rest of it, but to uphold the law.

***

The Federal agent, Halen Braun, turned from looking out the station house window. He glanced at the clock. "Soon now."

Carmody ignored him. The less he saw of Halen Braun the better. Carmody had not even known of the existence of Halen Braun until a few days ago. The Special Agent in Charge had driven over from Santa Fe and introduced himself. He explained the purpose of his visit was to establish "a working relationship" between Carmody and the FBI "in supporting the laws of the United States Government and Federal programs in the area."

"We're clamping down on illegal union activity," he said. "There's a union organizer coming out here to stir things up." He dropped a five by ten black and white photograph on Carmody's desk of a severely dressed attractive woman with a harsh expression.

"Her name's Yelena Ivanov. She's a Communist. We don't have any charges to bring against her, but we just want to keep her quiet. That's where you come in. When she steps off the train, we want you to put her in jail for a while."

"You asking me to arrest her without a charge? For how long?"

"Not really." Unaccustomed to being challenged, Braun had swung away from the desk and paced the office. He was a tall heavyset man, light on his feet. Unlike eastern agents, he had adopted wearing a large western style hat instead of a fedora and wore western boots. A wide snake skin belt with a large silver and turquoise buckle surrounded his girth. Against FBI regulations forbidding facial hair, he cultivated a thick brown handlebar mustache. Also, given the distance from headquarters in Washington, he openly drank bourbon, smoked cigars, and took his pleasure with Mexican whores. Were these activities known by J. Edgar Hoover, Director of the FBI, Braun would be out of a job. He was a man of appetites whose quick searching eyes squinting out from his florid face missed nothing.

During his early years with the Federal Bureau of Investigation., Halen had established an admirable record in his relentless pursuit and capture of bootleg runners in the hills of Tennessee and Kentucky. Although the austere J. Edgar Hoover thought the agent deserved a promotion, he had difficulty accepting Halen Braun's loud, aggressive, overbearing personality. He did not feel Braun fit in with the Washington Bureau, but was better suited to a part of the country Hoover considered uncivilized and where Braun would not overshadow him with publicity of his exploits. J. Edgar did not keep agents on the payroll who outshined him with the press, something Randolph Logan was told by another young agent, Howard Gimbel, coming to Mesa from Washington D.C.

Instead of being affronted by the assignment, Halen embraced it. He had free rein to pursue his beloved hunting and fishing and hedonist life style at the Government's expense with no one looking over his shoulder. He submitted his reports in a timely manner and no one from Washington ever bothered to come out and check on him, until now.

Agent Howard Gimbel was arriving on the same train with Yelena Ivanov. Despite correspondence that Gimbel would not have any direct dealings with the Santa Fe office, other than to brief him on Yelena Ivanov's activities, Halen was suspicious that Gimbel had been sent to spy on him. The dispatch had said that Gimbel would be working under cover with the Bureau of Indian Affairs in developing a law and order program and would only call on him if he needed Halen Braun's support. As Randolph Logan followed the story, things didn't happen that way.

There had also been some other incoherent murmurings about Gimbel's knowledge of Yelena Ivanov that Halen had considered irrelevant, as he evaded answering Carmody's questions about her incarceration. Yelena Ivanov's entry into Halen's territory had given him a mission. Under the Espionage and Security Act, he tossed Logan a tidbit to write in the local paper, "I am to be on the lookout for seditious groups and activity. We are a country about to go to war. Yelena Ivanov should be arrested and hanged on charges of conspiracy."

Randolph Logan hadn't heard any pronouncements that the United States was going to war with Germany. On the contrary, the Government and the country at large wanted to stay out of it, but the German threat was growing.

Santa Fe was a 100 mile drive from Mesa across open desert. Halen figured that Agent Gimbel would be hard pressed to run back and forth to the Santa Fe office and Halen could always arrange to be gone on "official Government business." In addition, Gimbel could come and see him only if he called in advance.

It was obvious to Logan that Halen Braun wanted little to do with Gimbel. In fact, he wasn't even supposed to be talking to Logan about him, as the reporter later learned by interviewing Gimbel. No one in Mesa was supposed to know he was an FBI agent working undercover in the Bureau of Indian Affairs. Gimbel had a reason for confiding in him.

Later on, as Logan became Gimbel's only friend, the agent opened up and told the young man about his assignment. Logan's story published by the United Press would be noticed by J. Edgar Hoover and place the young writer in the gunsights of the FBI Director as a communist and insurrectionist.

The Bureau had sent Halen Braun a photograph of Howard Gimbel. Halen expected to meet him that night when the train arrived, but he would leave and make the long drive back to Santa Fe. He would make it plain that he was a busy man and did not have time to "show him around" as the Washington letter suggested. Halen had no use for strait-laced easterners.

Gimbel appeared young and "pure" in his photograph to Halen's way of thinking. And Gimbel was probably married and religious, both of which proved to be untrue. He also probably "kissed ass" in the Washington Bureau and was a snitch to gain favor with the Director, also untrue. The photograph did not depict a man with whom you could toss off drinks, fuck prostitutes, and shoot desert quail. No, Halen wanted to see Gimbel as little as possible. It would be Randolph Logan who came to associate with Gimbel and to know him well.

The welcoming committee out on the platform noticed Halen inside the station waiting and watching, but they did not know what his position was with Sheriff Carmody. They resented Carmody's power as one man alone against them. They were even prepared to challenge him, but knew they could not overcome him. Drawing together, they continued to be rational, patient, their lives and purpose focused on the arrival of the train.

As Carmody sat now waiting in the railroad station office, Logan watched him.

Carmody was not in the pocket of corrupt corporations and politicians and never had been. He just wanted to get into his black Ford with the 'Sheriff' sign painted in scratched faded white letters on the doors and drive away anywhere, anywhere but where he was supposed to be according to the duty signified by his badge.

Carmody's fist slammed down on the desk top. The floor and walls shook with the ponderous rumble of the incoming train.

"She's here," Halen Braun looked with grim satisfaction through the window.

Carmody rose from his chair and with three steady strides was out the door. Logan noticed that the FBI man did not accompany him. Halen preferred to remain in the background. Let the Marshal do his dirty work.

Randolph Logan went out to the station platform with Carmody and watched the dark looming cars flow past with a heavy crunch of iron wheels. Brakes hissed. Shocks squealed long resistant cries that spiraled down through Carmody's head and twisted his guts into tight knots. Couplings caromed and slammed along the chain of cars. The train heaved a great dragon sigh with the final effort of bringing its long cumbersome body to rest.

The relief crew was already out there walking down to the engine to take over the next four hundred mile run. The porters were putting down the steps at two of the Pullman cars. The group of waiting men shifted with nervous anticipation and ground out their cigars underfoot.

A man, his wife, and a stumbling sleepy child stepped down from one car and walked away carrying awkward parcels and baggage into the station. A movement at the door of the second car, a woman's long dark dress, drew Carmody's attention. The other men strained, watching.

Carmody moved quickly across the wooden platform to reach her before the men surrounded her, creating a protective shield that would force him to challenge them with his authority. They saw him coming and hesitated, then jerked forward in a disjointed uncertain manner. They were too late. Carmody was there as Yelena turned from receiving her bag from the porter.

"Yelena Ivanov, I'm holding you under arrest. Come with me."

Logan was instantly smitten by her dark eyes boring into him with the hardness of cold granite. He struggled against a sudden rush of attraction to her feminine power, her independence and strength that washed over all of the other men, as well, but with a sour hate. She looked at the glowering intimidated men several yards behind Carmody and saw they were afraid to challenge him. She noticed that the Marshal had not drawn his gun and realized what his local reputation must be.

Logan saw her fix the men with a glittering stare, her welcoming committee. They looked like so many other welcoming committees. Her imperious expression fastened on Logan for only a brief moment. To him, she was incredible.

Carmody roughly clamped rattling handcuffs to her wrists with vicious snaps. She sent a mocking challenge to the others with her eyes. She did not need words.

Carmody picked up her bag and, placing himself between her and the men, pulled her forward, gripping her arm so severely she clenched her teeth with pain. The men trailed after them in the wake of their long swooping shadows.

Carmody muscled her through the door into the train station. Logan noticed that Halen Braun had disappeared. Taut, threatening, frustrated, and indeterminate, the group of men hovered after them and surged out the front into the parking area. Carmody jerked open the door of his car and jammed Yelena into the back seat behind the cage. He snatched away her purse, slammed the door, opened the driver's door, and tossed her purse inside onto the front seat. Watching for the sudden glint of metal, he glanced at the gang one last time and slid in behind the wheel. He maintained his momentum and force of purpose, giving them no sign of hesitancy or weakness.

As he gunned the engine into a start, he noticed the engineer shouting and waving his cap as he ran toward the car. "Marshal! Marshal! Wait!"

Carmody leaned out to let the engineer know he would wait to hear him. Trying to control his labored breathing, the man staggered up to the open window. "We hit a truck out at Red Rock. Someone tried to beat us to the crossing. We stopped. Looked around. Couldn't see much in the dark, only parts of a body."

Carmody looked beyond the throw of his car's headlights, playing the image of the collision in his mind. "I'll go out there in the morning."

"Not likely to find much. Coyotes."

Carmody nodded. "I can identify the truck."

"Sorry. I'm really sorry it happened. Didn't even know they was there."

The engineer stepped away. Carmody accelerated the car into a racing start, caught the cluster of men in the abrupt sweep of his headlights as he roared away, tires spitting gravel at their faces.

Before Logan got into his car and followed Carmody, he noticed Halen hidden in the shadows at the side of the building. He was watching Howard Gimbel walking quickly along the platform toward the Marshal's vehicle. Howard raised his hand. The car didn't stop. Halen must have decided there was no good purpose in welcoming Gimbel. *Let him figure things out for himself.*

Howard approached the group of men and asked them the way to the Harvey Hotel. Bags in hand, he then trudged off down the dirt street into the night. He would come back in the morning and find out why the Marshal had arrested Yelena .

Stunned, the welcoming party stared after Carmody's receding tail lights. Jolted from their inertia by the reality of Yelena 's arrest, they suddenly broke and ran to their waiting trucks. With a great slamming of doors and cough of engines, they drove away in a ragged convoy.

Logan was just coming through the jailhouse door as Carmody locked Yelena in her cell. Her attraction clearly influenced him, just as she did Logan, despite her stony stare. "Would you like some food?" Carmody asked.

She shook her head. He barely glanced at Logan, dropped the keys on the deputy's desk, "Make sure she has water," and walked out without another word.

Logan approached her cell. "Miss Ivanov, I was wondering if—-"

"Who are you?"

"I'm a reporter for the Mesa Independent."

"I don't talk to reporters. How did you know I was coming?"

"I know the sheriff."

"So you're one of them. I'm not here for the entertainment of your readers."

"I write real news."

"They can't hold me here. There is no charge. It's an unwarranted arrest. I don't suppose you might know who's behind this."

"I'm not privy to certain things."

"And you call yourself a newsman. This is politically motivated by somebody. Maybe you should do a little investigating and find out. Then you'll have yourself some real news."

Her stare was a summons to depart and sent the young smitten Logan stumbling awkwardly out the door.

II
Law and
Order

Chapter 10
OMEN

Yelena Ivanov's arrest did not come as a surprise to Logan. He was familiar with labor dissent among the miners at the Wooten Coal Company. Yelena's incarceration had occurred too late to make the morning edition of *The Independent* and now the fledgling reporter was stuck with the dilemma of either trying to interview her again or driving out to cover the investigation of the accident that had happened at Red Rock Crossing the night before.

After two cups of strong coffee that set his nerves on edge, Logan decided that Yelena Ivanov wasn't going anywhere in a jail cell and he should get on out to Red Rock before they scraped up the body parts.

Red Rock Crossing was thirty miles northeast of Mesa. Coming off Highway Route 66, the last twenty meandered along an old wagon road across Navajo reservation land. Overtaking the dust of the coroner's truck, he could see vultures circling ahead in the sky.

He reached the crossing at about ten o'clock. Sheriff Carmody was already there with the local Santa Fe Railroad Supervisor, Phillip Sweigart, brother of Noel Sweigart, the Indian trader. Two members from the Navajo track crew accompanied them.

The four of them were picking their way through rocks and sagebrush a few hundred yards from their trucks and Carmody's patrol car parked back at the crossing. They stopped from time to time to look at some object on the ground, then walked on. The coroner left the road and, paralleling the track, slowly followed them in his truck bouncing over the ruts.

Logan parked his car next to Carmody's, grabbed a note pad and climbed out with a camera dangling from a strap around his neck. He jogged along the track, boots striking the loose gravel with urgent grinding thuds.

When he caught up, the others barely glanced at him. His eyes followed where it was they were looking. The sight of the mangled corpse gagged him. Vicious black flies and bulging white maggots swarmed over the flesh working on its decomposition. The sight reminded him not so much of a human corpse as that of a coyote laid open on the highway. The head and face were gouged and smashed and barely recognizable, but he could make out the features to be those of Elmo Liggit. He took a photograph, although he wasn't certain Shreve would print it. There might be others, less shocking.

After an hour of searching, the coroner managed to piece together most of the remains of the Ligget brothers, whatever the coyotes hadn't carried off. He had to make an educated guess about the third corpse, the oldest brother, because they couldn't find his head, not even among the twisted wreckage of the brothers' old pickup.

The next major concern was how to best break the despairing news to the father of the young men, Jerome Liggit. They all knew how strongly he coveted his sons. The coroner suggested it would not be wise to allow the old man to see the severed bits and pieces of his boys. He would go stark raving mad and tear the town apart. He would probably do that anyway. Carmody said he would handle it.

Logan put a few questions to the railroad foreman, Phillip Sweigart as to how the accident happened. Sweigart repeated the sequence of events as related to him by O'Hagen, the engineer. He said he would never be able to account for what might have caused the Ligget brothers to "drive in front of a passenger express out in the middle of nowhere in the middle of the night." Sweigart did say they had discovered several broken bootleg whiskey bottles.

"Maybe they was just too drunk to know what was about to happen to 'em. Misjudged their distance and how fast they were going, maybe even tried to beat the train, drunk, joy riding, on a dare. They were a reckless bunch. We'll never know. That's all I can figure out."

Logan followed Carmody's patrol car back on in to Mesa to again try to interview Yelena Ivanov, even though she had warned him she didn't talk to reporters. He planned to follow her suggestion and investigate the political ramifications behind her arrest. He thought he might start with Howard Gimbel, since he would be interviewing him and writing a story about his addition to John Collier's team at the Bureau of Indian Affairs.

When they arrived at the Marshal's office, Yelena Ivanov was gone. Joe Moss, Carmody's deputy, sat in her place locked in her cell. He quickly described how five men, their faces smeared with coal black, had just walked in and got the drop on him.

"You better believe they had guns. I wasn't gonna argue with two double barrels and a Winchester starin' me down the throat. Don't give a shit if we was holdin' Hitler, let alone some god damn woman. Got some other news for you too. About an hour before those miners broke in on me, Jerome Ligget came into town with his tail on fire wantin' to see if his sons had been caught and arrested last night for runnin' bootleg on the reservation. They never showed up at the Ligget place all night. He could see for hisself we didn't have 'em.'"

Logan watched Carmody take all this in. The sheriff suddenly slumped into his chair. Having been up most of the night, he was too tired to give a damn anymore. He thought he must at least attempt to find and re-arrest the woman. In Coal Town, he knew that would be a near impossibility to even find her. She would be well hidden and protected. But in the forefront of his mind, the clear-eyed challenging way she had looked at him when he had arrested her captured his respect and admiration. He was sympathetic to her cause and to the cause of the miners. Carmody held no love for corrupt politicians and money men like Lee Stark, the president and overseer of the Wooten Mining Company. Now he was caught between Lee Stark, the FBI, and the union woman.

***

Three years ago, Lee Stark had taken the train south from Denver to follow a lead. Now that he had arrived in Mesa, he stood looking up and down the railroad tracks, then struck out for the center of town. Limping among the throngs of Navajo Indians that swarmed in and out of low adobe buildings along the streets, he realized he might have discovered the opportunity he had been seeking for years, if the information he had been given were true.

He took a room at the Harvey and inquired of the hotel clerk if the crowds of Indians outside were in town for some special occasion. The clerk handed him a copy of the local newspaper, *The Mesa Independent*, and pointed to the headlines which heralded a "NEW EL DORADO" under the Federal Government's Emergency Conservation Work Act.

The program known as the Civilian Conservation Corps or CCC called for the reforestation of Federal, state, and private lands where projects would contribute to the protection of resources on public property. Reforestation, in a sense, included soil erosion control, reseeding depleted range land, development of recreational facilities and other projects. Many were authorized on Indian reservations. They were considered Federal property and, therefore, qualified for conservation work and allotments.

$5,875,000 dollars of Federal Government money funded the program. Twenty-five out of seventy-two work camps had been assigned to the Navajo, which explained the massive influx to sign up for jobs.

The news story went on to report that Navajo livestock suffered from a shortage of water. The tribe would undergo a disastrous year unless rain fell soon. The CCC project was a virtual Godsend. There was a photograph of Louis C. Schroeder from New York. He was an expert on camp management and had recently arrived to organize the CCC administration for the entire Navajo reservation. Noel Sweigart, a local Indian trader, had been appointed as Schroeder's assistant. The article also included copious information on the new Bureau of Indian Affairs Commissioner, John Collier, praising his enlightened program and administration on behalf of the Indian's welfare.

Stark folded the newspaper under his arm and set out for the town hall to arrange an appointment with the mayor for that afternoon. As he returned to the street, the infesting excitement carried him along with an impending sense of fortune. The town was wide open, booming. He could see it, hear it, smell it, and taste it. He flowed with the emotion and searched the intense passing faces.

He stepped into an anglo saloon where business was brisk. Eyes studied him briefly, then glanced away. His business suit retained a western flavor. Although the dark beard and mustache seemed a little out of fashion, the Stetson and heeled boots identified him as one of their kind. He ordered a whiskey and lit a cigar. He drank with a great inhalation, absorbing the strong alcoholic grain fumes through his bristled nostrils. He set down the empty glass with affirmation and signaled the bartender to pour another.

Stark's taste in food and women were not shared by most men of station, wealth or esteem, which accounted for his eventual meeting and developing a friendship with Halen Braun. Their preferences led them to sordid saloons and cantinas and back alley cafes in Santa Fe and across the border.

Neither man felt a kinship with the usual variety of patrons in those places, but they were voyeurs. The rawness of low life behavior untarnished by the amenities and veneer of an elitist polite society fascinated both men. For Halen Braun, this interest had taken him down the road of law enforcement and into the realm of criminals and outlaws. For Lee Stark, his forays into debauchery sought to relieve recurring periods of apathy and emotional depression. Although he despised these people, he knew that he was one of them. To deny himself their association of smoke and drink, coarse language and crude laughter, the close-in stench of unwashed bodies, he felt would render him not fully aware and alive. But in these establishments, awareness left him to drift and drown in the sensations, to awaken late the next morning in the bed of some strange woman whom he had only a vague remembrance of meeting the night before.

Disgust and loathing for the woman displaced whatever he had done and the original sordid attraction. He despised himself for his weakness and desired to be gone from her room as quickly as possible. He would take a clean room elsewhere just to bathe and scrub himself, to rid himself of the odors of sex commingled with the lingering cheap perfume of the woman. He would soak his hair and beard in lye to kill the lice. While he soaked, what he remembered of the previous night he relived in his mind and increased through imagination.

His meeting with Halen Braun was not fortuitous or a chance incident. The FBI maintained a file on Lee Stark for tax evasion and graft bribery of Senators and congressmen for legislation favorable to the bituminous coal industry. The Justice Department had chosen to conveniently overlook the tax issues because of Stark's father's importance to the war effort in 1917. Thereafter, the son's continuance of the business was considered to be in the best interests of the country and the recipient bank accounts of many highly placed lawmakers. Halen Braun's job was to ensure that Lee Stark was assisted and protected from the intrusion of local law enforcers and from the encroachment of union organization. He was considered to be above the law.

Back in Colorado when his first western mine was in operation, he had kept three women in town. Since he was a major landholder and provided work for thousands, people did not question or challenge his behavior.

He remained aloof and a stranger to most, except for the miners he employed. He would mingle with them, a practice that was anaethema to his own officials. Coaltown was his creation. It was where he went to ward off his depressions. The miners and their families, their women, were a private zoo and he considered that he owned them. He was their keeper.

With sufficient capital, a man could enter the bituminous coal industry with ease. An abundance of mines, national resources and the insurance of great profits over the long run prompted Stark to leave Virginia in 1921 and migrate west to investigate the mining situation. Receiving only a small share of an inheritance at that time, he had sought a secure investment for rapid expansion of his capital.

Wounded near the close of the First World War, he had been convalescing at a military hospital when news of his father's death reached him. Realizing his shattered leg would never be normal again, confinement to a wheelchair increased his agitation. A young man of twenty-one, he was thankful to be alive and anxious to get on with his future.

His father had owned lands and mines in Appalachia. Lee and his three brothers had been privileged to accompany him on periodic inspection tours of the mine sites. The ruggedness of the men and the squalor of the women and children in the coal towns had always fascinated Lee. They reminded him of old photographs he had once seen at a museum exhibit of California gold miners. They were scenes of an earlier era that stimulated his imagination for romance and adventure in a time and place of few amenities and raw violence.

Tact and manners were foreign to him. As a child, he had spurned the social graces so readily adopted by his siblings. He was viewed as the scourge and embarrassment of his family. They called him the black sheep. The negative reputation he maintained was often painfully wrought.

Lee had welcomed the war. He had enlisted while his older brothers sought means of avoiding the danger and discomfort of military service. The war brought him closer to those elements he had imagined as a child from the influential photographs and from exhaustive readings about the Old West. He adopted the hard rock fortitude and independence of colorful men who were masters of their own destinies.

He looked upon his shattered leg as a badge or symbol of entry into their exclusive ranks. A veteran of the war, he identified more with the Confederate soldiers of the Civil War than The Great War of 1915. He grew a beard during an era that stressed fashionable trim hair and clean shaven faces. He drank strong whiskey and smoked black cigars on his mother's veranda. To the disgust of his family, he started packing a gun, a pearl handled western Colt .45. They grew concerned that his wartime experience had rendered him mentally unstable. As soon as his leg was strong enough to allow him to get around with the assistance of a cane, he bid them all farewell and boarded a train for Colorado.

His intention was to observe the management and operations of various mineral companies with an eye to seeking a partnership for an enterprise of his choosing. He did not possess adequate capital to totally finance the opening of a new mine on his own. A year later, he joined forces with Theodore Wooten as senior partner of the

Wooten Mineral and Resource Corporation, which owned copper mines in Arizona and Utah, as well as coal operations in Colorado.

With the additional working capital gained from his alliance, Lee hired a geologist and survey crew and went out in search of his mine. He sought a vein that would allow for an open pit operation which required the least expenditure of men and equipment. After a three month assessment, he purchased two-hundred acres of unused ranch land and began grading.

The rise of coal consumption during World War I had created a market of unlimited capacity. Lee undertook his operation with images of staggering profit margins without ceiling. Within one year, he decided he had made the wrong decision. He discovered a sudden limited market resulting from intense price competition with other operators. He could barely maintain a market share in the business. Wages had to be cut drastically to obtain lower production costs in order to survive. For a time, Lee thought his enterprise would collapse and he would lose everything.

Mine labor, like mine machinery, was relatively immobile. There were few alternative employment opportunities. As a consequence, his labor force was willing to remain in spite of a decline in wages. Lee quickly realized that the net returns from operating at a loss were greater than the net returns from not operating at all.

Between 1920 and 1929, coal consumption diminished in favor of a trend to the use of competitive fuels. Too many consumers had been plagued by interruptions in their fuel supply caused by work stoppages and the shortage of transportation facilities. The dependency on a single source of energy, coal, had come to an end.

In 1929, Stark closed down the operation of his mine and moved into a managerial position for Theodore Wooten until 1933 when, under the stimulus of Federal recovery measures instituted by the New Deal, the bituminous coal industry began to revive. Wooten sent Stark to New Mexico to investigate.

Since the reservations were considered Federal property, the mineral resources were claimed by the Government, as well. Wooten manipulated a deal with his cronies in Washington that gave him unlimited access to those resources as long as he purchased the land from the Indians at a nominal price. Jim Picker, an agent from the Bureau of Indian Affairs in Mesa, New Mexico became Stark's go between, his bagman.

Stark poked about the streets and large mercantile and general store and sized up the local population. He noticed only a few foreigners among the Indian faces. He would have to advertise in the East and in other regions of the West for experienced immigrant miners. The wealth of Indian labor would have to be overlooked. Indians knew nothing about mining. He might be able to hire some as slate pickers, but that would be the extent of work.

Finding a foreman and superintendent presented another problem. He would have to search and interview carefully to find skilled dependable men.

He stopped in at the Fred Harvey restaurant for coffee and a hot roast beef lunch. He returned to the hotel in an anxious and fidgety mood. His leg was bothering him. He didn't like having to wait for an interview. Promptly at three o'clock, he entered the office of Mayor William B. Chanson.

Stark's initial impression of Chanson was dislike for his foppish tailored mannered clothes, freshly barbered appearance, and political style in relating to him. But he detected the shrewdness and calculating nature of the man as he explained the proposed industrial intentions of the Wooten Corporation in Mesa and environs. Chanson asked pertinent and knowledgeable questions regarding financial and operational logistics.

"There is no doubt that the existence of a working mine would stimulate employment, taxes, revenue, local business and real estate," said the mayor. What was left unspoken was the extent to which the mayor could conceive the value of considerable personal investment. "I encourage and support your proposal. The name of the Wooten Corporation will soon be recognized as a cornerstone of the local economy. I am at your service, Mr. Stark." He rose from behind his desk and extended his hand.

After the traditional man to man agreement, they resumed their seats and relit their cigars.

"The major problem," Chanson explained, "is that the richest coal deposits lie on reservation land. Access to that land means negotiating with the Navajo tribal council for a lease. They're generally reluctant to let an outside corporation come on the reservation, let alone take their natural resources. Timing is a factor. Obviously you're aware of timing or you wouldn't be here. It's not likely they'll turn down revenue, even with all the Federal spending going on around them." He paused. "I have friends in the B.I.A.who carry some influence with Chee Dodge, He's the headman. It will cost you though. I can promise you that. Dodge is a wiley old cuss and drives a hard bargain. He's better at making deals than most white men. But, as you say, money is no obstacle."

Stark nodded with growing satisfaction.

"I'll arrange a meeting for you with Jim Picker. He's a regional superintendent at the BIA and a trusted friend. Having such friends is important to doing business. It's the only way you're going to survive out here. Anyhow, we've done a few favors for each other."

"I look forward to meeting Mr. Picker."

Three minutes later, Chanson concluded a conversation on the phone with Jim Picker. Hanging up, he pronounced, "Done. I'll take you over to the agency tomorrow morning and introduce you.."

"Looks like I came to the right man."

Chanson smiled at Stark's lack of subtlety, but appreciated the position of being one up on Stark. Chanson figured he could always exert control over people who lacked subtlety.

"Efficiency in government would be impossible without the cooperation of men like Jim. Living out here is like being on the border of a foreign country. The reservation has a life and economy all its own. Sometimes an obstacle like that can make things difficult, not for them, but for us. If you know what I mean." Chanson phrased himself down to what he assumed was Stark's unsophisticated level, knowing Stark would appreciate the reference. It didn't help to make a man feel less than you were even if he was in reality.

Stark smiled knowing very well what the mayor was about and let him think he was in control of their burgeoning business relationship. "I understand everything you're saying."

"Mr. Stark, Lee, I can call you Lee?"

"Of course."

"Call me Billy."

"Billy it is."

"Good. I'm throwing a dinner party tonight. It would give me great pleasure to have you in attendance. It's an opportunity to meet several important people who carry weight locally and in the state government. I know they'll want to meet you."

"I most graciously accept."

Chanson's twinkling blue eyes locked a moment at the spoken amenity. Stark's sudden manner of elevated speech caught him off guard and left him wondering if he might be underestimating the man behind the slovenly appearance. The brief condescending smile in Stark's eyes unsettled him. "I'll send a car around to your hotel at seven."

That night as Stark was chauffeured in the mayor's Packard into the low arid hills at the east end of town, he struggled to repress a gloom of apprehension that had overtaken him just before the arrival of the car. Being an advance man did not come easily, especially courting the favor of local prestigious social figures. But then, he thought, they would more likely be courting him. Chanson was certainly rolling out the red carpet. Wherever there was the smell of money to be made in these hard times, they flocked around like jackals. He would have to make a few deals. Not only would the Navajo demand a substantial rate and a profit percentage of production, there would be local investment and banking interest, as well. This would all be boring conversational matter. What he hoped to accomplish through Picker, however, was a special deal, something that would circumvent all the financial hoop-la.

Stark also did not look forward to the snobbery he expected to encounter. It might not be as pronounced as in the East, but he suspected the local ruling class would be intent on keeping themselves socially above the riff raff. He could accept that as long as their expectations of him did not interfere with his slumming expeditions.

He was to discover that in his own sordid way, he was more of an elitist than they.

Many of the people he met that evening had lived in Mesa since the turn of the century and before. A few of the original pioneers had established lands and businesses and amiably co-existed with the Mexicans and the Indians. Their graciousness did not encourage stiff formalities. He was surprised at their lack of pretension. For the first time in his life, Stark felt truly comfortable with a group of people who were his peers.

Among the twenty guests, he was introduced to a woman with whom he sensed an instant compatibility and attraction. He thought they had met somewhere before, but she might have only been an ideal he had dreamed about. Her composure impressed him. The direct meeting of his gaze with clear blue eyes rivaled her turquoise jewelry and intimated an earthy sexuality. Her dark hair was swept back in a chignon that accentuated the sharp strength of her features. Her Mexican style white dress embroidered and belted at the waist flowed to mid-calf length in simple elegance. Brown tanned feet tucked into a pair of soft leather sandals wriggled slightly from time to time as her only outward expression of an inner tension as they conversed. Her slender hand occasionally adjusted a crocheted black shawl that graced her broad shoulders. He watched the free easy motion of her body walking, sitting, and subtle shades of variegated expression surface across tanned features that denied makeup.

Stark wondered if Indian blood didn't figure somewhere in her background. In the course of getting acquainted, she corrected his misconception, explaining that she was born in Chicago, had lived most of her life in Omaha, Nebraska and was of Dutch-Scandinavian descent. Her maiden name was Larsen. She had married into the Degrood family fourteen years ago in 1919.

The Degroods were well entrenched in New Mexican society, not only in Mesa, but in Albuquerque and Santa Fe. The family had been there since 1879. Professionally and politically affluent, they were considered among the pioneer aristocracy.

This charming woman, Amelia Degrood, had been a widow for eight years. Her husband had died of head injuries caused by a fall from his horse. She had one daughter, Erin, fourteen, who mirrored her mother's beauty.

During that first meeting, Stark exchanged only brief conversation with the woman, but she was firmly lodged in his thoughts. His eyes kept seeking her across the room so that he continually lost the drift of more immediate talk with others. He decided that one day soon, he would propose marriage to Amelia. Becoming the adoptive father of her teenage daughter, Erin, would not be a deterrent.

He bluntly asked Billy Chanson about Amelia. He was not surprised to learn that this widowed woman of wealth and position, as well as exquisite beauty, was widely sought by many aspiring and established businessmen and politicians.

"She owns a vast cattle empire southeast of Mesa, about four-hundred thousand acres. She also maintains a residence in town. She's my neighbor about a mile down the road."

The Chanson name was still relatively new to the region. Billy had left a limited future in Chicago ward politics as a young attorney in favor of California. Leaving behind his bride of six months, he had traveled to Los Angeles to investigate the political and legal climate. Neither appealed to him. He finally admitted to himself that he was just small time and could only be effective in a situation suited to his abilities.

In 1917, he was still awkward and callow in a political sense. His affected style and polish would take several years to acquire. He had wanted instant success and thought he might discover the possibility in a small town.

After moving his distressed wife to the dusty little hole that was Mesa, he soon learned that complexities still existed, although scaled down. There was nothing simple about human relations. Losing the mayoral elections between 1922 and 1930 confirmed that fact. So he moved his law practice to Santa Fe.

The Great Depression with its desire for economic salvation finally thrust him into office. The local citizens wanted change. They turned their backs on the established old guard who could not even offer hope, let alone provide financial assistance and relief. Chanson campaigned on the promise that "what was needed now was new blood. Modern style politics would prepare them for the changing times. And they will change!" became his slogan and promise proclaimed with the fervor of an evangelist minister.

In an era of despair, the people responded to his convictions to publicly stand up and offer them hope. They believed his promise to lead them out of economic destitution. They elected the illusions they wanted to hear. Charming Billy, as he came to be called, gave them an earful.

In 1933, when Franklin Delano Roosevelt opened the floodgates of the meager Federal treasury to revive the dead economy, Billy was esteemed a hero for his faith. He shrewdly identified himself with Roosevelt and the new politics, The New Deal. The association was to sustain him through a long and prosperous career.

On that same evening, Lee Stark also met Clyde Shreve, Editor of *The Mesa Independent*. The two men fired up at Billy's well stocked bar and talked into the wee hours. Shreve dominated the discourse on subjects ranging from Federal fiscal policy to Indian herbal medicines. He requested that after Stark was established, he would like to write a feature about him and the proposed mining operation. Stark said "I'll be more than happy to oblige."

When he finally looked around the spacious hacienda living room to bid goodnight to Amelia, he discovered that only he and Shreve remained. Even their gracious host had gone to bed. Shreve drove Stark back to his hotel.

Stark woke the next morning consumed with waves of pain rolling through his skull. He panicked, grabbed for his watch and saw that he still had a half hour before the mayor's car and driver would pick him up. He ordered a pot of strong black coffee and tomato juice and consumed them while he haphazardly dressed. *Thank God it was only a preliminary meeting.* He'd never be able to discuss deals in an intelligent manner with his head banging like a claxton. When he went down to the car, he could only growl with disgust at Billy's fresh appearance and cheery "Good morning, Lee. Ain't it a beautiful morning."

"I should have warned you about Shreve," said Billy. "I guess sometimes it sticks better when you find out about people yourself."

"Shreve's okay. I'm a fool for trying to keep up with him though. I had a good time last night. You'd think some of that good feeling would carry over, not hang over."

Billy chuckled with appreciation. "Shreve's an old newspaperman and a good boozer from way back. I'd sure hate to have his liver."

"I thought he'd never shut up."

"At least you're a good listener. He'll try to corner you again sometime." Billy laughed.

"I was asleep on my feet."

"Doesn't matter. Shreve's been known to expound to an empty room after everyone has gone to bed. Likes to hear himself talk. You could have left and it wouldn't have made any difference."

"Christ," Stark clutched his throbbing head.

Chapter 11
THE MARSHAL

Eighteen years ago, as a young man in search of work, Everett Carmody sought out the DeGrood ranch near Mesa, New Mexico.

He arrived at the small adobe town at dawn and toted his bag to the Harvey Hotel a short walk down the road from the train depot. After a bath, shave, and breakfast, he went to a local trading post and outfitted himself with boots, Stetson hat, Levis, chaps, a Colt .45 rig, Wincester rifle, slicker, and a bedroll. His next stop was the Federal post office. He inquired of the postmaster the way to the DeGrood ranch and when their supply wagon came in for the mail. It would be there the next day.

Carmody wandered the streets of the sparsely populated town and found little diversion. There were two saloons and the railroad's Harvey House Restaurant. In conversation with a bartender, he learned "Things get pretty lively around here on Saturday nights. Stockmen come in from the ranches. Not much has changed over the years. Now if you're lookin' for a woman, there's a place just outside of town."

Everett shook his head reeling from the effects of eight shots of whiskey. He returned to the hotel and slept soundly until the following morning.

He checked out of the hotel and carried his duffle over to the post office to wait for the DeGrood supply wagon to arrive. The Mexican's driver's limited English and Carmody's Spanish eclipsed only a few words of conversational salutation, but Carmody was able to convey that he wanted a ride back with him to the ranch and that he was seeking work.

The slow-moving wagon allowed him the opportunity to look closely at the terrain and absorb the dry heat and pungent desert smells. His eyes squinted against the gritty dust blowing across the land.

A wide wooden gate stamped with a simple bronze plaque bearing the name Degrood and DD, the double D brand, marked the entrance to the ranch. The ride in the wagon took another hour to reach the main house. It stood among a grove of cottonwood trees near a silt creek fed by a natural spring. A tall windmill pumped well water which was piped to the house and into metal tanks in six large corrals and adjacent grazing land.

As the wagon pulled into the shady yard, Carmody's gaze roamed over the scarred white adobe contrasted with newer sections where rooms had been added to accommodate the growing Degrood family. Until recently, three generations had been living under the same roof.

Two spacious barns, including a dairy barn and a horse barn, stood back from the house near the creek. A network of corrals, chutes, pens and paddocks divided these from a hog barn and a large chicken coop.

Frederico, the driver, directed Carmody to the office at the main house, then drove the wagon to the kitchen at the rear to unload supplies.

As Carmody paused outside the door for a further look at the long shaded front porch, he saw a woman come riding in at an easy lope on a fine Palomino mare tacked with a Spanish rig and silver bridle. The woman wore a split leather skirt, white cotton blouse beaded with turquoise and a sombrero to ward off the sun. She moved rhythmically with the animal and directed her along the wide path of an expansive flower garden. Entering the yard, she pulled to a walk and rode over to him.

"Hello, are you waiting to see someone?" Amelia displayed a clear-eyed poise and serenity that matched the silent spaces of the surrounding country. She eluded the pressures of agitation and time.

"I'm Everett Carmody. Looking for work."

"My husband's in Santa Fe on business, but you can speak with the foreman when he rides in." The late afternoon sun was beginning its descent. "Expect him any time. You can wait in the office if you like, or you're welcome to look around."

"Thank you, Ma'am."

She nodded once and urged her horse on to the barn at a walk.

Carmody entered the cool shadows of the office and sank into a thick leather armchair in a corner of the room facing a massive oak desk topped with stretched cowhide. Heavy ledgers and rows of leather bound books filled the shelves along the back wall. Out of curiosity, Carmody went over to them and browsed through the titles. There were many classics, a few in the original Greek and Latin, a smattering of romantic novels, books on livestock, veterinary medicine, ranching, agriculture, economics, philosophy, history, many volumes on politics and government, a collection of writings on the Civil War, a history of the American Southwest and Mexico, and a ledger containing dates and facts relating to the Degrood family history.

Carmody opened it to the first few pages containing a land survey drawing copied from the original plat issued in 1779 to Colonel Charles Hampton Degrood from the provisional Government of New Mexico. The land grant totaled forty-thousand acres of what had once been Navajo Indian Territory prior to their incarceration at Bosque Redondo and subsequent confinement to the reservation.

There were several Brady tintypes of the family accompanied by dates of birth, honors, military and political offices held, names and birthdates of children and grandchildren, with an observable improved quality of the photographs recording the more recent younger generation. Colonel Degrood had sired an extensive family of five sons and six daughters. His second wife had outlived him by seven years, but she had not remarried.

Stephen J. Degrood, forty years old and the youngest of the Colonel's sons, had assumed the ranch operations while his brothers had entrenched the family in positions of power in business, the law and politics of New Mexico. Many of their sons, in turn, maintained the tradition in the interest of the family fortune and political influence of white cattle ranchers.

Amelia was Stephen's third wife. The first had died during childbirth, the second separated from him had since remarried. However recent their history, Carmody realized that they were a formidable dynasty as he reached the end of the massive volume.

Returning to the leather chair, he heard the clank of spurs outside. A moment later, the ranch foreman, Neil Bonnyman, crowded through the door slapping trail dust from his chaps. He paused at the sight of Carmody standing at the center of the room.

"Name's Carmody." Everett extended his hand. "Lookin' for work."

The shorter man accepted Carmody's with an exceptionally strong grip. "Neil Bonnyman, foreman." He removed his leather chaps and hung them from deer antlers on the wall, then sat in the high backed chair behind the desk. He offered a cigar. Carmody declined.

"Have a seat." Bonnyman lit his cigar with a cloud of white smoke.

The sight of the taut-jawed little man sunk down behind the huge desk like a child straining to see over the top amused Carmody, but he maintained a passive expression. He assumed that Stephen Degrood must be a much taller man.

In a quiet efficient manner, Bonnyman established friendly respect and authority. He listened to Carmody's delineation of past employment with the railroad, and his two years working on a Niobrara River horse ranch in Nebraska. Bonnyman was favorably impressed with the young man's answers to his questions. "I'd like to see how you work with two of our colts. They're green as grass. But you've got a job punching cows, if you want it."

Carmody grinned and nodded.

Bonnyman got up from the desk and grabbed his hat. "I'll show you around the place." He took Carmody over to the adobe bunk house and introduced him to seven of the hands who were not out tending stock. He said that supper would be served in the main house kitchen in one hour.

Carmody dropped his duffle on an empty bunk and joined the dusty trail weary men washing for supper. They were similar to cattlemen he had met in Ainsworth and the men with whom he had worked on the railroad, tough raw individuals whose direct manner was fundamental to judging and relating to each other without complexity and without tolerance. They shared the same work, the same food, and the same values. Their variations of personality were thematic within the structure of their work. They were basically men of the soil, men of the land, men of the earth who voiced a credo of individualism and freedom against exploitation that rivaled that of eastern labor and was comparable to Marxist political philosophy and the class struggle. Yet, what they might utter in one breath, they contradicted in the next through an undisguised prejudice against the local native Indians whose land they had taken and now worked as their own. Carmody understood the inconsistency. It was an issue of white supremacy in which he did not believe.

Out of his failure to comply with that code, a bitter conflict arose between him and several of the ranch hands close to his own age, Red Tasker and his followers, Warren Lillibridge, T.J. Hatman, Bob Greever, and Tom Clough. These were all Texas boys, skilled stock and horsemen, but *tejanos*, outsiders to New Mexico and to many of the local customs and social tolerance.

Red's grandfather had fought on the side of the Confederacy during the Civil War and his father had taken part in Indian campaigns in the Southwest against the Apaches in 1886. From family tradition, Red Tasker bore no love for Yankees, Niggers, Jews, Catholics, and Indians. An able fighter, he enjoyed stirring up trouble just to let off steam. His nearly constant state of tension created a congenital need to fight. A Saturday night rarely passed that he did not go into Mesa and throw a slur that was returned with a punch and the fight would be on.

Carmody assimilated well with most of the men. There were twenty hands in all and the chuck wagon cook, whom everyone made an extra effort to treat kindly. A conflict may well not have arisen between Tasker and Carmody had Carmody not developed a friendship with Juan Castillo, the Navajo half-breed ranch blacksmith and silversmith whose craft approached a high form of art.

Juan would not tell anyone his age. Carmody guessed him to be about fifty. What he did share was that, as a child, his Navajo mother had been sold as a slave to a Mexican rancher down near the Rio Grande during the time of The Long Walk in the middle 1860's. The rancher had sired him and Juan had taken his name.

For many years, he had also been a slave and had learned the trade of a blacksmith. When he became a young man, he had stolen a horse and returned to the homeland he had never known. He and his wife lived in a Hogan now about a mile from the main house. It could not be seen from the white man's adobe.

Juan taught Carmody the rudiments of the Navajo language and something of the history and culture of the *Dine'*, the People. He was often an invited guest at Juan's Hogan. Once, Juan took him to a sing. He was a medicine man and sang the Red Ant Way chant.

Red Tasker would not even allow Juan to touch his horses, let alone shoe them. He shod his own. Juan didn't much care because he could devote more time to other men's horses. Red's enmity was unmistakable. Juan avoided him until one day Red and his friends deliberately ran a herd of cows into the vicinity of Juan's Hogan. They destroyed his wife's outdoor loom and a rug she had been weaving for three months.

There had been other minor incidents in the past. Tasker had salted Juan's forge with gunpowder. The ensuing small explosion had so startled a horse Juan was shoeing at the time that the frightened animal kicked him in the chest. Red daily flung racial slurs and demonstrated his disrespect with marked attitudes of derision that did not go unnoticed by either Bonnyman or Stephen Degrood. But Red Tasker was a top hand. They never reprimanded him, even though Juan was equally valuable to the ranch.

Following the incident of the cows, Juan decided to work a little mischief of his own. He carefully collected mud that Tasker had scraped from his boots. He did it in such a manner that Red saw him. Red was curious and suspicious as Juan continued to collect and hoard small items that Red cast away, a broken rawhide *latigo*, an old torn red bandana.

Then one day, Red caught Juan pulling hairs from the tail of his favorite horse. He walked over to the old man and flattened him with a single punch. Carmody stepped up behind Red, spun him around and spotted him on the jaw. Red went down sliding in a pile of fresh horse dung. He came up swinging. The fight was brief. Bonnyman intervened. He would not tolerate fighting between his men. "If I catch you at it again, I'll fire the both of ya."

On the following Saturday night, Red went after Carmody while they were in town. The fight was brutal and bloody. It started in the cantina and crashed out through the doors into the street. Both men finished exhausted and barely standing. They both required medical attention. Red had not counted on Carmody's ability being equal to his own. The sheriff, John Stone, locked them in separate cells and the doctor, McAffrey, treated them in the jail.

After the encounter, Tasker would not rest until he had Carmody cold. He tried for him out in the open far from the ranch headquarters. He was unmatched with a rope. He succeeded in snagging Carmody from his horse and dragging him through the rocks and brush. He left him afoot fifteen miles from the main house. When he walked in, Carmody told Bonnyman and Degrood that he had fallen and been dragged. His boot had gotten hung up in the stirrup.

Neither believed him but they did not choose to intervene until the sudden appearance of iron. Carmody started packing a gun, which prompted Red to do the same.

Bonnyman argued with Degrood that either one or both men had to go before blood flowed. Degrood was more concerned about his wife's infidelities under the pretence of shopping and cultural trips to Santa Fe. She had been spending more time there lately than at home. He left the decision over the conflict between Tasker and Carmody up to Bonnyman.

The foreman favored Carmody. He made a few discreet inquiries among the men as to what might happen if he let Red Tasker go. The consensus was that Red was top hand. He had seniority over Carmody. Many of the men would undoubtedly quit at what they considered unfair treatment and go with him. Bonnyman could not afford such a severe loss of manpower. So he confronted Carmody in the privacy of the ranch office.

"That's the way it is and I'm sorry for it. I have to handle this for the well being of all concerned."

When Carmody rode into Mesa on the supply wagon, Juan and his squaw went with him and returned to the reservation. Degrood had not expected to lose a good blacksmith and blamed Bonnyman for mishandling the whole affair. Bonnyman threatened to quit on the spot. "You can git yourself another foreman."

"No, I need you here. I just didn't want to lose a good blacksmith."

With his personal life crumbling around him, Stephen DeGrood drank a half quart of bourbon. His wife had been sleeping regularly with a friend of his in Santa Fe. Now he might lose Bonnyman, his foreman, much in demand and locally the best in the business.

Stephen took his drunken rage out on his prize stallion by running him over rocky uneven ground. The horse stepped into a hole and went down with a snap of a foreleg and crushed his rider.

Carmody debated whether he should try another ranch or find a different line of work. After a conference with the local Santa Fe Railroad supervisor, P.T. Sweigart, he returned to the railroad.

At this time, he became fast friends with P.T. Sweigart (Phillip Thayer) of the Indian trading family and whose father, Noel Sweigart, who taught him about the *dine'*, the Navajo People.

Their friendship was to span sixteen years. They met while working freight runs between New Mexico and Arizona. Sweigart took Carmody further into the life and ways of the Navajo and Hopi tribes. His father was an Indian trader like his father and great grandfather before him. The accessibility opened Carmody to something more than tolerance and detachment from these people who formed the greater population of the territory both on and off the reservations.

Sweigart and Carmody were alike in physical stature and the respect accorded them by their fellow crew members. They differed in a sense of personal humility, a quality deeply ingrained in Sweigart from his youth and daily association with the Indians who came to his father's trading post, the only one on reservation land. The young Sweigart had been adopted into the Hopi tribe as one of only three white men to experience their rites of initiation into manhood. This knowledge was of such profound secrecy that he would carry it to his grave and never divulge it.

He was tall and angular with sharp chiseled features, high brow and cheekbones, a hawkish nose and penetrating blue eyes. His thin dark hair was swept back at the temples. He was an open man, without pretense. His manner was dignified, gracious, and almost formal in its simplicity.

The close friendship and understanding of these men had much to do with the attraction they held for two of the young Harvey Girls who worked at the local Fred Harvey Restaurant. Sheila Sloane from Chicago and Judith Ryan from Kansas City had each been there for little less than a year. After big city life, neither had imagined they would remain long in that desolate location. They soon discovered they never lacked for male attention.

Few women of quality and breeding flowered in that region. The strict supervision of young girls insured an impeccable image of good taste and Christian virtue. They were sought by bachelors and widowed ranchers, miners, and railroad men.

For the first few months, they frustrated the overtures of an army of suitors. They were a stunning pair, Sheila a statuesque graceful blonde shot through with shades of red and brown. Her distinguished features and elegance of movement seemed transplanted from a Viennese court of another era that was strangely foreign and unsuited to this rough locale.

In contrast, Judith reflected her Welsh mining family background. She exuded strength and energy that overwhelmed most men who came under her intense gaze. She was prized by many drawn to her white skinned beauty against her brunette hair. Her features were not so fine as Sheila's and she tended to be shorter and slightly buxom. Of the two, she possessed a warm motherly personality and steadiness of character.

Carmody held out six months longer than his friend, Sweigart, and deprived the girls of their cherished plan for a double wedding, for which they never forgave him. Carmody protested that he just wasn't ready to settle down. But influences from his past restrained him from a commitment to Sheila. What he feared most was the emotional void he felt when they were alone together. He did not understand its origin, because it conflicted with the genuine attraction she held for him and that he denied himself.

As a child, he had always been uncertain of his mother's sincerity and affection for him. What remained in memory was how she had encouraged devotion to herself and had doled out little emotional rewards. She had used them as leverage against him and his sister. Carmody did not possess a sense of what an honest, loving relationship was or could become. He perceived all women as basically egocentric as his mother. In that warp lay the unconscious reason he had denied Sheila her coveted double wedding.

He feared something reawakening in him. He had never in his life struck back at his mother, neither in memory or in reality. He believed that he had adored and protected her.

Carmody's decision to apply for the position of county sheriff upon the retirement of Jim Stone came as a surprise to everyone, no less than to Carmody himself. The opportunity opened the door to a hidden pocket of his mind. After seven years with the railroad, he had gone the way of many when The Great Depression swept across the country. Secretly, he was not unhappy at losing his job with the railroad. He felt the need for a change, a break in the routine of long hauls across the desert flats.

Even more to the point of his decision was the need to support his family and the conscious image he had of himself as a husband and father.

On the basis of Jim Stone's recommendation, Carmody was the obvious choice to become sheriff, given his reputation as a railroad man, as well as his knowledge of the people and places in that region of New Mexico.

Carmody stepped into the role of sheriff as though he had been born to it. Without seeming effort, he quickly established himself as law and order, a figure of respect and authority. His charisma was such that rarely did anyone refuse to cooperate with him whenever he arrived on the scene to make an arrest or investigate a crime. He was known to be fair and never used brutality as a means of coercion. He would first reason with a man or a woman who was being difficult. He never beat them into submission.

He sometimes depended on Noel Sweigart in law enforcement matters involving members of the tribes when they would come into Mesa to trade. Their laws and values were not the same as those of the Anglo and had to be considered in a different light. Noel, who ran the trading post, knew and understood them well. Through his influence, Carmody adopted a leniency in some matters he would not ordinarily overlook.

Nights in town tended to be moderately quiet during the week. To see the local people, you would not imagine there could be that many living out among the rocky hills and mesas, not including Indians. Though Indians were not allowed in the saloons, even they would come in and wander about the street as if drawn to a need for community beyond their own society. The need usually took the form of a search for a drink, which they were always able to find. They also sought to escape their misery and poverty and the low esteem they held of themselves and of their station in life.

By Monday morning, the knifings and fights and arrests were counted and recorded in *The Mesa Independent* as a measure of the enthusiasm with which the weekend had been celebrated.

***

Carmody's sharp look told Logan he was no longer wanted there at the jail. The young journalist apologetically bowed out and returned to *The Independent*. He felt sympathy for Carmody, an honorable lawman. As Logan started to work on the two stories of the day, Red Rock Crossing and the jail break of Yelena Ivanov, he decided to leave the one on Yelena open. He believed she would provide cause for a lot more newsprint before her presence in the Southwest was over.

Chapter 12
REVENGE OF A BOOT LEGGER

The fire had gone out. The slow condensation from the still's coiled copper tubing ceased with a final sliding transparent drop into the large wooden vat below. A concentric ring glided over the glassy surface like viscous mercury and halted at the edge with a barely perceptible quiver. The surface lay as quiet as the thoughts of the man who lay quiet.

The distant whistle of a passing train woke him, a clear haunting wail out of a dream. A swollen knot of pain and nausea blocked his despair until they oozed through him as his sole thought, his sensation, his life. The voice of the train lingered and faded, then sounded again farther in the distance, the ghosts of his sons calling to him.

Life was gone. The extensions of himself that gave purpose and meaning to his existence. Jerome Ligget cast about in his chaotic mind for something to grasp, an anchor. When he could not find one, he panicked, a sharp cry rising in his throat. He drifted alone in some terrifying space through which he perceived no end. He staggered to his feet and flailed disoriented into the cave wall. He must find something meaningful to hold him steady.

He had gone into town in search of his boys.

Phillip Sweigart was typing the accident report when a shadow blotted out the light at the window. He glanced up fearfully at the sight of Jerome Ligget peering in at him. He wondered if Carmody had yet told Ligget about the deaths of his three sons and if the man had come to take his revenge against the Santa Fe Railroad or any representative of it. He rose up, tense, ready to defend himself if necessary as the large man moved around to the entrance and stood like a hulking towering grizzly in the open doorway.

"Lookin' for mah boys. Been lookin' all mornin'. They never come home last night. Ain't like 'em." Ligget paused. His eyes searched the sparsely furnished office as though he hoped to discover his sons sitting there. His gaze settled a moment on an eight by ten black and white photograph of a Navajo track crew. "I been askin' around. Maybe you seed 'em someplace."

The last thing Sweigart wanted to do at that moment was to stand there trapped, alone, representing the Santa Fe Railroad and tell this man, knowing his reputation, what had become of his sons. Ligget would kill the messenger. He had obviously not talked to Sheriff Carmody.

"Come in. Ligget. Sit down. I have to run an important message over to the dispatcher. Then I'll see what I can do to help you out. I have seen your sons. I was meaning to call you, but you don't have a phone. Come in. Sit down. Have to get this over there. It's urgent. Be back in about ten minutes, if you don't mind waiting."

Ligget's rancid smell permeated the office as Sweigart maneuvered out past him and hurried along the adobe building to the dispatcher's office where he nervously snatched up the phone.

"Ev, Sweigart. Ligget's here. He don't know yet. He's waiting. Sitting in my office."

Sweigart hung up and waited, stared a moment out at the empty track, then turned and walked through the crew's waiting room to the ticket office just to keep out of sight. He hid there for ten minutes praying that Ligget would not come searching for him. A car pulled up outside on the gravel. Sweigart pushed through the gate into the passenger lobby as Carmody came through the door.

"Christ, he had me trapped in there alone. I couldn't tell him like that. He would've taken me apart. The strange thing about it, I'd just finished typing the accident report when he walked in. It's still sitting there in the typewriter. I don't think he can read."

The two men moved quickly along the platform next to the building. Ligget still sat half dozing in Sweigart's office. He startled awake and looked up with surprise at the sight of the sheriff. Sweigart went behind the desk and prepared himself for the worst. He carefully pulled the accident report from the typewriter.

Carmody nodded, removed his hat and sat opposite this large man whose world was about to shatter with the next few words he would hear.

"Joe Moss told me you came by this morning looking for your sons. I'm sorry to have to give you some bad news."

Ligget's dull gray eyes quickened with alarm. "What's happened to my boys? You put 'em somewheres?" His breath built in agitation.

Ligget, I want you to listen carefully and keep yourself under control. There's no one to blame. It was a freak accident. Happened late last night out at Red Rock Crossing." Carmody shook his head in sympathy and stared a moment at the scratched wooden floor to give Ligget time to contain himself and to expect the worst. He raised his eyes to the man's straining face.

"For some reason no one is able to explain, your sons were on the tracks. The express hit them going ninety miles an hour." He paused. "I'm sorry, Ligget. There's nothing left of them. I am truly sorry."

Jerome froze with a sharp intake of breath. His small eyes pivoted from one man to the other, distrustful, hoping they were lying to him. Their eyes expressed their wariness and their sympathy and told him, in truth, his sons were gone. His expression locked staring through the window as if he expected to see his boys come around the corner and through the door laughing that it was all a hoax. He would whale the shit out of them for scaring him like this. They did not appear.

He slowly rose and silently walked out into the sunlight. Sweigart and Carmody watched as he stood there shaking with his back toward them. Suddenly he began running and stumbled along the tracks. Howls and hoarse bellowing grunts and cries of anguish trailed behind him.

Sweigart and Carmody rushed out of the office and watched him until he reached the stockyards where he turned aside and ran from view out into the desert.

***

As Ligget emerged from the cave, sunlight struck him with a hammer of heat. His head swam. He fell to his knees, then to all fours and vomited with a coughing animal-like roar. When he was done, his stomach continued to quiver. Bile streamed from the corners of his compressed dry lips and dripped from his bearded chin. His breath wheezed in shallow painful gasps. The backflow of the acrid vomit stung his eyes and nostrils.

Bent over nearly double, he shuffled slowly on down the canyon to his shack. He stopped at the well pump. The metal was hot to the touch. Cold water gushed into a metal pail positioned below the spout. He splashed his face again and again, then finally lifted the pail and drank deeply. He came fully awake and his thoughts began to clear.

Late in the night, he stared out the window at the cold stars. He rose from the scratching tick mattress he called a bed and lifted his hunting rifle from its wall rack. His hands clutched the wooden stock and heavy lethal dark barrel ... his anchor.

While waiting for the return freight on the Kingman run, Charley Hughes walked into town to scour the shops for a birthday gift for his wife. Kate was a hard woman to buy for. She hadn't really cared much about the frilly nightgown he had given her last Christmas. She just wasn't a frilly sort of woman. One hell of a lover in bed though. He would not make the same mistake twice. This time, he would find something solid and strong like Kate. But, oh, how he liked to touch and handle those soft frilly underthings. He would see to it that his baby daughter had plenty of them as she grew up. Sturdy old Kate, what would be appropriate for her? He decided to stay away from dresses altogether. Not that much more to chose from in Kingman than in Mesa anyhow. Mostly Mexican designs. Now, if he had been on the Santa Fe run maybe. But time was short. She already had all the turquoise and cooking ware she needed.

He walked into a trading post. After several minutes, he settled on an intricate Hopi woodcarving of a deer and a beaded doeskin dress. He had it wrapped in plain paper with a bright yellow ribbon around it. Then he returned to the depot thirty minutes before his train was due in from the west,

Three hours later, as the train rolled across the Arizona–New Mexico state line, Charley felt a sharp sting followed instantly by an explosion into absolute blackness as the concussion of the high-powered bullet slammed him to the floor of the engine cab.

His foot flew off the deadman brake throwing the train into an emergency stop. The fireman staggered flailing against the control panel. He stared in horrible disbelief at the side of Charley's head crushed from the impact of the slug and now pooling the metal floor with blood. A moment before, he had been sitting at the open window thinking of where he would take his wife, Kate, out for a birthday dinner that evening.

***

"I'll tell her," said Carmody, his voice tinged with anger and sadness. "But we can't let her see him like this."

Dr. McAffrey pulled a blanket over the dead engineer's body lying on the floor of the crew's Mesa Depot waiting room. The coroner motioned for assistance. Gnarled strong hands lifted the corpse and carried it outside to the hearse. McAffrey and Carmody followed.

"My God, Ev, on her birthday. On Katie's birthday." McAffrey coughed to keep from weeping.

The fireman came up silently behind them. He mumbled incoherently as he handed Carmody the bloodstained gift, then wordlessly shuffled away in his grief.

McAffrey stared at the gift. "Who do you think did it?"

Carmody shook his head.

"And why? Jesus Christ, why?"

Carmody peeled away the crunching blood-stained paper. He would not hand the gift to his daughter like this.

"You going over there now?"

Carmody nodded and walked slowly to his car.

Later, remembering his daughter's tears soaking into his shirt, he never realized tears could be so hot. "Oh, Daddy, Why? Why?

Who would? Why? Why? Not Charley, not my Charley. Oh, why? Why?" Until she choked and could not speak.

Carmody suspected it could be Jerome Ligget, but he had no proof. "Your mother doesn't know yet. I'll go get her." He felt strange and sick and tender. "The Sweigarts are here. They'll stay with you 'til I get back."

Phillip Sweigart, who was the regional manager of the railroad, and his wife, Judith, came in. Judith went quickly to the couch and her arms encircled the moaning young widow.

Sweigart and Carmody walked outside onto the porch. A warm night wind blew across the land. The woman's pounding sobs rolled out to them through the screen door.

"What can we do?" Sweigart asked.

"It's such a waste. What you want is to prevent these things from ever happening. Once it's done, there's no recovering. There's no second time. We're here once and then we're gone and that's it. We have to get the man who did it but we've got nothing to go on."

"I'm so sorry for her, Ev. I'm so sorry. It's like she's my own daughter." He paused. "It could happen again, you know. Someone else. The word's out between here and Kingman. What if he decides to open up on a Pullman?"

Carmody shook his head. "If there's a pattern to this, maybe we can get to him. Train passing that region on the same schedule. I can be on it. Have a horse ready in a stock car. It might not happen again, but if it does, I'll go after him."

"Judith said she'll stay the night with Kate and for as long as she needs her."

"Thank you. Thank you, both. I'll bring Sheila over. She hasn't heard yet."

" That bastard will try again," said Sweigart. "We have to get him. Can't just let this go by. Know who I think?"

"Who? Ligget?"

"No, miners ... gunman anyway. Brought in special from the East."

Carmody stared at him.

"About a half mile of sideline track between here and the Wooten Mine was blown out early this morning. Dynamite. My crew's there now rebuilding the roadbed."

"Armed?"

Sweigart nodded. "Not taking any chances."

"The sniper was west of that area. Could be entirely different. Just seems like a bad coincidence. Maybe it was planned that way."

"You think that union woman organized 'em that fast? Don't make sense. They haven't made any demands yet," said Sweigart.

"Tell your train crews to keep clear of the windows when they pass through that sector. If it happens again, we'll have a place and a pattern ... at least a place."

When Carmody arrived at his house, he could tell from the expression on his wife's face that she anticipated bad news. He never came home during the middle of the day.

"What is it? What has happened? Is it Bobby?"

"No, our daughter. Charley was killed by a sniper on the Kingman run."

"No, oh no. Have you seen Kate?"

"I just came from her house. The Sweigarts are with her."

"There's something about the trains," said Sheila.

"What do you mean?"

"What they cause to happen. What they bring into our lives."

Carmody understood. "Let's go to Kate."

His wife nodded and preceded him out the door.

***

The horse's hoof repeatedly stamped the straw littered floorboards. He tossed his head, pulling impatiently at the restraining leather rein that held him tied to the paint peeled slats of the moving stock car. Suspended sunlight flashed through the spaces in rapid changing mottled patterns of whirling dust left in the wake of hot rushing wind.

Carmody sat alone at the front of the rumbling creaking car and looked back at the horse. He smelled the fresh droppings even though the wind blew the scent in the other direction. He shifted in discomfort at the raw hardness under his buttocks as the car swayed on its carriage with bolt shuddering cracks and groans and jolted with a sliding grind of heavy metal.

He picked at a sliver of wood while trying to scan the terrain surging by too quickly for the eye to clearly see through the narrow openings. He had been traveling now for two hours and figured the train must be approaching the region where the sniper had fired on the first train and killed Charley Hughes.

Bracing against the wall, he staggered up and paced the moving car. He paused to check the tightness of the saddle girth. His hand brushed the stock of the Winchester repeater and shoved it more firmly and deeper into its saddle mount. He stepped to the side of the car and peered out between the weathered slats.

Ligget was surprised to see the long freight train slow and come to a steaming halt with great clouds smoking from the black engine. He had not even fired a shot. He noticed movement at about the center of the train. A door on one of the stock cars was thrown open and a ramp thrust out and down to the gravel bed. A moment later, a man emerged from the gloom of the car leading a dun colored horse down the ramp. He lifted and shoved the plank back into the car, waved toward the engine, then mounted the horse and began riding at a walk in his direction.

Ligget did not believe the man could possibly have seen him or even suspected he was there hiding among the boulders on a low ridge about a half mile from the track. As the train slowly pulled away behind the rider and gradually resumed its interrupted pace, he saw the flash of a rifle barrel drawn from its saddle mount.

Ligget raised his gun to his shoulder. His hands shook so that he could not hold the oncoming rider steady in his sights. He fired too quickly and the rifle bucked. The bullet kicked up a spray of dirt several yards to the side of the horse. The animal reared shying away. Carmody spurred him into a leaping run toward a protective cluster of large boulders as two more shots rang out in rapid succession. The slugs nipped the dust at their heels.

Carmody dismounted and waited. He sighted up the rise between the tall rocks. He detected a blur of movement and saw a man scramble further up the slope and disappear over the rim. Carmody quickly remounted and set his horse charging up the rocky grade.

When he reached the top, he saw Ligget struggling to mount an old Indian horse with a scrawny ewe neck and large Roman nose. Ligget looked back in fear over his shoulder. With much effort, he pulled himself into the saddle, causing the horse to stagger and stumble under the sudden unbalanced weight. Ligget panicked at the sight of Carmody on his horse silouhetted on the ridge above against a cloudless sky.

Carmody recognized the large clumsy body and caught a clear glimpse of Jerome Ligget's face. He watched the heavy hunched over figure kick the old animal into a clumsy jarring gallop. The sight gave Carmody the strange sensation of watching a bear riding a horse. It occurred to him that going after Ligget was not unlike tracking down a ponderous and lethal bear. He put his own sturdy quarterhorse tucking and sliding on its bulging muscular haunches down the steep slope. When they reached the bottom, Carmody's booted heels touched him into a flat out run, leaping rocks and dodging in and out of the brush on small quick striking hoofs.

Ligget heard the steady thud of hoofs closing behind him. The earth suddenly opened before him in a wide arroyo. He pulled hard to the right to turn away, but threw his unbalanced horse off stride causing him to stumble. They fell hard at the edge of the drop. The sandy soil crumbled under their combined weight. The horse rolled, legs thrashing as they plunged with a rush thirty feet to the dry wash below. Hung up in the stirrups, Ligget took the full crushing weight of the animal on impact. His spine snapped with a loud crack like a dry branch. He lay staring at the stark blue sky in amazement as the animal scrambled up and limped away.

Ligget did not realize the girth had broken with the fall and his paralyzed legs still encompassed the saddle. He could neither sense nor feel anything, yet he could see blue sky and the hazy figure of Carmody on a horse looking down at him from high up at the edge of the arroyo. The image blurred. The sky slowly faded to a white film cutting off his vision. He tried to blink away the brilliant sun. His eyelids would not close.

Chapter 13
A MATTER OF INTERPRETATION

Much had happened since Yelena Ivanov's arrival in Coal Town. She had been taken to a house hidden deep within the ghetto of the mining community. She noticed how the eyes of the man's wife greeted her with honor and respect. Yelena immediately approached their children gathered in a shy curious cluster in a corner and gently touched their heads, then looked back at the parents. The adults understood her gesture, why she was there and what they would be plotting against and fighting for together.

She had not eaten since breakfast and felt slightly weakened as she slumped onto a quickly offered chair. The woman sensed Yelena 's need, but politely asked. "You hungry, ma'am?" Yelena nodded with a weak grin. As long as she took care of them, they would take care of her. Although still young, feeling old and tired concerned her.

It was important that she develop strong friendships here among these people. She was a fugitive and did not want to spend her remaining years in a cold prison cell. Coal Town was the last place for her to go before she left the country, but she had to pay her way with her services. She must make the inhabitants her people. She would waste little time in rest. She would begin at once, that very night. She would ask to meet some of the men and their wives. It was most important to know the wives and let them know her. She would listen to them with a supportive and sympathetic ear. The wives were the real strength behind their men. They were steady in their resolve and persevered where the men could easily be discouraged and intimidated with beatings and weariness and a bottle of whiskey. The women had power and influence over their men.

When she had finished her meal, Yelena said she would like to bathe and rest for a few hours. The woman sent the men and children outside. She heated a cauldron of water on the coal burning stove and filled a metal tub. Then she also withdrew and left Yelena alone to soak and contemplate.

Yelena stripped off her clothes and eased her thin frame into the water. She stared mesmerized at the steam rising around her still youthful flesh. At a young age, her personal enjoyments had been few, always tied to influencing the lives of others, persuading and motivating them to change, to better their lot in life, and strike back at their oppressors. Her occupation left only a small space for herself.

She finished her bath and toweled dry. Pulling on a loose shift, she lay on a hard narrow cot and closed her eyes. For as long as she could remember, except when she was a child, she had slept on hard narrow beds. She had forgotten the sensations of luxury and comfort that her mother had provided her and her sister. She had since become a warrior and led a Spartan existence.

There were moments when she longed for human comfort, holding her lover's body next to her own. Something had come between her and Damon Roikos after their initial relationship. He blamed her for her desire to avenge what had been done to her family. They had slept rigidly in isolation. She was saving herself for the people.

She had subverted her sexuality and channeled it into the sphere of work. She regretted never having children. There still might be time if she met the right man. She loved children, the frail children of the oppressed. They were so thin, suffering, and hungry. She felt a profound tenderness toward them. They were her own. All of them were her own.

Lately, an impulse had seized her to throw off the mantle of her revolutionary burden. She wanted to turn in some other direction. But her path had become a wide trench along which she could only trudge forward hoping to reach the end.

She despaired that there was no way out for her, no rest, no relief. The stirring excitement was gone, burnt out before crowds of anonymous faces. Now, she just went through the motions. Her speeches and exhortations had become a repetitive performance.

Later that evening, a small crowd gathered in the cellar of a local bakery. There were some forty men and women. These were her contacts, her messengers, her beginning. They were the first of the volunteers. She would use them to advantage because already their cause was mutual. There was no need to persuade and inspire them.

But it's no longer my beginning, she thought, as she moved to a position at the front of the room and faced them. It's their beginning, maybe. I give them their beginning. She slowly looked around at the worn silent faces of people who suffered and groveled in the earth for a living.

"I have been asked to come here and speak to you by some of your comrades." Her voice commanded attention. It was firm, far reaching in its strength, soothing, logical, and direct.

"Were I to ask the question, is there any man or woman here who does not want to better their station in life, I doubt that any of you would answer no.

"What we are about to do here is a simple act of faith … . faith in ourselves and in our personal value as human beings placed upon this earth as men and women, faith in our worth as human beings. Remember, that is what we are fighting for. We are going to demand that your worth be recognized."

In one part of his news story, Randolph wrote:

The main obstacle to the successful organization of the miners employed by Stark is the immigrants' acceptance of capitalist rule. The goal of the National Miners Union with communist party leadership is the collective social ownership and operation of all natural resources and means of production in order to end the economic exploitation of workers by management.

In a capitalist society, private ownership of economic resources gives rise to class divisions; and the state, using armed force, enforces upon the workers the will of those who possess the resources and hold the power over those who produce, but do not own the means of production.

In the old country, a man sought economic security. He was not concerned with personal, political, and religious freedoms, except with the advent of the war. Many came to America to escape military conscription. They wanted to make money, then return to Europe, their homeland, after the war and purchase land for themselves. Most of them lost interest in returning. The loss of employment security through the mine superintendent's blacklist causes fear among them and a reluctance to organize.

Knowing that Yelena Ivanov is or will be at work somewhere in the midst of Coal Town miners and their families, Stark has taken immediate steps to counter subversive union activity by hiring detectives and installing thirty mine guards who are heavily armed.

On the same day that a gang of miners had broken her out of jail, Stark had posted a statement of company policy that was read and translated in several languages to all miners. The preamble began:

> The company is unrelenting in its stand against the unionism as subversive and undermining the basic constitution of this country. We, therefore, consider it a conspiracy against the very foundations of the nation. Punitive measures, including execution will be taken against any groups or individuals who become involved in such activities. It is company policy to pay a fair wage for equal labor.

In another part of his news stories, Randolph wrote:

The average weekly earning of a coal miner is $35.00. It is Yelena's intention to point out to the men that the company engages in profit increase by wage reductions while raising prices on the market and cutting back on the cost of production. The wages paid by Stark are comparable to exploitive wage rates elsewhere in the country.

They do not receive pay for dead work not related to actual coal removal. These segments include waiting for material to arrive, bolts, props, ties, rails, pumping out water, and moving coal a longer distance from where it was taken. Men lose time waiting for tools and waiting for the cage to take them down into the depths and bring them back up from the mine.

The mine officials interfere in the election of the check weighman, who then does not record the correct weights for coal that was actually mined. He is employed by the company to increase company profits at the expense of the miners. Deductions for the use of blasting powder, fuse caps and supplies are also taken from the miners' wages.

Affiliated with the United Mine Workers during the 1930's, Yelena has successfully organized immigrants during strikes in the eastern states. Being one of them, she understands how they think and how they react to change.

They live in groups that retain their old cultures. Each group has a leader who interprets the new American culture for the others. He acts as spokesman for the group. Prestige and respect come with his position.

Immigrants are not leaders. They tend to be followers. They are fearful of doing anything that might bring them more trouble than they have already experienced. They are plagued with feelings of impermanence, of mobility, of not belonging as an integrated member of a community in which they have no interest and no investment in its problems. They are perpetual strangers on the outside looking in.

They view direct efforts to make them change as attacks on their customs that cause sensitivity and over-reactions and withdrawl. Those who try to assimilate encounter the hostility of their own ethnic groups.

Natives waylay and harass them on the way to church. Spewing self-righteous bigotry, they blame the immigrants for the war in Europe and associate them with Hitler. They accuse them of drawing the United States into the war because "hunkies and garlic eaters and Johnny Bulls can't fight their own battles or defend themselves. Yet they come to our country and make money and expect our young men to go off and fight and die for them."

Lacking the security and courage to sever their ties with the past and to face new unstructured concepts, they are willing to turn over their freedom and responsibility to their group leaders. They vote as a block according to the dictates of their ethnic leader.

Yelena wasted no time in seeking out these intermediaries and carefully persuading them to join the side of unionism. She could depend on them to hold firm in the face of even fearful opposition.

American Landscape

Local native miners are always first to cave in when a strike is called. They do not save money to enable them to weather the strike period. Not only are they afraid of losing their jobs, they're afraid of the violence they know willl come against them.

Chapter 14

INDIAN AFFAIRS

After twenty-five years as a newspaperman, the publishing editor, Junius Shreve concluded that he loathed writing as a profession, but he didn't mind editing the work of others. He often professed that his true calling was to be a critic, because as he told his young protégé, Randolph Logan, "I'm just far too intelligent and perceptive to wallow in the drudgery of writing."

When he carried on in such a manner, usually after a few belts of bourbon from the bottle he kept in his desk drawer, as one of his two young staff writers, Randolph was tempted to ask him what he was doing then editing a newspaper in a one horse town in the middle of the Southwestern desert, but Randolph valued his job and his hide.

Shreve also kept a loaded Colt 45 in the same drawer next to the bottle, "just in case," he said, "the power of my editorial rhetoric should incite the passions and antagonism of a vigilante force and cause them to storm this office."

This exact event had once happened to one of Shreve's senior editors when Junius was still a cub reporter in a small town in Texas. Junius said that "Texas was then, and probably would forever be the greatest hotbed of powerful, corrupt, ignorant, barbaric, uncouth, uncivilized megalomaniacs west of the Mississippi and that rivaled only in degree the mental midgets of the South and the preposterous, assumptive imbecility of those floundering idiots in Washington."

Shreve's opinions sometimes got him into trouble. To hear him talk, he should have been made king of the world, or at least God's right hand man. He had an opinion and a solution for everything. He claimed the only reason he had settled in Mesa instead of accepting an offer to be Editor-in-Chief of the New York Times was that he wasn't a yes man. Logan was convinced that Junius was lying about the New York Times, but never called him on it.

Junius often referred to his impending retirement and had done so for the past five years. Tom Bell, the grizzled stringy pressman, who barely spoke two words together, figured "It's not going to happen. He'll never retire. That gray-haired old fart will keep on saying another five years until he keels over. He couldn't live without that job." Bell communicated mostly with gestures and grunts. He believed he put more than enough words in print and didn't have to say much else. People seemed to understand his grunts anyway.

Logan had personal visions of leaving his "post" there after about three years and becoming a traveling correspondent in Europe and the South Pacific, both exotic locales in his mind. Although the South Pacific had beautiful available native women, Europe was fertile ground for a journalist where Hitler and German aggression threatened the continent. He figured he could make a name for himself as a war correspondent reporting in the face of danger. His itch to travel, however, had not turned into an initiative to leave New Mexico and risk his life.

With wide-set almond eyes, dark hair and high cheekbones inherited from his Irish mother and the sturdy body of a miner from his father, who had died in a mining accident, he cut a dashing romantic figure with nowhere to be dashing but in his own active imagination.

Since Logan and his mother had moved from Virginia, he had never stepped outside of his small town experience other than in reading novels and the newspaper and watching movies in Santa Fe, where they had the only theater within a thousand miles. He often saw the same film several times, since it was shown for one month before the next arrived.

Shreve had hired Logan when he sent an English composition as a writing sample along with a letter asking for a job. Although he would never openly admit it, Shreve recognized potential in Logan's work and agreed to hire him on a trial basis. Logan had now been with him for three years, learning the craft of news reporting from the old master who never planned for Logan's trial to come to an end.

Much of the news in *The Mesa Independent* was drawn from The United Press over the wire. National coverage usually took the headlines and page one, giving *The Independent* the appearance of containing important news. Events of Roosevelt's New Deal programs rolled daily off the press. Logan had written a good many features on local events.

Shreve had assigned Logan to keep a running story on the planning and implementation of the New Deal programs for the Navajo, the Civilian Conservation Corps. The New Deal was big news, national news, for that part of the country and was of particular interest to local business. It was a relief to know that once again there would be money flowing and it would change hands.

Logan spent a lot of time sitting in on John Collier's organizational meetings and following him around on side trips with survey parties out on the Navajo reservation. As a human interest element, he also interviewed a number of men involved in the project. There were a few locals, but Collier had recruited most of his staff from prestigious colleges and universities back east, such as Princeton, Harvard, Yale, and Columbia.

During an interview, Collier told Logan, "I wanted the top minds with the most current technical information on anthropological and cultural change and I got them."

The Civilian Conservation Corps headquarters had been established at Albuquerque. The local bureau superintendents were submitting project proposals for review by foresters and engineers.

Logan found Collier to be an unusual man, who cared little about his personal appearance, as though he didn't have the time to bother whether or not he shaved or if his clothes were pressed. He struck Logan as a fanatic, but his energy provided the kind of persistence and dedication necessary to accomplish the scope of such a massive undertaking. Collier called himself a social revolutionary. To J. Edgar Hoover back in Washington, that branded him a communist and placed him in Hoover's files as a subversive.

Logan learned that during Collier's career before he was appointed Commissioner of Indian Affairs, many Government and agency officials considered him nothing more than a rabble rouser. He was a graduate of Columbia University and the College de France and had done social work in New York, Georgia (his native state), and in California. His main concerns had been cooperative community action and planning in immigrant communities. Then, in 1920, he had attended the Christmas rituals at the Taos Pueblo in New Mexico.

"That experience sent me off on a whole new cause," he told Logan. "I saw the Pueblos as an example of everything I had sought to develop as a social worker for an effective integrated society."

Collier described for Logan how all the preparation going on around the Civilian Conservation Corps created a sense of confusion concerning priorities, where the money could most effectively be spent and on what projects.

After witnessing the ruggedness of the land and the non-existence of paved roads on the reservations, the Government engineers advocated the purchase of one-hundred large Caterpillar tractors and other heavy construction equipment. Here again, the locals knew better and advised against the expenditure. The most important needs were water reclamation development, wells, and dams to contain water and combat drought.

Logan had been present the day Sheriff Everett Carmody went out to the agency to discuss the organization of an Indian police force to help subdue the growing crime wave in the checkerboard area at the east end of the Navajo reservation. Portions of the land owned by the Santa Fe Railroad and leased to white ranchers for grazing and water rights had been the cause of much controversy during the past twenty years.

The biggest problem was the sale of bootleg liquor to reservation Indians which fostered gambling, illegal land speculation, and prostitution. Three killings had occurred over that way in the past week and Carmody was getting anxious to move in and clean out the area, but he needed armed manpower.

Collier believed the Indians should learn to police themselves. In a side meeting, Carmody told him, I want more men. The checkerboard area falls within my jurisdiction and I can't cover it all with one deputy. Things are getting out of hand."

That was the moment Collier told him, "The Government Commission is sending an expert to establish and direct the law enforcement program. His name is Howard Gimbel."

"What makes him an expert?" asked Carmody.

"He's with the FBI."

"That's it? Has he ever been out here? Does he have any experience?"

"I don't know anything about him. The Bureau wouldn't release any information to me. There seems to be some secrecy in his coming here."

Carmody stared at the floor. "This doesn't sound good." He looked back at Collier. "You expect me to work with him?"

"I'm asking you as a favor. These things come together only to the extent we cooperate with each other. I firmly believe you can work out any differences between you."

"Meaning you want me to look after him."

"In a manner of speaking. Share what you know. We have to teach each other."

"What I know is not something you can teach. You have to live it. He's probably never been west of Washington."

"That's possible."

"I'll know when I meet him."

"He'll be here in two weeks."

"Who picked the FBI?"

"Not me. But this is a Federal program."

"The Government has done enough damage."

"I'm here to change that."

"You'll have a fight on your hands."

"Nobody said this would be easy."

"It won't be easy but I'll agree to help him." Carmody pulled on his Stetson and stomped out of Collier's office. He knew Gimbel would fail without even trying. When it came time to select and train the men, he would need Carmody. People from the East knew nothing about Indians except the distorted images portrayed in Hollywood movies. Carmody figured Gimbel's main purpose was to forge a promotion for himself.

When Collier received his money from Washington, the field operations began in earnest. Eastern experts assigned Navajo crews to work on various projects. Logan drove out onto the reservation daily to observe and record the events for his ongoing news feature.

The men use teams of horses and large metal scoops in building dams across streams and arroyos to catch and store water for livestock and to prevent losses from flooding and runoff during the heavy rains.

In other locations, crews drill wells, construct windmills, dig springs, and install water storage tanks. One of the bigger projects is the building of a truck trail into the Fort Defiance plateau to provide access to the tribe's valuable timber resources and to act as a firebreak.

From time to time, Logan came across Indian crews of hundreds of men carrying bags of poison grain which they spread in a great crisscrossing of the Navajo range land in a huge rodent eradication and control program.

Thirty dollars a month per man wasn't much, but it prompted an economic boom for nearly everybody in that area of the Southwest, both whites and Navajos. At least now they could purchase food and clothing for their families.

One of Collier's projects that began with good intentions created more problems than it solved. The erosion control program quickly became a headache for Collier. It tampered with a Navajo tradition, the nature of their grazing and livestock practices.

Collier had coordinated with the Department of Agriculture for assistance in setting up an erosion experiment station. The report came in that the reservation was severly damaged by soil erosion from years of overgrazing. The land was pocked with scoops or "blow-outs," great holes and sand dunes where the topsoil had been scoured off. Water runoff from the uplands had cut deep arroyos across the fertile valleys. The livestock had eaten even young saplings and prevented the forests from new reproduction and growth. The survey report estimated the occurrence of erosion on seventy percent of the land, some of it beyond restoration.

In his process of reorganization, Collier explained to Logan that the Navajo's must reduce their livestock holdings. What he asked of them was tantamount to cutting away the basis of their economy, their social values and their way of life, a contradiction to Collier's own objectives. Ironically, he laid the seeds for the destruction of the very things he had wanted to preserve, the culture and autonomy of a unique ethnic society.

These were exciting and colorful times for Logan. Some of his copy even went back east through The United Press for reprint in major newspapers. In his analysis, he would say that all in all, many positive results were coming out of Collier's program. But as it turned out, while he covered local events during the next few years, he lost sight of his dream to leave Mesa. He discovered more strife and dissension attached to Collier and the Federal Government tampering with the Navajo way of life than he would have ever imagined.

***

What angered Indian Agent Jim Picker as he set out from his rambling adobe house on a summer morning was that the Collier contingent had not even bothered to consult him for advice based on his years of experience. He had come to the Southwest as a field worker for the BIA in 1913, when nobody knew anything about dealing with Indians and you had to learn it from the ground up. At that time, a Bureau job was considered about as low on the civil service ladder as you could get.

Picker had always resented the condescending attitude of Washington officials when they breezed through on a perfunctory annual inspection tour. Looking back, he wondered how he had managed to stay with this kind of work for so long. He was distrusted and despised by the Navajo on one side as the representative of a Federal policy of planned exploitation. On the other, a prevailing congressional prejudice held BIA staff workers in very low esteem as inept paper pushers in remote locales and not suited for more important Government appointed positions. *"Hell, what difference does it make anyway? We're thousands of miles away out here in the desert. What do they care?"*

Rather than adequate funding to improve faltering educational and rehabilitation programs, abuse and criticism was his daily cup.

More often than not, a BIA agent became a middleman for congressional figures and big business in usurping lands and resources from the tribes. No wonder agents were hated. *"Pretty soon, you begin to despise yourself for being nothing more than a lying, cheating unscrupulous lacky for some fat cat Senator."*

He had come to the job as a young man with ideals and enthusiasm. Time and cynicism had eroded even a remote hope for progress and personal recognition and advancement. Through sheer stoicism and endurance, he had gained the position of regional superintendent. His function was to maintain an administrative status quo of a low denomination while he counted off his remaining years until retirement.

Now Collier was bringing in eastern college graduates primed to the gills with fancy social development theories. These greenhorn upstarts knew nothing of the realities of Indian Bureau management. Picker believed that Collier favored them because he himself was a college Joe hollering around about anthropology and his great cultural experiment to take place there on the Navajo reservation. *"What the hell did college courses have to do with Indians anyhow? It was all bullshit. Just plain bullshit."*

Back in 1914, Picker had married the daughter of a local railroad worker. Two of his five teenage children excelled in school and had expressed ambition to attend college in Kansas or Chicago. They wanted to live in a big city where they could escape the provincialism of the Southwest. Picker's earnings could not support a family and put a son and a daughter through college, especially during those hard times.

Suddenly in 1934, Franklin D. Roosevelt had opened the Federal coffers to the Bureau. In addition to proposed new programs under discussion, Picker heard speculation as to sizeable increases in salary at every Bureau level. Only, Jim Picker and others of his staff were being side-stepped. Among his peers his bitterness did not go unexpressed. He heaped vilification upon Collier behind his back, but refused to go directly to him and seek what he considered just compensation. Collier had made his position clear by simply ignoring him. Picker felt he had already been kicked hard enough. It was just a matter of waiting to see where he would finally land.

The green-eyed wonders from the East were aggregated just down the hall from him in the council room at the end of the adobe offices. Picker wanted badly to be there among them offering advice, suggestions, directing activity, making the weight and substance of his experience and rightful authority felt. He could be effective. Instead, he ached with chagrin. What he knew and could offer could fill volumes. He was invaluable to the functional operations and just knowing how to handle special Bureau problems. He had considered walking in there on them, but no! Now it was a matter of pride. They would probably just ignore him anyway and he would end up making a fool of himself. No, they would have to come to him. Maybe eventually they would, once they discovered their own ignorance. He hoped. His experience with practical administrative history could not be ignored.

Collier's new principles of Indian management were counter to every attitude and procedure Jim Picker had learned and applied during his career. Even if Collier demoted him and kept him at the Bureau agency, it would be difficult to alter his old ways and habits and he knew it. In Collier's presence, he fronted his anxiety with a veneer of indifference. It was in such a state of mind that Lee Stark found him sitting morosely in his office that June morning of 1939 and presented him with a proposition.

When Stark entered Picker's office and closed the door, Picker instantly sensed something bad was afoot.

"I want the coal bearing lands in the Black Mesa area."

Picker studied him a moment, then shook his head. "You're about one year too late. The new commissioner, Collier, is going to stop the leasing program. He claims it's pulling off the tribe's natural resources. You can submit an application, but I'm telling you it would be just a waste of time and paper. Collier will throw it in the trash. He doesn't like people like you."

Stark grinned and spit a piece of cigar tobacco onto the floor. "Isn't there some way we can go around the commissioner and the Tribal Council?"

"Not if you intend to mine on tribal land," said Picker.

"What about private land?"

"There is some private ownership under the old allotment system, but you can't get anywhere with that. The Navajo have kinship groups that own the land together, see. They'd all have to agree to sell it, which ain't likely because there's a shortage of land for their livestock. The range is overgrazed. If you go in there and start strip mining, all hell will break loose."

"It doesn't require a large area," explained Stark. "Just the right one. I need about ten square miles."

Picker studied him. "There's also the problem of geological surveys to find the coal. Surveyors can't trespass on tribal lands anymore. They're likely to be shot, or at least arrested by Carmody. He's the Federal Marshal for the territory."

"The reservation lands are rich in coal deposits. Millions of years ago, this whole area was underwater," said Stark. "My enterprise would have to be tied into a profit system for the tribe plus the lease. That much is understood. I can provide jobs, simple manual labor. I'll have to bring in my own skilled people from outside to operate equipment. I'm sure there's some way we can manage this. I understand you've been with the Bureau for twenty years."

"Give or take."

"You must have influence."

"I don't have a pot to shit in. I'm not one of Collier's golden college boys." Picker delineated his situation.

After hearing the story, Stark knew that Picker was malleable and could be bought. He possessed valuable knowledge of certain Navajo kinship groups that might respond to an offer. Stark would have to move fast. Any arrangement was dependent on the length of time Picker remained on the payroll as a superintendent. In another few months, Picker might be fired.

"If you'll negotiate a deal for me," said Stark, "you'll have a permanent high paying position on my payroll as a technical adviser. How does that sound to you?"

Picker became intensely interested and began quizzing Stark for more information. Stark encouraged him, "Don't overlook any motivating factors including liquor, pocket money, bribes and gifts to convince them to sell out or leave. I'll pay top price for coal bearing land. One way or another, I'm going to take coal out. No one's going to get in my way and no one's going to stop me."

"How much money we talking about?" asked Picker.

Chapter 15
COERCION

"That's the way it came down from J. Edgar himself," Halen Braun sat across from Howard Gimbel at the Bureau of Indian Affairs agency in Howard's office.

"Something like that I need to see in writing." Howard retorted.

"They don't put orders like that in writing. They don't want a paper trail."

"Assassination is illegal."

"Doesn't have to appear that way."

"Yet, you say they want me to put a bullet in her."

"That's your assignment."

"I don't believe you, Braun. Why did they pick me? I'm not an assassin. I've never killed anybody. The only shooting I've done is on the range."

"Because you know her. You can get close enough to her. And she'll never expect it coming from you."

"You're wrong about that. I can't get close to her. I tried when we were on the train. She won't even talk to me."

"It couldn't be that you still have feelings for her."

Howard stared at him. "What did Tolson say to you?"

"I'm here to make sure you do your job."

"And if I don't, you're going to do it for me. Is that it?"

"No, that's not it. You'll be out of a job and that's it. Times are bad. This is a dirty business, Gimbel. You should have known that going in."

"Upholding the law isn't. Breaking the law is."

"Your job is to follow orders. Others make the law."

"Others also manipulate the law in their favor. I'm not a hit man. I'm not an assassin. I'm not even sure anymore why I was sent out here."

"Yelena Ivanov is a Communist. That's why. You must understand that."

"The Wagner Act makes it legal for unions to organize. It's not un-American. It's part of National recovery."

"I didn't stop in to have a friendly debate about politics with you, Gimbel. The fact is companies don't want unions and Reds ain't wanted in this country anywhere anytime. No one gives a damn about the Wagner Act. All I have to do is share this little conversation with Tolson about your reluctance to follow a direct order and you'll have to hop a freight to get back home."

Howard remained silent. There was only one way to get Braun out of there. "Do you know where she is?"

Braun's jowls quivered with his heavy nod.

"Tell me."

"You're going to do this."

"I have to know where she is first."

"Just between you and me, there's another option."

"Another option."

"That's right. You're not a hit man. But you can persuade her it's in her best interests to get out of the country. All she has to do is cross the border into Mexico and never come back."

"That's assuming I can even find her."

"You're an FBI agent. Be resourceful."

"What do you suggest?"

"I've giving you a chance. Find a way. She can join her own kind down there."

"That's a better option."

"It's not mine. We never had this conversation." Halen rose heavily from his chair. "Just don't wait too long in getting on with this. You'll be doing her a favor. There are others who won't hesitate to kill her. There's another thing."

"What's that, Halen? What's the other thing?"

"I wasn't supposed to tell you this."

"Then why are you telling me?"

"Because I'm looking out for you, asshole."

"My asshole or yours?"

Braun had all he could to contain himself from attacking Howard and strangling him. Howard enjoyed the rising red flush in the man's bull neck.

"Listen. I'm gonna forget you said that, Gimbel. You might not believe it, but I was once where you are, on the bicycle."

"How do you know I'm on the bicycle."

"Hoover would never put an agent on a shit assignment like he did you, unless you're on the bicycle."

"I take great pride in the assignment I've been given. You shouldn't denigrate it."

Braun's eyes bulged in disbelief. "You are shittin' me Gimbel. This is not an assignment to be proud of."

"Seems to be important to Hoover and Tolson."

"Listen, asshole. Yelena Ivanov is nothing to Hoover and Tolson. They want her dead."

"They think she's a communist. That's enough for them. They've got files and spy on everybody."

"She is a communist."

"Yelena Ivanov is not a communist. She is trying and even putting her life on the line to make a better life for people who are oppressed."

Braun's guffaw ended in a deep throated gurgle. "It's a damn good thing I'm not wearin' a wire or you'd be in the pen tomorrow."

"This is America, Halen. We're supposed to support the Constitution, not bury it."

"You took an oath to obey J. Edgar Hoover and don't forget it."

"I took an oath to uphold the Constitution and the law, not his majesty J. Edgar Hoover. As I recall, Hoover does not allow mustaches, imbibing spirits, and wearing other than the standard gray suit and fedora, not a Stetson."

"I wear what keeps me close to the people in the Southwest. They don't relate to ties, gray suits , and fedoras," said Braun.

"My point. Nice that we agree on something."

"What the hell you talkin' about."

"The people who aren't rich."

"I don't follow you."

"I know."

"Don't look down your nose at me, asshole. I got into the FBI without a college degree. I earned my badge."

"When did Hoover put you on the bicycle?"

Braun carefully thought through his answer. "I never thought of it as being on the bicycle."

"Your words, Halen."

"Making me SAC in Santa Fe was the career opportunity of my life . You couldn't pay me to work in Washington."

"So, life is good."

"It is unless you fuck it up for me."

"What weren't you supposed to tell me?"

"Hoover and Tolson are going to pay you a visit."

Howard suppressed a grin. "Are you concerned?"

"No, but you should be. They're checking up on you. That's why I'm talking to you. They expect to see that you have put an end to Yelena Ivanov."

"When?"

"When they call and tell me."

"Mmh—and if I haven't?"

"Then we're both out of a job."

"You won't be."

"Meaning?"

"You're close to Lee Stark. He's bank rolling you."

"That's it. Fuck you, Gimbel. Don't say I didn't try to save your ass." Braun grabbed up his Stetson and swept out of the office in the manner of his usual exit.

***

Howard came to consider Randolph Logan an ally, or more accurately, a sympathetic listener, which was the role of a journalist. He shared confidential information so that someone other than himself would know what was going on. "In case something happens to me," he confided. "I'm not going to do what I was sent here for. I'm going against a direct order from J. Edgar Hoover. Agents who defy him don't last long. Hoover is a very strange man.

"He's the head of the FBI and everyone thinks he's moral and upgright, yet I've heard he has a secret garden with statues of naked men and boys and he collects pornography. Hoover creates the impression about himself for the public that he's a tough crime fighter, but he tries to hide the facts of how he really is. The truth of the matter is the Government can't control crime."

"What do you mean, can't control crime?"

"The FBI couldn't even prosecute Capone. It took Eliott Ness to do that, a prohibition agent. My admiration for Ness is the reason I joined the FBI. I wanted to be like him and I thought he was the kind of law enforcer the FBI created. Turns out that's not so. John Q public believes Hoover can overcome crime single-handedly. It's supposed to turn us G-Men into heroes, but we can't take any credit for it. Only Hoover can be quoted in the newspapers. If there's any picture taken, it better be him, not yours or you'll find yourself out of a job.

"People want to believe we make a difference. We're supposed to be crime stoppers. Hoover created the idea of the crime wave and public enemies. It's a Washington idea, nothing like what your Marshal Carmody has to work with out here in the West. Hoover just wants people not to understand anything more complicated than the good guys rub out the bad guys. He's caught in the web of a myth he created for himself. No one wants to hear about the real causes of crime, the lack of moral education in families and the corruption in our public institutions. It's not sensational enough. It doesn't make good copy for the newspapers and Walter Winchell's radio show. Even if Hoover is a queer, it's pushed aside, buried. Nobody wants to hear about it.

"My concern is for the innocent victims. That's the only reason I'm in this business. Unfortunately, Hoover has misplaced priorities. Communists are not a threat to our country. We have the crime we do because of the economy and because crime is the fastest way for immigrants to get ahead and politicians and capitalists, like Rockefeller.

"Hoover doesn't even believe the Mafia exists. It's almost like they've got him blackmailed. He squashes any attempt to go after them. In fact, if you even bring up the Mafia, he's likely to can you. That happened to more than one agent I know of. He just wants to save America from the communists. He even believes there are Washington politicians who are enemies of their own Government. He's got wiretaps on just about everybody in the Capitol.

"Agents know the Mafia is real. The only reason he won't go after them is he can't control them. They're stronger than the FBI. There's a good bet they've got something on Hoover and can blackmail him too. His avoidance is too obvious. You probably never heard he runs a publicity mill down in his basement. It's all for J. Edgar's glory. Whenever something big happens with the Bureau, he takes the credit in the press like he did it himself single-handedly."

"And as for Clyde Tolson, his right hand man who sent me here. He's suspected of being Hoover's not so secret lover. They do everything together. You never see 'em apart. They even go on vacations together. Seems odd, doesn't it?

"Remember I told you about his speech at my graduation from the FBI academy, I know Hoover drinks. He drinks a lot and in public," said Howard. "I saw him and Tolson tossing back whiskeys with Babe Ruth at The Stork Club in New York City. He likes to be seen with celebrities. Hangs out with movie stars. He makes such a big deal about us agents not drinking, and there he is, a two-faced whiskey-drinking hypocrite.

"He's got everyone in Washington by the balls, so he can do no wrong. That's how he gets his power."

Randolph noticed a change in Howard as he gradually became aware of the nascent corruption going on in the BIA organization by observing his colleagues, who immediately distrusted this green newcomer. They figured he had been sent from Washington to spy on them. His frustration mounted, as he realized he could not act on his suspicions of graft, especially where it involved the Agent Jim Picker, who had a reputation for being underhanded.

Gimbel had heard the name of Lee Stark mentioned in discussions at the Bureau of Indian Affairs offices from time to time, but had never seen the man. He assumed Stark was of some political importance in the overall scheme of reclamation and use of reservation lands as it related to mining interests and, therefore, to union activity.

As Gimbel began to conduct a quiet investigation to better understand the context of collaboration between mine owners and the Federal Government, he believed he would gain some insights into the subversive rationale of Yelena Ivanov. He needed a vehicle to pursue his assignment and decided that Lee Stark might unknowingly open that door for him.

Gimbel thought of sharing his strategy with Halen Braun, his Special Agent in Charge based in Santa Fe, until he learned that Braun and Stark were close friends and until the day Braun threatened him. Howard knew that Braun was reporting back to the FBI in Washington on Howard's own activities. Hoover and Tolson always arranged for someone to be looking over your shoulder. Since Braun had a connection with Stark, there might be a link to a supporting committee or a political figure in the Federal Government. Lee Stark did nothing to conceal that he was a ruthless financial and political manipulator and opportunist. He was there in New Mexico because he had followed the trail of available Government money.

Chapter 16
THE PLAY SPIRIT

Jim Picker's sweat-soaked shirt clung to the seat backrest of the car and the scratchiness fused his irritation. He cursed the heat, as his old Government issue Ford bumped and swayed over the ruts and rocks along the dry wash that served as a road into the high desert back country. The worn tires sank into heavy dust. The sand sifted and spilled from the spokes lurching the car forward.

Christ, how could he have stayed on living in such desolation for so long. The car continued to run only because of his skill as an amateur mechanic. *Damn that Collier to hell. If it wasn't for Lee Stark's offer, where would poor Jim Picker be now? Maybe this would be the last time he would have to crawl along the damn dry wash. Maybe Collier would get his road built by the time the mine operation got underway. Collier could take his summertime college boys and stuff them. That's all they're doing out here anyway, playing at being camp counselors.*

It outraged Picker to hear them talking in their special little groups and meetings around the agency like this thing with the Indians was nothing more than a big lark. *Collier's the one who set the tone, the bastard. The Play Spirit. That's what they sit around and talk about, those experts in recreation and summer camp management. They don't know shit from shinola about the Navajo. That's their first serious problem. They're obsessed with outhouses and sanitation. The sight and smell of a human turd makes them gag.*

Some of the local white residents had privately come to Picker complaining that they should have the supervisory positions on the reservation projects. Picker had to inform them that on this particular issue, his hands were tied. He could not give out favors, since he could not even get one for himself.

Collier had an edge because he was able to pull large sums of Government money into the region. The whites supported him on that score, but they didn't like the way he was handling the organizing. Like Picker, they too felt great hostility toward those *eastern swells* who were running the Civilian Conservation Corps program amuck.

Only someone who had been born and raised in that part of the country and had grown up around the Navajo could understand and know how to deal with them. *Well,* thought Picker, *let the specialists fall on their educated asses. They'll be gone by the end of the summer and then the locals can run the project like it should be.*

As far as Picker was concerned, he was past caring anymore about the Bureau of Indian Affairs and its labyrinthine politics. Collier, The New Deal, all of it could go to hell. He had his own *New Deal* with Lee Stark and he wasn't going to lose this opportunity because of some age old agreement on some back-assed treaty that nobody worth anything gave a god damn about. That was why he would even risk carrying a trunk full of bootleg liquor onto the reservation to smooth the way in his negotiation.

The mine owner and manager, Lee Stark, and a geological survey crew had already been out scouring the countryside for the site they wanted. Nobody had thought anything was unusual about their activity. The Indians just assumed they were a group of Government officials, specialists, like the others swarming all over the reservation.

The tract Lee Stark had finally settled on was an allotment in the eastern region of the checkerboard area. In examining the land records for Stark, Picker had determined the Navajo family ownership and kinships involved. He had then investigated the extent of the family debt and inventory of livestock holdings. This information would be important in persuading the Navajo patriarch to sell the land.

Stark's blank check offer would be a second deciding factor. Picker determined that a sizeable portion of that should end up in his pocket for services rendered. Picker was adept at manipulating finances. He had to exercise extreme care now that Collier was in charge. Collier had ethics and moral integrity, one of the reasons President Roosevelt had hired him.

Considering the kind of man Stark was, as long as he got what he wanted, he wouldn't care about Picker's petty embezzlement. Picker rationalized that graft was a standard way of doing business and was a matter of personal necessity. Stark himself would do it if the tables were turned.

The road ahead grew torturous as it rose to a level stretch topping a saddleback ridge, then snaked downward twisting back and forth along the face of a red sandstone cliff. At the bottom, it disappeared over a bed of rocks and boulders, then resumed in another dry wash of sifting sand. The wind whipped up dust around the car, forcing Jim Picker to stop and close the windows.

After several more miles, he passed a wagon trail that wound away out of sight around a towering black granite butte. Further on he came to another trail that led to a cluster of low earth-covered hogans and lean-to summer shelters set back among scrub juniper, pinon trees and sagebrush near a running spring. In the distance, two young Navajo girls on fuzzy-eared burros watched over a small herd of ragged sheep.

At the sound of Picker's approaching car, a man, two women, one clutching an infant, the other in late pregnancy, and one teenage boy came out of the Hogan and watched the vehicle grind along the last few hundred yards to their homesite.

The women wore traditional dark full length skirts and moccasins with leather leg wraps. Picker noticed that the wives' silver squash blossom necklaces and other silver and turquoise jewelry commonly worn by Navajo women were missing. For him, that was an auspicious sign. That meant their jewelry would be in pawn at the local trading post so the family could have credit with the trader to purchase food and supplies.

Like most other members of their tribe, their economic situation was not good. Even though the husband, Anthony Zaragoza, had come to the agency to sign up for work under the Collier program, the factor of being in such great debt would be favorable in persuading him to sell the land.

The teenage son emulated his father in dress and manner. He wore boots, jeans, a plaid shirt and leather vest, a red bandana headband with his long black hair done up in a *chonga* knotted in a tight *chignon* at the base of his neck.

Picker's nose twitched at the smell of mutton stew that wafted from the cooking fire, as he stepped out of the car to meet them. His ability to speak the Navajo language was only functional, not nearly fluent when a conversation involved complex nuance and idiom. For normal business, he would have relied on a native Bureau interpreter, an English speaking Navajo. In a matter of this nature, using an interpreter would be out of the question.

After formally greeting first the men and then acknowledging the women, Picker walked Anthony aside out of hearing of the others and said he would like to talk about some important business. He knew of Anthony's weakness for liquor and that Anthony would understand when Picker suggested the two of them should drive away a short distance in the car.

Anthony's wives watched with curiosity and some anxiety, as their husband climbed into the agency car with Picker and drove back along the wagon track until they were out of sight of the Hogan. The appearance of an agent from the Bureau almost always meant trouble of one kind or another, a capricious disrupting of their lives. Witchcraft was in the making. It had always been so.

Picker stopped the vehicle and the two men got out, their heeled boots leaving gouged footprints in the sand. Picker opened the trunk so that Anthony could see the four cases of liquor. Anthony stared in disbelief at Picker for this incredible act. Picker grimaced a cynical grin, reached in for a bottle and handed it to Anthony. "It's all right," he explained, knowing full well he was breaking the law even bringing liquor onto the reservation. "Don't worry. I'm an agent."

Although Anthony strongly desired the liquor and took it with gratification, his already limited esteem for this corrupt white man of authority dropped even lower. He instinctively knew Picker could not be trusted.

Picker then reached back inside the car and brought out his briefcase. "Let's go sit over there," he pointed. They walked into the cool shadow of a cliff and sat on the sand. Picker waited until Anthony had enjoyed several good strong pulls at the bottle before he pitched his proposition to sell Anthony's land.

He approached the point slowly, emphasizing Anthony's debt to the trader and the diminished condition of his first wife's herd. He talked of the future of Anthony's son, Duncan, and his daughters. He suggested that conditions could be better for all of them. It would be nice to get their silver out of pawn and still have money for luxuries. What would Anthony think of having a truck of his own?

Anthony listened carefully to what the agent was saying. Through the growing buzz of the liquor, what he heard sounded good and matched the good feeling that was spreading through his mind and body.

Picker told him that the cases of whiskey in the trunk of the car were all for him. He could cache them somewhere nearby. This also sounded good.

Picker talked about the land, the poor grazing conditions and steady depletion of sheep and horses. Then Picker told him that a man wanted to buy his land and that he would pay a good price, a price so big that Anthony would never have to work again for the rest of his life. He would be a rich man and could live in a white man's house with a toilet and running water.

Even through the haze of his rapidly growing drunken stupor, Anthony was not sure he would prefer a white man's house to living in his Hogan.

When enough had been said, Picker held the papers on the hard surface of the briefcase for Anthony to sign. His signature would transfer the deed to Lee Stark and the Wooten Corporation. Anthony scrawled his name with an unsteady hand. Picker carefully tucked the deed back into his briefcase and snapped the lock shut.

He returned to the open car trunk and lifted out the four cases of liquor and placed them on the ground next to Anthony who watched him through blurry eyes. He was surprised to see that the agent had become a double image and there appeared to be more than four cases of liquor. He grew fearful that he had been bewitched.

Anthony struggled to his feet and staggered over to the car as Picker was climbing in. He wanted to tell the agent something, but the words would not come to him. Picker started the engine and drove off leaving him standing there weaving unsteadily in the ball of afternoon heat.

His son, Duncan, came and found him at sundown asleep in the shade of the cliff near the secret hiding place of the whiskey, a location that only Anthony would know. The boy crouched near his snoring father. He watched the quivering of his jowls with each labored exhalation. His father had lost the hard leanness of his youth. At the sings and tribal fairs, he could no longer reach down far enough out of the saddle from his galloping horse and pull the rooster out of the sand where it had been buried up to the neck. His father had grown stout around the middle and would risk falling off his horse.

Duncan watched him for an hour out of respect, not wishing to wake him in an abrupt manner. By then, the sun had dropped behind the trees on the mesa and was slowly leaving the sky. An owl hooted somewhere off in the brush. A chill rippled the boy's spine. He could wait no longer or both he and his father would be endangered by the presence of a witch who had assumed the form of the owl, a common practice for witches.

Being away from the Hogan after sundown was always unsafe. He had to keep his father awake and moving for at least one mile. The walk back was long and they could be overtaken by night. A coyote howled at some distance and was immediately answered by another nearby. Duncan stood up. The *Were People* were coming out into the evening. He must wake his father now and get him home.

He gently shook his father's shoulder with no response. He shook harder. The man rolled over with a groan, but his eyes did not open. His mouth did and a horrendous foul smelling belch exploded from deep in his guts reminding the boy of a loud fart from a horse as it leaps into a run. The smell from his father was sour, not the pure sweet smell of horse dung from the sage and desert grasses of its diet.

The boy leaped back away from his father as Anthony suddenly thrashed and sat upright with a coughing cavernous gurgle and a rush of vomit spouted and spewed down his shirt front splattering over his legs. He rocked forward gasping and strangling as more and more of the acrid russet fluid flowed and drooled from his mouth. His eyes closed, stinging from the salt tears. A whirling vertigo set in and pulled his mind catapulting into black space. Again he pitched into unconsciousness and lay still. His gut twitched and trembled. His heart thumped weakly. A slow steady stain soaked his pants with the rising ammoniac stench of urine.

The boy called to him. "Shizhe'e'! Shizhe'e'! My father! My father!" He stared in dismay as the man slept on blubbering long rolling snores. The boy was growing afraid now with the coming of the night and that his father would not wake.

He debated whether he should just leave him lying there and run back to the Hogan. His mother would be in a terrible rage when he told her of the condition in which he had found his father and that he could not even arouse him enough to stand on his own two feet, let alone stumble home along the wagon track.

He tried one more time to wake Anthony. Except for his snores and a twitching of his arms that reminded Duncan of a *hand trembler* who had located the source of an ailment in his younger sister, his father was like a dead man and did not respond. He was possessed.

The boy's stomach churned at the odor of the fresh vomit pooling in the dirt. He scrambled away several steps hoping the momentum would help him arrive at some decision. What would the other tribal members think of a fourteen year old boy who could not wake his father, drunk or not, and bring him home. If you could not even wake your father, you were not fit for other responsibilities, those of a man.

An idea occurred to him. He grabbed a handful of sand and gently sifted it across his father's exposed neck. Anthony brushed at the slight irritation. Suddenly his eyes shot open with fear as his imagination fixed on a terrifying image, the slow dry pulling movement of a snake passing across his neck.

He erupted from the ground with a howl of terror, galloped several staggering steps and fell gasping to his knees with a resurgence of vomiting. He was awake! His skin prickled with cold sweat.

The boy wasted no time and did not chance losing his advantage. He walked quickly around to face his father, who glared up at him out of dark jellied eyes. He saw his son as two boys, twins moving in and out of focus.

Believing he was being haunted by a witch, Anthony struck out at him in fear. The boy fell unhurt with a sharp grunt, scrambled to his feet and stood back out of reach of his father. Anthony mumbled and groaned unintelligibly and wiped a hand across his eyes.

Duncan spoke, "Father, it's growing dark. We must go home."

Anthony nodded and reached out for support. Duncan helped him to his feet. His father's weight came down heavily and rested across the back of the boy's shoulders.

As they stumbled along the rutted track, the putrid stench that came from his father nauseated Duncan. His muscles ached and trembled with the strain of holding him upright as their heeled boots dragged in the sand.

He could see the Hogan now and the streaked red battlements of rock fell behind them. The slowly dying afterglow of the sun continued to light the way. Blue smoke rose from the opening at the top of the Hogan. The scent of burning sage and mutton came to them on the evening wind. Duncan was gasping with exhaustion by the time they reached the open door.

The pungent odor of mutton stew seeped into his senses and unleashed his knotted stomach in rumbling throes and caused his mouth to water. He hesitated, watching his mother's mask of anger as his father lurched away and collapsed snoring in a corner of the Hogan.

His mother spat disparaging words of bitterness at the sorry condition of her husband. His mother's sister, who was Anthony's second wife, went to clean him with water and soap made from yucca so they would not have to smell his stench.

Duncan's mother motioned for him to sit and eat. Avoiding physical contact with his two sisters, as befitted their age and relationship, he circled to the opposite side of the fire and sat on his blanket while waiting patiently for his mother to serve him.

According to the incest taboo, he and his sisters were not allowed to even touch one another or to directly hand objects to each other. They would place them on the ground for the other to pick up.

The stew contained mutton, corn, onions, turnips, and potatoes and was supplemented with fried bread and coffee. Mutton was the family's main diet. They ate meat three times a day.

An hour later, Anthony woke and loudly demanded food. His second wife served him. Then, braving the dark against the pain of his swollen bladder, he staggered outside a few yards from the Hogan and relieved himself with a great gasp. He returned muttering that he had heard some creature in the brush that made a strange noise and said he suspected it was a witch.

He sat for a while with his family around the fire. Rubbing his head, he told them it was filled with pain like someone was beating a great drum inside.

When his first wife asked him what the man from the Indian Bureau had talked about, Anthony complained that the firelight hurt his eyes. He crawled away without answering and went to sleep.

"In the morning you will tell me," his wife snapped, "or you will sleep outside with the witches and they will have intercourse with you."

The family sat in silence, Duncan and his two sisters, his mother and her sister, and his ancient maternal grandmother, Adjiba To' dich' li' nii, on whose side the clan kinship was associated with the Black Mesa Group. During the great purge of the Indians of the Southwest in 1863, some of her clan had escaped to Navajo Mountain in northern New Mexico. She, along with many brothers and sisters had been captured and force marched, *The Long Walk*. To Fort Sumner for incarceration. From there, they had been marched to Bosque Redondo. She had told her grandchildren many stories of that ordeal. Lately, her memory lapsed and she did not talk as much. She was eighty years old.

Duncan's mother told him that now that he had returned from his first year at boarding school, a sing would be held for him to counteract the evil white influences he had learned that were not good for a Navajo. She had noted with disapproval certain changes in his manners and eating habits. He had even once removed his shirt to change it for a clean one in the presence of his two sisters. It was forbidden for them to see him so unclothed.

She was certain there were many other hidden contaminations since he had lost his gall bag or it had been forcibly taken from him. The gall bag contained medicine to ward off evil spirits at the white school. A message had been sent to the medicine man to conduct a sing. A Blessing Way chant was requested.

Duncan began to think back on his behavior since his arrival home from the boarding school. He realized that he had not been aware of his transgressions. The influence and power of the white teachers at the school must be very strong to make him forget the important matters of etiquette of his home life. He looked forward to and welcomed the Blessing Way sing and asked forgiveness for his unthinking behavior. Old Adjiba nodded her approval.

As they sat, the women talked of the increasing incidents of witchcraft and sorcery in the land. They considered the Government officials' announcement about cutting down the size of the sheep herds and destroying the horses. Too many things were out of balance, out of harmony. And that day, the man came from the Bureau to talk to Anthony and gave him whiskey. That act was very ominous.

The teachers at the boarding school had told Duncan and the other Navajo children about the new program. So he had some understanding of its goals and purpose. It was supposed to benefit the *Dine'*, the Navajo people.

In the face of his earlier transgressions, he could not now speak favorably about the white administration of Navajo affairs. His mother would think him seriously ill, perhaps even possessed. He would require more intensive treatment which would cost many more goats and sheep for the medicine man. He remained silent, wondering how he could reconcile what he had been taught at the boarding school with the elements of his home life.

Suddenly, they heard something scurry across the sod roof. Everyone froze as particles of dirt sifted down from the smoke hole. Perhaps it had been a small animal, but witches could assume any shape or form they desired. Considering what had already happened today, there could be no doubt that a witch was abroad in the vicinity of the Hogan.

His mother brought out prayer sticks and Adjiba led them all in a short prayer chant to ward off the presence of the witch who had just passed over the Hogan roof. In the morning, Duncan would go out in the surrounding brush in search of werewolf tracks. Witches frequently took the appearance of a large coyote. He would be able to tell by the size of the tracks. His parents and grandparents had told him about witches and how to avoid them. Sometimes it was impossible because of their many shapes, forms, and disguises.

It was common knowledge among the People that witches committed foul and atrocious acts. During the past month, a man and a woman had been caught and accused of occult practices. After much torture, including burning coals held to the soles of their feet, they had confessed to their crimes.

Another man who claimed he had been one of their victims had, with the sanction of the inquisitors, then split their skulls with an axe. The man felt he had been poisoned and cheated out of his horse and a roll of spring wool he had been taking to the trading post. He had stopped to visit and share a meal with the couple. He insisted that when he revived, he discovered he had been moved several miles away and left to die.

The couple vehemently denied the accusations, arguing that the man had merely lost his horse and wool to them to satisfy a gambling debt. He had then tried to walk home drunk a distance of twenty miles in the hot sun and become dehydrated and fell unconscious.

Under the influence of torture, the couple had confessed guilt and responsibility for other misfortunes whose cause people attached to them. The cumulative evidence of testimony had proved overwhelming. So they were executed.

Shortly thereafter, the fortunes of the People in that region began to change for the better, which confirmed the rightness of their decision and their act of killing the man and his wife.

The practice of witches described to Duncan by his grandfather had both fascinated and terrified the boy when he was much younger. As the family sat around the fire at night, the old man would tell of Witchery Way, folk tales, and about the history of the *Dine'*, the People, as the Navajo called themselves. His grandfather had been a medicine man of many years and possessed great powers. So he knew about such things.

"Witchery started out under the ground," he said, "after First Man and First Woman come out of the earth. First Man says, they forget something. It is medicine. They tell Diving Heron to go in water and get that thing. The bird bring it up and man and wife feel good again. First Man say it will make them rich easy. The thing is sheep and horses, the same as having goods. First Man and First Woman come out of the cave and build first sweat house. Witchcraft Woman gave all the People some corpse poison. Rattlesnake got some and didn't have no place for it, so he ate it. That is why you die if snake bites you.

"Witch people get together and talk about things. They are glad to kill someone because then they can make fresh corpse medicine. If they kill a good woman, they bring her dead into a bad Hogan and have intercourse with her. A lot of them have intercourse with her. Put a pot under her to catch the stuff.

"Sometimes they take body from grave and cut off little pieces of meat. Top of head, end of nose, then every place where there is whorls, thumb and finger. Then end of man's penis and woman's vagina. They take meat to witch's Hogan. Dry it up, pound it and make powder. That is corpse medicine. They tie it in little bundles.

"When a good man or good woman dies, they go to good place where our holy people go. Witches and bad people go to ghost land under the earth.

"Coyote prayer make some people rich. That is also witchery. These people are not afraid of snakes and bears and lightning. They kill their brother or sister. They use a stick with bad medicine on it. If it touches you, you will die unless you carry gall of eagle and bear and witchcraft plant. These protect you. You must carry it with you always.

"If you have a big family, nice girls, nice boys, you must keep this medicine, especially if you go to an Enemy Way or where there's lots of people. Witches can kill easy there. They can also send a snake after you or make lightning strike you.

"They meet at night someplace in mountains. They take off their clothes and put on paint, then make noises like coyotes and owls. They take hair, clothes, fingernails, spit, and they pray over them. The man who it came from will die."

As Duncan drifted off to sleep, he remembered how at the boarding school, when they cut his hair, he had gathered it all up and buried it away. Later he had stopped doing that, because they had beaten him until he was unconscious.

The firelight rose and fell through the skein of his closed eyelids. It felt good to be home. He slept.

Chapter 17
TRADING POST

Duncan walked slowly back to the Hogan. He would tell his mother how the coyote tracks had vanished out there in the dust of the mesa. As he drew closer, he stopped at the strident sounds of argument from within. The evil from the coyote's visit had taken effect.

Anthony Zaragoza careened out through the Hogan door to escape his wife. She raged and flailed at him in great torment, voice shrill and high wailing. She chased him several yards through the desert brush and stopped. Breathing heavily, they faced off apart from each other. She hurled threats and accusations of such force and vehemence that Anthony could not find space to reply. He thought it would be better to wait and say nothing, just let her anger cool down. It would be best to keep his distance for a while. A wife murdering her husband was not uncommon. He did not want to get in her way.

He truly believed he had done a good thing by selling the land. His hand clutched the check for five thousand dollars. *Crazy woman.* Had she forgotten how poor they were? Did she not realize how many things this money could buy? She argued that he was not entitled to sell the land. According to custom, the land and the flocks and livestock belonged to her and to her mother's clan.

"But I did not sell everything," he shouted back. "I only sold part of the ridge."

"How do you know what you sold? You were too drunk to know."

He had also violated the tradition of a clan decision. In the Navajo way, responsibility did not rest with one individual. Major decisions were arrived at only after much thought and discussion among members of the clan. What Anthony had done was unspeakable.

As far as his wife was concerned, no one had been consulted or agreed to the sale, so it was not binding. Yet, she knew the white men would come and take possession regardless like they always had when they cheated the Navajos. And she knew she would take that white man's money and spend it at the trading post to get their jewelry out of pawn and revive their credit with the trader, Sweigart, to whom they were in debt.

***

The two important necessities to Noel Sweigart's existence were a consistent source of drinking water and Navajo trade. He was one of the few traders in the Southwest to be blessed with an abundance of both. His grandfather, also Noel, had established the post in 1863 as the first white trader in that territory long before the major Indian wars and before their final incarceration and banishment to reservations. "Water and Navvie trade," he used to say, "the mainstay of my life."

The trading post was constructed of adobe mud bricks. With the assistance of Navajo labor, the modest structure had expanded over the years into a sizeable compound with three warehouses and additional living quarters attached to the main store as extended wings. Light crept into the dim store through two steel barred windows at the front and bled pale-gold over canned groceries, hardware, yard goods, men's clothing and Pendleton blankets stacked on the floor to ceiling shelves on three sides and on tall counters forming a bull pen.

It was not uncommon for several horses and wagons to be tethered outside the post while Navajo familes visited and gossiped, sometimes spending two or three days there while trading. The post was also a center for socializing after long periods of isolation at distant sheep camps.

Some families would travel from twenty-five to fifty miles and were in no particular hurry to make the long return trip. Therefore, the process of trading was very slow. The act of selection and decision-making often achieved greater importance than the final transaction itself. Such ways required infinite patience on the part of the trader. Patience was one of Noel Sweigart the Third's greatest virtues.

This land of windswept spaces had become an extension of his mind. Sweigart had blended with the terrain long ago. He was as leather-skinned and enduring as any Navajo with whom he did business and led his life. His tall brawny frame and white mustached countenance commanded respect and trust from all who entered his store. The Navajo called him Mr. Mustache.

The Navajo were a sensitive, but not a frail people. They could endure emotional and physical hardships far beyond the white and other tribal societies. Although Sweigart's own life bordered the vying cultures, he cast his lot with the Navajo. He was just as questioning and suspicious of encroaching white influences and agendas as the tribe that had assimilated him into their own time and system. He loved and cared for them as his own family. Over the years, the land, the tongue, the habits, beliefs and values had become his own.

Sweigart told Logan he thought there was something wrong with the man who introduced himself as Howard Gimbel, the law and order expert from Washington, D.C., who had been assigned to work with John Collier on the Navajo program. Gimbel did not seem able to concentrate. Although he was learning and he tried, Howard appeared ill at ease and did not always listen to the advice both he and Sheriff Carmody provided him.

During Howard's first few weeks at John Collier's side, Logan observed him going through the motions of being there, being seen, granting interviews for the *Mesa Independent*, insuring that he stood with the groups of the most important program officials when photographs were taken and sent back to Washington. There were also photographs taken with local state politicians and businessmen, including Senator "Charming Billy" Chanson and Lee Stark, President of the mining operations on the Navajo reservation and a partner with the Wooten Corporation.

As Sweigart observed and assessed the newcomer, he openly criticized Gimbel as a man overly concerned with his own visibility. Sweigart understood that in the world of the white bureaucracy and corporate politics, those affiliations were the road to advancement.

Collier's information about Navajo culture did little to help Gimbel with any kind of planned intervention. He told Gimbel to rely on Carmody, who, in the beginning, considered Gimbel as being only a suit, a greenhorn politician of some sort.

"With qualifications like that, a career in Washington should suit him fine," Sweigart shared his opinion of Howard with Carmody and Logan. That had been three weeks ago at one of John Collier's interminable New Deal organizational meetings held at Fort Defiance.

Collier had asked Sweigart to assist Gimbel and Carmody in recruiting dependable Navajo men to train as law enforcement officers to police the reservation. Having been around a while, Carmody understood the difficulties of how Navajo values and interpretations of the law differed from those of a white man.

Carmody had worked with Sweigart in the past in attempting to crack down on reservation bootleg operations. Also Carmody's close friendship with Noel Sweigart's son, Phillip, the railroad foreman, had brought them together on social occasions. He and the trader could work as they had in the past, but now had to bring Gimbel into the picture.

Logan rode as a back seat passenger with Carmody and Gimbel, who were scheduled to arrive at the trading post by noon. Gimbel had requested that Sweigart have a contingent of Navajo men from which to make the selection. Sweigart had six who had been waiting around the post since dawn. They had built a fire in a nearby wash and were sitting and smoking. Five more would arrive sometime later that afternoon.

He stepped to the door for a smoke and saw Anthony Zaragoza coming down the rim trail on his horse at a slow bone-shuffling walk. His son, Duncan, and two wives rode in their old flatbed wagon a few yards behind. They had left their daughters to tend the sheep. Sweigart could see bundles in the bed of the wagon. They had come to trade.

He greeted Anthony as the man rode in and swung down from his horse. Sweigart had not seen the Zaragoza family for six months. During the recent hard times, many of the people had shunned the trading post, which was heavy in pawn with their jewelry.

As the family filed in through the open doorway, they carried dust and sand on the blankets and wool pelts which they dropped and unrolled for inspection on the long wooden counter. Worn greasy and smooth over the years, Sweigart periodically scrubbed it with soap and water, hoping to maintain a basic level of hygiene.

When he and his wife worked at the counter, they conditioned themselves to avoid touching their faces with their hands owing to the prevalence of trachoma, a terribly infectious eye disease common with the Indians. Goods and objects in the store were always handled and rehandled many times by many customers before decisions were made about making a purchase.

In addition to fifty pounds of wool, the Zaragoza women had brought in four new blankets. Sweigart recognized two of them as the work of the eldest daughter, Raven. He was sorry she had not come. He would tell her mother to mention his admiration for the artistic work.

The girl's specialty was in creating complex designs, occasionally from sand paintings using a sheep gray background, a color simulating tan. The wool was taken from the backs of yellowish-brown sheep. The second blanket was basically an authentic gray, a shade arrived at by careful carding of wads of black and white wool to achieve an even mix. He foresaw in her ability the development of an artist. He collected some of her work, which was of a superior quality. He could imagine how it would evolve and improve in another five or ten years, considering the increase in the girl's maturity and skill.

At the New Deal meetings, Logan had heard discussions about the overgrazed reservation lands and prospective methods considered to remedy the situation. Reducing the size of the herds was the solution given the most support as advised by Collier's range management experts. Sweigart had tried to talk them out of implementing such a program. It would severely undercut the basis of the Navajo economy, which was sheep. Sheep were their source of meat and provided wool with which to trade and weave. Sweigart's own business depended on sheep.

Navajo sheep owners were already taking heavy losses on that year's crop because of the late spring weather. The sheep had been rubbing against brush and rocks to rid themselves of the wool during the natural time of molting. The weather had not been warm enough to begin the shearing.

According to custom, the women had entered the store and gone to the right side of the bullpen while Anthony and the boy, Duncan, mused over the shelved goods on the left side.

Anthony rolled a cigarette from the box of free tobacco and paper that Sweigart kept near the front of the counter to encourage business and good customer relations. Anthony knew the women would take a long time to arrive at a suitable price for their wool and blankets. That was strictly their business. Then he would show the check to Mr. Mustache Face and settle all their debts. They could regain their jewelry from pawn and load the wagon with the many things they would buy with all that money. He would even ask the trader about buying him a pickup truck too, go in to Mesa for a few weeks maybe. He did not want to be cheated when he bought the truck. That would happen if he tried to himself. He trusted the trader. No more horseback and slow wagons for him.

Duncan studied the candy jars so he would be ready with his choice when the trader came around to them.

Two of the Navajo men sitting in a sandy shallow cut of the dry wash left the fire and walked up to the post to visit and gossip with the new arrivals. Anthony did not want to tell them of the money he had made through the land sale. They would eventually find out through other sources. The two men were cousins in his wife's clan. If she started in again with her grievances against him, they would side with her and things could get pretty tense.

They talked about how they had signed up to work on the construction of water retention dams. Now, the white sheriff from Mesa and a man from Washington were going to come out there and talk to them about becoming law and order for the *Dine'*.

Anthony grew increasingly uncomfortable, because the trader was writing the amounts and credit on a brown paper bag with his stub pencil. That meant the transaction with Anthony's wife and daughter was drawing to a close. Now they would spend the next three hours or maybe more, maybe even a couple of days deciding what to buy. His wives' cousins continued to hang around exchanging amenities. Anthony thought for certain he would be caught in a crossfire of renewed accusations. Then the trader was looking at him and waiting and his wives were waiting.

Anthony carefully took the check from his shirt pocket and presented it in a self-effacing manner to the trader, who stared at the amount with great astonishment. His expression did not go unnoticed by Anthony's wife. Sweigart looked from Anthony to the women and back again and asked, "Where did you get this?" The statement immediately drew the attention of the two cousins hovering in the doorway.

"I sold some land," explained Anthony in a low voice. There was no getting out of this now. The trader should not have asked such a question.

The cousins crowded in demanding to see the check. They clamored to know the amount and insisted in Navajo that Sweigart tell them. Sweigart held on to the check and moved well out of their reach. He could see what was about to happen.

Anthony's first wife uttered the amount between clenched teeth, but loudly enough for everyone in the room to hear. Then unable to control herself any longer, she hurled fresh invective at her husband.

The cousins bristled for more information regarding the transaction. Realizing he had unwittingly opened a fresh wound in a family relationship, Sweigart quickly interrupted and said he would take the check. After subtracting the Zaragoza debts, they could either pay cash or have full credit. With the advent of her sudden buying power, Anthony's wife quieted down, much to her husband's relief.

The sound of an approaching car rattling over the gravel pulled the cousins to the door. The two Navajo men saw that the sheriff had arrived. They noticed Logan and another man, Gimbel, with them who looked tall and pink, sweating and irritated from the long rough drive and the hot sun. They had been told this was the man from Washington who had come to talk to them about law and order.

The two cousins went outside and the four other men left the fire and came up from the dry wash. Sweigart followed the cousins and walked over to the car. "Have to ask you to wait 'til I'm finished here. I'm in the middle of a transaction."

Carmody nodded his understanding.

After the strained one hour drive across the desert with Carmody, Howard wanted three things at that moment—- shade, a long cold drink of water, and to wrap up this selection business as quickly as possible so he could return to Mesa by dinner time. He didn't care to make the fifty mile trip across that arid terrain on a rutted wagon road in the dark, although Carmody seemed capable enough to navigate safely.

From the time they had set out from Mesa that morning, Carmody had responded in a limited way to Howard's attempts at conversation. Although Carmody smiled at him in a friendly enough manner, he made it clear that he didn't talk much and kept to himself. Howard wasn't comfortable with that sort of behavior. He liked to know what a man's thoughts and feelings were to be able to relate to him. *Quiet one like him, never know what he's thinking or what he thinks of you,* which concerned Howard more than anything else. Carmody was his key to getting this job done and he knew it, but he did have some ideas of his own. One of them was to ask Carmody to help him find Yelena Ivanov.

Howard splashed cool spring water over his face. Drops rippled down his chin and soaked in to his sweat-stained suit jacket.

Fanning himself with his fedora hat, he sat on a rock and looked back at the trading post. Carmody had gone inside. Howard's eyes roamed the rocky terrain and settled on the slender column of smoke rising from the dry wash. The four Navajo men had returned to the fire and now hunched around it. Their high crown black hats gave them the appearance of giant gnomes.

Howard didn't know how to act around these Indians. He didn't know what to say or how to say it. What he knew of them was cinematic images of howling savages on horseback attacking settlers in a wagon train. He felt compelled to raise his hand and say, "How." He didn't though, because he never saw anyone else do that and the gesture would make him look foolish. He felt awkward enough just being there with Carmody and trying to emulate him. At least Carmody understood English. The Indians just did not respond. Their silence blanked him out as though he weren't even standing there in front of them. "How the hell can you deal with that? What the hell can you say?"

"That's why we're working together," Carmody told him. "That's my job."

He turned, startled at a slight rustle behind him and nearly fell off his perch into the pool of water. A Navajo man stooped at the spring and drank water from his cupped hand. He glanced once at Gimbel, an inscrutable glance, then rose and walked back to where he had been sitting in the shade of a nearby pinon grove. Howard had not even seen him and there the man was in plain sight. *Nothing moves.*

"No wonder they're so bad off," he thought. *"Just sit around and do nothing. Mean looking bastards. Wouldn't want to cross them. Get them trained to keep the bad ones in line. What the hell's taking that trader so long? There's another strange one. Never understand why a white man with any sanity would want to come and live out here. Nothing but sand and rocks and rattlesnakes and savages who don't talk".*

He rose and Logan followed him scuffing through the dust over to the building. They paused in the doorway allowing their eyes a moment to adjust from the sun's intense glare to the musty illumination within.

Sweigart conversed in Navajo to his customers. Carmody sat on a bench in the corner drinking a bottle of Nehi orange soda pop. "Soda Pop!" Howard nearly lurched forward. "It's a mirage." Sweigart barely glanced at Howard and continued his transaction. "Where's he keep those?" Howard asked.

Carmody pointed to a wooden crate behind the counter. Howard walked around and pulled out a bottle while his eyes searched for a cooler. There was no electricity, therefore, no cooler. No ice. He spotted the bottle opener and snapped off the top, then returned to Carmody. "They drink it like this? Warm?"

Carmody nodded. Gimbel took a pull at the bottle and nearly gagged. "Why doesn't he keep it cold out there in the spring?"

"Get stolen." Carmody pointed to the rifles and revolvers hanging at strategic locations behind the counter. "That's not decoration. He's got maybe forty, fifty thousand dollars worth of merchandise in here plus all the silver in pawn. No insurance company's going to touch it. There aren't any now anyway. That's his insurance."

"That bad, huh?"

"Mostly it's a show of force. You kill a Navvy and half his kin'll come after you in reprisal. Stealing's not a crime to them."

"What?"

Carmody nodded.

"Then how do you go about setting up law enforcement when everyone of 'em is a potential thief, given the opportunity."

"Not everybody's a thief. Can't judge them the same as in the white man's law and order system."

"Sounds like there's a need for some education."

"You can't change a couple hundred years of their way of life. The white man hasn't provided them with a prime example either, other than to steal from them. So what good reason do they have for wanting to obey our laws? We can only show them a few things, then let them work it out so it's best for them."

"We're supposed to set up a formal program to manage and train them."

"You're not going to manage any Navajo. If you try, they'll treat you like you don't exist—- and you won't."

"They can't just magically make me disappear with their medicine hokum."

Carmody stared hard at him with a condescending smile.

"I've worked in special police training and investigation procedures in New York ghettoes," said Howard "What's all this out here but a ghetto of another sort. Poverty, boot legging, malingering. It's just spread out over a few hundred miles instead of being concentrated."

"You'll be making a big mistake, if you keep looking at it that way. It's not the same. As a matter of fact, they regulate themselves through their clan relationships without any outside interference."

"I'm not talking about interference. I'm talking about the correction of criminal behavior. You do things like an old time western marshal. Coming out here, I get the feeling I've walked into a Hollywood movie. My purpose is to be helpful, not perpetuate a kind of make believe." Howard's presumptuous gesture was meant to include Carmody and the entire Southwest.

"When a man is shot or knifed out here," said Carmody, "he bleeds and dies just like men in the East. The reasons for killing a man might be different. Not all are."

"The idea is to provide a working system of crime prevention, not just react from one crisis to the next."

"They have a system. It's called shame. Nobody wants to be singled out and shamed. They live by that. Someone gets out of line, they have ways of taking care of it. Almost everybody on the reservation is related to everybody else. A person doesn't do much without somebody knowing about it. And it gets around fast."

"Could be the basis for an effective surveillance or spy system."

Carmody shook his head. "You have to stop thinking like a white man. White law is not Navajo law. They know it and live by that."

"The Indians are wards of the Federal Government," Howard quoted from the documents that had been given him to read while on the train to New Mexico. "They are expected to learn and live by the white man's laws. That's an important aspect of the Federal program and everything that Collier's doing. We have to re-educate them to white law."

"White law has nearly destroyed them as a people. They have no respect for it."

"Collier said you could help me with this."

"You have to first understand how they see you and why. You represent everything evil that was ever done to them."

"But you don't and you enforce the white man's law."

"I'm not good news to them either, Gimbel. But I live here. I'm not Washington and the Federal Government."

Howard slugged at his soda pop in frustration. Nothing in life was easy.

An hour later, they still sat waiting for Sweigart to conclude trading with the Zaragoza family. Howard had walked out twice. He no longer attempted to mask his irritation. Sweigart took no notice of him and did not hurry his patrons.

The second time Howard returned, he complained to Carmody just loudly enough for Sweigart to hear. "Why is he doing this to us? Why can't he just tell them to wait or go away and come back later?"

"This is their land. He has a business here only because they allow it. They are more important than we are."

Gimbel slapped his hat on the bench and scowled at the earthen floor. Sweigart continued to be solicitous with his customers and three more arrived and walked in. At that point, Howard rose and shouted across the room. "Sweigart!"

The Navajos in the store turned and stared at him for his ill manners. But it was to be expected of a white man.

"If this is supposed to be some kind of insult, it's gone on long enough. I get the message. Now, I have a job to do and you're on the payroll to help. What's it gonna be?"

Sweigart motioned for Carmody to come over to the counter. He spoke quietly and briefly. Howard strained but could not hear what was said and he didn't want to appear to be trying to listen. Carmody returned. "He wants us to wait outside. We're making the customer's nervous."

"Nervous? I may be a greenhorn, but I know when I've been put on. Just tell Mr. Sweigart to have his boys at the agency tomorrow at nine o'clock sharp." Howard stomped out the door and stopped at the impressive sight of seventeen Navajo men waiting, some on horseback, others standing next to their mounts. A few were sitting with their horse's reins trailing in the dirt.

Flushed and humiliated, Howard turned to Carmody walking slowly out the door. "How long have they been here?"

"Most of them have been traveling all day. Some have been here since yesterday."

"How come I didn't see them?"

"You didn't look."

"Why didn't you tell me if you knew it all the time?"

Carmody grinned and spoke calmly, maintaining control, not letting himself be pushed by this young law and order man from Washington and the ghettoes of New York. "They weren't all here until five minutes ago. No point in repeating myself for just a few, is there?"

"No, I wouldn't expect that from you. But you could have at least said something. Can you talk to them? Obviously Sweigart can't be bothered."

"What do you want me to tell them?"

"Tell them who I am and tell them to come to the Fort Defiance Agency tomorrow morning at nine o'clock. I'll brief them there in an environment where I've got some control over the situation. Tell them this much. They'll be spending three weeks in training and orientation learning to be policemen enforcing the law, the white man's law, which is also their law, here on the reservation."

Carmody interpreted the message, carefully editing out what would have been distasteful to the Navajo men. They listened with no visible response. A long silence passed. Then several promptly rode away on their horses not to be seen or heard from again. The two white men said nothing more. A few of the remaining Navajos entered the store. Three returned to their campfire in the dry wash. None remained watching Howard and Carmody and Logan.

"Let's head back," said Carmody.

"Are they going to be there tomorrow? Will they come?"

"They don't have clocks but they'll be there in the morning, most of them. Some maybe not for a couple of days."

"But I can't have that kind of inefficiency. Police can't just come to work whenever they feel like it."

Carmody shrugged and they walked to the car. Howard did not say anything further to him during the entire trip back to Mesa, which suited Carmody just fine. Gimbel had already done enough damage, but he could learn from his mistakes.

Chapter 18
KILLERS

Ned Thompson and Paul Leuentky arrived on a night freight making its run east from California. Moments before the heavy wheels and grinding metal on metal of ear shattering brakes were muffled by a great dragon hissing of steam, the two drifters clutched their pokes and leaped from the open door of their slowing boxcar, landing with a stagger several feet from the track. They stepped quickly into the shadow of a warehouse and watched to see if any railroad bulls were on patrol with their vicious nightsticks before venturing into the sleeping town.

They had barely escaped being arrested and incarcerated back in California's central valley for the murder of a Pinkerton guard. They had been hired as lettuce pickers along with an army of migrant workers newly arrived from Oklahoma.

They were housed in a tent city encampment enclosed by barbed wire and patrolled twenty-four hours a day by guards and dogs. To come and go to the fields required a special pass issued by the foreman.

Although they needed employment, Thompson and Leuentky did not accept the surveillance and oversight of being treated like prisoners, especially when they were prevented from going out drinking and whoring in the nearest town, then barred from re-entry to the encampment and their jobs given to someone else who had been waiting to get in.

Thompson had grabbed the rifle from the guard, lifted him off the ground by the throat, and strangled him. They had run off into the night and remained hidden near the San Joaquin River near a railroad bridge.

The trains approaching Stockton always slowed as they crossed the bridge. The biggest concern for Thompson and Leuentky was to be discovered by a railroad bull and beaten and thrown off. So they positioned themselves to climb aboard a boxcar after the train's departure from the freight yard. They rode undetected for three days until they reached Mesa, New Mexico, not a planned destination, but convenient, small and remote enough to fade into hiding for a long time.

When they said they were seeking work, the bar tender at the cantina mentioned the new Wooten Mine that had opened out on the reservation in the eastern sector. A few months ago, the owner, Lee Stark, had placed an employment announcement in *The Mesa Independent*. "You could maybe get a job out there," he said. They talked it over and decided it would be worth looking into since they were both flat broke.

Taking the bartender's advice, Thompson and Leuentky rode the mine company bus from town out to the Wooten Mine to inquire about employment. Since they did not possess skills or experience in this line of work, the supervisor hired them to start as slate pickers on the separator. They would segregate the slate from the coal and assist in various other outside labor the foreman might call upon them to do. Only skilled men worked the inside or underground operations.

After an appropriate time, they could both apprentice for a better paying job with more prestige. They would start at twenty-five dollars a week and be glad to have it. Considering these were hard times, that was good pay. Skilled labor was pulling thirty-five dollars a week. They would aspire to reach that goal.

The supervisor told them they could find living arrangements in Coal Town. "Plenty of boarding houses. Might have to search some for a vacancy. Maybe share a bed on a shift. You report to the foreman at six A.M. Show up late and we dock your wages."

Leaving the adobe office, they wandered into Coal Town. Rising dust from the outlying open pit operation hailed through the dirt streets like fine sleet coating them with grit. They passed several crude hand painted signs advertising room and board, no vacancy.

They tried three and decided the lice-ridden beds weren't clean enough for the price. They didn't much care for the shrill suspicious women running the establishments.

On the fourth inquiry, they found a situation they felt they could live with. The rooming house provided bed and meals, and a guaranteed change of linen twice a week. For an extra dollar per week, a wash tub bath would be prepared in the privacy of their room. Otherwise, the nearest bathing source was the company bath house at the mine, a half mile from town.

Considering that the husband and daughter of the proprietress with two small children lived there, the food would prove to be palatable. They knew that other boarding houses served subsistence slop they suspected was made from contaminated meat. Because of limited rooming facilities, even if an owner skimped on meals in order to increase her profit, a tenant had little choice in looking elsewhere.

The only drawback was that Thompson and Leuentky had to share their room with a stranger. He was a foreigner at that, a Hungarian named George Sendak. He seemed friendly enough except that he talked incessantly and too loudly and too much about himself and the old country and how lazy Americans were and how he didn't have a lazy bone in his body. He would flex his arm right under their noses as if the sight of taut lean muscle proved his point. He worked inside the mine as a timber man and sometimes as a roof bolter to brace the caverns to prevent cave-ins. He had been a miner for twenty-two years, beginning at the age of twelve.

The experiences of Thompson and Leuentky hopping freights and living in hobo camps had taught them how to respond to men of a tough nature, all nationalities and kinds. They figured they could manage to endure "Hunkie George," They never called him a Hunkie to his face after the first time. George had leaped up from the supper table and threatened to cold cock Ned. He was more bluster than blister, but his howling vituperation was punishment enough.

"I'm more American than you are, you son-of-a-bitch," he had shouted. "I come here on my own money and paid my way ever since. I speak English. I even fought in the Great War when you were still shittin' your diapers. You, hell, you're nothin' but a bum. You come here with a bare ass and never done no better since except to show it. Every morning, I have to wake up in the same room with you and what do I see? Your bare ass. You're the laziest man on the crew. I know. I heard how you got caught sleepin' in the machine house. You're nothin' but a damn slug. I'm a loyal American citizen. At least I mind my own business, which is more than I can say for you, you bastard."

At other times, mellowed with beer, he would stumble in long after dark, having worked a double shift and stopped off at the all night saloon enroute home. "You know," he said, tugging off his boots, "we're just checkers on the board. It's like being a soldier in the army." The other boot clumped to the floor. Ned and Paul covered their heads with their pillows in a futile attempt to ignore him.

"If you're smart, you try to make a better situation for yourself.. But there is always someone higher up you have to watch out for. You have to keep guessing what his next move will be." His maxims terminated with a loud belch and gurgling snore.

Both young men tended to remain quiet and withdrawn. They let an incident develop, then reacted to it. A silent understanding flowed between them that allowed them to know what the other was thinking so they were able to extemporize situations. Ned Thompson usually tipped off his friend that something was afoot by falling into a sly sluggish manner, a departure from his thick, good-natured country boy. He stood tall and blocky in stature. After two days on the job, he had been dubbed with the nickname "Ox" by other members of the crew.

Paul Leuentky was also tall, but gawky. His joints flapped when he moved. His nearly permanent dour expression belied an underlying sense of humor of a caustic nature. Depending on the company, his remarks were usually accurate and acceptable enough to draw laughter, albeit sometimes bitter. He soon came to be both hated and admired by the men with whom he worked. Often both emotions occurred simultaneously in an individual who became a target of his ridicule.

As if by some congenital arrangement, the lives of Thompson and Leuentky became extensions of one another. This phenomenon occurred without rationalization and without understanding, similar to the complex network of biotic impulses between Siamese twins. They engaged in few activities on a solitary basis, including excretory functions. They could be in the public bath house or in the brush or sitting side by side over two holes in an outhouse. Communal in nature, they would always share the same paid for woman or the many unpaid women they had raped in California.

To the concern of those who became suspicious of anything other than the usual grunting insertion followed by a quick release, the two young men would watch each other perform this most private of acts. While one poked at the prostitute, the other hunkered down naked or sat on a chair next to the squeaking bed and stared with an emotionless gaze at the mechanical animal rutting while the woman's eyes rolled fearfully from one to the other.

The ejaculations were often soundless. There was no guttural portrayal, no sudden intake or loss of breath from the exertion , just a short series of quick spasmodic shudders from the tense groin and the penetration was over. The woman was nothing more to them than a conduit.

They never offered a word of response or an amenity. As the madam explained to the chosen whore, "They put down their money, you put up with whatever they want."

The miners prided themselves in being able to endure a harsh way of life. A motorman who nursed a grudge against a fellow miner had run him down on the track and severed his legs from his body. It was called an accident, an occupational hazard.

Nearly every morning, a fist fight broke out between men waiting at the cage for the lift to take them down into the mine.

At the local school, a strong belligerent boy, bigger than the teacher, had desecrated several rooms with coal tar. After fighting and overcoming the kid, the principal, tough in his own right, was unhappily visited by the boy's father and a small group of friends who ended the functioning of his academic life by damaging his brain from repeated blows to the head.

Intellectualism and self-improvement were held suspect. Anyone who applied themselves academically was considered suspicious.

Better that the community did away with schools. The only thing that mattered was working in the mine. Acts of humiliation overcame the bright ones and quickly eroded any value of scholastic pursuit in Coal Town. Resignation to life's conditions prevailed. People wanted escape from conflict and anxiety, to escape from the community. Close off all hope and aspiration and be sure to get the other guy before he got you.

Violence became a virtue. To call in the law or attempt to prosecute an issue in court was considered a sign of weakness.

The weak, the infirm, and the wounded attracted Ned Thompson and Paul Leuentky like fresh blood draws a weasel to its source or as a wolverine relentlessly seeks the delicate necks of young birds. They begat each other as gluttony and hunger increase each other.

In California, they had raped thirty-six women and never been caught.

Blackbirds had often landed in the Leuentky family's yard. They would eat the sowbugs and crickets. As a boy, Paul had always wanted to kill them because he could not stand the jerking motions of their heads and their shrill cries. He would throw rocks and run at them screaming to startle them away.

There was a recurring memory, a sound, the wind scraping a branch of a tree in the yard against another branch. They screeched like the screeching of chalk across a blackboard. Paul would always listen to the sound. It came to him often like the high pitched "mewl" of a kitten.

As a young boy, he and his family, a brother and a sister, had lived in St. Louis and were disappointed at the lack of opportunity the area had to offer. Paul had detected the sadness of his parents as he watched their floundering efforts, their comings and goings. He had listened to their high pitched hysteria vented through the windows.

In the beginning, Paul had avoided Ned Thompson, the bully, the fat one. Stay away from the fat one. The overwhelming image of Ned Thompson's shit stained ass revisited Paul nightly after he had witnessed its preponderance one evening toward the conclusion of a parent and student P.T.A. function. The great ass, smeared against the window at the local school, had held the adults and children in attendance spellbound as its lips undulated against the glass. The students knew to whom it belonged. Only one of their population was endowed with such a posterior beam. No laughter resounded, not even a titter, only stunned silence.

The daring nature of this escapade prompted Paul to seek out the owner of this displayed monstrosity. Within a short time, Leuentky and Thompson were an established duo: Thompson the slug, Leuentky the crazy one. Each supported and fed off the other. What one lacked, the other provided. Thompson, bull muscle and Leuentky a fertile imagination for felonious pranks. They thought they were invincible.

When they left home and traveled to California, Thompson's and Leuentky's normal maturity was lost somewhere in the California sun. Now they were linked, married by eccentricity. They had been on a long honeymoon. The wide open lawlessness of Coal Town would provide them their consummation.

From the moment they walked in to one of her meetings, Yelena knew they meant trouble. But they did listen attentively to what she was saying to the group of miners and wives in attendance.

When she described how a strike could shut down the mine operation and provide leverage for the union to negotiate better conditions, they stared at her with a lethal diabolic smile that chilled her. They were killers. In their pursuit of distorted personal thrills, they could easily undo her careful planning and accomplishments by permanently alienating Lee Stark and his officials when her organization of the miners finally reached the strike stage.

Incapacitating machinery, causing cave-in's and equipment malfunction was helpful to the cause. But bludgeoning mine guards would only create unbreakable resistance and armed retaliation.

Her primary concern was to organize and move toward a successful strike, not perpetrate murder and mayhem. But Thompson and Leuentky had unspoken ideas of their own.

Chapter 19
LAW AND ORDER

Logan received word about the killing of a Government range rider the day after the incident occurred. Shreve was gone from the office at the time and Tom Bell, the other reporter, was running down some minor local news about a planned church social the following Sunday. The lead came from Logan's contact, a member of John Collier's staff at the Fort Defiance Agency. He told Logan that one of the new Navajo policemen had come riding in and now all hell was breaking loose at the rumor of threatened retaliation if any of the suspects were arrested.

Logan left Mona, the recently hired secretary, in charge. He instructed her to tell Shreve where he was going and ran out of the office. He didn't want to miss Carmody and Gimbel when they went to investigate the scene of the murder.

Howard Gimbel had recently moved from his room at the Fred Harvey Hotel to a small adobe house at the edge of town and was in the process of hiring a Mexican woman as a cook and housekeeper. Lucia Rubio understood very little English and Howard did not speak Spanish. His instructions to her were largely a galaxy of arm wavings and pointing at objects while mouthing loud tones about them. The sudden silent appearance of Sheriff Carmody at his door brought Howard's sign language to a halt.

"There's been a killing," was all he said and returned to his battered police unit.

Howard went to the door and shouted after him. "Where?"

"On the reservation," Carmody called back over his shoulder.

"I'll get my hat. Be right there."

He told the stout middle-aged Lucia that he would explain about cooking for him and caring for the house when he returned that night. Lucia did not need instructions. She would clean the house until it was spotless and she would prepare the hearty Mexican food as she had all her life.

The mutter of Carmody's car Engine sent Howard racing out the door. The investigation would be his first case since the introduction of Navajo police under the new law. When they arrived at the Fort Defiance Agency, they went directly to Collier's office to be briefed on the available information, which Carmody knew would not be complete or perhaps even accurate.

Collier's pipe was steaming little puffs of smoke while he wrote rapidly on a document on his desk. Without looking up, he waved to Howard and Carmody and Logan, who had followed them in, to take a seat. He finally paused at the end of his letter and acknowledged, waiting impatiently.

"This has the makings of a major crisis," he said bluntly. "We have to be careful how we handle this. We can't afford to fail. The problem is this. The Navajo deputy told me that some people are accused of being witches because of my sheep reduction program. As you well know, Sheriff, when it comes to witches, the Navajo don't fool around. They just kill them. I've heard of such incidents in the past, but I've never seen it happen until now."

"Who's the deputy?" asked Carmody.

"Hiram Betinez."

"I want to talk to him."

"He won't say much about it. These extended relationships in the tribe are going to prove difficult for us. No one's willing to give out information."

"Taking their stock will guarantee trouble," said Carmody. "It's their livelihood."

The reduction was tied in to Collier's soil conservation program. His proposal was for the slaughter of 200,000 sheep and 200,000 goats. The Federal Government was to reimburse the Navajo sheep owners an income to offset their loss, only as long as they cooperated with the soil erosion and conservation programs. The plan was that in five years, the over-grazed range would be restored and the Navajos could revive their sheep industry.

Logan had attended the meeting where the Navajo tribal council had angrily rejected the idea.

From mid-November to December, Navajo sheep poured into the Mesa holding pens. The stockyards were jammed with sheep waiting to be shipped to packing plants.

Logan had written a story for *The Independent* of several incidents where the agency officials violated the agreement. The council had asked that no reductions be made in flocks of fewer than one-hundred head. The Government range riders, however, did not discriminate. They slaughtered sheep at will upon discovering that owners of larger herds had split them into smaller groups and hidden them up in box canyons where they were difficult and often impossible to find. The field men would ride into a sheep camp, pay one dollar a head and just indiscriminately shoot and kill fifty percent of the animals.

White ranchers were moving in to claim the vacant range land by right of use. The Navajo saw this as yet another maneuver by the U.S. Government to take their land from them. Tribal tension was high. Outraged Navajo men vowed they would fight back in the old way.

Collier's next step was to issue grazing permits and to give the Indians work on irrigation projects so they could earn some kind of living.

The killing of the range rider was a sign of resistance.

Logan had always had the feeling that Carmody did not particularly like him coming around to interview him and others during investigations. More than once, he had ordered him not to take photographs. Logan objected that it was his right as a journalist to gather information and statistics in any form to tell the story. His job was to get the news. If necessary, he would go about this task without Carmody's or anyone else's cooperation.

Carmody was clearly angry over something, but Logan could only guess. He was dead set against Collier's methods of manipulating the tribe to achieve his personal program goals, especially since they were not in the best interest of the Navajo way of life.

Logan watched Carmody, Gimbel, and a Navajo policeman walk to the Sheriff's car. Carmody had ordered the man to accompany them. Since he had reported the killing, he would have more information to provide than he had shared with Collier. Logan discreetly avoided them and rushed back to his own car. Gunning the engine, he set off after them in a swirling cloud of dust.

The two vehicles headed northwest out of town on one of Collier's new graded crushed gravel roads that tended to wash out during heavy rains. After twenty miles, the road dwindled to little more than a wagon track that followed a long winding canyon cut into the mountains.

Logan had been drinking with friends the previous night and shreds of a tequila hangover still clung like a sticky fog to his brain. His erratic driving with the car lurching over the rocks and ruts did little to soothe his stomach. For all the years he had lived in that region, he had never quite grown accustomed to navigating the adverse conditions of the mesa wild lands where, until recently, roads had never existed.

Logan's greatest apprehension was to have a tire blow-out and he not be carrying a spare. Also, the engine of his '33 Ford coupe was badly in need of critical maintenance, but he never had time or money to take it to a mechanic. He also could not afford to not have the car available while covering local incidents for *The Independent.*

His other worry was that he might be going up a dry wash and blunder into a pit of quicksand. Such occurrences were not uncommon out there for the unwary driver or a horse and rider. When a horse and rider mysteriously disappeared, quicksand was usually assumed to be the cause. If a man was alone and nobody was within shouting distance, he and his horse or car or truck went down and that was that. Where your tracks ended told the story.

Their vehicles were passing over a particularly rough area with many protruding sharp rocks when what Logan dreaded happened. His left rear tire blew out and he crunched to a rubber thumping halt. He leaned on the horn. He was closely following the shieriff's car and saw the red tail lights flash. He grabbed the canteen he always carried on the floor, leaped out of his car and ran forward.

"Blew a tire," he shouted through Carmody's open window. "I have a spare but no time to change. I'll get my car on the way back. Can I ride with you?"

Carmody's nod gestured Logan to get into the back seat with the Navajo policeman.

Red sand rose in scattered dervishes and smote the sheriff's car as it plowed along the twisting course of the canyon floor. Howard's arm crooked to protect his face from the dust blizzard that swept through the interior while his free hand rolled up the window until they had passed the whirlwind.

The unwashed smell of the Navajo man sitting in the back seat nauseated Logan and exacerbated his hangover along with the stinging dust, the lurching car, and the eye-reddening glare from the relentless rocks. He glanced at Carmody's sharp profile. His hat was jammed down low on his forehead as he hunched forward, hands firmly gripping the wheel. Grim as the hard set of his mouth, he concentrated on the shifting terrain.

Howard had pretty much shelved any ideas he had for training the Navajo police. He knew nothing about dealing with them. He couldn't begin to communicate with them. Like Carmody had told him, they ignored him as though he weren't even there.

Early on, Howard realized that the Navajo men selected for the special training listened and responded only to Carmody and went along with what he said. There wasn't any classroom time. Carmody spoke to them out in the open air. They sat on the ground. He could plainly see that they respected Carmody. They listened. He understood them and did things their way. They knew him and his reputation for being honest and tough.

Time and again, Howard had caught his jaw flapping the breeze until he became self-conscious and started listening to the sound of his own voice, his intense authoritarian manner that was more anxiety than authority. The Navajo men could easily read him. He was so overly concerned with impressing his listeners, his words spewed forth as a tirade.

Carmody maintained a steely calmness even in an argument. Howard was irked at himself for being so preoccupied with Carmody, who so effortlessly dominated him. He realized he harbored a grudging respect for the westerner. Carmody was skilled and did his job well. He just would not bend. Howard wished that Carmody would treat him as an equal, but you had to earn Carmody's respect. Few men had done so and Howard believed he himself did not deserve it.

His resentment bit deep, a sour geyser of envy. All he needed was an opportunity to prove himself.

The Navajo passenger tapped Carmody on the back of the shoulder and pointed to a small canyon pocket off to the left where a Hogan and sheep corrals nestled at the lee of a cliff. Two women came out from the Hogan and watched them with suspicion. From the nearby brush, the frightened inquisitive eyes of seven dark-haired children watched the approaching car.

No one had touched the dead man nor the dead man's horse, which browsed off to the side, reins trailing. Nor had they touched his rifle lying in the dust. The Navajo avoided touching a dead man, woman, or child. Should someone die while inside a Hogan, the remaining occupants would seal up the dwelling containing all its contents considered to be possessed by the spirit of death. They would move elsewhere and start over. This sheep camp where death now hovered was no longer habitable. The women were packing to leave. No men were to be seen.

Carmody understood their religious superstitions and realized what had taken place. He also perceived that the two Navajo women feared his badge and his authority.

Noel Sweigart had told Logan of several instances when Navajo families had come to the trading post and asked him to dispose of the corpse of a dead relative or of one in the process of dying. They did not want to be transporting a dying person to the agency hospital or even away from the Hogan and have him die while they were touching him.

They feared the Government and mission hospitals as houses of death. Only through patience and careful education had medical personnel made limited progress in preventive health programs. A hospital was viewed as a place you went to die, not get well.

Sweigart said he took great care to avoid having a fight erupt in his store or to allow an ailing individual to linger inside. If a person died in the trading post by whatever the cause, Sweigart would have to close up and go out of business. The Navajo would never trade any goods that had been in the store.

One time, a Navajo man had an epileptic seizure right in the middle of the trading post. The other terrified customers had rushed to get out through the narrow door. Sweigart had watched them fighting each other in their panic, claw and climb over each other like fear-driven sheep. He had vaulted the counter and hustled the poor man outside into the compound. The others feared their brother was possessed by evil spirits and thought to be in the throes of death.

Carmody, Howard, and Logan stepped out of the car. The Navajo policeman would not go anywhere near the dead man or his horse. He watched Howard and Carmody examine the body. The man had been pulled off his horse and clubbed to death with rocks and his own rifle. His head, face, and portions of his body were red and swollen from the blows and had turned blue with death.

Carmody walked over to the women and asked them in their language to where the three men had ridden who had done the killing. The policeman had already given him their names. They were brothers in the Zaragoza family. Carmody knew them. The women shook their heads with anger and fear tinged bitterness. The teen-age boy, Duncan Zaragoza, stood in the background near his sisters and watched and listened.

Carmody said that he would have to track them down. He said they may have believed they were justified in the killing, but they would have to be tried in the tribal court. There would be complications, because the range rider was an official of the Federal Government murdered on Federally regulated land. He turned to Howard and told him, "Put the body in the car and take it back to the agency. The policeman and I will go after the men who killed him. He won't ride in the car with a dead man."

"When we catch up with those men, I want to be in on the arrest," said Gimbel. "I wasn't sent out here from Washington to be a go-for and sit behind a desk."

"I thought that's what you people did in Washington," said Carmody with sudden bitterness.

The blood rose up Howard's neck, flushing his perspiring face. "You have the wrong impression. I was sent here to do a job and I intend to do it. It's important that these people know that."

"You're from Washington. The Government has double-crossed them at every turn. These Navajo don't trust you and they never will."

"What about Collier?"

"What about him. For a man who studies the way people live, he has sure gone and destroyed their livelihood. They barely tolerate him. They don't trust him and they don't accept him."

"That dead man's not going anywhere. We can pick him up on our return," said Howard.

"Corpses have a strange way of disappearing out here. That might not be for a few days. Coyotes won't leave much but bones."

"Can't be helped. We have enough horses."

"I suppose you want to go with us," Carmody spoke directly to Logan, "to tell the story."

Logan nodded.

"The range rider can stay here or walk home or go back to the agency. Doesn't matter," said Howard.

Carmody studied him. "We have to do this carefully, Gimbel. Without violence and bloodshed. Word gets around fast out here. What I'm hoping is that the rest of the clan will want to avoid any tough restrictions against them because of this. They'll advise the men to turn themselves in for the good of the people. We have to put pressure on them though. We have to track them. That's how we go about this."

Carmody walked away from him and over to the eldest of the two women. He told her he would have to take her horses and saddles but that he would return them. She started to protest. He ignored her and went to where the horses stood tied at the fence of the sheep corral. Leading one of the animals, he walked back to the car for a blanket and canteen. He strapped them to the saddle of the dead man's horse and mounted, then slowly circled the area in search of the most recent departing hoof prints. Finding them, he headed out across the canyon toward a trail that climbed the opposite ridge.

Howard and Logan grabbed the reins of the remaining two Indian ponies, clumsily mounted and followed Carmody. Howard had ridden horses only a few times back East and was not balanced or comfortable in the saddle. The horse's choppy gait jarred him. Resting his rifle across the pommel, he checked his handgun, a snub .32 Smith & Wesson, worn in a shoulder holster. Logan had been riding since he was a boy, so it was second nature to him.

Behind them, the women called to Duncan and his sisters who brought the smaller children out of hiding. Together they began to herd the sheep down the canyon. Duncan knew he must now take the man's role at the head of the family and protect the women and children.

The Navajo policeman watched the departing figures on horseback, then turned and walked away alone down the canyon after the sheep. He decided it would be best for him not to be law and order. A range rider, a white man, whose death he considered justified, had forced him to stand against his own people. When he reached the agency to reclaim his horse, he would also turn in his badge, then pay a medicine man to cleanse his spirit at a sing.

***

When he touched the neck of his horse, Anthony Zaragoza's hand came away wet and sticky and smelling of animal salt and lather. His horse had begun to tire during the last climb. Anthony noticed that his two brothers were lagging. He stopped and waited. His horse blew and heaved and stood with its head hanging low.

When the others came up to him, they stopped to rest their animals. One of the brothers, Fred Zaragoza, said they should not stay there long. There was not enough cover and they could be seen from a far distance. He knew of a spring another three miles ahead. It was a hidden place and they could rest there safely for a few hours. So they agreed and pushed on across the windswept open space.

They did not know for sure if they were being followed. The second day was coming to an end since they had killed the Government range rider who had come to slaughter their sheep. They had not expected to see him or even that the camp would be found. They had not planned to kill the man until he started firing at random into the herd without telling them anything.

Ason Zaragoza, the brother whose wife owned the sheep, had pulled the range rider from his horse. His intent was not to kill him, only to prevent him. The white man had grown afraid and fought back. He had even tried to shoot Ason with his rifle at point blank range. The bullet had grazed Ason's scalp and he thought he had been killed as the world spun in blackness.

When Anthony and Fred, the eldest brother, saw Ason fall with blood streaming down the side of his face, they believed the range rider had killed him. They had run screaming to the man and had overpowered him in the stupefaction of his remorse. He was shocked at seeing the blood coming from the man's head and yet had witnessed so much blood pooling from the heads of dead sheep.

Fred grabbed away the white man's rifle and swung it brutally as a club. The man folded and collapsed at the stunning impact to his abdomen. Then, as if arisen from the dead, Ason had staggered up in a rage that terrified even his brothers. He had picked up a large rock with both hands, raised it high over his head and brought it down with such force against the back of the man's head it crushed his skull and killed him instantly. The man's remorse leaked out with the fluid of his brains.

The three Navajos stood nearly unable to breathe as their rage subsided. They did not rejoice as warriors. They were shaken and afraid at what they had done as if they had been children caught in a forbidden act. After some frantic discussion, they decided they must leave the canyon at once and journey north to the region of Navajo Mountain where there were many wild canyons in which to hide. The men would go on ahead. After a suitable time, Duncan and the women and children would follow, herding the sheep and goats. They would take a peripatetic route and stay in different sheep camps so that no one would watch them with suspicion and foretell their destination.

On the morning of his death, before he rode out from the agency at Fort Defiance, the range rider had told the Navajo policeman that he was going up the canyon in search of hidden sheep camps. If he did not return by the end of the day, the policeman should come looking for him. When the range rider had not ridden back by nightfall, the policeman decided he would go up there into that canyon the following morning, at which time he had discovered the Zaragoza brothers making preparations to leave the sheep camp.

They described to him how the killing had happened. Even though he agreed with the motive for the killing and would himself have crushed the range rider's skull with such a rock, he told the Zaragoza brothers he must still ride in to Fort Defiance and report what had happened. He would give them plenty of time to make their escape. He apologized for doing what he must do. He told them, he was law and order. After this, he would give much thought as to whether he would continue to wear the white man's badge. A Navajo never wore such a badge in the past. The whites had given him money to wear it. He told the Zaragozas he would take most of the day to ride back to the agency. They should expect to be followed, but not until late the following day. He could not tell them when the track down would begin, but they wanted to have a good long start on anyone who might pursue them.

Nine months had passed since Anthony Zaragoza's wife had divorced him. His affairs had not gone well ever since the sale of the land to the mining company owned by Lee Stark. Even living with his brothers, Anthony had to exist in constant hiding like many other Navajos to escape the senseless slaughter of their herds to meet some white Government worker's foolish quota system. And now, his part in the killing of the range rider added to his bad fortune heaped upon bad fortune. He saw no end to it, unless they could all escape. A long time would have to pass to bury this incident among the many of the past two hundred years. Like the conflicts of the past, perhaps the white man would no longer consider it of importance. Only the

Navajo would remember. Given time, the white man tended to forget everything, especially the treaty.

Thirst and hunger grew like young raw shoots in the guts of the men, spreading from the pits of their stomachs like nutrient seeking branches until the hunger ached even in their limbs and consumed their minds with the desire to satisfy the cravings. But, for now, they must keep moving to outdistance whoever would pursue them.

The three Navajo sensed a familiarity to this fugitive existence. The pattern of what was happening to them originated back many years in the history of their people having to run and hide to escape incarceration. The three brothers paused at a hidden spring to refresh themselves and to refill their canteens. The cool water coursed down Anthony's throat. Again and again he dipped into the pool and drank and splashed the water's freshness over his face.

He talked with his brothers, Ason and Fred. They talked about their back trail and what they knew of Carmody or had heard about him, the white law and order. They knew Carmody would be the one to come after them. So they must disappear into the northern wild canyons of Navajo Mountain. The ride would take many days. They decided remaining any longer at the spring would not be a wise decision.

Chapter 20
DISGRACE

Straining for the horizon, a flock of dark birds swarmed across the blood red sun. A sudden cool evening breeze whipped up out of nowhere and struck Carmody and Gimbel and Logan in the face as they maneuvered their horses down a gradual rocky slope to a grove of aspen rising out of the mesquite.

Carmody paused, taking in the breeze. He shifted in his saddle to ease the momentary stiffness of his body's position. Heat and dust clung to the riders' clothes and skin. Logan heard Gimbel's horse coming up behind kicking loose stones. Then Gimbel was there beside him, hunched in aching discomfort, his face blistered from the sun, eyes dark and hollow with fatigue.

He tugged at his Fedora. "We stopping here for the night?"

Carmody nodded and dismounted. He led his horse to a nearby bush and loosely tied the reins. He turned back startled at Gimbel's loud moan of agony as the man slowly wrenched his body from the saddle and painfully lowered himself to the ground. He stood leaning against the horse for support and tried desperately to master the excruciating convulsions that shot down his legs as circulation was gradually restored. He saw Carmody look away and busy himself removing the saddle. He was affording Gimbel a space of privacy to recover without embarrassment. Logan tied his horse and quickly removed the saddle.

Carmody thought it wiser to make a cold camp, no fire. He had brought jerky and a canteen of water. He left these next to his saddle and stepped away into the brush to relieve himself. Logan watched Gimbel fumbling with the canteen. Upon returning, Carmody noticed that Gimbel had not bothered to unsaddle the other horse.

"Go easy on the water," he ordered and walked over to see to the Indian pony.

Caught gulping thirstily, Gimbel was again embarrassed by his own surprising lack of stamina and self-control. He was disturbed by his inability to measure up to Carmody, who had not yet taken a drink and had warned him to go easy on it. And now he was unsaddling his horse for him as if he, Gimbel, were a woman.

"I'll do that." Gimbel staggered to his feet and started off a few stiff halting steps.

Not waiting, pulling the squaw saddle from the tired animal, Carmody ignored him and dropped it a few yards from his own. Taking the canteen from Gimbel's tight grip, he sat on the ground, drank quickly, a small amount, cut off two hunks of jerky and offered them to Gimbel and Logan who nodded their thanks as Gimbel worried his sore body to the ground.

"Aren't you tired?" Gimbel reached out and took the dried meat. He bit off a mouthful and chewed slowly. His saliva began to flow, digesting the spicy flavor.

"Yeah," Carmody belched, took another sip of water. "We'll sleep a few hours. Clouds moving in. If they pass, should be light enough to track them in the dark."

"If they know we're after them, won't they just keep moving?"

"Not at night. Too superstitious. Witches come out at night. We could surprise them."

"We're lucky because they're so damn ignorant. But they must have guns."

Carmody nodded. "They're not ignorant. They have a different kind of intelligence that matches their way of life."

Gimbel remained silent for a while, thoughtful. "This is very different for me——this." The slight motion of his head included the horses and the desert twilight. "When——we come on them ... "

"They could surprise us."

"They already have a killing on their hands."

"They believe it was justified. The range rider was destroying their sheep."

"But that's part of Collier's program."

"Nobody told them and they don't agree. From their view, the range rider is the criminal."

"It doesn't justify killing him."

"They aren't your sheep."

"You sound like you're on their side."

"I understand their side."

"They're subject to the law like everyone else."

"They had their own law before we came along. White law is hard to accept when it takes everything they own, even their dignity."

"So they might ambush us."

"They could."

"But they won't," said Gimbel. "You know what you're doing."

The comment surprised Carmody just as much as it did Gimbel and Logan that the words had leaped so easily from his mouth. "There's also a chance they can make it. Hide away so no one ever finds them."

"We'll find them. I know you'll find them." Gimbel paused. "I've never killed a man. Never had to, yet. I've seen gun battles in the city streets. Fired as a backup on raids a few times in New York. But never just killing face to face where it was either him or me." He waited. "You must have done that ... out here in the West with things so–different."

"Bullets and death are no different here than anywhere else."

"It is. Not like the city. Out here it's a different time, a different place. People are different, independent. They don't need anybody. Maybe it's the history out here."

Carmody remained silent. He considered Howard an ignorant fool. At least he was willing to listen and to learn.

"I've always wondered what it would be like, what it would feel like to have a show down. What we see in the movies isn't real, but out here I suppose it's likely to happen that way." He paused. "What was it like for you, the times it happened?"

Carmody stared off at the rounded tip of the glowing sun ball as it sank steadily into a dark murk, extinguished. The portent clouds pressed steadily onward, a massive army on the horizon.

"What did you feel?" Gimbel's weary insistent voice pressed him. "What was it like? Were you afraid? Afterwards, what did you feel?"

"Why are you asking me this?" The question stopped Gimbel.

After a long pause, he said, "It's you. I suppose I want to know about you."

"I never killed a man like that."

"You never killed an Indian? Nobody ever pulled a gun on you in a saloon? Like in the movies?"

"No."

Disappointment settled in Gimbel's dirt-lined face. He didn't believe Carmody, didn't want to believe him. This was just another of his refusals to accept Gimbel by an impregnable reluctance to talk and share who he was. He offered bare amenities only.

Logan knew Carmody would never encourage this FBI agent who sought with foolish envy a sense of worth and self-esteem in the eyes of a western lawman based on Hollywood movie depictions of a heroic archetype.

***

The delicate desert perfumes of night closed in around them like the drawstrings of a soft doeskin purse. They listened to the night creatures prowl forth. Logan identified the rustlings and stirrings within earshot of the camp, the long slow dry passage of a bull snake, the piping of a kangaroo rat, the whispering glide of an owl, the click of a beetle, the sudden buzzing rush of a bat.

Over the years, Logan had learned from Carmody through friendship with his children to love this land and the life it sustained. Logan was intimately familiar with its moods and seasons from violent storms and the bitter death blanket of winter to flowering springs and hot blistering summer winds that sucked the moisture from all living things.

From the many fishing and pack trips that Carmody took Logan on with his son, Bobby, and with Phillip Sweigart, his son, Kemp, and the trader, Noel Sweigart, Carmody had integrated the sweeping topography of the reservation lands. He could navigate the dry sea of mesas, mountains, forests, canyons, springs, the shifting Navajo camps, and endless miles of twisting sand bottom river beds. The geography was imprinted on his mind. He was familiar with the clans and knew many of the Navajo people by name. They knew him and respected his authority.

Gimbel shifted seeking a comfortable position he would never find on the hard ground. Neither he nor Logan had a blanket. He complained wondering how long it would take to recover from the sore stiffness of this long ride. His body throbbed and he manuevered his limbs as though he were crippled. Every time he moved, excruciating spasms shot the length of his raw inner thighs. He would have to invoke a supreme effort of will to mount his horse again in the morning, the squaw pony ... he, Howard Gimbel, riding in misery in a squaw saddle. No matter how he might falter, not by any stretch of the imagination could he ask Carmody for assistance. Carmody would render it directly and simply without causing him embarrassment. The embarrassment was of Howard's own making, but he could not help himself out of his pride and the behavior he thought he must exhibit to be heroic, to be a man.

It was the acknowledgment of Carmody's quiet graciousness in this matter that angered Gimbel and intensified his envy. "He's always one up on me, the noble bastard." Gimbel mentioned to Logan. His thoughts dwelt constantly on comparisons between the two of them when they were together. He wished he could flush Carmody from his mind once and for all, but Howard still carried the baggage of childhood, the repeated influence of his own father in awe of men who were stronger and more substantial than he. Now Carmody was entrenched in Howard's mind and always would be as a reminder of what he, Howard Gimbel, was not and could never be.

Why should he, Howard Gimbel, be trying to measure himself against another man in the first place when he himself was a leader in his own right, an FBI agent on the side of the law. Other men measured themselves against the persona J. Edgar Hoover had created for the agents who fought for law and justice. But it was an eastern form of law and order. They were heroes in the eyes of the general urban public. Howard did not feel like a hero and longed to know what that feeling would be.

Gimbel admired Carmody for embodying the qualities of a lawman that he, Gimbel, would like to possess. For the past two months, he had studied Carmody and tried to understand the essence of his behavior. The realization that he did not have the capability, spirit, emotional makeup and the frontier savvy to even emulate Carmody caused Gimbel deep frustration and fomented a rising discontent with himself and the purpose of his mission in the Southwest. He felt he must redeem himself to himself and, hopefully, in the eyes of other men, especially Carmody. He stifled a groan as he again rotated his hips and turned his body. He wanted so much to sleep. God, he wanted to sleep but he was overly exhausted and uncomfortable. An insidious chill consumed his body. Who would have thought the desert could be so cold at night.

Snakes were another thing that terrified him and would not permit him to close his already leaden eyes. Scorpions and rattlesnakes could nestle up to him during the night. And there was Carmody over there sleeping like a baby, not a care in the world. He'd care fast enough if he woke up with a rattler coiled on his chest staring him in the face. But Gimbel knew that wouldn't happen to Carmody. And even if it did, he would probably get out of the situation, probably heroically and without disgrace.

Gimbel could only see himself screaming hysterically like a woman, were he in the same situation. Disgrace, that was something Howard Gimbel did not handle well. He would go to great lengths to avoid it. There was no element of disgrace about Carmody. He was like an Indian. That was it. He was a savage, like an Indian.

Howard could no longer control his insistent yawns. His eyes swam like gritty jellied liquid in their sockets. He succumbed to a restive, tossing sleep filled with nightmares and groans of pain he had suppressed while conscious. To his relief, he did not wake the next morning to discover any desert creature anywhere near him, except for a single red ant which he squashed with his calloused thumb.

The trail led the party northeast with the sun coming up on their right. They reached the fresh water spring before noon and found signs of the Zaragoza brothers having spent the night.

A glance at Gimbel told Carmody the man was weakening fast and was badly in need of a rest. Gimbel should not even be there. He was in no shape for this. He should not have come.

Storm clouds had been building since dawn heading up from the east. He did not want to lose time and have the tracks wash out, at least not until he had accurately determined their possible destination. He told Gimbel and Logan, "We'll rest here for a short time." He pointed to the threat of the impending storm.

Howard refilled the canteen in silence. He then plunged his face into the spring and drank deeply of the fresh cool water. He would have preferred to remain there by that clear water for days and rest and recuperate, then have someone take him out of there in a jeep or small aircraft, even better. Lift up and fly the hell out of there. Forget all this. Go back to his home in Washington, a terrain with which he was familiar. He could relate to people back there and he was respected. He could not understand the people here and their way of life.

He was beginning to learn that out here, too much talk is energy wasted. He sought the shade afforded by a large boulder. Moments later, Carmody had to wake him from an all consuming doze. Howard muttered a startled "Sorry" and used the rock to support himself staggering to his feet.

A moving mountain of thunderheads multiplied layer upon layer. The churning pure white mass towered above the three tiny figures on horseback moving slowly across the miles of open parched terrain. The advance storm wind swirled the dust about the animals' legs and rattled the thirsty brush.

The horses quickened their walk as large cold drops pelted their hot dusty hides. Intricate ghoulish webs of lightning danced spider-like across the black horizon now thrusting forward as inevitable as the sea. A bolt struck the earth. The horses shied into a run. The scorched smell of ozone stung the nostrils of men and beasts. Like the spilling crest of a towering wave, rain poured over them in a drenching wall. Infused with the onslaught of a hurricane wind, the choked air left the men and their horses gasping, ballooning their laboring lungs with dense humidity.

They pulled the horses to a walk. The storm raged over them with multiple explosions and echoing reports of thunder upon thunder that coupled a trembling earth and sky with roars that reverberated mile upon mile. Black clouds bellied low over the land and burst, strafing the dry arroyos with muddy running rivulets.

With one hand Gimbel clutched his horse's slick wet mane. The other slipped holding the dripping leather reins and pommel of the squaw saddle. He no longer attempted to guide the animal by any means, but let him have his head to drift with the storm just as he was adrift in his mind and in time. The rain struck in such blinding sheets he could only hunch his shoulders and not look back into the gale. The riders remained bunched close together until Logan grew aware that Gimbel and his horse had drifted away.

Early during the whirlwind, Howard had lost sight of Carmody, which concerned him, but not as much as having his horse plunge into a hole and snap a leg or pitch headlong into a flash-flooded arroyo. For the first time, he admitted his fear to himself and hoped that Carmody was looking out for him.

The storm passed on, tailing an intense glistening calm, a sudden enchantment of triple tiered rainbows and bee infested bright flower blossoms that had not existed before the falling rain.

Man and horse came to a halt, stood dripping in bedraggled bewilderment and inhaled great lungfuls of fresh pure air washed clean of dust.

Howard looked around. Carmody and Logan were nowhere in sight. He called out and received no answer. Carmody would not be one to call back. Howard turned his horse and attempted to retrace the route taken during the storm. But he had not been able to discern any landmarks then and the terrain was totally unfamiliar.

Topping a low rise, he called out again. How far could he have gone in the storm? Howard could have sworn that at least for a time, Carmody and Logan had been right there beside him. Gimbel acknowledged that could have been in his imagination. Carmody and Logan were gone without leaving a trace, as cleanly as if the rain had washed them away.

Gimbel wondered if Carmody's horse had stumbled with him into a wash and they had been swept off in a flash flood. That event would not be likely to happen. He did not believe that Carmody was capable of making a wrong turn. Even if he had drifted with the storm, Carmody would have maintained control and known where he was going, where he would end up and how to get back.

Gimbel was beginning to think that nothing short of a violent confrontation could move the man. Even then, he imagined Carmody would be cool and deadly. Where was the son-of-bitch anyhow? Gimbel forced his eyes to scan slowly. He paused to refocus at the disconcerting distance and visually vacuumed the terrain in his mind. Nothing out there moved that look like two men on horses. In fact, nothing moved at all. How was it so easy for them to disappear? To no longer even be figures in a landscape.

Gimbel blinked rapidly. He blamed his eyes and his inability to yet perceive anything in that country with accuracy. He was in a foreign land. Time and again with his first trip out with Carmody to Sweigart's trading post, he had been startled by what he originally thought were giant boulders or large earth mounds that turned out to be Hogans of various structural design. Here, everything blended in harmony with the landscape—- the life, the people, and he could not see them. He began to think that maybe he was losing sight of who he was himself.

He conjectured that Carmody and Logan might have deserted him. They could have tired of his company and the burden of having to help him along. Maybe they were holed up in a sheltering pinon grove and had just let Gimbel wander on for miles out of sight. Would Carmody do that? Was the man up to it? Or down to it? Testing him?

After a period of strained searching, the hills out ahead began to look the same to Gimbel. They began to look even more the same as he rode up and down through the brush calling Carmody's name and hearing only his small lost echo. He could no longer even discern which mesa rim or distant mountain range toward which they had originally been headed. He fired off a rifle shot. There was no answering report. Now Gimbel began to panic. Where the hell was

Carmody? Why wasn't he looking for him? If he had been, they would have found each other by now. Gimbel was sure of it.

When Carmody and Logan first saw him, the storm was tailing off to the west. Gimbel was seven miles away and beyond shouting distance. Then he disappeared and they did not see him again until more than an hour later as a tiny dot. The horse and rider were moving farther and farther in the opposite direction headed back the way they had come, probably according to the instinct of the horse. Carmody figured Gimbel would eventually come across a wagon track and did not pursue him. Gimbel would find his way home. Carmody's primary concern now was to put himself in the minds of the Zaragoza brothers, whose tracks had vanished in the rain.

After leaving the fresh water spring, the trail had gradually wound away through the rocks and brush to the northwest in the direction of Canyon de Chelly and Black Mesa which stretched for five hundred miles across the broad center of the reservation. The terrain would place the Zaragoza brothers somewhere in Arizona. That region would normally have been out of Carmody's jurisdiction, but he was employed now by the Federal Government and the reservation was considered Federal domain.

At mid-afternoon, they came to another spring and rested their horses for an hour. If the Zaragozas continued to follow the springs, as Carmody believed they would, then he had assessed their plan correctly and would eventually discover them at Chinle or hidden somewhere in the Canyon de Chelly. He would have to rely on the cooperation of local Navajos in that area, not as informers, but to convince the fugitives that it was for the good of the *Dine'*, the people, that they turn themselves in to the Government authority.

They feared the Government because of its tradition of mass reprisals of one kind or another. If officials determined that a crime had been committed against its absolute authority, other tribal members would inevitably suffer. Such treatment had happened in the past and would happen again. Perhaps the policy would be to increase the number of Government range riders in armed strength and create a traveling posse resembling a military patrol. That would not be good for the *Dine'* and would further plague the already tainted relationship between the U.S. Government and the Indian.

Carmody knew the Navajo would consider these realities. They would not physically coerce the Zaragoza brothers into turning themselves in. The power of social ostracism for noncompliance could prove strong enough to accomplish that. He hoped the men would come in voluntarily without violence or bloodshed.

Carmody allowed their horses a long drink before beginning the arduous climb to a promontory from which he and Logan could see twenty miles in any direction. The tiny figure of a horse and rider moved unerringly toward them from the south. Gimbel had turned around. Three miles short of the ridge, they veered off to the east. Carmody said the rider was Gimbel traveling in a big circle. He fired his rifle into the air three times, causing his own horse to tense and prepare to bolt at the sudden loud cracks that echoed over the landscape. The distant figure hesitated, then changed direction and continued coming toward them.

They rode back down the steep trail and met him at the spring. An hour later, shaking his head, Gimbel slid down from his horse and collapsed in the wet cool sand and shade near the pool of water bubbling among the rocks. Carmody said, "They're headed to Chinle. It's about thirty miles." Gimbel was too weary to ask how he had arrived at that conclusion. He just wanted to get there and be done with his personal ordeal.

An epidermal paste of grit and sweat caused Gimbel to itch incessantly. If he reflected on Carmody's rumpled, scruffy unshaven appearance, that was also intolerable. Gimbel prided himself on personal neatness and a sense of efficiency, none of which mattered out here. He had lost touch with those qualities, which increased his irritation with himself, Carmody, and the whole damn Federal program.

The monolithic beauty of Canyon de Chelly's red sandstone cliffs penetrated even Gimbel's fatigued and jaded attitude about that region of the country. A spiritual impulse fluttered up within him at this awesome natural scar in the earth that dwarfed their figures.

They arrived at Chinle during the night. Upon consulting with the agency official, Carmody learned that the Zaragoza brothers had been seen in the canyon the day before and were probably staying with clan relatives or else camped in the northern passage.

Since the death of the range rider, the Fort Defiance Agency had sent out couriers to alert all the posts. The Chinle agent acknowledged that a good deal of concern and speculation as to resultant Government action, including the abortion of financial assistance, was rumored among the Navajo living in his jurisdiction. He provided the searchers with a meal and put them up for the night.

Early the next morning, they rode along the northern sector of the canyon so that their presence was noticed and registered with the local Navajo residents. From time to time, Carmody would stop in the vicinity of a Hogan. Long waits ensued before a man or a woman came forward to inquire what he wanted. That day, Carmody established that law and order rode in Canyon de Chelly in search of the three Zaragoza brothers.

As they traveled the winding passage, Carmody continually looked for extra saddles outside the Hogans, but they might have been hidden along with their owners.

By nightfall, ten miles outside of Chinle, they unexpectedly came upon the brothers' camp. The three men barely moved or even looked up as Carmody, Gimbel, and Logan stopped their horses within the circle of firelight. It was as if the Zaragoza brothers had been waiting for their arrival. Suspicious of an ambush, Gimbel leveled his rifle at them until he noticed that Carmody had not drawn a weapon. Gimbel immediately lowered his rifle.

They dismounted and stood opposite the three Navajo men. Carmody watched closely for any signal or movement that might erupt into sudden violent resistance. He shot Gimbel a warning glance at his threatening manner of again pointing his rifle at the brothers. Gimbel noticed, but chose not to heed. Carmody deliberately kept his own rifle pointed at the ground without threat or provocation. This arrest could go smoothly. He could see that the brothers had merely been waiting. Someone from their clan had obviously talked and reasoned with them. They had reconciled themselves. Ultimately, they had no place to run to, no place where they could safely hide.

Anthony spoke in Navajo. He told Carmody they were willing to put their trust in him that they would not be mistreated and they would be given a fair judgment. They explained that the range rider's acts of provocation must be considered in judging their acts to defend their lives and property. They knew of Carmody's reputation for being fair and of his understanding of the *Dine'*. If he would promise them these things, they would surrender their guns and go with him peaceably.

Carmody assented and requested that they hand over their rifles.

The smoke and erratic shadows thrown by the fire confused Gimbel's already sleep deprived distorted perception of what was happening. What was to him a guttural strange incomprehensible parley intensified his nervous fear of these Indians as savage killers.

When Carmody reached over to shove down the rising barrel of his rifle, Gimbel refused. He was locked in to the illusion that these Indians could not be trusted and would pull some sudden lethal surprise and overcome them. So convinced was he that had the Zaragoza brothers not even made a suspect move, Gimbel would have interpreted anything they did at that moment as suspicious.

Wary of Gimbel's insecurity and sensing the final threat of the man and his fear of them, they slowly and cautiously brought up their rifles to pass across the fire to Carmody. Believing this gesture was the beginning of an attack, Gimbel opened fire, but the shot went wild.

Ason and Fred plummeted back, and with a single leap, followed Anthony, who vanished into the surrounding darkness.

With a sharp cry, Carmody knocked the rifle from Gimbel's shaking grasp. He hesitated an instant, chilled at the paralytic intoxication of the potential killing he saw in Gimbel's sleep deprived expression. Carmody saw himself, a moment of fascination with the killing he had done long ago, the power of death he had wielded in his own hands and savored, reflected upon, that he had forced from his mind but that continually returned to haunt his dreams. This needless shooting reminded him of the reason why he had sought the position of Sheriff. To control. Yes, to control. He had the socially sanctioned power to take life. But now it was not revenge as that act had been when he was still a young man, not much more than a boy. The attempted killing by Gimbel was an urging on the borderline of a primitive impulse that was part man and part beast.

It was no longer necessary to hunt and kill to survive. A suppressed drive, it was still an existing force that manifested itself in periodic wars, a venting, a release of man's innate savagery. Man hunted for sport and created vicarious gladiatorial games of ritualized violence. The release was an emotional necessity, to fight, to kill, to master, to overcome by the death of another, literally or symbolically.

In an instant, Carmody saw himself in Gimbel's eyes. What he saw disgusted him.

Carmody looked around across the erratic fire into the hole of darkness where the prisoners had disappeared. Carmody knew he would never catch them again.

A hot bolt shot through him, because he did not feel an immediate remorse at their escape. He realized that what Gimbel was experiencing was posturing without feeling, without tolerance. The whole world postured without pity, without love, without compassion.

He feared that something was terribly wrong with men and that they had a need to kill to prove meaning and existence. He could not reconcile the two sides of who he was as a man, the contradictory impulses to love and to destroy. There were no absolutes in his life except the continual flow and changing of the states of matter. The only absolutes he could know as a man were love and death. He wanted desperately to control them. He feared death as much as he feared fully embracing love, because love would be taken from him. He became an enigma to his world and to himself.

As he turned, Gimbel's eyes burned with the smoke and dancing flames in them of hatred, pain and incomprehension, and a deep abiding sadness. He had truly believed that Carmody had seen the ambush about to be sprung on them. He had fired at close range and had missed.

He had wanted to share the instant of glory such as he had never known before in his entire life, the spilled blood, the savageness of the primal fire and surrounding darkness, and the two of them together unseen in the firmament of time, supreme in mastering life by delivering death.

Carmody had represented an unattainable ideal for Gimbel. He was not an illusionary hero of film and fiction Gimbel could cope with. Society and the world did not expect of a man to attain such an unreal status. They expected emulation, to dream about the possibility, and to imagine and identify oneself with the image.

To have believed that here such a man lived in flesh and blood, to have realized it was truly possible, that the hero even existed was something. But Carmody had denied the side of right and he had not slain the enemy. Gimbel's disappointment and despair with himself, his own failings, was bottomless. Carmody had shown pity and compassion for savages. Carmody was human. Had Gimbel really known the heart and mind of Everett Carmody, the irony would have staggered him.

They stayed camped there that night. Carmody slept briefly. Gimbel said nothing and endured Carmody's disparaging silence and the hard ground. He dared not sleep for fear the Indians who had gotten away would steal up on him and slit his throat.

At dawn, they rode back to Chinle. Carmody reported the incident. He would not pursue the escaped prisoners.

In returning to the Fort Defiance Agency, not a word passed between Gimbel and Carmody. Bitter, humiliated, Gimbel wanted to submit his resignation and board the next train to Chicago. He did not, because he remembered his purpose in the surveillance of Yelena Ivanov.

Word spread quickly across the reservation of the escape of the Zaragoza brothers from the white police authority from Washington. As Carmody had feared, because of his association with the incident, his credibility and respect by the Navajo were seriously undermined. The Navajo men dropped out of the law and order program and the training of Navajo police came to an end. Except for his mission to spy on John Collier and Yelena Ivanov, Howard had to fabricate some reason for his staying on at the Fort Defiance Agency.

All trace of the Zaragoza brothers vanished the moment they disappeared from the light of the fire in the canyon. Government officials speculated they had gone underground and were being kept well hidden and cared for by their clan. The consensus was that Federal authorities should not pursue and prosecute the matter.

Halen Braun informed Howard that the Bureau had smoothed things over with the B.I.A. when John Collier had requested that Howard be removed. But when the news reached J. Edgar Hoover, he was not a happy man. He informed Clyde Tolson that the only thing keeping Howard Gimbel on the payroll was his assignment to stop Yelena Ivanov.

One month later, three Navajos identified as the Zaragoza brothers, were struck by a large Civilian Conservation Corps truck at night on a desert road near Tuba City in the western sector of the reservation. The driver reported that the Indians had been staggering drunkenly along the road shoulder, then had suddenly stepped out waving their arms in the blinding glare of headlights of the oncoming truck.

Officials of the Tuba City Agency handled the disposal of the remains.

With no further reason to be associated with Carmody, Howard saw him infrequently at the agency or occasionally about the streets of Mesa. Carmody refused to look at him and they stopped speaking to each other. Howard filled his days with meaningless bureaucratic paperwork for John Collier so he could appear to have a sense of purpose. He had become what he despised most, a worthless suit at a desk.

That all changed and his relationship with Carmody was renewed the day Duncan Zaragoza walked into his office at the Bureau of Indian Affairs to see him about his father and what was happening out on the reservation.

III
COAL
TOWN

Chapter 21
THREAT

Yelena thought about what Howard Gimbel could do to further her cause and make any difference. He had no influence over the Governmental powers above him, especially the FBI. He could not protect her or interfere with the politicians and capitalists' private agenda of greed through exploitation of working men and women. So, she asked herself, what do I want from him?

At first, she did not have an answer. It came to her one morning as she drank her coffee while staring out the window at a group of small children playing in the narrow street. Using short sticks, they were drawing pictures in the dust.

Howard Gimbel was the only connection she had with her family and her past, with the exception of lost relatives in Russia. He was a link to her identity, to the dynamic young musician she had been and since repressed when her family was destroyed by Hoover and the Palmer Raids. The irony of Howard's reappearance in her life did not escape her. She depended on her keen intuition about others and their motives to accomplish her objectives, to avoid and counteract those who worked against her and wanted to eliminate her. She was equipped to survive.

She realized that through Howard Gimbel, she might rediscover what she had lost. But she could not openly go to him and she had no means of approaching him without raising suspicion among the workers she was organizing and whose interests she was sworn to protect. An opportunity presented itself in an unexpected way.

Randolph Logan learned these things about her when she finally agreed to grant him an interview.

***

Even with the windows rolled down, the night wind streaming through the car did little to cool Yelena and the four dark clad men who had broken her out of jail. She smelled their reeking body odor and the scent of whiskey and tobacco on their breath. The Ford coup tires bounced over a rut in the dirt road, jostling the passengers, throwing two of the men hard against her pressed between them in the back.

She caught brief glimpses of sage and mesquite flashing by in the yellow cast of headlights. That no one spoke suited her. She assumed that, under their current circumstances, they did not know what to say to her, not even to ask a simple question. In addition, they feared that they were breaking the law by having her in their possession and protecting her.

Breaking the law is how you change the conditions under which you work and live. She had spoken those words to thousands of laborers, men and women, over the years. *Your labor is for hire. You are not servants and slaves to capitalistic lords. It is the responsibility of your employer to pay you a decent wage and provide you with safe working conditions.*

"Ain't nothin' safe about minin', lady." That voice would always be raised. *"You risk your life every damn day goin' down in the mine."*

There are things they can do better.

Her thoughts reverted back to the marshal. Carmody, she had heard someone call his name. He had briefly hesitated when he had looked into her eyes while arresting her back at the railroad station. She had seen a flicker of recognition, not as a person or identity, but perhaps her own inner strength. Perhaps it was an expression of surprise and respect for who she was and what she represented. She did not drop her gaze. He did not intimidate her.

She wondered if he were married and had a family. She imagined he did. How did he relate to them? Did he understand the importance of family to working class men and women, their need to pull together, to protect and survive.

She preserved the memory of her family by striving to establish and shelter the rights of other families. What she had told Howard Gimbel on the train was a lie. Her sister, Lilya, had died, but not in her memory. She fought on for Lilya, and for her mother and father who had been forcefully deported by J. Edgar Hoover's Red Guard and never seen nor heard from again.

She and Lilya were obviously still strong in Gimbel's memory, although she was suspicious of the circumstances that he had recognized her on the train, that he was even on the same train. She had grown too sensitive to the bludgeoning transparency of company goons and Federal agents to miss the coincidence of their chance meeting. What could Howard Gimbel possibly know about *"Indian Affairs?"* He looked like a typical young Government bureaucrat, but he acted and smelled like the FBI.

If he were an agent, why wouldn't the Bureau use him to try to get close to her. After what J. Edgar Hoover had done to destroy her family, he would stoop to any device to discredit her.

Little Howard Gimbel, her childhood admirer, was now all grown up and upholding the lies and deceit of J. Edgar Hoover's shadow government as a member of his secret police.

There must be some way I can use him to my advantage, she thought. *He can't be entirely comfortable with what they've assigned him to do. I could detect his uncertainty in his voice and in his eyes. He was too innocent and gullible when we were childhood friends. At heart, he might still be a decent human being, and that's what corrupt people do. They exploit decent people for their own political and economic gain.*

If I can rekindle the friendship, I can get him to cross over to my side. He doesn't fit with who I am now. But perhaps in his trust and innocence, he can be helpful to me, a collaborater. I too have to use others. I'm an opposing force and Howard is caught in the middle.

***

Halen Braun believed that a journalist could become an effective and unwitting spy, if manipulated in the proper way. He had used news writers twice before while conducting investigations. They could often get inside an organization and acquire information that a covert agent could not. A journalist did not try to hide his identity. In fact, there were a few who openly hob-nobbed with crime bosses, mutually enhancing their fame and notoriety.

Logan returned to *The Mesa Independent* office early one afternoon cogitating on the lingering luncheon aftertaste of sausages simmered in onions and hot Mexican peppers served with pinto beans and rice. Fighting off a post prandial desire to catch a snooze at his desk, his interest was instead piqued by the black Ford Government car parked at the entrance. He came fully awake on seeing the recognizable bulk of Halen Braun conversing with Shreve inside the editor's glass-enclosed office. Logan considered the glass pretentious, a bubble of arrogance and condescension for a regional non-descript news publisher.

Logan admitted that Shreve occasionally wrote a mean editorial to accompany a story taken off the wire from one of the Eastern rags. But of late, he seemed to be writing less and drinking and socializing more with local and state politicians and wealthy ranchers and corporate mining officials in Santa Fe. He told Logan that inviting him to social affairs was their way of courting favor with his influential newspaper.

"News is made by the movers and shakers in this world," he said. "To be a successful news publisher you have to be in their midst."

Logan's first meeting with Halen Braun, the night that Yelena Ivanov arrived on the train, prompted him to pursue the story, but in a cautious manner. In the first place, Braun's physical demeanor and predatory gaze did not engender a feeling of trust. His dark hard-as-marble eyes reminded Logan of a malevolent male grizzly he once encountered while hiking in the mountain wilderness north of Mesa. Rearing up to his full eight foot height on his hind legs, after much snuffling at Logan's man scent, the grizzly decided he wasn't a threat, dropped to all fours and ambled on past Logan's petrified form.

Logan wanted to avoid Braun and spend as little time with him as possible, but Braun was the gatekeeper to an underlying conspiracy that allowed the Federal Government and the Wooten Corporation to exploit the natural resources of the Southwest and the men and families to mine them.

At the time, he had only a superficial awareness of the political forces that determined what was being done under the encroachment of global war. Where he would never challenge a grizzly, Logan took it upon myself to quietly resist Halen Braun.

When Shreve introduced them, Logan sensed that Braun looked at him as though he were some kind of insect he could easily squash under his size fourteen western boot. The corners of his pouchy eyes cracked like an eggshell in an unsuccessful attempt to convey warmth and conviviality. The introductory mention of names went unheard and unheeded.

Logan inwardly recoiled at Braun's menacing demeanor, while Braun was trying desperately to break through his shallow self-serving facade and convey a sense of partnership and good will. Logan gripped Braun's extended paw with all the strength he could muster and succumbed to having his arm cranked up and down like the handle of a water pump.

"He's from the FBI," were the words that fronted the proximity of what Logan heard spoken by Shreve, who faded into the wings like a secondary player on a bare stage. Logan wondered at the redundancy of Shreve's comment other than to emphasize the importance of Logan's response. They both well knew who Halen Braun was.

At that moment, Logan realized that a secondary player was all that Shreve was and would ever be. He boasted and pretended to greater achievements, but his written words did not move and shake anybody. The newsprint that contained the editorial expression of his vaulted opinions on one day became the paper that the butcher used to wrap cutlets of meat and fluttered on outhouse floors for occupants to wipe themselves the next.

Thoughts expressed by the juxtaposition and configuration of words were always a wonderment to Logan. The words written or typeset on a page did not endure. The abstract thought they might have expressed hopefully carried on.

The more Logan obsessed on his yet young life and the more he observed of people and larger social and political forces in the world, the more he realized that written language played a part in the historical fate of mankind. What he was being asked to do was to prostitute himself as a spy on the pretense of the written word. He remembered his dialogue with Shreve and Braun and later wrote it down word for word.

"Junius and I have been discussing a situation."

Junius, Logan thought. *On a first name basis. How casual, how assuming, how arrogant, how in charge.*

"Mr. Braun has brought a tremendous feature story to my attention," said Shreve from the wings, "and I want you to write it."

Their ploy could not have proceeded better had they rehearsed the encounter. Logan nodded and reserved any expression of enthusiasm, since he didn't feel any, and contained his suspicion. Both Shreve and Braun were a little put off by his lack of enthusiasm.

"You know of Yelena Ivanov." Braun's deep voice rolled over him.

"I saw her arrested the night she arrived on the train."

"Do you know what she does?"

"I've heard she's a union organizer."

"That's right. That's exactly right and a communist to boot."

"We want you to do a story on her," said Shreve.

"The story is a cover to get you close to her," said Braun. "The FBI wants to know where she is, who she's talking to, and what she's doing or plans to do."

"The FBI?"

"As of this moment, you're working for me."

Randolph let that unsettling thought sink in. "You mean you want me to spy on her."

"Yes, that's exactly what I want you to do."

"What if I can't find her, or, if I do, what if she refuses to talk to me?"

"Be resourceful. You're a news writer. Find a way."

"And if I can't?"

"I don't accept failure, Logan. I'll assume you don't either. And if you do fail, I'll put your ass in prison for conspiracy against the United States Government in a time of war."

"I didn't know war had been declared."

"It will be, any day now. The Brits can't hold out any longer. The air raids have flattened them. France has been overrun by the Nazis.

They started with Poland and Austria. Now Italy joined with 'em. They've got Europe wrapped up."

He looked over at Shreve, who nodded that Logan had no choice. He did have a choice, but didn't care much for the alternative.

"What are the arrangements?"

"You'll report directly to me."

"And the story...Do I actually write one."

"To keep up appearances."

Shreve interjected, "We'll publish a series on the mine and its importance to the economy and the war effort. It will need some human interest, as well, something you're good at writing about."

"Just remember your choices" said Braun, "and don't try to double cross me. Yelena Ivanov has a reputation for being persuasive. Act like you agree with her, but that's where you draw the line. Got it, Logan?"

The young man did not waver under the agent's threatening stare. "Yeah, I got it."

"You call me when you have the first installment. Shreve has my number. I'll set the meeting place. Can't be here. Too open. Any questions?"

Logan remained silent. He did have questions, but there were no answers.

With a single brusque motion, Braun moved toward the door, causing Logan to step aside or risk being knocked down. When Braun was gone and Shreve and Logan heard his car roar away down the main street, he cast Shreve a long sour look. He responded with a lopsided grin.

"I could say I'm sorry, but I'm not. This will test your mettle as a newspaperman. You'll do fine, Logan. You'll do fine. Young lad like you has a way with the ladies."

"Yelena Ivanov doesn't sound like a lady."

"Maybe not, but she's a woman and a strong one at that. You ever known a strong woman, Logan?"

"Yes, my mother, but otherwise, no. I suppose now you're going to tell me you have."

"My mother too, bless her soul. Where you think I learned to be such a hard ass?"

"If it's true, then she did a good job."

"Thank you, Logan. I take that as a compliment."

"You gonna help me out on this?"

"Wouldn't touch it with a ten foot pole. Braun's mean as a bull rattlesnake and twice as deadly."

"Coward."

"Don't yellow me, you cub you. I've been close to danger in my time. I've paid my dues. I dodged bombs and bullets in two wars for the sake of a story. You're in a thankless profession. What people read in the paper on one day——"

"I know. They use to wipe their ass on the next."

"Sounds almost Biblical, don't it, young Logan? The power of the written word can take you places you never imagined."

"How about you pay me before I get started on paying my dues."

"You write any copy the past week? You put anything on my desk?"

"I'm investigating a story."

"Looks like your story found you."

"I have to eat to stay alive and to write."

"Doesn't your mother feed you?"

"Oh, she feeds me all right, as long as I bring money home. It's not a free ride anymore, now that I've growed up."

"Well, all right, since you insist." Shreve reached into a desk drawer and pulled out a wad of bills. "Just a test of your perseverance. Don't get nothin' out of life 'less you ask for it and, in some cases, outright take it. And you sure as shootin' don't get a story unless you go after it in an aggressive manner. Here." He handed Logan the bills. "Now, don't go and make this your last supper. You ain't Jesus Christ. Don't sacrifice yourself to this Ivanov woman. She's likely to hypnotize you like starin' into the eyes of a cobra. You don't want to fall in love with a cobra and get your ass thrown in prison all on the same outing, if you get my drift."

"I get your drift all right. You're goin' senile. Why would you even bring romance into this? This is about politics, not love."

"You're young and single and she's young and single and somewhat heroic and challenging. Spirited is what I call it. It's easy to fall in love with a spirited woman."

"How do you know she's young–and single?"

"Braun told me her age."

"How old?"

"Twenty-nine."

"She's older than me by three years. I don't mess with older women, Shreve. I'll leave them for you to do that."

"You're still wet behind the ears, young puppy. She's only three years older than you, mama's boy, and she has a stronger personality than you. She can dominate your life and that would suit you just fine, because you will fall in love with a woman who will dominate you. That's why a man falls in love, to serve a woman."

"So you make yourself a prophet now that you can't write anymore."

"I'm beyond writing, cub. I'm an editor. I make what you write readable."

"I can't fall in love with a woman like that, Shreve."

"Sure you can. Why the hell not? It would make a hell of a story. Think of it. Think of the dilemma. You spy on her for the FBI and fall in love."

"You couldn't print that."

"No, but you could write it in your memoir someday."

"You writing a memoir?"

Shreve magnanimously thrust his hands behind his head. "Maybe. I need to wait and see what happens to you first."

"Whether I live or die."

"That's right."

"I can't fall in love with a woman like that, Shreve."

"Sure you can. Why the hell not?"

"Why would I need a woman like that when I've got you?"

"Watch your insinuations there, boy. Don't blaspheme in my court."

"I work to serve you. You're the master."

"That is an accurate statement. I speak from experience. I was married to my wife forty-three years until she died and she was a spirited woman."

"Any advice on how to approach Yelena Ivanov? What questions to ask?"

"Not a one. That woman and I are birds of a feather. Just don't be a smartass which I know is hard for you not to do, since you believe you've been endowed with all the Lord's wisdom and his personal fountain pen. And don't try to take charge or she'll show you the door, like I'm about to do. Get the hell out of here, young Logan, and get to work. You have food and gas money. It's a long drive out to Coal Town and gas is on ration. You don't want to run dry in the middle of the goddamn desert."

"Thanks," Logan stuffed the bills into his pocket. "Your kindness is exceeded only by your generosity."

"The door is closin' fast. Don't let it hit you in the ass."

Logan raised his right hand and extended middle finger as he walked out the door.

***

Logan's mother wore a floral print dress and open-toed leather sandals like a Mexican woman. She was not a heavy *mamacita*. Her straw blonde hair hung in a long dense braid that accented her lean features and translucent blue eyes. Logan liked to think her eyes looked that way because of the hours she spent working in her vegetable garden out in the sun. She was a quiet creature of the desert landscape.

She always spoke kindly to her son in endearing phrases. He could not recall her ever raising her voice in anger at him or at anybody even though she certainly had cause to once in a while. He didn't think he had been spoiled as a child, but he had been the center of her love. He had barely known his father, who had died when Logan was quite young. His death now brought Logan's mother rarely, if ever, to the subject she chose to ignore. She had once to satisfy her boy's then seven year old curiosity as to why she never talked about his father, even in memory. She kept a faded black and white photograph of the two of them framed on her dresser.

"His life was cut short," she had explained. *"He was killed in a mining accident. What you should remember is that you were the center of his world. He loved you more than anything in this life."*

"But he loved you too."

"He loved us both."

"I'm going out to Coal Town to do a story," Logan said.

"Shreve sending you out there?"

"Yes 'm."

"Well, it's not like you haven't been out there before."

"No, Mum."

"As long as you don't go down into the mines. They said your father died in a mining accident. They said it was his fault. That was just so the mine bosses didn't have to pay anything to his widow and his son."

"I won't be going down into the mines. Have no reason to."

"You don't have to write anything good about the mine bosses either."

"It's not likely I will. I'll be talking to a union organizer."

"Oh, they're allowing a union now?"

"Don't think so. They want to stop it from happening."

"So, what is the point of your story?"

"Don't know yet, Mum. Don't know. Won't until I talk to her."

"Her? The union organizer is a woman?"

"Yes, her name's Yelena Ivanov."

"Yelena Ivanov—A Russian. She must be a brave-hearted soul."

"I'm told she is."

"When will you see her?"

"Don't know that yet either. Have to find her out there in Coal Town."

"The law don't look kindly on union organizers. She's likely to be suspicious of you. I would be."

"Mum, how could you say that about me, your only son?" He laughed.

"Not aimed at you. Your profession. She would be suspicious of how you used the information she gave you."

"And well she should be. Writers and journalists are a callous lot. People and events are just story material. The story is everything. But the next day, that same newspaper is–"

"—used to wipe somebody's ass."

"You've heard this before."

She nodded. "You mentioned it to me once when Shreve butchered one of your articles. I told you it wasn't worth getting angry about. And then you said–"

"—the next day."

"I want this story to work for you, Randolph. It's important that it comes out in support of this woman."

"I know."

"Yes, you know, but the press is a tool of those who have political power. They think they own it as their personal mouthpiece."

"I didn't know you thought about all this."

"I tend to be a private person. You never asked," she said.

"And I'm sorry for that."

"I want to help you, son."

"Help me? How?"

"It's not likely Yelena Ivanov will ever let you see her if you try alone. Let me find her with you and help open the door. I want to do this for your father. We need to do this for your father, the two of us."

After a long thoughtful pause, he said, "I can't let you help me."

"What are you saying?"

"It's too dangerous."

"If it's too dangerous for me, then how dangerous is it for you? What is the danger?"

Logan inwardly squirmed. He wondered if he had deliberately brought himself to this point as a plea for help or if what was to come was fated to happen. He would never have imagined his mother being involved, of all people. He thought that maybe he was looking for a way out of his dilemma. His mother had offered assistance and he could not refuse her. After all, she was his mother. *You don't refuse your mother's help. But the danger,* he thought. *What about the danger?* He couldn't tell her about Halen Braun. But he had mentioned the word danger. She had asked, what is the danger? He had not answered her directly, which made the situation worse. She would wait for the answer. She expected it. She would demand it. He was her only son.

"You know," she said, "We get pushed and pulled in different directions in our lives. What happens to us forces us to make choices. So what difference does danger make to me? None at all."

"Mum, I don't want you to get hurt in all this. You've been hurt enough."

"Who's going to hurt me? Do you know?"

"I don't know, but there is danger."

"Life is risk. It's as simple as that. There are no guarantees."

Logan quelled a sudden rising emotion to cry.

Chapter 22
JOURNEY TO COAL TOWN

Logan and his mother departed before dawn, driving out slowly on a rutted road toward the sunrise cresting the mesas and dissolving the desert shadows.

The smoky aftertaste of mesquite flavored bacon with eggs and salsa that his mother had prepared for breakfast left him feeling ambivalent about their journey. Her being next to him on the passenger seat underscored his continued dependence on her. At the age of twenty-five, he still lived at home. She cooked his meals and washed his clothes just as she had when he was a child. He did not know whether to feel grateful or resentful. He did not dislike her looking after him. He couldn't cook to save his soul and he hated to wash and iron clothes. He had paid to have those chores done when he was in college. Now, he had had to rely on his own resources for two weeks a year while his mother visited her sister in Santa Fe. He was always pleased and relieved to have her return and met the train promptly at the station upon its arrival.

He imagined that if Shreve saw the two of them driving out of town together in the battered black Ford coupe, he would have howled with laughter. In reality, Shreve would have wept with sympathetic admiration. It was a side of himself that he would never openly reveal to Logan. He would die first.

A slight morning breeze carried the sweet sharp scent of sage and chaparral through the open windows of the moving car and kicked up a fine powdered dust in its wake.

"It's a beautiful morning," his mother commented.

He nodded his head toward the wide radius of the steering wheel. *She is not that much older than myself,* he thought. *Twenty years, makes her forty-five. Still looks young. Few wrinkles at the corners of her eyes. Sees things the rest of us don't notice. Probably talks to Dad everyday, out there in her garden or walking in the desert. You're spiritual, Mum. So if you say Dad is with us, then it's so. Seems appropriate, considering what we intend to do. Not quite sure what that is myself yet, but you are. Just have to go along and see and hear it and write about it.*

Coal Town fanned out seven miles in length with three main dirt streets connected by a gridwork of connecting side streets and alleys three miles across. The lines of adobe and tin shacks housed four thousand miners and their families. An incessant cloud of black coal smoke fed by a multitude of cooking stoves rose in a steady stream from corroded metal chimneys where an east wind dispersed the coagulant dust out over the mesa rendering the town the appearance of slowly progressing westward like a battleship at sea.

Entering the town, they maneuvered slowly through a mob of soot encrusted men coming off the night shift and infiltrating the streets. They grew to an army of dark creatures dispersed among the unsoiled men streaming from the side alleys and onto the main road where the dominant mass trudged toward the mine.

He stopped the car and turned off the engine to avoid bumping or running down any of the pedestrians.

Curious grimacing faces peered in at Logan and his mother through the open windows. With the exception of those cars driven by the mine managers and migrant families, automobiles were seldom seen on the streets of Coal Town.

Logan perceived the miners as an army of worker ants wearing boots and coveralls streaming in and out of the colony in frenetic disarray. He had no idea where to begin their search or to whom they would likely inquire about Yelena Ivanov without arousing suspicion.

"There's a post office down there," he commented, catching sight of a limp American flag draped from a pole that extended twenty feet above the tin roof of a weathered adobe building.

"Not likely she established an address," said his mother.

"I was thinking she might have posted an announcement about a meeting."

"The mine owns that post office."

"The Federal Government owns that post office."

"The Federal Government and the mine owners have their hands in each others' pockets and they want to keep it that way," said his mother. "There's a different law out here. Yelena Ivanov is a threat to their private arrangement."

"Understood."

"I'm thinking that as soon as the streets are clear, we might try a few boarding houses. She could be staying in one, but maybe not. Too public. It's a start."

An hour later, the throng had subsided, but as Logan restarted the car and began to move forward, they were approached and their way blocked by three civilian suited men wearing prominently displayed badges on the left breast of their dark coats. They wielded police batons and Logan could detect the bulge of side arms at their hips.

While one of the goons remained standing at the front grill, the other two sauntered around to each of the open front windows. They were unshaven and smelled of whiskey and the sweet acrid scent of chewing tobacco.

"What business you got here?" barked the one on Logan's side of the car.

Minerva leaned across the seat and fixed the man's menacing stare with one of clearly equal strength and challenge. "We're out to visit my sister."

"Don't allow no visitors."

"We might also be lookin' for work. My son here is young and strong. Ain't that how you like 'em?"

"You want work, you go to the mine office to sign up."

"Need to find lodgin' first."

"We just want to know who comes in here, lady."

"Name's Flynn—Minerva Flynn," she gave out her maiden name. "My son's Randolph."

"Long as yer lookin' fer work, you can stay."

"That's our purpose."

"There's a fee for drivin' a private automobile in Coal Town, just so's you know. It's payable to me."

"We didn't see no sign comin' into town."

"Don't need no sign. We're the law."

"I thought the law was back in Mesa."

"Out here, we make our own law. We work for the mine boss."

"And just how much is your fee?"

"One dollar."

She nudged her son. "Give him one dollar."

Logan shuffled his hand into his back pocket and came out with his wallet. He positioned it out of the men's sight below the window ledge where their prying eyes could not see its contents. He snapped up a one dollar bill and thrust it out the window at the man, while at the same time, putting the car in gear. It rolled forward causing the man in front to leap aside with a shout of alarm and a curse as the wheels accelerated their momentum and quickly put distance between them and the three men.

"You're brave," Logan laughed to expel his nervous tension. "But don't think I'll be signing up at the mine office."

"Have to call their bluff on men like that," said Minerva. "Need to get us off the main street, out of sight back in there with everyone else. We'll find someone we can talk to."

Logan made a sharp left turn that took the car onto a narrow unpaved side street. They passed along a row of closely packed adobe dwellings and had to be cautious of small children dodging in and out of open doorways.

"Where there are children, we'll find mothers. They will be the first to know, because they are the foundation of their families. They will persuade their husbands."

"You sound like you've done this before."

Minerva shook her head. "But if I did, this is where I'd begin."

After several minutes, they came to a break in the long line of shacks. "Pull in there," Minerva pointed to an opening.

Logan maneuvered the car onto the lot shared by three battered trucks resting heavily on soft wheels. He turned off the engine. With a brief nod at his mother, they opened the doors and stepped out of the car into ankle deep dust. The foul air stung their nostrils. He followed his mother, who tucked her woven basket purse under her left arm and appeared to know where she was going.

Hordes of black flies rose from garbage and buzzed about their faces, as they trudged along the street. Minerva paused to speak to a haggard young woman with stringy brown hair and dull dark eyes. Three small children, a boy and two girls, clung to her dress as she stood barefoot at the doorway of her hovel.

"Excuse me, we're looking for Yelena Ivanov. Do you know where we can find her?"

The woman stared at Minerva as though not understanding either the question or even the language. "Don't unnerstan. No speaka da English," she finally uttered with a heavily layered Italian accent.

"That's okay. Thank you. Grazi." Minerva continued on. Logan winked and waved at the little children gazing up at them.

"Not goin' to be easy, this, " said Minerva. "Like tryin' to find a needle in a haystack."

They saw a miner limping toward them from the main street. Soot encrusted him so that he was only recognizable as a human by the occasional rolling flash of the whites of his eyes. He momentarily paused to listen to Minerva's question, then shook his head.

"Don't know no union woman and don't wanna know her. Could lose my job."

"But she is here," Minerva insisted, as he brushed past leaving a sour odor of sweat and grime in his wake. "You know about her. You heard about her."

He waved his empty hand in dismissal. Within a moment, he disappeared into the rabbit warren of hovels.

As soon as he set foot inside the door, the soot coated man spoke to his wife. "Beth, there's a woman outside askin' about the union woman. Man along with her."

Beth went quickly to the door and looked out down the street where Logan and Minerva continued to query the residents they encountered. "I see 'em." She had soft brown eyes and a long nose tipped sharply upward over a wide generous mouth. Her skin was smooth and young and clear.

"Didn't say nothin'. Said I don't know a union woman."

"Wonder what it is they want. Don't look like Government agents, 'though the man could be. Yelena warned us to be careful."

Beth continued to watch the pair inquiring from door to door without success. People were careful not to divulge what they knew. She saw a neighbor leave her hovel and thrust her plump form toward her while glancing back in the direction where Minrva and Logan had passed.

"Did they come to your door," she wheezed.

Beth nodded. "Yes."

"They seem firm in their purpose."

"They do that."

"What do you think?"

"We should let Yelena get a look at 'em first."

"Want me to fetch her?"

"I'll go."

Olga's dark head wobbled in the pool of fat flesh that collared her neck. "Don't look like they're gonna quit their search."

"Don't look like it." Beth called to her husband inside. "I'm going fer Yelena."

"Yep!"

She stepped around the corner and jogged the length of two alleyways to a shack deep within the labrynthian maze. She paused at the door and gave three measured knocks followed by two quick sharp raps. A solid muscled woman opened the door. "Beth." "Mavis."

"Someone come into the street lookin' fer Yelena."

Mavis peered up and down the dirt track.

"Over my way. Two of 'em. A man and a woman. She's older."

"What they wantin' with Yelena?"

"Don't know. Think they're okay, but best not to bring 'em straight on over here. If Yelena wants to see 'em, might be better she come to my place."

"I'll ask her."

Mavis stepped inside the shadowy house and spoke to Yelena silhouetted at the rough wooden table toward the back wall. Beth saw her rise and come to the door.

"Hey, Beth."

"Hey, Yelena."

"What do you think they want?"

"Can't tell, but they look harmless enough. Thought you might want to take a look at 'em."

Yelena nodded. "I'll follow." She trailed a few steps behind Beth on the return walk through the alleyways. They paused at where the alley merged with the dirt street. The two inquirers were becoming distant figures.

"Want me to bring 'em back?"

"Best for now." Yelena watched Beth hurry away through the dust after them. When she reached them, they conferred briefly, then quickly returned. Yelena's perceptive gaze recognized them as a mother and her son, whom she found mildly attractive, but youngish and immature in appearance. The graying mother was like so many others she encountered in her meetings and travels.

Minerva and Logan stopped a few steps short of her. He recognized something about her beyond her hard cold demeanor and the barrier she communicated between herself and men.

"You're the Union Woman ," said Minerva. "I'm Minerva Logan and this is my son, Randolph. You're not what I expected. You're young enough to be my daughter, if I had the good fortune to have had a daughter. But I feel a kinship to you more like that of a sister. You see, my husband died in a mining accident back in Virginia. Randolph was only three at the time. My son and I want to help. That's why we've come. Randolph is a journalist, a writer for *The Mesa Independent*. He can expose the conditions under which the people out here live and work. He can help carry your message forward."

Yelena frowned at Logan. "We met. At the jail. I don't mean to discourage you, but nothing you write will ever convince the mine owners to change how they treat the workers. It takes stopping them where the most damage can be done. The only pain they feel is when their illegal profits are prevented."

"So, you don't believe they care about the workers."

"No, not ever in my experience and not with others, here and in other countries."

"A lot has been written about injustice," said Minerva.

"A pen doesn't draw blood."

"Depending on who holds it."

"How so?"

"Different ideas can be set against each other. Information can be written for a purpose."

Yelena shook her head. "Almost everything written about our struggle has not happened. Ideas aren't enough."

"It's what we have to work with."

"Well, we don't have to stand here in the street." Yelena turned and moved away in a direct manner back the way she had come.

"We have food in the car," said Minerva.

"I'll get it," said Logan. "You go along."

"I'll need your help to find the way," he nodded at Beth. "Car's down the street."

"I'll wait." She watched his receding back.

Yelena and Minerva disappeared into the gloom of the alley.

A half hour later, they were sitting around a wooden kitchen table in the shack where Yelena was housed as a guest. Together they shared Minerva's picnic lunch of tortillas with fresh fruit and dried meat washed down with clay mugs of well water.

"What's most important," said Yelena, "is that there is no unusual or noticeable activity to draw the attention of the goons. We keep things quiet and out of sight. No meetings."

"How do you communicate with the mine workers?"

"I don't directly. Information is passed along through the women. I rely on them as a network to lay the foundation with the men for a strike. They are far more persuasive than I can be alone."

"What about timing?" Logan was scratching rough notes on a pad.

"That will be established in the same way and everyone will know."

"Is it just work stoppage?"

Yelena nodded.

"No sabotage?"

"Not necessary."

"No violence?"

"Only if the goons perpetrate it."

"And if they do?"

"We will fight back."

"How? Miners don't have weapons."

"They have the law."

"The goons have their own law," Logan reminded her. "They'll just shoot and kill until the crowd breaks and runs."

"There won't be a gathering. There won't be a crowd. The miners just won't show up for work. There will be only a negotiation committee. No threat of force."

"How do you make sure all the miners will cooperate."

"Through the influence of their women."

"Surely there are spies."

"We know who they are and they see and hear only what we want them to see and hear."

"You said you have the law."

"There is a Federal law that supports unionization," said Yelena.

"Who enforces it?"

"Until recently, I wasn't sure. No one."

Logan looked at her and waited to hear more.

"The Federal Government is supposed to."

"But it doesn't," he said.

"Hoover runs his own government with the FBI."

"So I've heard."

"I need someone who's sympathetic. No, that isn't right. Someone who has the strength and integrity to stand against corruption."

"Is there someone like that out there?" Logan paused in his writing.

"Could be."

"Do you have a name?"

"Not that I want to see in print."

"Okay, I understand. He could be eliminated."

"He could." After a few moments of silence, Yelena continued. "I want you to take me to him."

Logan stared at her in shock. "And keep it quiet."

"Then you understand."

He nodded.

"Then you might know of him."

"Do you have his name?"

"Gimbel... Howard Gimbel."

Logan again registered surprise. "He works at the Bureau of Indian Affairs."

"It sounds like you know him."

"I do. I've spent a great deal of time at the Bureau writing about Collier's program. And there was an incident."

"What kind of incident?"

"He came here to set up the law and order program on the reservation."

"What happened?"

"He almost killed a Navajo."

Yelena took a deep breath and released it slowly. "Was there just cause?"

"There's never a just cause when it comes to a white man killing an Indian, as far as the Indian's are concerned. No one knows the details except the sheriff...Carmody."

"Carmody—the one who arrested me when I got off the train?"

Logan nodded.

"Strange–all this."

"Where do you know Gimbel from?" asked Logan.

"He's with the FBI."

"And you want to go see him? That sounds crazy."

"I know Gimbel from a long time ago," said Yelena.

"But he works for the Federal Government."

"He does and, in an odd sort of way, I suspect there is an association with why I'm here and what I'm doing."

"Because he knows you from the past?"

"I believe so."

"Does he even know you're here?"

"Yes, he was on my train. That was more than a coincidence."

"What is it you want with him?"

"I want you to take me to him."

Logan's eyes squinted with a quizzical expression. "Why?"

"I'm going to ask him to help me."

"I got the impression you didn't think highly of him," said Logan.

"That may not be true."

"Isn't the FBI trying to stop you?"

"All the time."

"You could be arrested."

"He won't arrest me."

"How do you know? And what about the others?"

"He can keep them away from me. I'm not going to be visible in public. I won't be holding a town meeting."

"When do you want to see him?"

"Do you know where he lives?"

"I do," said Logan, "but I don't think it's a good idea for you to go there."

"That's my decision, not yours."

"I don't want to be responsible for you getting caught."

"The risk is mine."

"It's too dangerous."

Yelena stared at the young man through a long silence. "I live with danger all the time."

"I'm sure you do, but some risks don't have to be taken."

"I have a Russian name. My life is a risk. There is nothing else."

"Maybe–maybe not."

You sound hesitant," said Yelena.

"I'm not hesitant, just concerned. I–we–my Mother and I don't want anything to happen to you."

"That's refreshing. Someone is concerned."

"I'll take you to where he lives."

"That's all I ask."

"We need to wait for nightfall."

"Were you followed coming from town?"

Logan shook his head. "No reason for anyone to follow me."

"So–you said you need a story."

"They're expecting one."

"They?"

Logan again hesitated. "Well, my editor."

"What's his name?"

"Clyde Shreve."

"He sent you out here to find me."

"Where do you come from, Yelena?"

"Does it matter? Why?"

"Are you from Russia?"

"I thought you wanted to report on the need for a union."

"Getting to know who you are can make a difference."

"In what way?"

"For readers of the newspaper. It gives a face to what you're doing and why."

"People don't have any problem relating to what I'm doing. They understand. They're being exploited. That's personal enough."

"Well, let me put it a differently," said Logan. "I would like to know who you are, at least something more about you."

"My parents came from Russia. I was a professional violist. My sister played the violin."

Logan stared at her, yet another surprise. "What?"

"I answered your question. When I was a girl, I played the viola. My sister and I played in concerts with orchestras. At the time, we were considered child prodigies."

Logan quickly jotted a note. What Yelena said was an odd and indirect opening to the information he sought, but he followed her lead. "I'm listening."

And indeed, they all were listening.

As Yelena unfolded the story of her creative young life, a profound discovery came over Logan. He would do anything to protect her. He had instantly fallen in love with her. His feelings for her tended to interfere with his promise to deliver her to Howard Gimbel, whom Logan suspected held some attraction for her. She had not mentioned him in the story of her past, but she had alluded to a boy who had been a close friend of hers and her sister. Logan also worried that Yelena could easily walk into a trap. Gimbel might pretend to be sympathetic to her cause, then arrange with Halen Braun to arrest her. Logan vowed to never let that happen.

Chapter 23
REUNITED

Yelena's unwavering stare met Logan's repeated glances in the rearview mirror. The fact that she was always looking unnerved him. *Why is she staring at me,* he wondered. In reality, he imagined she was looking at him. Only twice during the two hour drive through the desert night did she catch him watching her in the rearview mirror. At that, the brief interludes occurred when the car veered off the dirt track due to his lack of attention on the unveiling dark road ploughed by the headlights yellow glare.

At such moments, Minerva also noticed his distraction and once uttered, "The road is narrow, Randolph."

He grunted and restored the errant tires to the ruts.

They rode with the windows open and the sweet smell of sage swept over them.

The scattered lights of Mesa emerged as a low cluster through the brush and cactus and did not appear to appreciably increase in size as the vehicle drew closer.

Yelena spoke. "Just take me directly to his house."

Logan looked up sharply as though he had been poked by a sharp stick. "We were thinking you might like some dinner first. You must be hungry. I know I am."

"I appreciate your hospitality, but I'm expecting Mr. Gimbel to feed me."

"Expecting? What if he places you under arrest?"

"He won't arrest me."

"What makes you so sure?"

"Something I know about him."

"Well, I can't just let you walk in there alone."

"When we arrive, I don't want you to stay," Yelena ordered

"You mean just leave you and drive away?"

"That's what I want."

Logan thought a moment. "I can come back in an hour. Of course, you'll be staying with us for the night."

"I will be staying at Mr. Gimbel's."

A sharp silence cut between them. "We have a spare room."

"It's of no concern."

Logan was grateful for the darkness that masked his rising blush and the cords of anger that strained his neck. "You sure you don't want some dinner first?" He croaked.

"I'm sure."

After another mile, Logan suddenly pulled to a stop and left the motor idling.

"What's wrong?" asked Minerva. "Is something wrong with the car."

Without responding, he opened the door, stepped out onto the dirt road and paced back and forth in the dual beam of the headlights breaking their swath with his giant black shadow.

"What's the matter, Randolph?" His mother craned her head out the passenger side window. "What are you doing?"

He stopped and gazed off beyond the dusky haze of the lights with his back to the car. Then he slowly turned and walked to the open door, braced himself in the doorframe and looked in at Yelena.

"There's something I have to tell you." He waited.

"I'm listening."

"The FBI is forcing me to spy on you."

"Someone is always spying on me, Randolph."

"Not like this. If I don't help them–well, at least one of them. He'll put me in prison."

"For what?"

"Conspiracy."

"There is no conspiracy. What I'm doing is according to the law."

"His name is Halen Braun. He's a law unto himself, if you know what I mean."

"I do. I've been fighting men like that all my life. So now that you're spying on me, what does he expect will happen?"

"I don't have an answer for that."

"I do. He wants me out of the way."

"That's what worries me," he said, "what he might do to you."

"This is not the first time I've been in this position."

"But you're risking your life."

"We are all at risk. We're all vulnerable. There are no guarantees."

He wasn't certain how to respond. What came out was, "How do you know you can trust Gimbel?"

"I don't. But he'll trust me and that's what I need."

"I'll be there if you need me."

"It sounds like you need to watch your back, not mine."

"I'm aware of that. I know I'll have to deal with Halen Braun somewhere down the road. At least for a while, I can stall him."

"You'll have to do more than that."

Their eyes met and held. He reseated himself at the wheel, pulled the door closed, and looked at her in the rearview mirror. A moment later, he put the car in gear and continued on into the town.

He left the motor idling as Yelena stepped out of the back seat. She paused to lean in at the driver's window. "I want to thank you. You have both been very kind."

Logan looked straight ahead. Minerva raised her hand in farewell. They watched Yelena walk to the front door of the adobe house.

"It's time to go," said Minerva. "We have to let her do this in her own way."

"What can I do?"

"Protect her. Write your story carefully in support of her and expose the FBI for their fascist conspiracy."

Logan turned the car and they drove away slowly down the quiet dirt sweet.

Yelena knocked lightly and waited. She heard a chair scrape back and footsteps coming to the door. When Howard opened the door, he involuntarily stepped backward in shock.

"Yelena, what are you doing here?"

"Is that any way to greet an old friend?"

"What has happened? After the train, I never expected to see you again."

"May I come in or do I have to be interrogated standing in the doorway."

"Of course, of course, come in. Please, come in and sit down." He offered her the chair he had just vacated.

"Thank you." She stepped into the room while he peered out into the night at the receding tail lights of Randolph's car, then closed the door.

"Who brought you here?"

"Friends, the young newswriter, Randolph Logan and his mother. I believe you know him." Yelena loosened her comb and allowed her hair to fall about her shoulders.

"His mother? How did you come to meet them?"

"Stop acting like an agent, Howard. This is not an investigation. They came to see me so Randolph Logan could write a story for his newspaper. Why don't you offer me a drink."

Howard stared at her in disbelief. "There must be something going on here."

"There is, Howard. You and I are going to start over. We're going to talk. But first, we're going to have a drink."

"What would you like?" He nervously hovered away toward the icebox.

"Didn't think you'd ask and, also, I'm quite hungry The family I'm staying with does their best to keep me fed. Food is not always plentiful in my line of work."

"I'm not much of a cook. My housekeeper makes a meal for me before she leaves at night. But I have leftovers I can heat up."

"Who is your housekeeper."

"Rosa...Rosa Guiterrez. She was recommended."

"Is she a good cook?"

"Actually, yes, but it's all Mexican. That's all she knows. She doesn't speak any English so I can't explain to her about other ways to prepare food."

"Not to sound ungracious, but the sooner that food gets on the table, the better. All I've had today is a cup of coffee and a piece of stale bread."

"Yes, of course." Howard pulled open the door of the icebox. He reached for a cup hanging from a wall hook, then hesitated. "Whiskey–tequila–wine?"

"The FBI must pay you well to keep a fully stocked bar."

He stared at her. "How did you know I'm with the FBI?"

"Oh, Howard," Yelena's lovely mouth angled into a smirk. "You have no idea how obvious you are. First of all, you look and dress and act like one of them. I'm surprised they didn't think to send you undercover as a coal miner. Are you supposed to assassinate me, the evil union organizer?"

"For god's sake, Yelena."

"What is it they told you to do to me?"

"They weren't clear about that. They just wanted me to keep an eye on you."

"They who?"

"The Chief."

"Is that what you call Hoover these days, the Chief?"

"I don't call him anything. I never see him. None of the agents do. We get our orders through his assistant director, Clyde Tolson."

"And what orders did Clyde give to you?"

Howard turned to face her from where he was pouring two tumblers of tequila. "Yelena, you have nothing to fear from me. I would never do anything to harm you. That's why they gave me this assignment, to test my loyalty to my sworn duty and to the Bureau."

"And now you've failed the test. You're standing here talking to me and you haven't done a thing. Anyone else would slam me with a billy club and throw me in jail."

"I'm doing my best to protect you. Coming here tonight was not a good idea."

"That makes two of you who want to protect me, you and the reporter. He's head over heels in love with me. What's your excuse?"

Howard handed her a drink. "I guess I don't have one. I valued our friendship."

"Is that all this is about, our childhood friendship?"

"I don't expect anything more. It's enough for me."

"So you just want to be my protector, my body guard of sorts."

"I would believe in anything you do, Yelena."

"Then you're in trouble, my friend."

"How is that?"

"I'm your enemy. You fraternize with me and you're a traitor. Hoover can put you away for the rest of your life or even have you executed."

He took a long swallow of his drink. "There was a time when I believed in what I was doing, but that involved going after hardened criminals who had broken the law. You're not a criminal and the people you're trying to help aren't criminals. I grew up with them. I was one of them. I lived like them."

"The law changed, you know. It allows me to do what I do."

"I know."

"But the FBI and the big companies, the big money they shield don't care about that law."

"I care about you."

"Then you must care about that law."

Howard finished his drink and poured another. "I don't think I'm cut out to be an agent anymore."

"You were until they gave you this assignment. You still are. They placed you in a difficult position. It takes a special kind of person to stand against them. You show a sense of humanity and they can't have that."

Howard stared into her mesmerizing brown eyes. She held out her empty glass.

"The pay stinks," he said. "But in these times, I'm lucky to have a job."

"In these times, anyone is lucky to have a job."

As he handed her the refilled glass, their arms touched. Howard felt he should pull away, but Yelena did not move. Her searching gaze never left his face. He felt edgy and self- conscious, like she dominated him with a glance when he was a boy.

"You're a good kind man, Howard. There aren't many of you in the world. You're what an agent should be." She paused. "I want you to know that I'm glad you're protecting me."

She reached up with her other hand and touched the side of his face and tenderly pulled it to her own. Their lips touched in a tenuous kiss that opened into a sudden groping passionate embrace constrained only by their each holding a glass in the other hand.

"It's more than friendship," muttered Howard. "I love you. I have always loved you."

They frantically slammed their glasses down on the table and made a clumsy stumbling waltz to fall onto his single bed. Their kisses probed deeply into their mouths as their hands grabbed and tore off each other's clothing. As they finally came together, their breath heaved in desperate gasps until they lay quietly entwined in each other's arms and fell asleep listening to the crickets serenading them beyond the open window in the vast desert night.

***

Howard pulled two clay crockery bowls containing albondigas soup in one and rice and beans in another. He shoveled the casserole into a large iron skillet, poured the soup into a saucepan and turned on the gas burners. He brought Yelena a clay mug filled with cold water from the tap. She drank thirstily while he went to the cupboard for a clay bottle of tequila. Pulling the stone stopper, he poured each of them what he estimated to be two shots into separate mugs. He plucked a lime from the fruit bowl on the counter, sliced it in half and squeezed the tangy juice into the tequila. He handed her a cup and raised his own drink in salute. She acknowledged and put the strong liquid to her lips. The acrid fumes caused her eyes to water and she coughed.

"You all right?"

She nodded. "Never been better."

Howard stepped back to the stove and stirred the soup and the casserole with a large wooden spoon. "Why wouldn't you talk to me on the train?" He remained with his back facing her.

"For many years, I've tried to forget the past. Seeing you on the train was a painful reminder. I couldn't talk to you then."

"And now?"

"We can talk about anything."

Howard continued to stir. "I have a confession to make."

"I'm interested."

He turned to face her. "I should never tell you this, but my being on that train was not a coincidence."

"Of course not. I knew."

"You knew. How?"

"You were always uncomplicated and transparent when I knew you as a boy. You haven't changed. You don't make a convincing spy."

He smiled. "Mm, I had a feeling you suspected something."

"From the moment you walked past me and turned around. I've had far too many men spy on me. Usually they're obvious by trying not to appear obvious. As soon as you told me you worked for the Federal Government, the Bureau of Indian Affairs, you confirmed my suspicion. You were never west of the Allegheny River. What would you know about Indians?"

Howard remained silent for a moment. "That obvious."

"That obvious." She took another sip of tequila and sensed a slow spreading warmth and release of tension as the alcohol diffused into her bloodstream that still coursed with the alive sensation of their love making.

"I really don't know why the bureau sent me out here."

"You work for Hoover and you haven't figured him out. He's afraid. He's afraid of life, of anything different that threatens his narrow view of the world. He's a sick crunched up ugly little toad who's been given the power to ruin people's lives. All people want is to live a good life, Howard."

"I know. I know."

"Do you?"

"Yes, I know what poverty is. I know what it does to people."

"Do you know what wealth and power are and what they do to people?"

Howard's silence acknowledged that he knew.

"It corrupts them, because they're afraid of losing it. So they will do anything to keep it and to increase it. They have everything, but they don't care. They don't care about the conditions that others live and work in to support them. They want to keep the workers in fearful servitude, under control. The workers are the producers. Without them, there would be nothing, not even wealth, nothing." Yelena wiped a tear. She had never cried before. *It must be the tequila,* she thought. "What made you want to work for that man?"

"I don't think I've ever worked for him. I worked for the ideal that he stood for. I don't think of myself as working for him. From what I've learned, what I know, I despise him as just another bureaucratic despot, only worse. He's a fascist who does real harm."

"How close is that food to being ready?" she asked. "I need to eat something."

Howard stirred the soup and casserole and steam began to rise. "Almost ready."

"It smells good."

"Rosa is a good cook. I've gotten used to Mexican food. Took a while to get used to chili peppers, but I did. Actually developed a taste for them, as long as they aren't too hot."

Yelena tossed back the rest of her tequila and set the cup down hard on the table, causing him to turn sharply.

"I'm serving it now," he said. "Should be warm enough." He grabbed a plate from the cupboard and piled the rice, chicken, and beans on it and set it in front of her.

"Well, I could eat with my hands or just stick my face in it like a dog," she laughed.

"Oh, of course, just in a rush here." Howard snatched a fork and spoon from a drawer and placed them in her outstretched hand. She dropped the fork and dug in with the large spoon, ravenously shoveling rice and chicken and beans into her mouth.

"Do you like it? Does it taste okay?"

She mumbled and moaned.

"You don't have to answer right away."

"It's good. It's good." Half masticated food spittled from her lips.

Howard thought her ravenous attack of the food made her all the more beautiful. He spooned soup into a large bowl and served it slightly aside.

"That smells delicious. In a minute... I'll get to it in a minute. Oh," She shoved her cup forward. "Another."

"Another?" "Yes."

Howard poured her two fingers more of the tequila and squeezed in another lime.

"More," she said. "Just pour it in."

Twenty minutes later, Yelena's rapacious ingestion slowed, faltered, and came to a halt."

"Feeling better?" Howard watched her closely.

"Feeling full. Ate too fast. Sorry about my manners."

"No need to apologize. Whatever you do, whatever you want is fine."

She looked up at him. "You're not drinking." She raised her cup.

He gulped his tequila and grimaced at the long sliding burn flowing down his gullet.

"Good, Howard, that's good. You know, in spite of the years, I think we're going to get along."

"We're friends, Yelena. I've always been your friend."

Yelena nodded, took another bite of food, then stopped. "We're more than friends now, Howard. Too late. We're lovers. You need to change your way of thinking. Can't eat anymore."

"You did a good job."

"A good job. Can't ask for more. So, tell me what happened to you, Howard. What brought you to where you are?"

"I was a law student. I needed a job. The Bureau recruited me."

"I mean before that."

"Before that?"

"One day, we were gone–my mother, father, Lilya and me. What did you do? You told me on the train you tried to find us?"

"Yes, I did try to find you. I asked people. I looked everywhere. You said Lilya died. How did she die?"

Yelena could not speak for a minute. "She took her own life. They found her in the river."

"But why? She had you."

"Having me was not enough. I was just part of something larger in her life. Mama and Papa and her music were gone. She saw them all brutally destroyed. I always thought of her as a musical spirit. She was far more a musician than I ever was."

"You were good. You were wonderful. You were both wonderful."

"At that time, we lived for the sound we made together and with the orchestra. We became a single existence, a single being. Experience and memories are all we have and I do cherish them. So what became of you, Howard? What did you do?"

"I didn't want to be poor. I didn't want to live all my life in the poverty I saw around me. In studying economics, I came to understand some of the causes of where we are as a country, the financial pyramids and holding companies whose stock was worthless. Most of the population was in debt buying on installment plans before the crash. We have too many small banks and no deposit insurance program. And there's more, much more, an imbalance of trade. The Government has to put money back into circulation so people can buy again. But even the President won't get behind deficit financing so we can restore employment to the people. But if you look at Europe, like it or not, we're going to be pulled into that war, and we will be spending money in a big way. Unfortunately, a war needs production. It stimulates the economy."

"You sound like you should be on FDR's staff instead of working for that fascist, Hoover."

"Roosevelt wants to get us into the war even though it's not our war. He's an odd and interesting man, a great leader on the one hand, and he has some personal ambitions and agendas on the other.

"I'm also here on one of his recovery programs. At least that's my front. Now that I am here, I believe in what he's trying to do for these people, for all the people. We've seen the banks fail. People rushed to reclaim their money and the doors were closed and locked in their faces. The foreclosure of mortgages and liquidation of companies made us into a destitute country. I've seen riots at garbage dumps. Starving people fighting over scraps of food. I've seen armies of unemployed men and women lined up at the cities' breadlines and soup kitchens for a meal. I've seen the suffering and disillusionment on their faces because our Government has failed them. I counted myself among the fortunate few who have a paying job.

"There's something about people though. They don't give up. They'll do anything to survive. There are armies of peddlers on the streets. Have you seen the white duck caps sold by hawkers. Crowds look like fields of cotton. Vendors are selling every kind of merchandise they can along the sidewalks—-jewelry, clothing, books, pencils, apples, toys and games and even small animals.

"President Herbert Hoover did nothing to help the country. He just let it sink. He wouldn't do anything about the depression. He ignored what was written about him in the newspapers. Thanks to no Government intervention, the industrialists profited. If FDR had not been elected, we wouldn't have any financial system. We needed him to bring the country out of economic paralysis."

He had just won a landslide election by more than seven million votes. The people believed in his campaign song, "Happy Days Are Here Again." The citizens of America were going to get a "New Deal," and "The only thing to fear is fear itself."

Howard had been among the amassed cheering thousands at FDR's inaugural address and parade. The cold biting wind that swept over the immense crowd that stretched for miles along Pennsylvania Avenue did nothing to diminish their upward looks of hope and expectation of deliverance from the social and economic despair in which the people of America floundered.

"It was his voice," thought Howard. "The way he spoke, the words he said, the confidence he gave us. He is our leader. I will go anywhere and do anything he asks of me." Like the rest of America, Howard had succumbed to the charisma of this man with crippled legs and a brilliant mind, a man who truly cared about the people of this country. This tall broad-shouldered bespectacled imposing man with the fatherly god-like presence and calm sensibility of a long awaited messiah. The inspirational words FDR spoke on that day were burned into Howard's memory, as the newly inaugurated President addressed the silent crowd focused on him.

"This is a day of national consecration ... I am certain that my fellow Americans, expect me to address them with candor and decision. Now is the time to speak the truth, the whole truth, frankly and boldly. Nor need we shrink from honestly facing conditions in our country today. This great nation will endure as it has endured, will revive and will prosper. So, first of all, let me assert my firm belief that the only thing we have to fear is fear itself—- nameless, unreasoning, unjustified terror which paralyzes needed efforts to convert retreat into advance. In every dark hour of our national life, a leadership of frankness and vigor has met that understanding and support of the people themselves which is essential to victory. I am convinced that you will again give that support to leadership in these critical days.

"If I read the temper of our people correctly, we now realize as we have never realized before our interdependence on each other; that we cannot merely take, but give, as well; that if we are to go forward, we must move as a trained and loyal army willing to sacrifice for the good of a common discipline. For the trust reposed in me, I will return the courage and devotion that befit the time. We do not distrust the future of essential democracy. The people of the United States have not failed. In their need they have registered a mandate that they want direct, vigorous action. They have asked for discipline and direction under leadership. They have made me the instrument of their wishes. In the spirit of the gift I take it."

Howard identified himself with the throng of men and women who rushed to contribute their ideas and talent to re-stabilizing the country. FDR opened his doors and welcomed their energy and integrity in conceptualizing and implementing the programs and initiatives of his administration. These New Dealers were largely Democrats who believed that the collective will of the people with faith in their Government could accomplish the goals set out by their President.

Conservative critics and elitists labeled them communist sympathizers and spies, and Howard found himself an unwilling accomplice on the side of the law imposed by J. Edgar Hoover to repress people Howard admired.

As he drove through the Washington streets to his home in the suburbs, he became acutely aware of his surroundings, the many blocks of stolid monolithic gray Government buildings that housed the managing mechanism of the country. He would be leaving this significant influence on his life and following his destiny into the American interior.

Recent movie entertainment was filled with the reversal of sex roles and strong feminist models. In *Female*, Ruth Chatterton played the CEO of a large automobile manufacturing company with the management style of a commanding drill sergeant by day and sexually sampling various male employees by night, then casting them aside when they mistook sex for love.

Audiences responded to the use of sex to break down class barriers in *Red-Headed Woman* with Jean Harlow seducing her wealthy respectably married boss.

In Government politics, the behind the scenes maneuvering and deal-making to either push a bill through Congress or to prevent its passage were always associated with the needs and wants of special interest groups represented by lobbyists who bribed and prevailed upon the Congress to cast votes in their favor while his party endorsed and supported the industrial elite.

Yelena realized it was a world in which women held no influence until the visible emergence of Eleanor Roosevelt, who became Yelena's second hero.

Eleanor had been speaking in public on her husband's behalf for years during his convalescence from polio that crippled him, but did not deter him from his goal to become President.

Yelena admired Eleanor Roosevelt for becoming a National leader in her own right, not just being the hostess at the White

House. The President's wife championed the National Child Labor amendment against the exploitation of children in the workplace and ensured they received an education. She spoke out against hazardous work environments that threatened the health of factory workers and people affected by the proximity of toxic dumpsites and picked up the banner of The National Consumers League with the words, "There is something fundamentally wrong with a civilization which tolerates conditions such as many of our people are facing today. We talk of a 'New Deal' and we believe in it. But we will have no 'new deal' unless some of us are willing to sit down and think this situation out. It may require some drastic changes in our rather settled ideas and we must not be afraid of them."

In Meridel Le Seur's book *Women on the Breadlines*, Howard had read about the plight of homeless women who "suffered in silence" and "tended to disappear." The editor of the magazine *New Masses* exhorted readers to read *The Working Woman* and join the Communist Party. Eleanor Roosevelt took up their cause to establish a New Deal for women and redirect their options from a widespread revolutionary movement. Her radical demands and involvement with the Women's Trade Union League made press headlines and met with sustained resistance, as she campaigned for equal rights for women in the Civil Works Administration and the Works Progress Administration.

Howard knew about the plight of women, but typical of the men of his generation, he did not comprehend the significance of the social problem and was not concerned, since he had no authority to affect it. In fact, his new assignment, under direct order from J. Edgar Hoover, was in opposition to the plans of the President of the United States and his wife. Howard was to prevent an influential woman from promoting unionism and the welfare of workers, men and women alike. A conflict existed even between FDR and Eleanor with FDR's failure to acknowledge women in the formation of the Civilian Conservation Corps which provided jobs for three million men. Women were not included.

Hoover was notorious for placing bugs and wire taps in people's residences and phones for the slightest personal grievance or suspicion he might hold against them. Howard's partner at the time, Tim Landon, believed that Hoover was a voyeur and just wanted to listen in on husbands and their wives having sexual intercourse.

He remembered hearing, as a boy, that the Charleston and the foxtrot were sinful and wild because they were dances of carefree and amoral people, many of them rich and many of them criminals. So at an early age, Howard was imbued with the belief that wealth and criminality went hand in hand with that kind of music, which it sometimes did in night clubs and speakeasies. As he grew older and wiser, he learned to discriminate and to appreciate the prowess of legitimate success and the laws that supported it to the extent he had become one of the enforcers.

Swing had developed out of the earlier ensemble playing style of Dixieland and hotel room and concert bands into a dense rhythm driven sound using a hard riff against which the melody could be played with long improvisations by the sidemen. As the reed-based sounds of the smaller hot jazz ensembles evolved into larger bands, trumpets and trombones were counter-balanced by saxophones and clarinets with the rhythm carried by piano, expanded drums, and guitar supported by a string bass.

Among band leaders, Howard had many favorites—- Benny Goodman, Glenn Miller, Tommy Dorsey and Artie Shaw. The music varied from ballads to frenetic jump tunes played in the ballrooms and dance halls that Howard and Tim Landon and his wife would frequent on Saturday nights, outings that soon came to an end.

"Did you know FDR gave Hoover the order to spy on American citizens? You, me, anybody and everybody that Hoover held any suspicion about or even disagreed with Roosevelt. Hell, Hoover even spied on Roosevelt's wife."

"Eleanor?"

"Yes, Eleanor. In some ways, she's a bit like you. She worked for people who are less fortunate. She's an advocate of the rights and needs of the disadvantaged and the poor. She's in the League of Women Voters and the Women's Trade Union League."

"No wonder Hoover spies on her. Does she know her husband set her up?"

Howard laughed. "It's not funny, but the irony of it is. I met her once. She's a graceful, attractive, and charming woman. She gave FDR advice on The New Deal. She lobbied for the National Labor Relations Act and the Fair Labor Standards Act. She visits people wherever they are living in poverty and enduring hardships. She's more personally in the front lines of The Depression than anyone else in the Government. I've read her articles. I've heard her speak."

"And Hoover's trying to rub me out."

"Have you ever thought of going to her yourself? If you worked for her, you wouldn't have to put up with Hoover and his goons and chasing you and spying on you all the time and the Pinkertons busting heads at your rallies."

Yelena shook her head. "I don't think that would be possible. Hoover has me branded as a communist. If I even tried to approach the White House, I'd be arrested as a bomb throwing radical and deported. The only reason Eleanor isn't is because she's the President's wife."

"I never wanted to become a man like my father," said Howard, "especially because of what he did to you and your family. He wasn't alone in this. There were many others, an army of men recruited by Hoover when he was just a small time bureaucrat. He was a file clerk working for the Attorney General, Mitchell Palmer. I didn't understand what was happening, but thousands of innocent people were being arrested and deported on the suspicion of being communists. Hoover has been on a witch hunt ever since."

"Yet, here you are working for him."

"When I was a boy, my father always pointed out to me that the important men wore suits and bowler hats and smoked cigars."

"Do you smoke cigars?"

"No, and I hate bowler hats."

"So what was the attraction?"

"Those men didn't work in the factories and they didn't do rough labor. They were businessmen. They were smart enough to have other people work for them and brutal enough to exploit them for their own personal profit."

"Or more likely, corrupt enough," said Yelena, "but go on. You're more sophisticated when it comes to business and politics since you were a child."

"I went to law school. Anyway, I hated my father after what he did in the Palmer raids. I never forgave him right up until the day he died in a factory explosion, not caused by terrorists. But I was also realistic when it came to survival. I started off working in a bakery. I sold newspapers on street corners, then graduated to working as a stock clerk in a grocery market. It was good to be close to food. Food is what everybody worked to be able to have, except those who took food for granted. It didn't take me long to realize that whoever controlled the production of food had power.

"I was never interested in power. I was just supporting my mother and me and making sure we had food on the table. But I wasn't going to be a boy forever and I did not want to go work in a factory. I wanted to change things. I wanted to make a difference."

"Did you set out to become an FBI agent?"

"No, the thought never entered my mind. I hated and despised J. Edgar Hoover."

"Do you still hate and despise him?"

"I think I understand him. I don't agree with him. I despise him for what he did and the kind of man he is."

"In your mind, does that justify what he did and what he's doing now?"

"No, of course not. But I didn't join the bureau because of Hoover and what he stands for. I'm an agent for what he doesn't stand for."

"And what is that, Howard? What do you stand for?"

"When we graduated, we took an oath to uphold the laws of the Constitution."

"And you think Hoover stands for that?"

"No, he doesn't even believe in the Constitution. But I do. He has distorted it for his own political purposes. Hoover considers himself above the law."

Yelena suddenly rose from the table. "Would you hold me? Now, I want you to hold me now."

Howard stepped over to her. She raised her arms and encircled his neck and shoulders as he slipped his arms around her waist. Her body pressing up against his aroused him again. She nestled her head against his chest. He detected the smell of sage and smoke in her thick dark hair. They remained still and quiet for several moments. Howard suppressed the impulse to talk to her. He decided to just follow her lead, as he had done when they were children.

***

Randolph Logan determined he was the only obstacle between Halen Braun and Yelena and he imagined, as infatuated writers do, that he would compete for her love. So he distrusted Howard Gimbel as an adversary. He believed Yelena could not possibly love Gimbel, because he represented the forces that wanted to crush her. The perception was a manifestation of his own envy.

He wrote his story about the history of the Wooten Mining Company in a manner that factually presented Stark and his politicians and did not shade their corruption. His coverage of Yelena Ivanov and her union organization activities exposed the collusion of the FBI in circumventing the Constitution and repressing the right of workers to join unions.

Halen Braun, on behalf of the FBI, had not told him to not be identified in the story. So Randolph took a risk and included direct quotes attributed to Braun. After all, Randolph reasoned, he was supposed to find the facts and tell the news.

Being a writer, he could make up anything he wanted about Yelena and Braun would never know the difference. More importantly, as long as Braun believed he was reading what was described as the truth, he would not throw Logan into a Federal prison, a proposition that did not sit well with the young man. Braun never read the story before it went to press. Shreve warned Randolph there would be harsh repercussions. A few months later once The United Press published and widely distributed his story, the truth came crashing down on his head.

Chapter 24
PRESSURE

Lee Stark was incensed at what was happening out in Coal Town and he let Halen Braun know the extent of his rage. His words still rang in Braun's ears as to how uncertain his future was with Stark's company once he resigned from the FBI

"You're supposed to be the Federal Government here, Braun. Not Gimbel. How did he turn things around? Answer me that?"

Like some raging potentate, Stark had summoned Braun. With a full black beard and wearing a black shirt and short tailed black suit of an 1890's cut and with an ever present pearl handled six shooter revolver slung low on his right hip, he looked more like a fierce desperado than the president of a modern mining company. Whenever he came into town, he stalked along the street as though expecting to engage in a gunfight at any moment.

Braun did not like to be summoned. He was always the one to order others, to be in charge. He did not like situations that did not go as planned. Now as he drove across the desert flats from Santa Fe to Mesa, he seethed with anger.

Braun had sworn to uphold the law, but he had learned early in his career that the law was selective. Those who controlled the wealth of the country were exempt, unless they came by their wealth by clearly illegal means. Going after gangsters, bootleggers, and killers did not require sorting out as to the degree of violation. The more subtle manipulation of finances by corporate robber barons and their exploitation of the labor that propped them up was supported by private interests and influence in the Government as The American Way termed *laissez faire* economics.

In time, Braun had come to feel like a lacky, a legal servant to the privileged class. Rather than continuing to look the other way, he aspired to join them. His salary not being sufficient, he endeavored to increase his personal capital by encouraging certain criminals to offer him bribes to avoid arrest. These arrangements were always negotiated alone. He ensured that he rarely worked in the company of another agent. His acts went undetected and certain big and small time criminals went free. He concluded a sufficient number of arrests so as to divert the attention of his superiors. Eventually, he rose up in the Bureau ranks to become a Special Agent In Charge.

His assignment to the remote region of Santa Fe, New Mexico removed him even further from the control of the Washington Bureau office. He was perceived by Hoover and Tyson as being an ethical and reliable self starter who did not require close supervision. Meeting and negotiating with Lee Stark did not change that perception. Stark's interests were the interests of the Federal Government monopolies and pork barrel legislation, despite the aggressive anti-corruption tactics of Secretary of The Interior, Harold Ickes, to destroy that influence. Ickes was a man of integrity on FDR's staff in designing The New Deal policies of the President.

Braun knew he would remain in Stark's favor only as long as he successfully did his bidding. His dream of gaining wealth and affluence rode on his ability to keep the way clear for Stark to continue his exploitive operations unhindered.

Lately, there were moments when his father would appear to him in his dreams. Braun would wake wondering at these visitations. He had always been a boy in the presence of his father, Augustus Braun, an imposing iron-willed man who quoted scripture and was ideally suited to his job as a prison guard.

Though Augustus was long deceased, his dark-bearded image and the influence of splintering blue eyes and deep commanding voice ebbed and flowed in Halen's mind like the resounding knell of his conscience. It was to prove to Augustus that he was worthy of his father's approval that Halen had worked his way through college and joined the FBI.

"The laws of man are the laws of God. I uphold the laws of God." How many times had Halen heard his father speak those words. They were emblazoned in his memory like a scriptural canon.

After his father died, of a stroke, Halen felt freed from the invisible chains of his influence. The immediacy of his father's death was followed by a conscious attempt to block Augustus from his life. At first, he hesitantly experimented with the illegal pleasures of debauchery in opposition and defiance of his father to prove to himself that he could live independent of the force and the fury that had dominated his young life and the lives of his mother and three brothers and two sisters.

They had been born and raised on a small farm at the outskirts of Rockmart, Georgia, a remote mountain town in the southern foothills of the Appalachians. For every day of his childhood years, Halen watched his father ride off on his horse at dawn to the state prison at Emerson, ten miles away. Halen's mother and brothers and sisters were relegated to growing crops and raising hogs and chickens and keeping a small dairy herd of five milk cows.

In addition, they were expected to attend school, which meant a two mile walk each day over a rutted dirt road that muddied with spring and summer rains and froze in the winter.

Because of the farm and the steady income his father provided as a prison guard, the family lived in a consistently well-provided manner until the sudden unexpected death of Augustus. The farm alone was not enough to sustain the large family. One by one, the children migrated to Atlanta in search of their individual futures.

Halen worked in a textile mill by night and attended college during the day. He graduated near the top of his class, but could not afford law school. He took a job in law enforcement and his record opened the door to employment with the FBI.

When Halen arrived, Stark shouted at him as he walked through the door. "Braun, you son of a bitch, I have some news for you. You've been trying so hard to find that union bitch and she showed up in my office this morning."

"What? She just walked in here?"

"Oh, yes, she was here all right."

"In Mesa? She came all the way here into town?"

"No, she was at the mine office in Coal Town."

"And you let her walk away?"

"Spare me, Braun. Just spare me. She had an FBI agent with her who works for you."

"I don't believe this. Who was he?"

"He showed us his badge and said the miners have a right to form a union and to collective bargaining under the Federal law that fucking asshole Roosevelt signed."

"The only law out here is what we decide. You know that. I stand one-hundred percent behind you and so does J. Edgar Hoover. Did he give you his name?"

"Gimbel–Howard Gimbel."

"Jesus Christ! That rat fucker. His days are numbered. Don't worry. I'll take care of him. He'll be out of here on the next train east or someone is going all the way to get his wallet at a time he shouldn't have been walking alone down a dark alley. You understand what I'm saying?"

"I understand. Sure, I understand. But what about the goddamn woman. What're you gonna do about her?" Stark hunched aggressively forward across his desk.

"I have someone working on it. He's a spy and I have a lead on an assassin, Clayton Byrne. Lives in Coal Town. Works in the mine. Did you actually see her?"

"See her? Shit, I could've reached out and touched her. I wanted to kill her with my own bare hands."

"No, I've got someone who can take care of that matter. But we need to find her."

"The people in Coal Town keep her well hidden."

"Well, Braun, let's celebrate your failure, thus far. Have a drink. Have a cigar."

The blood rose visibly from Braun's neck and spread across his wide face. "She'll be gone soon enough."

"Not soon enough for me."

"There's nothing she can do. They won't strike."

"She's already doing it. The goddamn workers are going to strike if I don't meet their demands."

"It won't last. They can't demand anything. She won't last. We arrest Communists and put them away."

"She's there and she's doing it right under our goddamn noses."

"It's only temporary, Stark. She's only temporary."

"I'll believe it when I see her dead or behind bars. If that doesn't happen, you'll be temporary."

Braun turned on his heel and slammed out of the office..

***

Unlike Halen Braun, their Special Agent in Charge, Agents Ken Ferguson and Melbourne Stuart complied with J. Edgar Hoover's G-man dress code of wearing a gray suit and fedora hat. Their only concession to living and working in the Santa Fe, New Mexico office was to wear matching pairs of black leather western boots.

After six rings, Ferguson answered the phone that had interrupted his nap. Unless Agent Braun was in the office, Ken dozed off after lunch on a regular basis. He lurched to an upright position in his chair. A lack of physical activity coupled with his wife's cooking had increased the sag of his gut and heaviness in his legs.

"FBI Santa Fe. Agent Ken Ferguson here."

"This is Clyde Tolson speaking."

Ferguson's sharp intake of breath was audible over the line. "Yes, yes sir, Agent Tolson, how can I help you, sir?"

Realizing the assistant director was on the line, Melbourne sprang energetically to his feet, a move that left Ken feeling envious. Mel was an athelete. He ran miles in the desert in the cool mornings before dawn. He possessed a lean body and a prominent clean jawline and chiseled sun-burned face. Ken's bull neck was morphing into a fold of bewhiskered fat pulled downwards by gravity. His rosy alcoholic cheeks had begun to fade to a precipitating gray pallor. He was still strong as an ox, a large man, just slow. Melbourne was divorced, single, and pushing thirty-five. Ken was married, the frustrated father of two older heavy-set teen-age girls, and pushing forty.

Most of their cases had occurred in and around Santa Fe, a quiet town dominated by political and ranching interests, which were the basis of the state's economy along with mining and the recent discovery of oil reserves.

The strategic location of one federal and two state banks had attracted robberies several times during the past five years resulting in shootouts and harrowing car chases after bandits determined to reach the U.S.–Mexican Border.

Their most challenging case had been to discover the source of a counterfeit ring. The investigation had lead them across the Southwest following a trail of banks to San Antonio, Texas. They had coordinated with the FBI office there to set up a sting and finally caught the gang of eight.

The most frequent occurrence of crime was the traffic of bootleg liquor across state lines. There had been two killings, one by a rival suitor over a woman, and the other, the murder of a state congressman by a small rancher who had been cheated out of his water rights by a legislative maneuver that financially benefited the congressman.

Occasionally, a transient would be discovered murdered and left along the tracks or thrown dead from a moving train.

Drunken brawls and disorderly behavior in the local saloons the agents left to the sheriff and deputy to handle arrests and prosecution.

"I would like to speak with Agent Braun."

"He's not in the office right now."

"Well, where is he?"

"On a case somewhere. He didn't say."

"When do you expect him to return?"

"He didn't say, sir."

"Well, what the hell does he say? Does he tell you anything about what he's doing?"

"On occasion, sir."

"Well, I want you to give him a message."

Ferguson grabbed a fountain pen and flipped open a notebook. "I'm ready. What's the message?"

"Director Hoover and I will be arriving on the 10:20 morning train that stops in Mesa on Wednesday."

"You're takin' the train, the 10:20."

"After we fly to Chicago."

"You're takin' the train from Chicago."

"That's right, Agent Ferguson, from Chicago."

"Will you and Director Hoover be stopping here in Santa Fe?"

"Unfortunately, we won't have time. We have business in California and will be on a tight schedule."

"I understand, sir. What would you like me to tell Agent Braun?"

"Tell him to have Howard Gimbel waiting for us at the Mesa station."

"Howard Gimbel," Ferguson quickly jotted down the name and waited for more. "That all, sir? Just Howard Gimbel."

"Just give him the message as I've dictated it."

"I'll do that, sir, as soon as he returns to the office."

"That will be all, Agent Ferguson."

"Yes, sir, thank you, sir."

The line went dead.

Ferguson held the silent receiver at arms length and stared at it. "Can you beat that? It was Tolson himself. He and the Chief are stopping in New Mexico on the way to California."

"Comin' to our office?" Melbourne squinted.

"No, they want Braun to set up a meeting with someone in Mesa. You ever hear of Howard Gimbel?"

Melbourne shook his head.

"Must be someone important."

"How you gonna get the word to Braun?"

"I sure wish to hell he'd tell us where he's goin' half the time. Now we have to go find him."

"I overheard him talkin' on the phone to that mine owner, Lee Stark, a couple days ago. I think he's been spendin' a lot of time there."

"You mean the Wooten Mine?"

"That's the one."

"We got a phone number?"

"Around here somewhere, maybe on his desk." Melbourne entered Halen Braun's sanctuary, ruffled through a few scattered pages on his desk, and returned to Ferguson. "You read this? Can't read his writin', but looks like there could be a phone number in all that."

Ferguson took the offered page and studied it. "I'll try this." He put the receiver to his ear and dialed.

American Landscape

***

J. Edgar Hoover savored the smoky liquid hickory flavor of charcoal filtered fine Kentucky bourbon sluicing over his fat tongue and sliding down his gullet. He loved Kentucky bourbon. He was addicted to it. Only Clyde Tolson knew that about his boss, and maybe the bartender at the Stork Club in New York City. But now Tolson had to work on Hoover to remain sober during their long train journey from Denver to Los Angeles, California, where they would mingle with movie stars, then drive south to Palm Springs to their favorite spa and golf resort for two weeks of vacation.

By the time their DC4 touched down on the plane trip from Washington to Chicago, Hoover was in a foul mood after enduring a tension-filled ride through turbulent weather. The local FBI director had met them at the airport and Hoover had declined his invitation to have dinner and stay the night. So he and Tolson were driven directly to the train station. Hoover was badly in need of a drink, but could not express his wish or certainly not go against his own rule regarding drinking on or off the job, not in front of the local agent.

Tolson knew that Hoover was a binge drinker and, in private, would often subvert his public persona of toughness and sobriety to engage in sordid masquerades of homosexuality involving blonde young boys. As Hoover's assistant and guardian, Tolson took precautions to protect his boss and their own personal relationship from discovery. He would track down the source of any negative rumors and eliminate the information and the informant by incarceration.

Like no other man, Tolson understood the emotional polarization of his boss, who devoutly believed on the one hand that middle-class Protestant morality was at the core of American values, but on the other, in his personal life, he engaged in its opposite. He knew Hoover as two different people, accepted him and loved him for the man he was, and worked with him as a loyal servant.

Tolson had arranged the side trip by rail mainly so he could make a stop in Mesa, New Mexico to personally check up on and confront field agent Howard Gimbel about his lack of progress in neutralizing Yelena Ivanov. Special Agent in Charge Halen Braun had confided in a phone conversation that Gimbel was holding back and not getting the job done.

Tolson suspected that his concern that Yelena still held a romantic attraction for Gimbel was being played out.

Tolson had contacted Warner Bros. studios to prepare for the arrival of America's number one G Man to meet Edward G. Robinson, star of the film, *Little Caesar*, depicting the heroic exploits of FBI agents against a public enemy.

J. Edgar Hoover especially liked Edward G. Robinson, because the movie star bore a physical resemblance to him, the pushed-in face and arrogant pugnacious personality. Every time a film came out with Edward G. Robinson, Hoover personally bought a copy for private screenings in the basement of his home. The irony escaped Hoover that Robinson played a gangster character who ended up being killed by the end of the movie by a good guy.

The actor Robinson's aggressive no-nonsense characters, especially *Little Caesar*, reminded Hoover of himself, even though Caesar Enrico Bandello, a small-time hoodlum took control of the mob and pushed his way to the top.

An exception was Robinson's depiction of an FBI agent in *Confessions of A Nazi Spy*, a film that combined documentary and fictional events to tell a story. The movie had just been released into theaters and Hoover wanted to personally congratulate Robinson on his performance. Hoover also wanted to use the film as a propaganda piece to promote his domestic spying on anyone and any organization he considered subversive. The list was long and kept Tolson busy working with field officers to create a policy of fear of a Nazi threat to the United States that did not exist. The President, Franklin Delano Roosevelt, was more concerned about Nazi dominance in the world economy over Britain and the U.S. and less so about the repression and genocide of European Jews. But FDR collaborated with Hoover to propagate leaks to the press about public officials who supported neutrality as being anti-Semites and fascists disloyal to the U.S. Government.

With the support and approval of the President, who was seeking a way to enter the United States into the war with Germany, Hoover had cast a wide net.

"We have all this information coming in to us," he commented to Tolson. It flowed in from the use of wiretaps on phones and electronic surveillance. "We've got the President standing behind us. We can do anything we want. We've got this country by the balls." They used their knowledge, both real and fabricated, to create a culture of fear among public officials. What Hoover and Tolson knew could destroy political careers.

***

Hoover slept in an inebriated stupor through most of the hill country and plains and across the high desert of New Mexico. The sudden slowing of the engine and sound of the whistle woke him, as the train approached and pulled into the Mesa station. The first thing he saw looking out the window of his Pullman was a family of Navajo, three women on horseback, and two men driving a flatbed wagon pulled by one swayback paint with prominent hip bones and knobby knee joints. A young boy and two teenage girls sat on the wagon among piles of wool and blankets.

"Look at that, Tolson. A whole family of Nigger Indians. The men ride in the wagon and make the women ride horses. Whatta ya think of that?"

"A bit unusual."

"It's a shame the Government didn't get rid of all of them when it had the chance."

Tolson knew Hoover's aversion to any people of dark skin color. Just as with curbing and hiding any references to Hoover's aberrant sexual behavior, Tolson had also been assigned to track down and eliminate an allusion to Hoover's possible ethnic origin. He was a virulent racist, yet there lingered in his background the taint that there was Negro blood in his family ancestry. His face bore evidence of mulatto characteristics and Tolson had arranged for the tampering of historical census records and destruction of any of Hoover's boyhood family photos, substituting and identifying his older brother, Dickerson Hoover, Jr., as John Edgar Hoover.

Among his many tasks, Tolson traced back any written lineage and ensured that it was destroyed. But the oral history provided by his actual father, a slave owner who had likely impregnated the young Negro woman who had given birth to Hoover, and the handwritten change of Hoover's birth date on his birth certificate escaped Tolson's notice. Doubt and aspersions were cast as to whether the white woman Hoover knew as his mother was actually his birth mother. Tolson made certain that any reference that Hoover was passing as white was buried. Hoover had never applied for a birth certificate until after his white mother's death the prior year, 1938, and it was statused as a delayed filing.

One drunken night as they lay in bed together, Hoover had confided in Tolson his need for protection of his identity. Tolson supported the values of his Chief and benefactor and kept Hoover's personal historical records clean of scandal and innuendo.

He had been alienated from his father and never discussed him. Dickerson Naylor Hoover had died in 1921 in a sanatorium from mental depression.

As Hoover's confidant, Tolson also learned of Edgar's fear of separation since childhood and excessive dependency on his adoptive mother, Annie Hoover, with whom he lived in their Washington house on Seward Square.

Hoover had not handled her death well the previous year in 1938 and his dependency on Tolson as friend and lover had deepened.

When the train pulled into the station, Braun told Gimbel that the meeting with Clyde Tolson was intended to be private and he would be leaving the two of them alone. In reality, Braun was anxious that Hoover not spot him from the train window and see him wearing a western hat and boots and sporting a full handlebar mustache.

As Tolson stepped down from the Pullman, Gimbel came forward along the platform to greet him. "Welcome to Mesa, Agent Tolson. It's a nice to see you in this far away place."

Tolson said nothing in return, but ushered Gimbel by the elbow to the far end of the station platform where their conversation would be overshadowed by the loud muttering idle of the engine and periodic blasts of steam.

"I understand that Yelena Ivanov is still active. You have a rare opportunity to explain yourself. The Chief wants to get rid of you. Under other circumstances, I would be taking away your gun and badge here and now, but I have convinced The Director to let you continue with your assignment, mainly because you are close to Yelena. You know her, perhaps intimately."

"We are not intimate, Tolson. I have not been able to even find her, let alone contact her," Howard lied.

"Did you meet her on the train?"

"Yes, she refused to talk to me. I'm sure she recognized me for who I am, an agent. We're easy to spot."

"Are you in love with her."

Gimbel's hesitation gave Tolson his answer.

"Whatever your feelings are about her, your assignment is to get rid of her in whatever means that can be done. The order from the Chief is to be innovative in doing your duty. You understand what that means, don't you?"

"I do understand...innovative."

"Is there anything else you need to be able to complete that order?"

"I have what I need."

"The Chief and I changed our itinerary just so you and I could have this little talk. So you must realize how important your successful completion of the mission is to The Director, to me, to the Government, to the Wooten Corporation, and to yourself."

"I understand."

"And what about John Collier? You haven't sent me any reports on him. We know he's a communist."

"He's doing his job. Not everyone agrees with him, but he's doing the best he can. I haven't seen him engage in anything you could call subversive communist activity. I will say from personal experience the Navajo are difficult to work with unless you really know what they believe and how they live. It's not like the white man. I've depended on the Federal Marshal here, Everett Carmody, to assist me. The Navajo do respect him. He speaks their language and understands their ways."

"Halen Braun informs me your law and order program has not gone well."

"Law and order here has a different meaning than in the East."

"What did you say?"

"There are cultural differences."

"If someone breaks the law, it doesn't matter who they are," said Tolson with a grim tightening of his lips. "They are to be arrested and prosecuted. It's that simple. That's the law you have taken an oath to enforce and uphold."

"It's not that simple here. There are no public enemies."

"Anyone who is a subversive and does not comply with the laws of the United States Government is a public enemy. The Navajo live on Federal land. They must obey those laws."

Howard acknowledged with a slight nod.

"Just to make sure, there is no room here for compromise, Agent Gimbel. Should you fail in your duties, you risk spending the rest of your life in an asylum for the insane or a penitentiary of the Director's choice."

"An asylum for the insane?"

"For your beliefs and wrong way of thinking."

"This is America, Agent Tolson, not Russia. And I'm not a communist."

"You live in The Director's America, Agent Gimbel. If you believe and act according to anything less, you will be prosecuted as an insurrectionist, a spy. Is that understood?"

"Understood."

"Good day, Agent Gimbel." Tolson turned abruptly and walked away to the Pullman.

Howard caught a brief glimpse of Hoover watching him from the compartment window. Howard smiled and waved. The wrinkles of Hoover's sordid face folded in upon themselves in a sudden purple rage. This would be the last time Howard ever saw that face.

As Howard left the station platform and approached his car, Braun stepped out from the shadow of the building and confronted him.

"I know you're protecting her, Gimbel. You know where she is. I made a phone call to Clyde Tolson. That's why he stopped here to talk with you. As the Special Agent in Charge, I am giving you a direct order to stop collaborating with Ivanov. That makes you a communist."

"You're in violation of the law, Braun." Howard was incensed, but remained calm. "And I take my orders directly from Washington, not from you."

"Not anymore you don't. You're collaborating with a Communist and, as far as Hoover and Tolson are concerned, that's a punishable offense. You'll go to prison for the rest of your god damn miserable life."

"I was threatened with an asylum and Yelena Ivanov is not a communist."

"What makes you so sure?"

"I know why she's an organizer and it has nothing to do with Communism. It has to do with J. Edgar Hoover. When she was a child, he deported her parents without cause. They were caught up in the Palmer Raids."

"Do you mean to stand there and tell me you are disobeying a direct order? You are challenging J. Edgar Hoover?"

"I am upholding the law, which is more than I can say for you. I don't know about Hoover, he's blinded by his paranoia and private spying; but it's clear you're in bed with Stark and the Wooten Corporation." He did not flinch under Braun's threatening stare.

"I could place you under arrest now for saying that, but I'm going to wait until later, when I can do it in my own time and my own way."

Howard did not know how or when Braun would come after him, but the encounter would be quiet and deadly and remote.

***

Frustrated by Gimbel's insistence to treat Yelena Ivanov in an ethical and honorable manner, Braun had determined he would get to her by a different means, the coercion of the young news reporter, Randolph Logan. It was time to get a report from his trip to Coal Town. Braun strode down the street and entered the office of the Mesa Independent.

"It was the only way they agreed to take me to her," Logan explained with some trepidation. "And with my hands tied behind my back. They didn't trust me not to rip the mask off my eyes. It was triple folded black cloth. Didn't let in even a beam of side light. I couldn't see anything."

Logan stood at partial attention in deference to the overbearing Braun, who had unceremoniously jerked him out of his desk chair that Braun was now sitting in.

"Who are these *they* you keep referring to?"

"Some of them were women and some were men. The men were all armed."

"I thought you said you were blindfolded."

"Oiled gun metal has a recognizable smell."

"Did they give you their names?"

"No names. Why do you think they would give me their names?"

Braun glowered at the reporter. "I'll ask the questions. You give me answers."

"I'll do the best I can," Logan hesitated just enough to imply his dislike and lack of respect for Braun, "sir."

Braun's eyes narrowed. He did not miss the inference. He suspected Logan might be duping him. The behavior was not uncommon when he put someone under pressure. "So you did get to see her. Isn't that right?"

"They drove me around blindfolded in the back of a truck for a long time. There was always a rifle barrel pushing me in the gut. Then they had me get out of the truck and led me up and down an alleyway somewhere out in the middle of Coal Town. They took me into a shack and sat me down on a wooden chair and told me not to move on the threat of being shot. The chair was not at all comfortable."

"Do you think I give a shit? I don't need a blow by blow description of how your ass hurt. Did you see her? Did you talk to her?"

"They made me keep the blindfold on, but I did talk to her."

"And what did she have to say?"

"She told me about when she was a girl growing up in Philadelphia."

"Oh, Jesus fucking Christ, what's the matter with you? Did you get any information about union activity. Are they planning a goddamn strike like I heard from Stark."

"I don't know."

Braun lunged up out of the chair sending Logan sprawling backwards. "You don't know? What the hell did you ask her?"

"She did say—she did say the law supported the formation of unions by workers."

"The hell it does. That is not what the law says and I'm the fucking law."

"She seemed to be quite familiar with the law, like a lawyer would be familiar."

"Go on, asshole, what else did she say?"

"She said the mine workers have the right to bargain."

"They have no goddamn rights. They take orders, do their job, and get paid. That's it. If it wasn't for Lee Stark, they wouldn't have a god damn job."

"I'm not arguing with you. I'm just telling you what she said."

"So it sounds like she is planning a strike."

"She wouldn't come right out and tell me."

"Did you think to ask her?"

"In a roundabout way. She knew what I wanted."

"This is getting me nowhere." Braun paced the office.

Shreve observed all this from behind his glass enclosure. He was enjoying how Logan was handling this arrogant bear. But he had to be careful and not irritate and anger him to the point where the bear would charge and take his head off.

"You need to find a better way," said Braun. "You need to go and see her again. She is planning a strike. I know it. The word you want to get to her is that when they have the strike, you want to be with her to write the story. You tell her you sympathize with her and your story will support her position."

Logan took a deep breath. "What's your point?"

"You will draw her out into the open and I'll be waiting."

Logan shuffled his feet. "Then what will you do?"

"That's my business."

Logan acknowledged his comment with a slight nod. "I suppose it might work."

"She'll trust you if she thinks you're on her side. So you convince her of that. Can you do that?"

"Like I said, I'll do what I can."

"You have five days."

"But I'm not promoting a strike. I can only be there if and when it happens."

"Don't take me for a fool, Logan. That woman's not out here in the middle of this Godforsaken place to have a picnic."

"I still think they'll blindfold me again."

"I have an informer. He'll get in touch with you."

"A spy? How will I know him? What's his name?"

"Wesley Zuber. It's his job to tell you when there's going to be a strike. It's your job to bring Yelena Ivanov into the clear out of hiding. The strike is how we'll get her breaking the law."

"What if she doesn't come out? Maybe she just works behind the scenes."

"You make sure she's right out in front so we can grab her."

"She didn't impress me as a woman who is easily swayed, based on my interview."

"You fuckin' better sway her any way you can, Logan boy, or you know where I'll put your skinny ass."

"I'll give it some thought."

"You do that, Logan. You do that." Braun swept his hat from Logan's desk and stormed out the door to his car parked in the street.

Logan's eyes met Shreve's twinkling at him.

"Not bad, Logan. Not bad."

IV

ENDLESS
TRAINS

Chapter 25
HARMONY LOST

At first, Gimbel did not know what to say to the tall, proud Navajo who had quietly slipped into his office unannounced. Although he looked familiar, Gimbel's first impulse was to be on guard in the event the man had come to kill him. Then he noticed the man was still a boy, but with intensity of purpose. He was surprised to hear him speak in perfect English with only a slight accent of the Navajo tongue.

"My name is Duncan Zaragoza. I have come to see you about my father and his brothers. I know from my relatives that you and the Marshal, Carmody, were tracking them because they shot a range rider from here who was killing our sheep. The practice of killing sheep is not good for our tribe. We cannot live without their wool and mutton."

Howard gazed at the handsome young face, the calm coal dark eyes that assessed him with such certitude. Howard thought he must look somewhat older because of the *chignon* knotted at the back of his neck and the blue bandana around his head. He wore a beaded blue denim shirt and jeans that touched the tops of his scarred leather boots. Howard's eyes were drawn to his large silver and turquoise belt buckle. He politely cradled a black Stetson hat in his large slender hands.

"My name is Howard Gimbel." Howard rose and extended his right hand. Duncan did not respond. Howard decided it would be best to remain standing behind his desk. "I am truly sorry about your father and his brothers. We never did arrest them. They got away and we did not pursue them."

"Then you let them go."

"Yes, we let them go."

"They have not returned. We do not know what has become of them."

Gimbel hesitated, wondering what he should or should not tell the Zaragoza son. He decided it would be best to just be honest and tell him what he knew. To do otherwise would be to disgrace himself further.

"There was some news of three men who were run over and killed by a truck. I have not seen them. I don't know who they are. Their bodies disappeared. We suspect they were taken and hidden by members of your tribe."

"So even though you did not kill them, this," the sweep of his extended arm holding his hat encompassed the Bureau of Indian Affairs building and all that it represented. "This that you are doing here killed them."

Gimbel wished that Carmody were there to help with the difficult situation. He wondered if he should suggest that they go together to see Carmody, who was recognized as the real law and order.

"I have no authority over what they are doing here."

"The *Dine* tell me you are law and order."

"Not anymore. I'm law and order in Washington, not here. Marshal Carmody is law and order here."

"But you are together."

"In some way we are. But I am just coming to learn about your people, the *Dine*. The white man's law is not your law. You have your own ways and we should respect them."

"You are not like the others."

Howard felt a rush of gratefulness at hearing Duncan's assessment of him.

"I'm not all that different from Marshal Carmody, except that he knows you and your people and I don't. Just because I'm sitting in this office doesn't mean I agree with what they are doing."

"Will you help me, Howard Gimbel?"

"I will do what I can."

Duncan nodded once in acknowledgement, placed his hat firmly on his head, then started out the door.

"Duncan."

He stopped and turned.

"What do you want me to do?"

"You will know when the time comes."

"How?"

"It is good to wait and see."

Howard smiled. "Well then, I'll wait and see."

Duncan smiled, then walked quickly out of the office. Howard listened to the hard staccato clunk of Duncan's boot heels on the wooden floor diminish to silence until he was gone.

***

Duncan Zaragoza's eyes popped open at the rush of cool morning air that brushed his cheek. A sadness suddenly replaced the thrill of morning. He missed his dead father and focused his thoughts on preserving his memory.

Someone had pushed open the hanging door blanket and stepped outside of the Hogan. He searched the lumpy sleeping forms stretched about the floor in the shaft of dim gray light swirling down from the smoke hole. His father was missing.

For a moment, Duncan thought he might still be dreaming and what he really saw was the gray dawn through his dormitory window at the boarding school. He would wake and lie still, often with his eyes closed, and imagine that when he opened them he would be here as he was now among the dark sleeping forms of his family. He savored the moment, the smoky rough smell of the wool blanket pulled up to his chin.

His mother rose, grunting, went out briefly and returned. Duncan remembered his father going to sit in the sweat house to cleanse and revive himself.

His mother stirred the coals and started a small cooking fire. Minutes later, the smell of meat and fried bread accompanied by the agitation of his straining bladder caused him to squirm in discomfort. He stilled himself, controlling the urge to spring up and dash out of the Hogan until he could no longer endure the sensate pressures of hunger coupled with the prickling need to relieve himself.

American Landscape

He recalled how, as a young child, his parents had made him and his sisters leap up from their beds on cold winter mornings to roll about and run races in the snow.

"It is to build strength for later life," they were told. It was to teach them discipline. Now, through some interpretation of his own making, by forcing himself to lie there, Duncan practiced discipline and self-denial.

He thought of how different his life was now than when he had been a small boy. Then, he had spent most of his time at home playing with his sisters and herding his mother's sheep. Sometimes, his parents had taken them to the trading post or to a sing. Those were the most exciting occasions. During those early days, he and his sisters had chased each other and often wrestled. Now, they hardly spoke and were not allowed to touch each other.

One day, his father had given him a rope. He had gone chasing his sisters and tried to rope them around their necks. They had screamed and laughed until he pulled the rope too tight. Then they had knocked him down and kicked him. He left them alone after that and tried to rope the goats and sheep, but was not successful. They always lowered their heads and dodged away from him. Other times, while they herded the sheep, he and his sisters would make a bet to see who could hit a rock a short distance away by throwing small stones at it.

Neither he nor his sisters had ever been severely punished. Sometimes their mother would shout at them. When he was singled out, he could always go to his aunt, who was also his father's wife. She would hold him and pat him and make him feel better. He called her mother, too.

He didn't like his mother's brothers. Every time they came to visit, they would find some excuse to punish him. They would ask his mother about his recent behavior. If he had been bad, they would whip him.

His parents said that people would not think well of them if he did not act right and the big gray *yeibichai* spirits would carry him off and eat him.

The worst thing happened during a severe rainstorm. He had taken shelter under some rocks and had lost the entire flock of his mother's sheep. His uncles had shouted at him and whipped him until he could hardly stand.

He had been herding the sheep alone most of the time when he was six and his older sisters were eight and ten. His mother had been keeping his sisters at the Hogan to learn how to cook and to card and spin wool. She was teaching the oldest one how to weave. His mother was one of the best weavers in the clan and the trader paid her high prices for her blankets.

When the children had been small, they had built a little brush Hogan while out herding sheep or guarding the cornfield against raiding crows. They would take some corn and get inside the Hogan. The oldest sister would grind up the corn with rocks, but they could not make bread because they lacked a fire. They were not allowed to carry fire around. Then they would all lie down beside each other and giggle and sing songs and tell stories.

One day, a white man from the Indian agency had come to their Hogan. Duncan and his sisters had run off to hide in the brush, but they crept back to watch and listen. After the man had gone, their mother told them he wanted to take them away to the Indian school. She said they could not go because she needed them to help with the herding and weaving and cooking and keeping the garden. She warned them that whenever they saw a white man coming, they were to run and hide until he was gone.

That year, Duncan's second eldest sister, Little Dance Step, became very sick. Her parents brought two medicine men. One of them was a hand trembler. They gave a long sing, Hand Trembling Way, that cost the parents many sheep and goats. Little Dance Step did not improve. Her illness grew worse and she was going to die. The white man from the Indian school came and saw her and said she must go to the reservation hospital or she would most certainly die. Since the medicine men could not make her well, she was taken to the white hospital.

The white doctor told her parents their daughter was very sick and would have to stay at the hospital for a long time, maybe one year, maybe even two years. She had tuberculosis and should not be around her brother and sister. He told them that Duncan and his oldest sister, Raven, would also have to be tested to determine if they had the disease.

They stood in front of a machine that could see inside their bodies. It was something like the Big Fly in the Hand Trembling Way chant who could go into the body of the sick person and come out and tell Gila Monster where the disease was located and what it was. Then the medicine man would know what ceremony to perform to make the person well. For Little Dance Step, the medicine men had made all four Gila Monster sand paintings. But they still did not succeed in making the child well.

The white doctor instructed them that they should not spit inside or near their Hogan, because that was where the disease lived, the evil spirit that entered their bodies. He called them germs. They had never heard that word before. Duncan's father was offended that the white doctor told him he could not spit around his own Hogan. It was a common practice.

A year and a half later, when Little Dance Step returned home, she spoke a few words of English. She had gone to school and now wore a white girl's dress. Her grandmother made her take it off and put on the clothing of a Navajo woman. The white woman's dress was burned far away from the Hogan so that none of them would breath in the smoke and be contaminated by the evil white spirits. They punished the girl if she spoke English around the Hogan and they did not allow her to return to the Indian school.

Little Dance Step taught Duncan and Raven some English words, but never in the presence or within hearing of the adults. She told how, for a long time, she did not understand what the teachers said to her. But she had a friend, Slim Schoolgirl, who helped her to learn things fast. First, she learned how to spell cat and dog and pig, boy and girl and words like that. Small words.

In the afternoon, they would fall asleep for a while in the schoolroom. Then they would play outdoors and have milk and bread. They would learn more words, then march to another building and line up to go inside and eat. Then they would play outside again for a while until they were ordered to go inside and sleep.

"We say a white man's prayer, then get in bed. We cannot talk to someone who is next to you or all get punished. If one talks, everybody gets punished. In morning, we all brush our teeth so we don't have dirty teeth. We go to eat, then come back and get ready for school. We go to school room and sit down and wait for teacher to tell us what to do."

When Duncan heard about her experience and other things that his sister had learned at school, he asked his father if he could go too. Enraged, his father whipped him, then told him it was time for him to learn how to break horses. Duncan did not mention the Indian school to him again.

His father told Duncan that Hosteen Begay, his brother by kinship, had agreed to apprentice Duncan in the art of the silversmith to determine if the boy possessed the aptitude. When Duncan turned fourteen, between horse breaking and working silver, maybe he could go to school and learn English for one or two years. Then he would be able to interpret for the family in their dealings with whites so they would not be cheated. But for now, it was more important that he learn skills that a Navajo boy must know for when he became a man.

His father owned fifteen horses. They ranged many miles in their open range grazing. Anthony often spent hours trailing them and herding them back to his corrals. Except for two or three favorite horses he would keep penned to ride or to pull the wagon, he would allow the others to roam free as was the custom. So it was always necessary to be breaking those horses from time to time, because they did not like to be caught and ridden.

Duncan rode out with his father on a second horse, a hammerhead bay with a jolting trot that jarred the boy's spine. Duncan had learned to ride a year before. He did not like this horse and the horse did not like him. The animal would sometimes snake his head around and try to bite the boy in the leg. Duncan had to be watchful and snap him across the nose with his rawhide quirt. All Navajo riders carried such a quirt. In their style of riding, they would appear to rain the horse with blows to make him move on rather than using leg commands. Much of this was just noise and flurry and slapping of saddle leather and most blows did not land on the horse's flesh. The Navajo rarely whipped a horse to punish him.

Duncan's father rode a roping saddle with a horn. The boy rode a squaw saddle with a rounded pommel and no horn. It was this kind they used in the breaking of horses. When the animal bucked, the rider would not impale himself and injure his gonads if he should come down hard while the animal was leaping and kicking and twisting and turning.

They did not find all the horses on the range, only nine. The other three were probably off on someone else's range or had joined another herd. That frequently happened. His father often discovered some neighbor's horse in among his own. It took Duncan and his father a full day to round them up and bring them back to the Hogan. So they did not start the breaking until the following day.

In the morning, two of his uncles came to help. One by one, they roped a horse from the herd as it charged round and round the corral raising a great cloud of dust. One man would keep the loop tight around the animal's neck, but not enough to choke him badly. The second man would blindfold the horse and hold him by the ears while the third strapped on the saddle and bridle. It often took several tries with the horse thrashing and squealing and kicking out trying to resist the men and the saddle. The best rider in the clan did the breaking. He had even won awards and bucking contests at white rodeos. Breaking Navajo range horses was just practice for him.

Duncan was too small yet to get into the corral and help with those crazy wild horses kicking and rearing and trumpeting all about with their eyes rolling, ears laid back and snapping at the men with their large teeth. Then, toward the end of the day, his father called Duncan over from his perch on the corral gate and lifted him onto the back of an old gelding who would buck as hard as the younger horses. Duncan was frightened and shaking, but tried not to show his fear in front of these horsemen and be shamed.

Listening to the instructions of He Who Breaks Horses to watch the direction of the horse's head and go with him, Duncan pulled his over-sized hat down tight. It was a replica of the big black ten gallon hats worn by the men.

With one hand he gripped the smooth pommel, because his legs were not long enough or strong enough yet to hold him on securely. His father pulled away the blindfold from the horse's face and Duncan was left sitting alone up there on that big horse waiting for something to happen. It did.

The horse's head went straight down and disappeared between his front legs where Duncan could not see to follow its direction. And he did not want to go down. The animal's rump exploded up and nearly knocked him in the back of the head. After three jumps, the boy weakened and lost his grip and followed that horse's head straight down.

He lay on the ground for a moment unable to breathe or to see. Dust filled his eyes and mouth and the wind had been knocked out of him.

The men did not come running over to help him or to see if he was all right. When he finally staggered to his feet, they laughed and he felt red with shame. He did not understand they laughed out of amusement and relief that the boy was not injured.

He retrieved his fallen hat and told them to "get that horse." They stopped laughing and did it. He walked over and climbed on without assistance. This time when the men stepped away, he rode the animal until it was exhausted and stood snorting and gasping. Duncan made him move into a trot and then an easy lope. The men nodded their approval and called him Little Breaker of Horses. He was proud and felt like a man.

Now, lying there in the Hogan, he felt like an infant who would wet his pants if he did not get himself outside there and piss. The strain of holding back was so terrible, it began to sting. He threw off his blanket, leaped up and dashed out of the Hogan as if he had discovered a rattlesnake coiled near him.

Standing off behind a bush, he gasped with relief as the hot yellow urine gushed splattering to the ground. He aimed his penis so that the stream arced several yards until the force of the pressure dwindled, then ceased. He rubbed his organ with satisfaction as it grew limp.

The massive spread of the sun startled the night shadows which fled swiftly and silently like coyotes through the brush. Duncan watched the great eye peering at him over the rim of the mesa. He filled his lungs four times with a deep drink of the cool morning air. His bare hand brushed a leaf. It trembled and fresh dew leaped and clung to his brown skin in clear precise cold drops. The chill traveled up his arm, then plunged deep inside so that he quivered with discomfort and joy like the ecstatic quick shaking of a ground squirrel.

Birds chattered and sang to him and he began to sing out of sheer exuberance, although his song was personal, low and quiet. His *Ha tothli*, grandfather, the medicine man, had taught him the prayer sung over a newborn infant.

Spirit of the dawn
Voice of the dawn
Head of the dawn
Go in beauty

Let him drink from all the springs of the earth
Let him eat pollen of all the plants of the earth
Let him eat of the pollen of the water
Let him eat of the pollen of the mountains

Son of Changing Woman, go in beauty
Pollen Boy, go in beauty
Everlasting One, go in beauty

He saw a ghost image of his father walking slowly from the sweat house. They each raised a hand in greeting across the way.

When Duncan had returned from the Indian school, the men, his father and two of his uncles, including He Who Breaks Horses, had invited him to join them in the sweat house. Clouds of hot whirling steam cleansed their skin and went deep inside them while they sang chants. Duncan was still shy and embarrassed to sing with the men. But the next time he went to a sing, he thought he might be better.

His voice was beginning to change now, which was a sign of becoming a man. Soon his voice would be strong and blend with those of the men, not squeak out weak and high-pitched. He would continue to sing and practice new songs when he was off alone working in the garden or riding his horse or herding sheep. There were many songs. One man could not learn them all in a lifetime.

He returned to the Hogan. Using yucca suds, a soap made from the yucca plant roots, he washed his hands and face, then sat and ate the breakfast of mutton, fried bread and coffee his mother had prepared for him.

He remembered his father deep in contemplation. Duncan figured it had something to do with that Bureau of Indian Affairs agent from Fort Defiance. His mother had already asked her husband three times what he and the agent had discussed. Anthony said he would eat first, then tell her.

When they had finished the meal, Duncan's sisters went to take the sheep from the corrals and herd them to the grazing area. They had to travel far now, two or three miles. All the grass nearby had been eaten and spring rains had cut great arroyos that snaked back and forth across the plain.

His mother had told him to go out and search for coyote tracks near the Hogan. She greatly feared they had been visited by a witch during the night. She sprinkled pollen in the doorway and on the roof from a medicine bag to ward off evil spirits.

Duncan found tracks. He followed them for a while until they disappeared a half mile to the north of the Hogan. He stopped and looked out across the land. A flush of embarrassment rose up from his neck and heated his face. He believed he had conquered the doubt and buried it forever. When Reverend Sims had told him those words, Duncan had tried not to listen.

He and the other Navajo children had been forced to go to the white church for an hour every day where Reverend Sims would shout at them about the greatness of the white man's God and how their Navajo gods were heathen and came from the Devil. Duncan was angry that he had listened to that shouting man who had cast doubt in his mind. He wondered if he, in fact, were not being foolish, following the tracks of a coyote who had come as a witch in the night.

He was angry because, as he looked back at the Hogan of his family, he felt different. His sense of who he was had changed. He was not the same person as before he went away to the school. Something he had felt before was gone from him. It had been taken from him as though an invisible hand had plucked out his soul. A hole existed where that something used to be. A unity had been destroyed so that he was no longer completely one of the *Dine'*, The People. Soon they would sing the Blessing Way chant for him. Maybe then, what was missing inside him would return.

He looked out over the *Dinetlah*, the land of The People. He saw what his parents and grandparents had told him. It was not just the yellow day coming up over the miles and miles of sage and chaparral and touching the distant rise of the blue mountains. No, the land flowed as a sea of shifting currents of purest light and colors.

To him, a Navajo, the earth was Changing Woman, who grew old and young again with the cycle of each year's seasons. The rising sun was himself a Being. He and Changing Woman created a warrior that cleansed the earth of most evil forces and used his power to help The People.

He had prayed to the first light of day, another being, Dawn Boy. He looked to the north from where First Woman, bitter and unhappy, sent colds and sickness. He then looked to the south, from where Gila Monster helped the *Ha tothli*, medicine men reveal the unknown. The lava flows from ancient volcanic cones were the dried blood of a giant killed by the Sun's Warrior.

Duncan could still see these images, but he was not certain now that he totally believed in them. "Manifestations of Devil worship!" That was what the Reverend Sims had called the Navajo and Hopi ceremonials. An impulse to destroy the Indian religion consumed him. He never realized he attacked those very concepts he espoused. The Indians believed in a Supreme Being, the divine origin of the universe, the immediacy and responsiveness of a deity to human needs through prayer, hymns, chants, and supplications. And they believed in the immortality of human and animal souls.

Duncan observed that no one liked or even respected Reverend Sims, not even the other white teachers at the school. They did not go to his church. He was one of those Methodist preachers. *Shouters,* the Navajo called them.

Different missionaries worked at different schools. Some had Baptists or *put under the water.* Others had Roman Catholic or *crosses himself* or *drags his coats* or *long skirts.* The Congregationalists and Presbyterians they called *short coats.* All of the missionaries talked about the same God, but none of them agreed with each other.

The *Dine'* realized this inconsistency about the Missionaries. The Navajo and Hopi also understood the delusion perpetrated by the white priests who said their God was one of peace and brotherhood. Yet, for a long time, white soldiers had killed and slaughtered Indians, nearly driving them into extinction. The *Dine'* did not believe the white priests. They were perceived as the mouthpieces for the Federal Government and other whites to cheat and exploit them and steal their choice lands. So very few went to the white churches except the children at the schools who were forced to attend and listen and recite the senseless things the *shouter* demanded of them.

***

Duncan had arrived on a hot afternoon after a bus ride of ninety miles. His head nodded. He was exhausted like the other thirty-four Navajo children who had been recruited to come to the Government school. He stared out the dusty window at the cluster of adobe buildings that were to be his home for the next year.

A tall man carrying a clipboard crossed the compound to the bus. Duncan noticed that he was thin and his hair was cut high on the sides. He thought the man had small ears for being so tall. The sleeves of his white shirt were rolled above his elbows. The dry wind flipped a large plain neck tie back over his shoulder as he approached walking with a slight limp. He wore thick-soled brown shoes with dark laces and his tan trousers billowed slightly with each step.

The driver opened the door and the man came up the steps into the bus. Looking over the shaggy dark-headed passengers, he and the driver talked for a few minutes. Duncan studied the man's angular face for some sign of how he should relate to him.

Except for the limp, his movements were brisk and businesslike at one moment, then suddenly he would lean down in a slow manner with a slyness that generated fear in the silent boy, even though he had never seen him before nor heard him speak.

The man exchanged a joke with the driver. They looked with condescension at their passengers and laughed about them. Duncan did not understand at what they were laughing, but the hollow sound coming from the man and the cackle from the driver caused Duncan to slouch down in his seat and avert his eyes in embarrassment. He sensed that the two men were looking directly at him and not at any of the others. The eyes of a white man could do that even if you were one in a great number of people. He was sorry that he had listened to the stories about the school told him by his sisters. He would escape and make the long walk home.

He glanced up in surprise as the man wearing the tie spoke to them in the Navajo language, instructing them all to leave the bus. Duncan rose and crowded along the aisle. He shuffled against the others and they stepped carefully down the steps that raised a metallic noise from their clatter. Then they were standing in a tightly huddled group like sheep on the hard baked ground. The bus engine sent heat and gasoline fumes in a vaporous wave over the boys. Duncan wrinkled his nose at the sour air and sneezed loudly.

The man ordered them to line up and follow him single file into one of the slope roofed adobe buildings to be processed. Duncan was surprised that the white man could speak Navajo so well. He could speak it almost as well as the white trader, Mr. Mustache. Duncan wondered where he had learned it. The line moved as the man walked on and entered the building. Duncan fell into step with the boy just ahead of him.

Inside the building, they were ordered to sit on the hard dirt floor. They waited patiently while being taken one at a time into a closed office. Duncan grew increasingly anxious at what might be happening in there.

Through the briefly opened door, he had glimpsed a woman with long yellow hair like the silk on young corn. Her hair was tied back with a ribbon. She was writing something at a large desk.

Each child spent a few minutes being asked questions by the man and the woman, then returned and continued to sit on the hard floor. None of the returning children spoke a word and Duncan was afraid to ask what had happened to them.

The unsmiling man beckoned to him. Duncan rose and followed him inside. The door closed abruptly behind him and caused him to jump. Trembling slightly, he stood facing the woman with yellow hair. If he had not been so afraid, he would have liked to reach out and touch it and feel its texture between his fingers. He had never before seen hair like that.

She looked up and smiled. Duncan immediately felt relieved. The pressure of not knowing how he should behave and what he should do had been building in him so that his stomach clutched in a tight knot.

The white woman spoke to him in his own Navajo tongue, asking his name. He did not know his age. She wrote down a figure in her book. Then she told him that Mr. Graham, the man with the tie, would take him along with the other boys to the place they would sleep, a large Hogan. Mr. Graham was the disciplinarian in charge of the boys. The woman, Miss Cort, was the matron in charge of the girls.

Mr. Graham marched them out of the first building across the compound to the barracks. He ordered the boys to strip off all their clothes and bathe. They looked at each other in great distress, for it was not proper to expose themselves before one another.

Mr. Graham told them in a harsh threatening tone that if they did not strip at once, they would be whipped. He slashed the long supple hickory stick so they could hear it cut the air. Reluctantly, with great shame, the boys undressed and stood hiding their genitals with their hands.

Mr. Graham prodded them several at a time into a room at the end of the two long rows of cots. It contained four large metal tubs filled with water heated on a wood burning stove. The rising steam reminded Duncan of his father's sweathouse. There were soap and brushes. The foam resembled the yucca suds that he used to wash himself at his family's Hogan. Rough bristles bit into his skin, but when he stepped out of the tub, his skin tingled refreshed and clean.

As Duncan returned to the sleeping room, Mr. Graham thrust a towel at him, although Duncan's body dried quickly in the heat. Duncan was directed to one of the cots where he discovered a clean shirt and a new pair of denims with his boots. His old clothes along with those of the others had been stuffed into a large sack to be taken out and burned.

Duncan observed how the other boys sat patiently waiting on their cots. He did the same. They watched the last few of their brothers come from the wet steaming tub room. Each one discreetly turned his back while toweling dry and putting on his new clothes.

Mr. Graham spoke to them. He said that as long as they followed his orders and did as they were told, they would not be punished. They would each be assigned certain tasks for which they would be responsible every day in addition to attending morning classes. Anyone who failed to do his job would be whipped, a form of motivation he personally enjoyed. The boys intuitively understood that about this man. To receive a whipping from him would not be the same as being beaten by their uncles. The intent of the man was different. He cared less if they learned than for the opportunity to inflict bodily harm.

They would all eat at the same time with the other students who were away doing their work on the farm plot. Others labored in the kitchen, the dairy, or the laundry, wherever they had been assigned. The children provided the labor that kept the school operating.

Each morning, they were expected to rise early, wash themselves, brush their teeth (a foreign experience for Duncan who had never conceived of his teeth as being dirty), then wait to march in formation to the dining hall. They would then march back again as a group that had its own identity, clean and straighten up the barracks, then march to class. The work assignments would be given after the first day of class.

Duncan's stomach churned with hunger. None of the new arrivals had eaten since early that morning. He wondered what all the waiting and marching was about. If he just did what the white man said, he would not be struck with that ominous whip. He feared the man and his whip as much as he feared witches. He so sensed that the man liked to use it that he would find reasons to do so, or create them. Duncan determined to do his best and to not antagonize the man.

They heard the voices of children coming from the schoolhouse. Mr. Graham said, "All right, stay in order and follow me." He led the way out.

The other children looked with interest at the newcomers as they converged, but did not call out greetings. Miss Cort brought the girls from their dormitory. They mingled at the cafeteria line and among the tables. Duncan noticed a few Navajo girls serving food. He stared momentarily at the shy dark eyes and small attractive face of one, Sara. He took the plate of beans and biscuits she handed to him and a mug filled with milk, then walked away to one of the tables.

The children sat four abreast on wooden bench seats across from one another. Duncan ate quickly, scooping beans onto the biscuits using his fingers. He suddenly stopped. The other children who had attended the school for a while were using either forks or spoons to do the same task. Since Mr. Graham was standing over against the wall closely watching them, Duncan decided it would be best to follow the example of the others.

After he had finished his meal, he sat waiting, looking surreptitiously about the dining hall. Then Miss Cort rang a bell and everyone rose in unison. They dropped their soiled aluminum dishes and utensils into a large bin near the door as they filed outside.

Sam, the boy just behind Duncan, said that now it was free time and he would show him around the school. Each day after supper, they were allowed one hour to themselves for leisure and recreation.

The smallest children swarmed chattering to the single rusted swing set and monkey bars. Sam took Duncan by the arm, "Come on. I'll show you the barn. Maybe you can work there with me."

"Do they have horses? I can work with horses. Back home, I am called The Little Breaker of Horses."

Duncan asked many questions that Sam was able to answer from experience. He had been at the school for nearly one year. He said he did not like being there and missed his family, but he was learning many new things and now could speak some words like a white man.

The long dairy barn housed twenty Holstein milk cows. Sam told him that Mr. Hunsaker was the boss there. Mr. Hunsaker also taught the boys about farming. The school didn't own more than a small flock of sheep, which was the Navajo's main livestock. Under his supervision, the boys fed and milked the cows and mucked out the barn every morning and every night. The milk was consumed by the children and staff at the school. The crops grown on the irrigated farm also fed them. The school depended on what it produced in order to survive. Little or no funds filtered down to them from the Federal Government through the Bureau office.

Sam showed Duncan a small rock and earthen dam that he and the older boys had helped to construct. The dam caught and held water that flowed from a natural spring into a small reservoir. By opening a little gate, they could allow water to trickle into the surrounding fields of corn, squash, beans, tomatoes, onions, peppers, and a few acres of cotton. The backwater also provided for a healthy population of trout, turtles, and frogs.

Duncan experienced some difficulty pronouncing the word that Sam called this system, *irrigation*, but he would remember about this dam holding the water and tell his parents and relatives about it when he returned to his home. It was much better than hauling water in clay pots and leather bags on the backs of stubborn burros.

The boys returned to the long barn. Sam introduced Duncan to Mr. Hunsacker, who smiled and shook Duncan's hand. Duncan thought he might like this white man. He and Sam helped him drive the cows out of the barn into the corrals for the night. Then they and three other boys cleaned away the soiled straw and manure.

Darkness had settled over the compound when they trooped back to the boy's barracks. The newcomers were talking and becoming acquainted with those who had been in the school during the past year.

Sam and Duncan washed at the metal basins which had spigots and running water fed by gravitational pull from the reservoir. Duncan was fascinated by being able to control the flow of water by turning a valve. Then he and Sam sat on their cots and talked for a while about their families, about home.

With only a few highly positioned windows to afford ventilation, the stale air was stifling. Mr. Graham walked into the open bay and started turning out the lanterns, a sign that all the boys must go to sleep. Sam warned Duncan that if even one of them should talk after the lights went out, they would all be punished.

Duncan twisted and turned restlessly on the uncomfortable cot. After two hours, he still had not fallen asleep. He quietly slipped off onto the floor. A harsh light glaring in his eyes awakened him at midnight. A heavy hand jerked him to his feet and flung him across the cot. The cane whip lashed down across his back and legs with stinging blows as though he were being repeatedly cut with a knife. He was so stunned, he did not cry out.

When the beating ceased, his body throbbed with pain. His body and the cot were soaked in sweat. His limbs and back twisted and jerked with spasms. He did not dare to move or to look upwards. Mr. Graham's voice spoke to him in Navajo.

"You are here to learn to live like a white man. A white man does not sleep on the floor beside his bed."

The light went out. Duncan listened to the limping steps fade away. The door opened and closed with a distant thump. The man was gone. Still Duncan did not dare to move. He fought tears of rage and humiliation. *You are here to learn to live like a white man.* The deep harsh voice echoed in his mind. That was not why he had come. He had come to learn some things and then to go home. He would always live like a Navajo.

After a long time, he inched his sore body around into position on the cot. He must learn to live like a white man. He must at least do it while he was there at the school or be whipped because of his ignorance of their ways.

No one had come to his aid. No one had come to help him. No one had even opened his eyes, while Duncan was being whipped and reprimanded. Duncan decided he would learn quickly. He did not want to be whipped again.

***

Stark's drilling crew had driven their trucks onto the Navajo range land two days before. Duncan Zaragoza's sister had seen them while she was out herding sheep. She told her brother when she came in at dusk. He went out after dark to see the operation. His relatives anxiously advised him to wait until morning. He told them he no longer feared the night. There were far greater fears than those they imagined. They did not understand him.

He rode out alone through the pinon groves in the moonlight to the low ridge where his sister had seen the men and their trucks. The lights from their construction trailer were visible from a great distance.

He rightly believed that this land still belonged to the Navajo. His mother's clan had grazed their sheep here for over a century. Now these white men had come here. They had paid nothing to the Navajo and they were gouging the land for coal and drilling for oil.

Duncan had heard too many words in the council sessions. He had witnessed too many broken promises. Many of his Navajo brothers were joining the white man's army. They would be sent to countries that were far away and would never return home. They would die in the fighting. He no longer had faith in the white man's words. Only actions were believable and final. Once implemented, they were irretrievable. What had been done to the *Dine*, the exploitation of the Navajo people was irretrievable. He would not waste time and energy with empty words, empty promises. They possessed no strength, no power, and no conviction.

Chapter 26
THE RETURN OF CLAYTON BYRNE

To the eye of the lone traveler, the heat pressed down like a giant unseen iron descending over the Kansas plains. The endless terrain of grass wilted and shimmered before the onslaught. Even the rolling hills seemed to flatten out like wrinkles in the oven-brown landscape.

When Clayton Byrne was released from the prison, he had neither food nor water. Only an old felt hat yanked by the wind from some farmer's head and deposited at the edge of a field where Clayton had chanced to pass shielded him from the sun.

His scuffed brogans rose and fell in the dust. That he was on a road and that it must lead somewhere away from the stone walls of Leavenworth Prison kept him going. His heavy denim clothing sucked the moisture from his body like a dark enveloping parasite feeding on his skin.

His hope for a passing truck or wagon had diminished much as the deceptive visions of water in the distance that continually evaporated before him mile after each trudging mile.

Although Clayton was not philosophical by nature in his own basic way of thinking, life for him was a gross deception, like the disappearing water. He had nothing which he could grasp and hold. His tenuous sense of self and his place in the world had been beaten out of him long ago by the prison bulls. He believed he could never endure any greater torture than what they had rendered him. His six year sentence had been extended to twelve when he had killed another inmate in self-defense. Eventually, his mind had slipped into a recess of non-existence to escape the pain and abuse. Only one thread linked him to the reality of his past.

Clayton Byrne had never forgotten Everett Carmody. Each day of Byrne's incarceration at the Leavenworth Federal Penitentiary had been devoted to nurturing his hatred of the man who had put him there. He envisioned the various ways he would destroy Carmody. Feeding on his dream sustained him for twelve years.

He was an uneducated, undisciplined man. Discretion of speech and manner were foreign to him. The repeated beatings had taught him to remain silent and to be submissive to the will of the guards. He hated and feared them, because they had the power and sanction of the warden to cripple him. He had witnessed their brutality against other prisoners. More than anything, he feared being crippled. That would make finding Carmody and killing him a difficult undertaking.

Time had blurred for Clayton. One day was indistinguishable from any other. He had exited through the prison gate with a quickening of his heart. He feared that his release was only a cruel trick being played on him by the warden. At any moment, the guards and dogs would chase him down.

For many miles on the flat plain, the walls had remained visible behind him. Each time he looked over his shoulder, they were still sitting squat and gray on the horizon like a bad memory he could not completely push to the furthest compartment of his mind.

He had only a dim recollection of his family. The journey by wagon they had made from Missouri and Nebraska to seek a better life had faded into the past.

The slow bleak entourage crawled over the tops of wet grassy hills against a gray Nebraska sky of steady rain. The worn iron rims of the wooden wagon wheels caromed skidding on the soaked matted down weave causing the black mules to jerk and lunge in their harness. Their hoofs chopped the soft earth kicked up in clods of mud that clung to their gaunt bellies in streaming dark rivulets melting from thin hides. The two wagons reached the bottom of the distant hill and came on at a sluggish pace slipping and sinking in the mud. Finally, sprung and overloaded, they bogged to a standstill. The hot mules steamed in the cold rain.

Clayton Byrne had not worked all winter long. The Wooten Corporation had closed down its coal mining operation in Arkansas the previous October because of low yield. On the verge of starvation, he and a neighbor, Marvin Sykes, who had worked as his partner in the mines, decided they would leave when winter broke. They loaded their wagons and headed out into Nebraska farming and ranch lands in search of work and maybe find a place they could homestead. After several weeks of travel, they were prevented from going on by the flooding waters of the Niobrara. They built makeshift shelters from cut logs and tarps and braced themselves to wait out the floods and spring rains.

Clayton and Marvin had never provided well for their large families while living back in Arkansas. As soon as their sons were old enough to wield a pick and shovel at age twelve, they had followed their fathers down into the slavery of the black mines.

The sight of rolling green range lands aroused the hopes and expectations of both families. They were certain that if they moved far enough west into the state, they would discover an opportunity to homestead several hundred or maybe even a few thousand acres. After two weeks of constant rain and being mired in the miserable muck of a spring thaw, their optimisim lapsed and their spirit drained away to a low ebb.

Clayton talked of turning back. His wife had given birth to their fifth child three days past and both were sick from the intense chill and dampness. "This river ain't goin' down for weeks. Not with it rainin' like it is."

"Ain't nothin' to go back to." Ignoring the rain, Clayton had ridden out on one of the mules to survey the terrain for the hundredth time. "Been thinkin' maybe we can convince them people to give us a little hunk of land. They got plenty, more'n they need. Runnin' good stock on it too. I seed it." He spat into the fire.

Their rheumy eyes and noses ran constantly from the choking smoke and dankness that knifed into the tight enclosure shared by the two families. A cacophony of coughing, blowing, sneezing and farting punctuated and blended with the dull drumming on the leaky tarp roof. The stench of lard, children's excrement and unwashed bodies permeated all they owned. Lice infested their clothes and bedding. The odor of wood rot from the green wet logs that formed the sides of their meager shelter hung in the air.

"Got me a plan how it can be done," said Clayton, stroking his scabby dark beard.

Clayton stared at the hollow sagging red eyes of his partner. He thought back over the years and hardships since he had been twelve. He wanted to never return to that life again. "We're all beginning to look the same," he thought. "We're all beginning to look the same." He listened to the rain and the mewl of a sickly child.

***

Clayton's children would be grown now. He wouldn't recognize them if he saw them. His wife had turned against him at the time of his arrest for rustling cattle and shooting at the marshal. He never wanted to see her again. Like as not, he would never find them anyway. They would have been evicted from the land where they had been squatters. Who knew where they might have gone.

What Clayton didn't know was that the country was in an economic depression. He wouldn't have understood what that meant even were it explained to him. He had always lived in poverty. He accepted poverty as his fate.

Feverish from dehydration, he tried to piece together incoherent thoughts and impressions that would give him focus. His mind wandered in somnolent patterns to which he had grown accustomed while in the prison culture where there was no need to think. Thinking was discouraged. Thinking was beaten out of you. Just go where they ordered you and do what they told you like a dumb animal. Clayton had forgotten what it was like to reason and to plan ahead. He was out of practice. The many blows to his head had caused some internal damage.

Swimming in delirium, he believed the weathered farm buildings off the road ahead were another part of the endless mirage through which he traveled. He was nearly abreast of them before he realized they did not disappear as he approached.

He stumbled up the broken steps of the deserted house and through a door that sagged on a single rusted hinge. He heard the scratching nails of rats that scurried away at his entrance. He looked for a place to sit, but the former occupants had taken every piece of furniture when they quit the land and joined a caravan of migrants enroute to California.

With a groan, Clayton supported himself against the wall, then braced and settled his agonized body to the scarred wooden floor. The close air was stifling and made breathing difficult. The stench of rat dirt and decay pervaded the few spare rooms. That the house shielded him from the sun was a blessing to Clayton and, for the moment, was all he cared about.

He woke in darkness. Through the fragmented glass of a window, he could see stars. With great effort, he pushed his aching limbs to a standing position, stepped out onto the porch, and took in the cool wind in great lung-filling gulps.

Thirst and hunger twisted his stomach. His body throbbed from dehydration. The dark spindle shape of a well pump drew him across the yard. Once long grass in loamy soil had been converted to dunes of sifted dust. He tried the pump handle, slowly at first, then in a short frenzied burst. To his relief, water gushed forth.

He fell to his knees and placed his open mouth under the spigot. The cool liquid flooded over his gaunt unshaven face and down his throat with a metallic taste. He cried out and pumped the handle again and again and drank until he could hold no more.

Gradually, his heart stopped beating so wildly. His fever subsided. He sat next to the pump. His skinny arm embraced the spigot like a long lost friend. After a time, he drank more, then thought about food.

In the darkness, he could not see clearly enough to search for something edible. He doubted he would find anything if he tried. The high winds had stripped and choked the land, leaving the soil parched and sterile.

He considered what might lie ahead of him. He reasoned that this farm could be within a few miles of a town or a settlement. The people who had homesteaded here would not likely have been living in total isolation. He knew he could not survive another day in the open sun. The heat would kill him. He had no means of carrying water. What he drank here would have to see him through. He rested a while longer. Three more times, he gorged his belly with water. Then, once again, he set out on the lone road through the vast prairie night.

A glistening dawn split the seam of the dark horizon at Clayton's back. The impending heat of the day stalked him. He had walked for most of the night and had not come to a town.

A plume of black smoke suddenly billowed from beyond the rise ahead. A hoarse cry escaped Clayton as he plunged forward. Too weak to sustain the pace, he slowed to a stumbling walk. He knew he could stay on his feet long enough to reach the source of the smoke. The whistle of a train called to him. With renewed purpose, he climbed the last low hill. Breathing heavily, with shoulders bent slightly forward, he gazed down at a railroad depot to which a small prairie town had attached itself. He rubbed at his gritty eyes and blinked several times to assure himself that the town and the depot and the train were not just a chimera of his imagination induced by hunger and exhaustion. The vision did not dissolve into a mist. He would have raised a cheer, but had no breath for a voice. Lacking the energy, he could muster only a dull grunt.

Wracked with pain and stiffness, his legs and joints propelled him forward in a jarring shuffle relying on gravity to pull him down the hill into the valley. He stopped next to the burnished steel rails east of the station.

The long train extended fifty yards to either side of the depot. Clayton saw the engineer climb down from the cab and cross the deserted platform to enter the station master's office. With the way clear, Clayton considered the possibility of slipping into a boxcar, but knew he did not possess the strength to haul his tired body up over the high edge of a trailer bed.

No one stirred on the dirt road that became the front street of the settlement. Clayton passed a hand-painted wooden sign that posted the town's name, Daleton, Population 57. Not even a dog rushed out to challenge him as he entered the outskirts of the town.

He paused upon seeing a tall lean woman come out the back door of a double story wood frame house whose paint-chipped siding was eroded and gray. She carried a large basket of wash from which she peeled off articles of clothing and hung them on a thin rope line stretched taut between a T-bar on a pole and a tree. As Clayton approached her from behind, he cleared his throat loudly in order not to surprise her. She whirled, clutching a damp denim shirt in front of her as a shield.

"'Scuse me, ma'am. Didn't mean to come up on ya and give ya a start. Name's Byrne–Clayton Byrne." He tentatively held out his hand, which the woman did not take.

Her quick, beetle-dark bird's eyes darted over his clothing, then returned to his dusty unshaven face. "Yer a convic'." She began edging away from him toward the house.

"No–No, I ain't. Now wait! Jus' wait! I was a convic', but I ain't no more. I done my time and I been set free."

Her eyes flooded with fear. Had she wings, she would have lifted off to the rooftop to escape Clayton's reach.

"You didn't 'scape?"

"No, No, I didn't' 'scape. I'm clean and I ain't gonna hurt you none. Ain't gonna set a hand on you. Been on the road for two days. Ain't had no food and I'm gonna drop dead if I don't git me some quick. Kin ya spare me a little?"

"Cain't hep ya. There's a hobo camp t'other side of town. You go on now and leave me be. You go on now."

"For God's sake, woman. Show some charity. I ain't gonna hurt ya. Cain't ya spare me somethin', some soup, bread, anythin'? I'll chop wood fer ya."

She stared at his desperately pleading eyes and realized how much he was suffering. "All right, then. You stay here and I'll bring it out and set it on the porch. But don't you come close 'til I say."

"Bless you, woman. You have a kind heart. I won't move. I promise I won't move. I'll stand right here 'til you call me over."

Watching the woman walk away, Clayton began to salivate in anticipation. He fretted inwardly, fearing that she had tricked him and would not return. He suppressed a rising urge to run to the house and pound madly on the door. After ten minutes, he moved his feet in a dance of impatience, much as a child whose bladder is painfully full.

The back door opened. "Hey!" Clayton called. The woman came out, stooped down, and placed a large bowl of corn and beans, a chunk of bread and a mug of cold cider on the top step. Like a well-trained dog, Clayton did not move until she beckoned him. His breath came in quick explosive gasps as he limped and hobbled to the porch. The woman withdrew and locked the door.

Clayton lowered himself to the steps, grasped the bowl with both hands and placed it in his lap. His fingers fumbled with the spoon that stuck half-buried in the thick paste of dark beans, molasses and pork fat. He shoveled three successive spoonfuls into his mouth. His desperate chewing and swallowing were interspersed with grunts and moans. He was saddened when his spoon scraped the bottom of the bowl. His stomach bulged from the rapid ingestion. He could not have forced any more down without becoming sick.

He reclined back against the porch steps, sipped at the mug of cider, and stared at the woodpile. He owed her a meal's worth of splitting logs. "I'll get to it," he thought. "I'll get to it." A sudden drowsiness came over him. His head nodded. His eyes would no longer focus. His chin lodged against his chest.

The heat of the afternoon and flies buzzing about his greasy face woke Clayton. He was surprised to discover a blanket cushioning his head. With a strenuous effort, he staggered to his feet. His ribs ached where the edge of the steps had pressed into his side while he slept. His mind and body felt refreshed, but hungry again.

The woman came out with another bowl of beans and molasses and a plate of muffins. "When ya et these, ya need to be on yer way. Ya can have the blanket."

Taking the food, Clayton looked up into her face, eroded by time and personal hardships, but her eyes still piercing and strong. "I said I would chop wood for ya."

"Fergit the wood. I want fer ya to be on yer way."

"Thank ya. Yer kindness shall not be forgot."

"Jesus said to be kind to the traveler, fer we are all travelers on the road of life. Ya come a long ways and ya got a long ways to go. Best ya be at it."

Clayton nodded and began eating the second bowl of beans. "I have to say these here are the best beans I ever et."

"The Lord provides," she said.

"Amen," mumbled Clayton. "Amen."

Clayton crouched in the tall dry grass and watched the rail cars of the freight train slide slowly past. The grinding wheels screeched over the steel tracks. Empty stock cars clanged against one another with shattering explosions, as the train rolled unevenly out of the station and began to build momentum.

He selected a boxcar then quickly closed the one hundred yard gap between them. He scrambled up the gravel roadbed and ran alongside the train. Gauging the distance, at the last possible moment, he flung his body up over the edge of the trailerbed, then kicked one leg up to secure his position. He rolled over into the center of the car. Gasping from the exertion, he looked through the slatted sides at the flashing brilliance of the morning sun.

A drifter at the last hobo camp had told him that there was work to be had in the New Mexico mines, if you could survive the food and harsh conditions. For Clayton, work would be his salvation. Nothing could compare with the conditions under which he had lived for the past twelve years. As for Carmody, wherever he was, revenge would have to wait.

Chapter 27
THE INFORMER

Red dust tailed from his car as Howard Gimbel and Logan followed the winding dirt road on its long gradual rise to the mine site. The wood frame and adobe houses of Coal Town clustered together began to materialize, emerging from the scrub brush and desert rocks and boulders they so resembled.

The town perched along the ridge of a vast open pit mine five-hundred feet deep and several miles across. Here, sub-bituminous coal was quarried and trucked to a railroad loading point at the top of the pit. The vein ran wide and deep and after three years, still produced a record annual tonnage.

The strip process consisted of a series of steps, beginning where the earth or overburden was the most shallow. To expose the coal, this soil had been scraped and bull-dozed aside downhill into dikes or piles called spoils. Where the mining progressed, following the coal vein, the thickness and density of the overburden increased so that the machines had to dig deeper into the earth.

They could see large crane shovels and haulage trucks moving around at the base of the pit. At other levels on the roads that formed giant steps along the wall of the pit, head frames marked the shaft entrances to subterranean mines.

They continued on the main road past the town laid out in regimented blocks along the slope. The meager dwellings housed some one-thousand miners and their families. On the level plateau, they paused to wait for the mine guards to open the gate. They drove inside the compound surrounded by a ten foot cyclone fence topped with barbed concertina wire and stopped before the network of adobe buildings that housed the offices of the mine officials.

Lee Stark's chauffeur nodded to them from behind the wheel of a green Phaeton parked among the trucks and lesser vehicles. Gimbel parked his car and he and Logan entered the largest building bearing the sign MINE OFFICE.

Logan first noticed the proliferation of firearms which struck him as being inconsistent with a working business office. Even Lee Stark packed twin Colt .45's with pearl handles. His two bodyguards bristled with shotguns and sidearms. The prospect of an impending strike obviously caused Stark some concern. Firepower did not seem to Logan to be the best way to manage a company. The office looked more like the command center of a war zone.

Gimbel recognized the superintendent and a foreman, but the last man, a coal miner, was a stranger to him. Stark introduced him as Wesley Zuber. He was the informer Logan was supposed to contact.

Zuber was a local homesteader who had failed at farming and raising livestock.

Beginning outside work as a slate picker, separating impurities from the mined coal, he had since become a hoist operator of an underground lift.

A facile man of simple wants and low ambition, he was not equipped for an industrial routine. He was an ineffective laborer with a record of chronic absenteeism. He earned in two days what he used to make in a week of grubbing an existence from the land. He could not stand to have so much money without going to Mesa and spending it on liquor and whores. Because war production was ramping up and there would soon be a manpower shortage, the company tolerated and retained him.

***

Although Zuber looked remotely familiar to Carmody, who had arrived only minutes earlier, he was just another unkept miner His rust-colored hair and beard were shaggy and his stained clothes hung on him in shapeless wrinkles.

According to Zuber, the cause of the whole problem of unions in the first place was "them God damn furriners."

As Gimbel and Logan sat across from this man only half listening to his prejudicial ramblings, Logan fought down an urge to walk out on the entire lot of them. But he controlled himself and waited, wondering when they would get to the subject of Yelena Ivanov.

"Now the reason I'm tellin' all this," said Zuber, "is that so y'all unnerstand what 'tis yer up against." He unleashed a string of invective against foreigners and immigrants who had come to work in the mines and monopolized the better jobs.

Overlooking the fact of their skill and years of experience in the mines of Europe, he allowed his envy to get the better of him and barely averted stepping on Lee Stark's toes by blaming him for hiring "them God damn Johnny Bulls and garlic eaters in the first place when we have the best men we need right here at our own doorstep."

Stark considered silencing him and prompting him to get to the point, then decided to let the man rant a while longer. Zuber would likely end up dead anyway for all his trouble.

"The problem with these damn hunkies is they ain't never satisfied. They keep wantin' more and more. And fer the life of me they never spend the God damn money they earn. They're always savin' fer this and savin' fer that." He spat tobacco into a tin cup. If I had as much as some a them got saved up, I could retire right this damn minute. Wouldn't' have to work a lick fer the rest of my goddamn life.

"What's goin' on here is they want to take things over, see. They really want the whole damn company fer theirselves. They'll do anythin' to make more money than they already got. That's why that damn Communist woman's here in Coal Town, you bet. The hunkies 'll do whatever it is they're told if it means more money's comin' to 'em. They'll do it even if it's the wrong thing, even if it's un-American. That's the whole point of it. They ain't Americans like the rest of us. They come over here and try to git away from a war that ain't our doin'. And we're goin' over there and fight their battles for 'em while they're soppin' up the gravy here gettin' rich as Croesus and preventin' a deservin' man like myself from havin' a better life.

"Now it's a fact that some a them hunkies even pay so they kin have better jobs. It ain't no secret. That's what I'm warnin' you about. That's communism creepin' up on us. It's a conspiracy. That's what it is. They come right over here from Europe and we let 'em right smack dab in the middle of us. And they don't even try to talk American. That way we can't understand 'em, see. They can say anything they want right under our noses and we don't know what the hell it is they're sayin'. They could even be plannin' to cut our throats.

"And another way they're gettin' in to take over is by marryin' up with our people. Soon there won't be any true Americans because they'll all be married up with these furriners.

"Do you know when an American shovels coal and he has to take a piss, he stops a while to do it. That's only natural. A God damn hunkie just keeps right on workin' and pisses down his leg. That's a fact. Now only a communist would do that."

"What about the woman, the union organizer?" Gimbel had finally reached the end of his patience.

"Yeah..." Zuber wiped his lips with the back of his fleshy hand. "The union woman ... Yeah, she pisses down her leg too. I told Mr. Nash," he referred to the mine superintendent, "that if he made me a machine runner, I could git around better and pick up on things people say, you know? There's already suspicious talk here and there, but the men are afraid of what might happen to 'em and they're bein' careful what they say. Far's I kin make out, the union woman might not even be here in Coal Town no more. She jist moves in long enough to organize, then she'll scat her ass on to the next place to make trouble for honest folk. I'm still workin' on it, but I kin find out where they got her hid. Jist give me a little more time. But as I said," his weasel eyes graced Nash, "I kin find out a lot more and faster if I was to be made a machine runner."

Gimbel turned to Stark. "Let me know when you do find her. Remember, she hasn't broken any law. There's no need to physically harm her."

"The need as I see it is to make certain she never opens her mouth again, anywhere." Starked sucked his Cuban cigar. "If my men find her first, then you can find her dead for resisting arrest."

"Your men aren't the law here."

"Did I hear you right? I make my own laws here. My men are the law here? I made 'em the law."

Stark chewed voraciously on his cigar. He wanted to punch out this FBI upstart, this Gimbel. "Odds are something's gonna happen because of what that woman is doing. We can't let her get started."

What Stark didn't realize was the extent of cultural factionalism that existed, not only among the immigrants, but even between the locals, like Zuber, and the immigrants. His imagination supplied him an apocalyptic vision of what that crawling mass of sub-humans living down the slope might do to the mine and to him and his officers.

He had ordered his own officials to not associate with the rank and file workers and, therefore, surrounded himself with men of comparable management ignorance who fed his paranoid fantasies. Their fear alone would be enough to precipitate powerful antagonism from the miners by enforcing new regulations to keep them under harsh control.

As they returned to Mesa, Logan's thoughts played over the scene of the men and their guns and their filthy ignorance and Zuber's prejudices. In the back of his mind, he dearly hoped they wouldn't find Yelena. A new attitude had crept in. He had the sense that Stark and his lackeys were depending on Carmody to make an arrest, since Gimbel had already made his position clear that Yelena Ivanov had every right to organize.

Another influence was about to arrive on one of the many trains that passed through Mesa with the release of a convict by the name of Clayton Byrne.

Although Carmody did not remember the man, Clayton Byrne was just another miner who had come into town to get drunk on a Saturday night. The hardships of prison life had aged him. His dark receding hairline rendered his gaunt features a skeletal cast, like a man slowly dying of a terminal disease. His disturbed feverish eyes darted and stared with the intensity of a fanatic.

Clayton's instant recognition of Carmody rekindled his long dormant desire for revenge against this man who had put him in prison. Like an unkind fate, Everett Carmody had descended upon him and set him on the course of the rest of his life.

Clayton didn't think Carmody remembered him. Even in a crowd, he would have shown some reaction as they passed on the street, but the sheriff had barely noticed him.

Clayton had exacted revenge many times in his dreams and distorted fantasies as he wielded a pick or a sledge, breaking up rocks or heaving lumps of coal ore into a car in the dank semi-darkness of a mine tunnel.

Chancing on Carmody again after twelve years was cause for celebration. Clayton entered the nearest saloon and ordered three shots of rye whiskey. As he drank, the whiskey loosened the drawstrings of his memory and, once again, his fantasies of vengeance raged like demons released from hell. He would watch and wait for the right opportunity, the right moment. Even if it were to be his final act, he would find some way to kill Everett Carmody and bring fate full circle.

Later, as he walked through the desert night back to Coal Town, he thought of the words of Yelena Ivanov, the union organizer whose secret meetings he attended. He didn't understand everything she said. Some of the words she used and the ideas were beyond his simple comprehension. But he did understand how he and the other miners were making the owners rich and that the law was on the side of the owners. Carmody was the law. So Clayton had another reason to kill Carmody.

Chapter 28
ENIGMA

Logan had learned many things about Carmody. He had been friends with his children and spent time in their home and in the one room adobe school house where Logan's mother was the teacher.

He genuinely liked the man. He had always made Minerva, his mother, and Logan feel welcome and kind of looked out for them when they had first arrived on the train from Virginia. Minerva had wanted to put distance between where they settled to start a new life and the place where her husband had lost his.

Carmody was not a shallow man. His emotions ran strong and deep. In many ways, he was a caring man. He loved his wife and children with a passion he rarely expressed. Logan recalled family outings, awards given at the school, watching and sometimes participating in the Navajo ceremonies, even though they were *anglos*.

***

Without her full realization, Sheila Carmody's visits to the Fred Harvey Restaurant at the railroad station had become a daily ritual. Logan could see her through the front window of *The Mesa Indendent* news office. Shortly after her husband's departure for work, she would roam the all too familiar streets and stare into the few shop windows with no intention to buy. She would look at the passing faces of people she knew and nod in greeting or recognition. Then she would go to the restaurant and sit in the same chair and sip black coffee.

Her pilgrimage had a twofold purpose. She remembered a time and a promise of happiness that she had known in her Harvey Girl days. She had waited on tables in that same restaurant in the 1920's when she had met Carmody during his railroad years. Since then, they had reared a son and a daughter who were now caught in the throes of a world in upheaval. The prospect of their son, Bobby, joining the army brought her back to this table in this place where she watched the almost daily parade of young men in uniform in the windows of the passing trains.

She noticed that more and more troop trains were beginning to roll through Mesa. Most of them stopped briefly, discharging soldiers who swarmed into the old adobe hotel restaurant adjacent to the station to dine on the famous gourmet meals or to invade the local cantinas and get drunk for the final leg of their journey to points of debarkation in California, then onward to South Pacific islands.

An endless sea of faces came and went. Their differences began to blur because of the sameness of the brown uniforms they wore.

Being short on staff waitresses, the restaurant manager asked her to work and was grateful to have a former Harvey Girl he would not have to train. Her old uniforms needed a few adjustments, but in wearing them, the memories of a younger happier time returned to her.

At the sound of the gong announcing meal service, she moved expertly and swiftly among the tables serving the soldiers with an expression and a smile that belied her age.

She joked and bantered with the young men who tried to flirt with her and the other waitresses.

As the short meal time rushed by, soldiers paid and hurried out of the restaurant. Others checked their watches to ensure they did not miss the departing train and stood outside on the porch smoking Chesterfield cigarettes and commenting about the food and the town and the surrounding desert, the long train ride ahead, and the future.

When the room was empty, the waitresses began to clear the tables. The second whistle blew and the final whistle shrieked from down the track followed by the ringing bell and heavy rumbling passage of the train as it slowly pulled out with resisting screeches and groans of the undercarriage trucks and wheels.

***

Bobby Carmody opened his eyes and sat up slowly. He eased his swollen right ankle to the edge of the bed, then his good left leg. He planted his right foot firmly on the wooden floor and gingerly put weight on it. An electric shock of pain flashed up his leg. He leaned out of bed. Supporting himself on the low window ledge, he peered out at the gray morning light slipping away across the desert hills leaving a soft rose pink glow in its wake. A dog's cavernous bark somewhere in the distance punctured the stillness.

He sat down heavily on the bed with a loud grunt. Someone stirred in another section of the house. The scrapings and dull bumps, the opening and closing of a door, muffled flush of the toilet were subliminal sounds of the waking household that rushed into focus. He had heard them every morning for the eighteen years of his life.

He tried to twist his right foot. The snug bandage wrap held it firm. He had misjudged his leap from a high boulder. He and his best friend, Kemp Sweigart, son of Phillip Sweigart, the railroad agent and Carmody's friend, were always attempting dare devilish acts. Of late, however, Bobby did not share his friends hope and enthusiasm that the United States would enter the war against Germany. Kemp had suggested to Bobby that they enlist so they could be among the first, just in case Roosevelt changed his mind.

Bobby had read the Mesa Independent news stories Logan had written of what was happening over in Europe. It was a distant continent on the far side of the ocean. The military aggression of Adolph Hitler did not bear on Bobby's young life.

Bobby thought that his friend, Kemp Sweigart, acting so bold and posturing was a desire to escape the provincial isolation of their lives in New Mexico and see and gain experiences out in the world. Kemp had even traveled to Santa Fe to talk to the recruiter and returned with high hopes that he and Bobby would enlist and be in the same unit. "We can look out for each other," he crowed. "No Nazi jackboot can get us if we cover each other's back."

Kemp had been Bobby's best friend since the time they could crawl. Their mothers had raised them together so that they felt equally at home in either the Carmody or the Sweigart households.

Bobby perceived their families as being a blend. The emotional sustenance he did not draw from his own, he found with the other. To him, his parents were withdrawn unexpressive people. Phillip and Judith Sweigart were giving people. They showered love on their children.

Bobby did not resent the trait so much in his parents as it saddened him. He knew that he and his sister, Kate, were loved. Demonstrative affection was just not their parents' manner of relating, or so Bobby had constantly justified to himself until he half-believed the deception.

Their family had not been that way in the beginning. The deterioration had crept up on them slowly so they were unaware until one day Kate had pointed out to him how all of them had changed. It was as if they had begun their lives as a healthy young tree that was slowly consumed by some inner blight.

The enticing odor of coffee and frying bacon leaked into the room and was absorbed by the dry musty smell of the wool Navajo rug and blanket Bobby had shoved to the floor. His mother was the first one up in the morning. The movement he had heard came from his father.

His father was an enigma to him. His quiet commanding strength did not awe his son like it did most men. Bobby sensed that his father had grown taciturn for some unknown reason, perhaps just age and the passage of time.

"What's wrong? What happened?" Bobby and Kate asked Sheila, their mother. But she did not understand any more than they. The change had come over their father three years ago and the depression had not lifted.

"You should have seen him just before we were married," said Sheila. "He was just like you, Bobby. He was nervous and worried. It took a lot of encouragement to get him to make the leap. But we had fun, lots of fun. I was working as a Harvey Girl waitress then."

Carmody feared something reawakening in him. He had never in his life struck back at his mother, neither in memory or in reality. He believed that he had adored and protected her and his sister and ultimately he had killed for them. He would fight down the impulse to hurt again and again during the years of his married life. The inner battle manifested itself as an emotional distance, an inability to always be free and open with his own family. For years, he had repressed the nature of their death and how, as a young man of sixteen, he had avenged them. The memories would erupt with uncontrollable fury as though, in his own mind, they foreshadowed what would happen to his son and the young woman he would marry, Erin DeGrood.

***

Upon returning from his walk, Everett connected signs of a struggle and his missing mother and sister with his encounter with Lonnie Coleridge and the hound. Lonnie had baited and intimidated him, using the dog as a threat, then had forced him to take a wide detour from his planned route.

Everett had gone to the sheriff without hesitation and a small search party was quickly organized. When the nude mutilated bodies of his mother and sister were discovered two days later several miles upriver, Everett was summoned to identify them. He held himself in control with a sudden quick blocking of the reality of what he saw. He had walked away alone down near the waterfront and had vomited into unconsciousness.

When he woke the next morning and returned to the house, he realized that the Colridges had a two day head start on him. Inquiring of a neighbor, he learned the direction their wagon had headed and he set out with the intent of overtaking them.

The road swung south out of town following the main twists and turns of the river for a number of miles, then cut abruptly inland to circumvent a large delta region of mud flats and tall reeds. Here, the open vista allowed a clear view over a vast distance. Far across the massive delta where the road began a long gradual curve of fifteen miles back toward the river, over the tops of wind tossed reeds, Everett barely discerned their tiny hunched figures like small dark birds on the slow moving wagon. He figured they must not have left Hampton until that day. They probably gathered belongings, fighting among themselves about what direction to travel, getting drunk and doing nothing in their confusion. He had witnessed enough of their behavior over the years. They were people slow in realization and consequence and must have felt reasonably safe, believing they had gained time in hiding the bodies. He was certain they did not bargain on what was set in his mind.

By the time he reached the point of land where he had first spotted their movement, they had long passed from sight into a forest that paralleled the river for twenty miles. With the setting sun at his back, he walked on.

As he walked, the memory, of the naked mud-encrusted ravaged corpses of his mother and sister floated at the forefront of his mind leading him on.

He tried to force the image from his thoughts and find peace and rest from it. He knew there was only one way he could purge their memory and so he embraced it.

As dusk crept in off the river and invaded the woods, he worried that he might pass the men he was following, should they pull away from the road to make camp in some grove or hollow where he would not be able to see their firelight.

The distant lights of the next small river town winked from the dark riffles near someone's private dock He hesitated and looked back along the tunnel of trees where he had come. His stomach knotted with pain and nausea from hunger and sickness and fatigue. His head burned with fever. He fought the impulse to lie down right there in the middle of the road and sleep, wake up fresh in the morning from this dark dream. He squinted at the distant curve of the high cut bank. Tall black trees loomed beyond the scant wooden buildings of the town whose existence clung tenaciously to a small general store.

Mosquitoes stung his hands and face as he walked on. He suddenly stopped and concentrated his gaze on a small flitting light set apart from the river's bauble reflections. A fire was five hundred yards downstream where the river swung out around a point creating a sandspit. At that distance it appeared no larger than a glowing lantern bug.

The hunger and fatigue sharpened his resolve and he pressed on. At one point, he broke into an urgent jog that brought him to the backwater town. He walked through, his eyes searching. They finally settled on what he needed, an axe resting against a door stoop near a woodpile. As he approached the house, a dog barked once from the back yard, but did not deter him. He walked on, letting his hands caress and mold to the smooth wood grain of the axe handle.

The Coleridge hound kept looking back through the dense brush in the direction of the road and huffed and growled deep in his quivering throat. Lonnie figured it was probably a possum or coon moving along in there and told the dog to quiet down. His noise and nervous pacing were keeping Lonnie awake. Jake Rilling and his father lay in a drunken stupor, having shared the remains of a large jug of corn whiskey. They heard nothing.

Recalling the sensation of the girl's tight cunt and the underbelly softness of her flesh, he pulled and scratched at his crotch. By drinking more and more, he was able to flush away his sickness and disgust and accept that his father's idea had perhaps been a good one, to set the dog on the two women. That way, when the bodies were discovered, it might have looked like wild dogs had attacked them. Nobody could trace the killings to the Coleridges. Half-burying them had gained them time.

At first Lonnie didn't understand why they had to kill the woman and her daughter. But Jake said the old lady had died of suffocation while he was on top of her. They couldn't let the daughter go back and tell who had done it. There had been no other choice.

The dog leaped up from his investigation of fleas and growled. Straining at the rope, he thrust his snout at the briars.

"It's jist a goddamn rabbit. Now shet up and lie the hell down."

The roused dog let loose a cavernous bark.

"Shit, if it'll shet you up, go run the sum a bitch down." Lonnie slipped the thick rope from the dog's collar. The animal sprang into the brush. Succumbing to the soporific effects of the corn, Lonnie settled down and within moments of starring at the blurred stars, he slept.

In his dream, he and the hound chased a white rabbit across a field of tall grass blowing in a warm wind. When they finally caught up to it, the dog mounted it, fucking it from the rear as if it were a bitch. The rabbit screamed. Then the dog and the rabbit disappeared and then he was fucking the girl, only her face looked like that of the rabbit and he saw that his face looked like the dog. But he knew he wasn't the dog, because the dog was howling somewhere off in the distance, then was abruptly silent. The rabbit face suddenly rose up at him growing larger and larger, suffocating him until he could not distinguish himself from the rabbit whose head was now severed from the body in an endless silent scream.

A shaft of sun beamed through cracks in the weathered barn siding and moved in a slow spray over the rust green hay until it touched the sleeping boy with a latticework of light. His eyes fluttered open at the gentle rousing warmth. His arms and legs moved stiffly. The blood had dried, soaked into everything he wore. He touched it caked in his hair. When his mouth stretched in a sudden yawn, the skin cracked the encrusted blood smeared thickly across his face. The smell of raw beef liver clung to him and lingered as an aftertaste in his mouth. He lay back, head sinking into the hay with a dry rustle. His throbbing eyes searched the cob-webbed rafters clotted with seeping black pitch. The thin shredded roof would not keep out rain and in some places he could see narrow patches of morning sky.

He relived the cutting crunch of the plunging heavy double-bladed axe through cartilage, bone, and flesh. His grip had been strong and sure on the curved wooden handle as he raised it high overhead, held it balanced a moment, then swung down with a terrible rush of wind. Moving from one sleeping form to the other, he had swung the blade until three heads tilted away severed from the bodies of the men. Their blood gushed high raining over him like oil in the firelight until he fell back slick and wet with sucking sticking noises.

He grunted at the consuming urge of elation that had swept through him from the contact of the thick angular blade, a smooth complete electric shock, an aliveness, a quickness he had never known before. The feeling assaulted him again and again four times, first the dog whose skull he had split and splayed its brains among the leaves and brush, and then the three men. The blade had driven down without resistance through their exposed unsuspecting necks. Then he had chopped savagely into their bodies and torn organs whole from their viscera with his hands. He could not remember rising and walking away into the night or coming upon the barn where he sought shelter.

He sensed something crawling over his coagulated face and did not realize until he tasted them that they were tears, the first sign of his returning to reality. The joy was gone. His stomach churned. He rolled over and heaved vomit that filtered sluggishly into the loose hay that formed the rim of his sleeping nest.

He crept down from the loft. Pressing himself to the wall, he carefully peered around the door jamb and scanned the narrow dirt road back in the direction he had come. He recalled how he had deliberately chosen the hay storage barn as a place to stop and rest, because it stood far out in the fields away from any other farm dwellings and outbuildings. He sensed that a few days would pass before the dead bodies were discovered. Someone out cat fishing might pass near the sandspit on the river and go ashore to investigate.

The mule he had turned loose in the woods would wander into some hay field. A farmer would catch it and maybe say nothing. But if word got around, the animal would be associated with the wagon. Everctt knew he must be gone a long distance from the county by then, north at least as far as Hampton. He would not be able to remain there. There was nothing for which to stay. He would have to quickly move on, but to what or where he did not know. He could not walk abroad in the daylight looking like an animated human carcass that had slipped off a meat hook. He would have to return to the river, clean his clothes as best he could or steal new ones. He had no money. He didn't even have the axe to sell. It lay at the bottom of the river.

There was no movement in sight. He crossed the road and plunged into a corn field that curtained his progress toward the woods along the river. Coming upon a secluded feeder stream affording him several clear pools, he stripped and submerged. The cool liquid depth seeping against his skin revitalized him. The smell of the stream and the pungent plant growth along the banks erased the odor of blood.

Repeatedly wringing out his clothes, he rubbed them with sand and gravel. The abrasive action further eradicated the stains. After spreading the garments on rocks to dry in the sun, he picked wild blackberries and slapped at the mosquitoes that worried his exposed white flesh.

A wall of trees and brush screened him from the river. He froze at the creak of oarlocks and splash and dip of the blades as a boat headed downstream passed near the bank. Not wanting to risk any chance of discovery, he quickly pulled on his still wet clothes. Keeping to the woods, he followed a game trail upstream for five miles until impenetrable brush and a swamp made further passage impossible. He cut inland hoping to find the road.

Toward late afternoon, ten miles farther to the north, a farmer driving a horse-drawn wagon saw him resting in the shade by the side of the road and offered a ride. Everett had not successfully washed out all the blood stains, but figured he could explain them away by telling the man he had been out picking berries and fell in swampy water. Other than a casual glance at Everett's clothes, the man expressed no further interest in his passenger. To Everett's relief, few words passed between them. The ride lasted all the way to Hampton.

Late in the day, he returned just as he had left. Approaching the house, he struggled against an impulse not to enter. He feared a sudden onslaught of memories generated by the artifacts of what until then had been his life and that of his mother and sister. As he passed through the rooms, a heavy inertia dragged at him and he finally sat, unable to move. He could point neither his mind nor body in any direction. A matrix of weariness and an irrelevance of existence mired him as if he floundered in a sinkhole. Finally, that he must turn to someone occurred to him, at least someone who would listen to him.

He changed his clothes and packed a few belongings. He did not linger. Coming back and walking through the rooms for the last time was far too difficult and painful. Even in memory, he sensed the dear forceful presence of his mother and sister. Now that they were no longer alive, he wanted desperately to escape the piercing wounds of love and memory and of death. The images of blood leaked through his thoughts. He wanted to seal off the mayhem of gore and brutal tearing of flesh, but what he had done had become a part of who he was.

Chapter 29
SONS AND DAUGHTERS

Carmody thought he had recognized Clayton Byrne on the streets of Mesa, but could not be sure. The image of the convict gnawed at his conscience and caused him an underlying fearful awareness as though he were being stalked by a hidden beast of prey. Memories of violent acts tumbled back upon him. When his children were grown and gone, Carmody considered he might retire from being a Federal marshal and find a new line of work.

At first, his children blamed themselves. They believed they had done something terribly wrong to alienate their father. From time to time, a fleeting glimpse of his joking, fun-loving old self would nudge him through his emotional encasement. But his attempts at spontaneity rang false. They could see him struggle in fits and starts trying to recapture the feeling of something he had lost. Then, failing, he would slide back into the deep folds of that protective suffocating cloak, exacerbated by heavy drinking.

Concerned, Sheila had consulted their close friend, Doctor McAffrey. The three of them sat and talked, but could not thrash out or exorcise Carmody's demons. He was unwilling to talk about himself. He said he was just fine, and in his own mind, he was.

Fatigue and stress and depression were terms McAffrey used in reference to Carmody, a condition of life. Carmody declined any recommendation of change or rest. He was locked in to his life, its patterns, and what he was doing. He did not even comprehend his emotional void as it was perceived by those who loved him and were close to him. He professed to love his family as he always had and did not understand this altered view of him. Sweigart didn't see him differently. Why all of a sudden should his own family. "Maybe you are the ones who are changing," he said.

At his comment, they ceased probing Carmody and began to assess themselves. There could be some truth in what he suggested. Looking back over her married life, Sheila realized that for many years her husband had exerted a vibrant power that knit them into a tight family circle. They had drawn from his life force, his vision, even his laughter. When the change came over him, they wondered who or what had siphoned off his soul. Was it them, a weariness stemming from the passage of time and events, a weariness of the familiar with no new doors to open. A weariness of the violence and dregs of human behavior he encountered every day.

She wondered if her husband had some kind of illness, but was keeping the knowledge to himself. McAffrey would know, if anybody did. McAffrey told her that Carmody had never consulted him about any personal medical problems since he had known him. To all casual appearances, Carmody was in excellent physical health and didn't appear to be deteriorating in any way and he and McAffrey held no secrets from one another.

When McAffrey not so subtly put the question to his friend, Carmody laughed and accused him of being in cahoots with Sheila to have him examined. He said he felt fine and asked if the good doctor wasn't pulling in enough revenue. "Trying to rope me into some imaginary ailment so you can slap on a fat fee for the treatment?"

McAffrey laughed with him. But the memory festered and from time to time erupted in Carmody's dreams.

"You know what I miss and remember most," he told McAffrey. "I had a chum name of Duke Boswell. When I see my son Bobby with Kemp Sweigart, they remind me of the friendship I had. Never found it again."

"Sure, Ev, who would want to be your friend?"

They laughed.

"Don't sell yourself short. I'm your friend. Sweigart's your friend."

"A boyhood friendship is different."

"I know that. We're just a bunch of grumpy old men who like to throw back a few together. So tell me about Duke Boswell. I'm surprised you never brought him up before."

"We did the Chatauqua circuit together."

"Chatauqua? That must have been an adventure. Saw one myself back east."

"We went to small towns out on the plains. Had us some good times."

***

Kemp Sweigart came by for Bobby in his Ford truck. The vehicle showed evidence of heavy use after many forays over nonexistent desert roads on the rangeland surrounding Mesa. Along with Kate, they had been rock hounds together and had enjoyed poking around old Hopi ruins and hunting for fossils and artifacts. They talked of someday traveling around the world together on anthropological expeditions.

Some of his father's good natured defiance pervaded Kemp's boyishness. He had assumed natural leadership of their little group with Kate monitoring and mothering after them if she surmised they were taking excessive risks or letting themselves in for trouble of one sort or another. Kemp called her their chaperon, but rarely had he and Bobby gone off on a jaunt without including her.

She was their senior by two years. She occasionally exasperated the boys when she pulled age superiority on them. They rarely sassed her back. She was nearly as strong as they were and was a skillful wrestler. She refused to teach them her tricks and moves or to reveal from whom she had learned them. But one day, they caught her talking to the captain of the high school wrestling team.

When she did a complete turnaround and married Charley Hughes, Bobby and Kemp cussed her out for ruining their plans to travel around the world. How could she give up all that to raise babies and take care of "the Gorilla" as they called her big muscular husband.

For years, the three of them had poured over maps and brochures and read every book and magazine they could get their hands on about foreign countries. They had accumulated a whole trunk filled with information. So people change. Times change. The world changes.

From all Southwest High School Wrestling Champion, "the Gorilla" had turned down scholarships and offers by professional managers and had gone to work for the Santa Fe Railroad. As an engineer, he made the twice daily run between Mesa, New Mexico and Kingman, Arizona. He was the proud father of two small children who bullied and beat him up mercilessly. "They're ruining my reputation," he said.

Charley's death from a sniper's bullet had devastated Kate. If it were not for her children, she said, she would go crazy. Carmody's chasing down Jerome Ligget did nothing to allay her emotional suffering. Ligget's death would not bring Charley back. He would only live on in their children.

What sense is there in planning anything, Bobby brooded, as he and Kemp drove slowly along the congested main street of Mesa on a Saturday night. People from all over the West and Southwest and a few from the East had congregated for the annual Intertribal Fair held at Window Rock several miles north of Mesa on the Navajo reservation. The fair was a high point of the summer in that region with members of all tribes gathering to feast, celebrate, and sell their art and crafts. The two boys would head out there as soon as they picked up Erin DeGrood and Sara Sims, their high school sweethearts for the past year.

The boys had not developed such a close friendship with the two girls until they had met at a church social. Given the Reverend Sims or his recent wife's approval, the boys took the two girls on their desert ramblings and revived their dream of world travel.

Erin had instantly paired herself with Bobby and Sara had attached herself to Kemp. Toward the end of their senior year, the prospect of marriage occupied much of their private conversation and Kemp became less concerned with enlisting in the army. He had good reason now to stay close to home.

Erin was the step daughter of Lee Stark, President of the Wooten Corporation and owner of the mine out at Coal Town. He had married Amelia DeGrood, a widow. She had inherited one of the largest ranches in New Mexico with the passing of her husband, who had died in a riding accident. Unable to endure Lee Stark's roughshod behavior, Erin had left her mother to live with the local minister, Reverend Sims, and his wife Sylvia. Reverend Sims would preside at the wedding of Erin and Bobby. At odds with her mother for marrying the fortune hunter, Erin would not invite her to attend the wedding. Of course, Logan did not include that private information in the announcement he wrote for the Mesa Independent. In retrospect, he wished he had never written any announcement of the wedding at all.

Chapter 29
POLITICS

A case of nerves had plagued Lee Stark for the past three days. He blamed it on the fact that he was trying to overcome nature by going on the wagon, with little success. So far, three days had been an agonizing record. He had finally decided to take Doc McAffrey's advice, since he was decidedly interested in the continuation of his life.

The blackouts had thrown a scare into Stark. He'd been drunk every day for nearly five years with no dry spells, no relief for his liver and his brain. His body was trying to tell him something. The realization that he had no control over his habit and that he was literally drinking himself to death panicked him.

Since his marriage to Amelia Degrood-Stark (To his consternation, she had retained the Degrood), he had gained considerable wealth and land holdings as well as the ear and partisanship of both state and Federal politicians who solicited his money and his favor.

The thrill of power clutched Stark. Since he had experienced every other sensation he considered of any personal value, he followed the pull of that cunning inexorable grip wherever it might lead. The blackouts were the first warning to change. He was still new to political power games. He played business games well. He knew he wanted to continue to play but he had to be sufficiently alert to function.

Many of the Degroods' who were blood relatives were direct descendants of the "original family." They considered Amelia and her hell-raising husband an embarrassment and a blight on the family name. A few of the Degrood men who held legislative office shunned Amelia's social affairs and would not by any stretch of the imagination engage in political transactions with Lee Stark. This snobbery so infuriated Stark that he lent financial support to the opposition at election time just to spite the Degrood tradition. This state of affairs provided Editor Shreve of *The Mesa Independent* with grist for his newspaper.

The Degrood oligarchs and their parliament decided it would be better to tolerate and placate Stark rather than parade the family division in public. In reality, Stark did endorse and support their basic policies.

More than one of the Degrood brothers would have liked to have Stark eliminated, but he was so much in the public eye that foul play would be traced back to them. Besides, Stark wore sidearms and surrounded himself with bodyguards day and night. Instead of fighting him, it behooved the disenchanted Degrood brothers to use his growing prestige to their own advantage.

His friendship with Halen Braun, the FBI Agent In Charge in Santa Fe, was also worth consideration where Stark was concerned. Braun attended all the Degrood social occasions and went quail and deer hunting with Stark.

Their association did not go unnoticed by Howard Gimbel. Stark and Braun made frequent trips out to the Wooten Mining Operation on the reservation. Howard was never asked to accompany them. He assumed that Braun was Stark's link to Washington when it came to mining on reservation land considered to be the property of the Federal Government.

At the moment, Stark's most urgent requirement was for a drink. He paced the study back and forth in front of the liquor cabinet. He had locked it and told the maid to hide the key somewhere so he would not accidentally find it. If he did, it would mean her job. The gesture was not entirely convincing of his will power.

A second key lodged in the top right hand drawer of the desk would allow him to make a scapegoat of the woman. If he had to deviate from his regimen, which he fully expected to happen, he could manage to do so without even requesting the first key and so save face at least in his own house. He could always claim the maid had not hidden the key from him well enough.

On an impulse that he later sorely regretted, he had also had the liquor removed from his limousine. He had difficulty accepting his mortality. In spite of what the doctor had explained, Stark did not believe he would die from drinking. He could not, should not, and would not.

He had cut back on the necessity of frequent inspection trips to the mine operation and drilling sites by hiring the best foremen and superintendents in the business. He had recruited them from the East at a high price.

The 400,000 acre ranch thrived under the capable management of Red Tasker, the man whom Everett Carmody had stopped from punishing the blacksmith at the DeGrood ranch when Carmody had worked there seventeen years ago.

From the beginning of his marriage to Amelia, Stark had recognized a likeness in Tasker's character to his own. He often invited Tasker to join him and Braun for a drink and when they went hunting. He trusted Tasker and Braun and confided in them as friends and allies regarding his concerns. He could use Tasker as his force, his muscle, and Braun for his authority.

The newly elected Senator, Bill Chanson, treated Stark with respect. Chanson would have liked to become a close associate. Stark cut a colorful figure. He was a powerful and rich man, the kind of friend the Mayor liked to cultivate, especially since he had ambitions to run for the Senate at the next election.

Stark's dislike for Chanson hindered the opportunity for a strong bond between them. Stark thought of Charming Billy as being too much of a dandy. He didn't consider him trustworthy. He had a scheming, conniving oily manner, like a professional gambler whose cheating at cards could not be detected. Stark did not perceive him to be a man's man. Billy was too fastidious, too conscious of his image in the public eye. He primped too much. But Stark did recognize his political acumen and contributed to his campaign fund.

Stark acknowledged that he himself did not possess the appropriate image to successfully run for public office. He didn't care for the responsibility required of a public servant anyway. Public service was merely a tool of the private sector. Stark's responsibility was to Stark. Chanson had followers state-wide. He may not have been a man's man, but he was popular, a people's politician.

Since few in the capital at Santa Fe cared much for Stark, he figured he'd better have a substantial arrangement with an insider to keep him informed as to what was going on behind closed doors. Who was making the deals. By supporting Chanson's election to the State Senate, he would essentially be placing the man on his private payroll as his informer and personal representative in the legislature. Using Chanson as his liaison, Stark could exert influence as he deemed necessary. He thought of it as being a Senator by proxy.

Stark's geologist had discovered extensive oil reserves on Navajo reservation land adjoining the Stark-Degrood Ranch. Stark intended to take possession of that region comprised of several square miles and begin drilling for oil on a vast scale. He would reap immense profits, especially as war with Germany expanded in Europe.

For the present, dabbling with a few wells that were not big producers was a start. With the advent of a continental war, the demand for coal and oil would spiral dramatically. He would capitalize on that opportunity and increase his fortune. It didn't concern him which side he sold to. He would sell to both sides, Germany and the allies. Profiteering and patriotism were not incompatible.

Stark rarely saw his wife anymore. She had moved to her residential mansion in Santa Fe. Her trips to Mesa had become increasingly more infrequent until she had stopped coming altogether.

Stark had sated his ardor for her some time ago when he finally realized she considered him a buffoon. He was her trained bear on a chain leash. What angered him had been her refusal to sign over more than twenty-five percent of her financial interests. He then set out to acquire by influence what she would not relinquish by marriage. He refused to be a rich woman's diversion to be cast aside when she tired of the novelty. He would not just be part of her continual social act. He would not play her fool. Ever since their farce of a wedding staged like a Bohemian opera in Santa Fe, she had not slept with him other than when it suited her.

To counter her liaisons, he and Halen Braun would arrange private parties with high class prostitutes brought in on the train from

Los Angeles and San Francisco. The ranch foreman, Red Tasker, was always invited to join them.

Stark oddly and unexpectedly felt a slight remorse that his step-daughter, Erin Degrood, despised him, as well as her own mother. Her youth and innocence flowering in that jaded society eluded him. Erin's reaction to their depravity was to embrace a puritan ethic of morality. She found its epitome in the Methodist teachings of Reverend Harrison Sims, the Navajo reservation missionary. Through this religious association, a sisterly bond of love and friendship had flourished between her and the minister's adopted Navajo daughter, Sara.

Erin had moved out of her mother's sprawling hacienda in Mesa where she had been raised and now lived in the Sims's small house adjoining the Methodist church on the other side of town.

Erin and Sara had met in a physical education class during their freshman year at Mesa Union High School. Erin had refused to move back East and attend a private boarding school. Sara stood out as one of the few Indians in the predominantly mixed white and Hispanic population. Most of the Mexican teenagers attended a Catholic high school.

Although Sara excelled in girls' athletics and earned high grades in the classroom, her shyness was an obstacle to establishing friendships. She felt low self-esteem at being an Indian. Yet she considered herself blessed and fortunate to live in a white family, attend a white school, and worship in a white church.

Erin broke through Sara's isolation. Erin was the most attractive and admired girl in the school and Sara could not understand why Erin would seek her friendship. She tried to escape the white girl's overtures by acting noncommittal and aloof. Then one night, Erin came in tears to the church house seeking refuge from the madness at her own home.

Erin's mother had been throwing a party for the usual strange Bohemian crowd when her stepfather, Lee Stark, had burst in raving drunkenly. "What the hell do you think you're doing with my wife, you fucking wetback? You call what you do art? It's nothing but shit! Anybody can throw paint at a canvas!"

He had slashed the artist Berto Cabeza in the face with a broken whiskey bottle.

Erin had run out of the hacienda to the stable. She saddled and bridled her horse and rode him down the long gravel drive in the blue shadows of moonlight to the main dirt road. The town of Mesa was five miles away. Determined, but trembling, she had galloped through the night amid the howls of coyotes loping through the surrounding brush. She smelled the sweetness of sage coming in off the desert on the morning breeze, as she turned uphill toward the church and the home of her friend, Sara Sims.

Her frantic knocking brought the Reverend Sims shuffling in his slippers . He quickly knotted his bathrobe and stroked back what remained of his balding hair, then pulled open the door.

"I can't stay there with them anymore," she said.

In hysterics she poured out descriptions of the ugliness and abusiveness she had witnessed and had to live with almost daily. She wanted deliverance from that wallowing hell.

To Erin's relief, and surprise, her mother never missed her.

Chapter 30
MURDER OF A BRIDE

Randolph was convinced he was responsible for the death of Erin Carmody on the day of her wedding, because he had written a front page story about them for *The Mesa Independent*, including a photograph. He had identified Erin as the daughter of Amelia DeGrood and step father, Lee Stark. He had made them visible to the killers who would have otherwise not even known about the wedding.

***

Charley Hughes' death by Jerome Ligget's sniper bullet had strengthened Bobby's resolve. He saw how his sister, Kate lived in a state of irreparable suffering at the loss of her husband. The transient nature of life had been steadily growing within him. He feared the proximity of death hovering out there, indiscriminant, waiting for him. The uniformed soldiers he saw coming and going on the trains were a daily reminder.

He had walked Erin to the door at Reverend Sims house after a stroll arm in arm in the adjacent desert landscape. "We have to talk," he said.

"We could talk now."

"Not now, it's not the right time. I'll come by later."

She held on to is arm. "Sara's gone. She disappeared the day she got that letter from Kemp."

"Where did she go?"

"Nobody knows. Did he tell you he wrote that letter?"

"I didn't know about the letter. He's different now. The army changed him. Something happened to him at Fort Bliss. I can't explain it. He's not like the kid we used to know. We'll talk later. Things have changed. So many things have changed. It can never be like it used to."

Their boyhood friend, Kemp had excelled in basic training. He had become a squad leader. He enjoyed sounding off marching commands and thrived on playing soldier games. He took to them naturally. He was a crack marksman and demonstrated leadership ability. They had even talked to him about training to become a combat officer. He had responded with enthusiasm and done well on his written and practical exams. Following his leave, he would go to Florida to Officer Candidate School. The long friendship between Bobby and Kemp disintegrated. Kemp was gung ho and highly motivated to go into battle. He wanted to kill Nazis.

In his letter to Sara Sims, the Reverend's adopted Navajo stepdaughter, Kemp had severed their engagement. There would be no double wedding. For Kemp, the impending war provided him a time and opportunity to become a man, to leave his boyhood behind. He said he didn't want any attachments, nothing holding him back, filling his mind and weakening his resolve.

"Do you still love me?" asked Erin.

Bobby could not believe she would say such a thing. "Yes, yes, oh, my God, yes. That is the only thing. That's the only thing that matters." He held her in his arms. "I have to go now. I'll be back in a while. I'll be back."

She watched him walk away.

Carmody had organized a search for Sara Sims. "If she left town, she didn't go out on a train," he said. "She's still somewhere around."

"You should forget it," said Bobby.

"What?"

"Forget it. Call it off. She doesn't want to be found."

"Call it off?"

"Yes, she ran away because of Kemp. He wrote her a letter."

When Bobby arrived home, he didn't realize how much he would miss his mother until that moment. He would miss the full rich smells of a fantastic meal permeating the house.

He could not deny reality. He wanted to cry out his anguish, blame his father, but he remained choked and silent. He could no longer concern himself with the destructive adult world. His own life, survival was his primary concern.

Bobby heard his father leave. He lay on his bed a while longer, then rose with the quick resiliency of youth and moved purposefully to the closet. He selected boots, denims, and a western style shirt.

He stopped to eat quickly at a café before going on to the Sims's house. He wanted nothing to detain him. The aftertaste of black coffee and spicy chili rose in his throat. He glanced around with the nervousness of a fugitive.

He did not want to talk with the Reverend Sims and his wife. He hoped Erin would be watching for him and come out to the street when she saw him. He passed the house once slowly, then returned. He waited straining like a dog on a leash at the end of the sidewalk. Finally, he went up to the door and knocked . Erin appeared from the rattle of dishes heard from the kitchen. "Come in."

"Let's walk. I want us to be alone."

"It's okay," she said. "The Sims drove out to Fort Defiance to try and bring Sara back home. She's at the hospital. We're alone." She held the screen door wide, then let it gently fall shut behind him. "They left only a few minutes ago. They'll be gone a long while. I'm washing the dishes."

He followed her in to the tiny kitchen. It was so small he wondered how anyone could even cook and serve a meal in there. Everything was cramped about the house, the space and the furniture that crowded that space. It reminded him of the sparseness of religion, the squeezing out of individuality to believe what could not be proven, the sacrifice of self in the name of blind faith. Not since he was a boy had anyone sold him on the idea. It had never appealed to him. The minister did not know how to persuade him.

Sitting at the oilcloth covered table, he watched her back as she plunged her hands into the suds and water. She paused a moment without looking at him directly, conscious of the posture and movement of her young body as it affected his perception of her. He loved the grace with which she bent from her narrow waist, the slight uplift of her breasts as she reached high to place a saucer in the cupboard. Seeing his reflection in the window over the sink, she said, "We have to think of ourselves now."

"I know. I know. That's what I want to talk about."

She turned to face him at the sudden sliding note of despair in his voice. "You too?

"No, no, not that! God, not that! We'll get married just like ... just like we planned. I'm afraid, Erin. If I go away, that will be the end of everything. We'll never see each other again. They'll send my parts home in a coffin because I won't be able to survive. I won't be able to take it. I know that. Half of surviving is that you set your mind to it and you will. Out there, no."

Wiping her hands on her apron, she came slowly to the table and stood opposite him. "What are you thinking?"

"I'm not going to let them take me."

"The army?"

He nodded. "I'm not like Kemp. I can't do it. I can't go out there knowing what will happen to me."

"What can you do?"

"The military draft is going to happen soon. We, us, you and I ... we'll get married. Then we'll leave the country. Go live in Mexico."

She stared at him with uncertainty.

"If you say no, if you won't, if you can't follow me, I'm going anyway. I have to. I'm afraid of dying. I don't believe in what they will try to make me do. I'm not a killer. There's a whole world of death going on out there. I have to get away from it. I'm not like my father. I have to."

Erin's gaze dropped to her hands.

"I'm not a coward either," he said. "I would give my life for you."

"I know. I know," she was quick to reassure him. "But how will we live?"

"I don't know yet. But I can find some kind of work. Maybe start up a business."

"You don't have any money."

"You do."

"It's in a trust. It's doled out to me. I can't claim all of it until I'm twenty-one."

"That's only three years away. We can go with what we have. Erin, I want to leave now, tonight, before anybody suspects anything. Just grab a few clothes. We'll take a bus to Juarez and cross the border."

"Do you realize you'll never be able to come back. You would be arrested and put in prison."

He looked down and nodded. "Does it matter. At least we'll be together."

She reached across the table and gently took his hand. "I'll go with you," she paused. "But I do want us to have our wedding here."

He searched her luminescent eyes and momentarily doubted the beauty of their blue milkiness as if they deceptively drew him closer to death rather than to love. His personal fear was all-consuming. "All right, but you can't talk about our plans to anyone, not even Sara, if she comes back. Nothing about Mexico."

Erin nodded. A pact had been made. She rose. "Let me finish these. It's a beautiful evening. We'll take a walk."

"I'll help. I feel like I should be doing something."

"There are only a few left."

He stood and came over to the sink. His arm slipped around her waist. They kissed lightly. "I want it to be like this," he said. "I really want it to be like this for us ... quiet, the two of us washing dishes in the evening. Am I asking too much?"

"No," she whispered. "No."

***

Carmody wanted to give his son, Bobby, and Erin a wedding gift that would endure and cause them to remember him. Bobby had been avoiding the house, specifically to avoid his father, coming in late after Carmody was asleep and not rising in the morning until after he was gone.

On the eve of the wedding, Carmody was determined to talk with his son, confront him if necessary. He sat up and waited for him in the dark. When Bobby walked in, his father's deep voice from the gloom startled him. He stood for several moments without speaking and sorted through his mind why his father would be there at such a late hour. Then, resigned, he asked, "Why are you sitting in the dark?" He touched the wall switch.

As the lamp came on, Carmody smiled and motioned him to a nearby chair and leaned forward to push an empty glass and a bottle of bourbon across the coffee table. "I'd like to have a drink with my son the night before his wedding."

Bobby reluctantly accepted the half-filled glass. He sat back staring at it without touching it. He slowly directly raised his eyes to look at his father. For the first time in many years, their eyes met and held. He wanted to confide in his father, tell him his fears and his plans. He wanted approval and support for what he intended to do, but he did not trust him to not interfere.

His father was made from a different mold. His tradition was founded on the values of an earlier generation that expected their children to obey and follow on, not lead. Conduct their lives in the manner of their parents.

Bobby's eyes drifted to the badge resting on the lamp table next to Carmody's armchair. Now that he planned to go against the law, he could not distinguish his father, the man, from the role of law enforcer.

"It's ... " Bobby's voice faltered. He had always felt intimidated by his father. He had never been comfortable with him. "It's hard for me, all that's happened," he paused, "and all that will happen."

Carmody nodded, encouraging him with gentle keen interest to continue. "Not a happy note to get married on." He waited. "Those were good days for your mother and me, the early days."

Bobby glanced up surprised at his comment. He felt like he was looking down at an object through clear water that refracted and distorted the actual position of the object. He wondered and half hoped to discover, even now this late, a restoration of the man he briefly remembered as a young boy. Bobby kept the memory alive so that he could tolerate the later man his father had become. His father had said "the early days." For whatever reason, those same memories for him were now gleaming through. Bobby suddenly realized his father must be a lonely man.

"I remember that spring you took all of us on a pack trip to Taos." Bobby picked up his drink and self-consciously grinned.

Carmody smiled, a small smile, but one that broke through the pain, the stress, the weariness of his life seamed across his face. "We never had such fishing, did we?"

Bobby fought the sudden tightness around his eyes to prevent from crying. "Everything happens so late," he finally croaked out in defensive anger to mask his emotion. "We never ... " he shook his head. "You know when Kate and me used to go out and dig around the old desert ruins when we were kids?"

Carmody nodded. He watched and listened carefully to his son to treasure these moments that would never be repeated. He also listened for what was not said, but what he knew he was meant to hear. These were the messages that Bobby would be able to communicate to him in a direct way. After so many years, they were both struggling.

"Well, I never quite believed those ancient tribes had been there and that was all that was left of them. Maybe I just didn't want to believe it, because that's all that could be left of us someday, and I didn't want to think that. I still don't, but if that's all there is, if that's all we come to ... " His shoulders lifted and settled with a nervous shrug. "I don't see much sense in following the way we're going."

They sat unmoving through a long silence. Carmody took in what he heard and carefully placed the thoughts in his own mind. He was in agreement. Through a gift, he would let his son know of the agreement. What his son did with his life was his own decision to make.

"I have a gift for you and Erin," he rose. "I'll get it."

He disappeared down the dark hall and returned a few moments later with a package wrapped in plain white paper. Almost shyly he handed it to his son. Bobby removed the wrapper with care and placed it aside. He opened the box and stared at its contents.

A large silver plate gleamed up at him in the dim light. He recognized the plate as the work of a Hopi silversmith. The Hopi's symbol of emergence, the Mother Earth symbol, had been painstakingly carved into the silver.

Bobby understood why his father had chosen the gift. In exploring the old Hopi ruins and in witnessing religious ceremonies at the Oraibi Pueblo, the trader, Noel Sweigart, Kemp's uncle, had explained to them the significance and meaning of the mystic ritual. The chants and dances told the creation myths.

In the beginning, man had been created in perfection in the image of his Creator, Taiowa, and had fallen from grace by succumbing to his human impulses. He had to climb upward. At each stage of his evolution, through the destruction of the world and mankind, he passed on to the next. The fourth world was the present one. It represented the full expression of man's ruthlessness, materialism, and imperialistic will. Man himself manifested his excessive appetites.

Then man rose upward to the higher centers. The crown of his head opened and he merged into the wholeness of creation from where he originated. It was a Road of Life traveled according to his own free will. He satisfied every capacity for good and evil until he came to know himself as a finite part of infinity.

Reverend Sims married Bobby Carmody and Erin DeGrood in a small private ceremony in the Methodist Church. Bobby's widowed sister, Kate Hughes, Carmody, Dr. McAffrey, the Sweigarts', Randolph and his mother, Gimbel and Sybil, the reverend's wife, attended. Sheila Carmody stood next to her husband. When she placed her arm through his and looked up at him with a smile, he felt a sudden wave of emotion. He was overcome by love and grief. He smiled in return and patted her hand.

Sara Sims had refused to return from the reservation. She was going to work at the hospital as a medical aide and interpreter. She had told Reverend Sims and his wife that she was a Navajo, not a white woman. She had been wrong in trying to become a white woman all her young life. From that time on, she would live like a Navajo and be proud of her heritage and who she was. She told Sims it would have been better for her to never have left the reservation with him when she was a little girl. Her remarks had hurt him deeply.

At the conclusion of the ceremony, Carmody passed his hat and handed it to the new young couple generously filled with cash to send them off on their honeymoon. Judith Sweigart silently noted that the wedding was particularly functional and dry-eyed, but the final embraces, good wishes and congratulations were bestowed with full sincerity. Sheila and Erin, mother and daughter-in-law embraced in tears.

Kemp and Bobby saw the hopes and fears in each others' eyes. They were leaving behind a portion of their lives. There was a possibility they would never see each other again. Kemp would be leaving on the troop train the next day to begin officer training at Fort Lauderdale, Florida.

Judith and Sybil injected the only moment of genuine gaiety in the otherwise solemn ceremony by showering the newlyweds with handfuls of rice prompting them into a self-conscious shuffling lope to the Reverend's car, which he was loaning to them for the duration of their honeymoon.

As they pulled away with a sudden aggressive blaring of the horn that sounded out of place in the quiet afternoon, they were unaware of a pickup truck that detached itself from the shade of a tree down the street and followed them. Logan believed he was the only one who noticed the truck. He didn't recognize who was inside and it did not occur to him that anything was unusual.

As Carmody shook hands all around with the well-wishers, they moved to decorated tables that had been set up for a reception barbeque.

***

Thompson and Leuentky had been cruising the main street of Mesa and stopped at the Harvey restaurant. While eating lunch, Leuentky's glance had fallen on a copy of the Mesa Independent left behind by another customer. He had read Randolph Logan's article about the wedding and an idea had occurred to him how he and Thompson could further the cause of the union organizer, Yelena

Ivanov. Erin Degrood was the step daughter of Lee Stark, the owner of the mine.

The truck had followed the newlyweds, hanging back for six miles, then had surged forward and passed them and continued building speed until it was gone from sight over a low lying hill far ahead.

Bobby leaned back as the hot wind plowed over him in rushing erratic gusts through the open windows. He smiled at Erin snuggled in at his side. He relished the touch of her slender hand resting gently on his thigh. For the first time in months, a lightness of spirit invaded him. A future filled with life and promise, and struggle, rather than death, lay ahead down the road.

They had not figured on having the car. They thought they would have to take the train. Reverend Sims's offer surprised them. Bobby would rather not have accepted it. It thrust an added responsibility on them and made it easier to identify who they were. Now they had to find a way to dispose of it. He decided not to abandon the car at the border. They had enough gas to get them to Las Cruces, then take the bus to Mexico City. The trip would be long and exhausting, but he would be free to begin a new life with his bride.

They traveled light, carrying one small suitcase each. Erin spoke a functional idiomatic Mexican-Spanish that she had learned as a child from her mother's housemaids and servants. Bobby believed it would not take him long to pick up more of the language than a standard greeting and a few schoolboy obscenities that had been integrated into local English usage. Once they were settled in Mexico, he would be immersed in the language on a daily basis. Erin had already taught him a few common words and phrases and he tried a couple on her as they drove.

"Buenos dias, Senora."

"Buenos dias, Senore."

"Como esta usted?"

"Estoy bien, gracias, y usted?"

"Muy bien, gracias."

"Estas casado.?"

She laughed. "Si, estoy casado."

Coming over the hill, they saw the pickup truck about a half mile ahead now pulled over onto the road shoulder. The hood was raised and two men were poking around the engine. As the car approached, the taller of the two stepped out onto the narrow road and waved them to a halt. He leaned down at the driver's window with a nervous anxious grin.

"Hi, havin' some engine trouble here. Could be the carburetor. Maybe a valve burned out on us. Don't know yet. We ask you for a lift to the next town? Looks like we're gonna need a tow in."

Bobby glanced at Erin to catch a thought or response from her eyes. At her sudden mask of terror, his head whipped around and he stared into the muzzle of a .38.

"Hey, listen, we're not."

"Shut your fuckin' mouth and get out of the car."

Bobby then noticed through the windshield that the other man, with the physique of a large ape, had a shotgun leveled at them from the other side of the truck under the hood.

The man at the window spoke. "You have about two seconds to move your ass or I'll blow your fuckin' head off." He cocked back the hammer to demonstrate he meant what he said.

Bobby opened the door and cautiously stepped out frantically searching for a sign of some other approaching vehicle. But he had chosen a seldom used road across desolate back country. As it was, few people traveled by car anyway because of the restrictions of wartime gas rationing.

"Take the car if you want it. You can have the damn car. Just leave us alone. That's all I ask. Please leave us alone."

The gun's heavy metal smashed against bone and cartilage, crushing his nose and shattering his upper teeth. He pitched backward into a black void studded with flashes of fire. Blood thickly scented his tongue. Erin's fading scream rang distantly in his head as it bounced on the rough road surface and he sluiced into unconsciousness.

Pulling the key from the ignition, Leuentky aimed the revolver at Erin's fear struck eyes bordering on hysteria and screamed at her to shut up and get out of the car. He himself imitated her hysteria knowing that it created an impression of insanity in his own eyes.

Thompson slammed down the truck hood. Placing the shotgun on a rack in the cab, he lumbered up into the driver's seat. Leuentky's free hand clamped Erin's arm. He walked her to the other side of the truck and forced her roughly into the cab where Thompson immediately pressed a heavy arm around her. She recoiled at his beady pig eyes so close to her face and the smell of liquor on his breath.

"Oh, God, let me go, please."

Thompson belched a sour vapor of chili and cheap whiskey. Erin's stomach rose in her throat, but she controlled the nausea precipitated more from fear than from the rotting body odor of the man. Through the dirt-streaked windshield, she watched the tall thin man drag Bobby into the back seat of the car. Then he jammed the gear shift at neutral and pushed the car to the opposite side of the road where it heaved and rattled heavily into the deep dry ditch. Leuentky then came around and leaped up into the cab squeezing Erin between himself and Thompson whose coarse hand explored the contours of her breasts.

"Let's go," Leuentky barked. "You can fuck her later."

Silent tears burst from Erin's eyes and streamed in coursing glistening waves down her face as Thompson started the truck. He made a tight U-turn and headed back in the direction of Mesa.

After several miles, they pulled off the deserted road onto an old wagon trail and followed the track's spine jarring ruts for three-hundred yards to where it angled down into a mud-cracked riverbed that placed them well out of sight of the road.

Holding his gun pressed into Erin's neck, Leuentky led her down out of the cab. Thompson walked around the other side to the back end and dropped open the tailgate with a clang of chains and metal. Leuentky pulled Erin to Thompson, who grabbed her by the wrists. Leuentky glanced around. He was anxious to get back. "Make it fast."

Thompson released Erin, grabbed her dress at the neckline, and with one brutal pull, split the garment from her shaking body in two pieces. She screamed and tried to twist away. His enormous hand encircled her throat. He shook his head. She did not scream again. He suddenly lifted her from the ground. "Get her pants off and the fuckin' bra. I want to suck her titties. She's got nice titties."

Leuentky snapped off her bra and rolled down her panties into an elastic band that tangled about her small feet until he impatiently jerked them free.

Pressed against Thompson's wide heavy body, Erin struggled for breath until he suddenly lowered her to the ground. Keeping a grasp around her waist, he unbuttoned and dropped his coveralls and underwear, exposing his erect cock, slimy with a partial anticipatory ejaculation. He lurched the rolls of his fat white buttocks onto the rear end of the truck, then lifted Erin, spreading her legs and forcing her to straddle him.

Her pink bare feet gripped at the hot metal ribs of the truck bed, as Thompson pulled her tightly against the tallow of his great body, probed and thrust hard and deeply into her. She cried out and hung limp, rising and falling with the motion of his upward goring penetration. He came with a long moan of relief, his hot labored breathing panting in her ear.

"I like virgins. Their pussy is nice and tight. How's that for being fucked on your wedding? Bet your husband couldn't fuck you so good. 'Course, you ain't never gonna know unless you already done it with him." Then to Leuentky, who had been observing the act of violation with a mien of emotionless attachment, he said, "I've got her good and greased. You can slide in easy like fuckin' liver."

Leuentky shook his head. "I want to get on back."

Thompson lifted Erin slightly from his lap and alternately took each of her breasts into his mouth, sucking and chewing noisily before he let her down. She clung to the side of the truck in suspended shock. Filth and defilement consumed her. In her mind, she kept withdrawing further and further away from them, escaping that reality into another of her own creation. Soon, they and what they had done would no longer exist for her. The truck rose on its springs as Thompson slid off the tailgate to the ground.

While Thompson pulled up and fastened his coveralls, Leuentky vaulted into the back of the truck and quickly unrolled a tarp. He motioned for Thompson to hand Erin up to him.

"Lie down," he ordered.

She sank to the truck bed. Leuentky proceeded to loosely wrap her in the tarp so that she was totally concealed. He kept her head near the open end so she could breathe without too much difficulty.

"Now, I'm going to be sitting right here next to you," he told her. "You shout or scream and I'll open up your head. That's a promise."

But she had already drifted beyond him. He could not discern from her vacant stare that she had not heard nor understood what he said.

***

A dust storm several hundred miles to the west sharply defined the emblazoned copper ball of the sun riding low in the rusty atmospheric haze. The headlights of the truck glowed dimly in the purple twilight of Coal Town. It followed a zig-zag route through the narrow streets and finally pulled to a stop at the rear door of a bakery that backed on an alley.

Thompson cut the lights and engine. He climbed down and walked to the rear where Leuentky was quietly dropping the tailgate. A pair of eyes peered out through the barred curtained rear window of the bakery. A moment later, the door opened, as Thompson and Leuentky slid the tarp containing Erin from the truck and carried her inside.

Dressed as a baker woman, Yelena Ivanov stepped down from the flour storage bin which she had established as her office. Here, all documents, business correspondence and union literature were kept hidden, sealed in plastic and buried in various sacks of flour specifically marked with coded baking terminology.

As Thompson and Leuentky pulled the bruised numb girl from the folds of the tarp, Yelena noticed the dried blood and semen that had leaked down Erin's legs. She turned on the two men with wild rage.

"You imbeciles! You cretins! What is this? Why did you do this? Why did you bring her here? My God, what have you done?"

"She's Lee Stark's step daughter." Leuentky thought his logic obvious. "We read in the paper that she was getting married today. We thought it would be a good idea to hold her for ransom so Stark would have to sign the union contract. That way, we won't even have to strike."

It was not even so much the blood and semen as the girl's haunted staring expression that Yelena recognized as madness. "You shits. You God damn fools. You've ruined everything I've done, everything I've set up. The FBI will come out here and tear the town apart until they find us. You have to take her to the reservation hospital at Fort Defiance. She needs a doctor."

Erin suddenly staggered to her feet and lunged away screaming in hysteria, slamming pots and pans to the floor and throwing them against the walls seeking escape from images in her mind. She did not know where she was and that she could have run out through the front door of the bakery. Thompson's looming bulk cut her off. She could no longer discriminate him from the pressing shadows in her mind.

Her eyes flashed on a sharp carving knife. She clutched it like a dagger and slashed at the mountain of oozing flesh. His viselike hand clamped her wrist with such pressure, the knife clattered to the wooden floor. His other hand slick with blood from the deep cut she had inflicted on his arm closed around her throat. The pad of his thumb cracked her larynx like an eggshell. Her eyes bulged. Her body thrashed, then went limp, hanging there in his grasp like a rag doll.

"Oh my God, no! No!" Yelena clawed at the man, going for his eyes.

"She tried to kilt me," said Thompson.

"You deserve to be killed," Yelena screamed. She turned to Leuentky.

Thompson released Erin's body. It slumped to the floor. He grabbed a handful of dish towels to staunch the flow of his blood.

Yelena stared at the nude corpse. She reached down and quickly closed the staring eyes. The girl's face and body were beautiful, even in death, the beauty of a child at rest, not the dark hollow eyes of miners' children haunted by poverty and deprivation.

"Where is her husband? What did you do with her husband? You didn't kill him, did you?"

"He's in his car somewheres in a ditch," said Leuentky.

"Did you kill him too?"

"Naw, we didn't kill him. He was breathing when I put him in the car."

"I hope he kept on breathing."

"What you want us to do with the bitch?" asked Thompson.

"She's not a bitch. She's a woman, a human being."

"She's a whore, a bitch."

The edges of Yelena's mouth curled downward in disgust. She wanted to grab the knife and carve up the beast Thompson.

"We can make it look like someone else done this," said Leuentky, ever open for an opportunity to redeem himself. "Like Injuns."

Yelena knew that her time there had come to an end. She must leave as soon as it was safe and she would not be detected. She didn't want these moronic psychopaths to know when or where she was going.

"We can make it look like Injuns done it."

"I don't want to know what you do again, ever."

"Then it's okay."

"Nothing you've done is okay."

"Well, shit, lady, we thought you'd 'ppreciate all this."

Yelena's eyes were dark coals.

"Looks like she's leavin' it up to us."

"Looks that way. We ain't gonna git ourselves caught."

"What about you, union boss? You gonna skedaddle?"

Yelena turned away and walked out of their sight into an adjoining room.

A trail of blood trickled after Thomson and Leuentky, as they staggered outside and stumbled through the dark alleyways back to their lodging.

Yelena considered her next course of action. She decided she would have to leave the country. She would take the baker's truck and she would take the poor murdered girl with her. She needed Gimbel. Together, they would take Erin Carmody to her father-in-law, the marshal. She would return to Coal Town with Carmody and identify the killers.

Then with Gimbel's help, she would cross the border into Mexico. She had received information that the Nazi party had established a cell in Mexico City. She was a pawn in the swinging pendulum of political forces. Although she despised Hitler and everything he was doing, she began to form a plan of how she could redeem herself for her involvement in the death of the young woman who lay on the floor.

Chapter 31
EMPTY PROMISES

The morning after his meeting with Howard Gimbel at the BIA, Duncan Zaragoza rode thirty miles to talk with four other Navajo men. They too had been out in the world and understood there were greater demons than the ghosts and witches and superstitions of the desert night.

A man who owned a truck drove Duncan to the general store in Mesa. Duncan purchased a pick and shovel, fuses, blasting caps, and two cases of dynamite. To all appearances, he planned to blast away hardrock and do a little mining, maybe for turquoise, as he told the store proprietor. "Navajos have their own secret places where we get the precious stones."

On the next night, he and the men rode out to Lee Stark's oil drilling site on reservation land. They carefully laid a network of fuses and explosives among the pipes and grid of the drilling rig. The ensuing blast shot a geyser of fire into the black sky and shattered the trailer windows of the sleeping crew who scrambled out into the brush as a second explosion followed, leaving the rig an impenetrable mass of hot steaming twisted metal.

Two days later, the same crew returned with six armed guards. They were Red Tasker's men from the Stark DeGrood ranch. They had orders to shoot and kill anybody, white or Indian, who approached the site in a suspicious manner. Tasker left that interpretation to the discretion of his men.

He suspected the sabotage was the work of the Navajos. He had experienced a running feud with several Navajo families in a range land grazing district that Stark had illegally purchased from the Federal Government. The Navajos had refused to leave the land. They had cut Stark's barbed wire fences and butchered his cattle that strayed into the canyons. Now, with the dynamiting of one of his drilling rigs, Stark gave Tasker the authority to retaliate and to show no mercy.

Raven, Duncan Zaragoza's sister, hummed softly to herself. Her horse meandered through the desert scrub behind the small foraging herd of sheep at a lazy walk. The noon sun warmed her back. She thought of the spring up ahead where she would have a drink of cool water and eat a meal of cold beans and friend bread. She also thought of the design in a new rug she had started weaving back at the Hogan, now three miles behind her spotted with sage and mesquite whose deep roots clutched the gently rolling terrain of drifting sand. A warm steady wind lifted dervishes of dust that whirled briefly among the scattered flock and settled on their gray wool.

She watched the sheep spread out along the narrow stream that bubbled from the spring among a stand of boulders. She dismounted and secured her shaggy spotted pony with a long halter rope that allowed it to wander several yards and nibble at coarse tufts of grass that thrust up from the desert floor. Removing a beaded leather bag from her squaw saddle, she walked in an unhurried manner to the spring. She dropped the bag and knelt at the clear pool formed by a concavity in the granite rock formation. Her hand dipped and scooped the water to her lips. Her tongue savored its purity and mineral flavor. Her dark eyes tracked the sudden movement of a lizard that emerged from a crack and briefly stared back at her before scuttling away to another place of hiding.

Pushing at her long dark skirt, she sat cross-legged and reached for the bag containing her food. A rifle shot rang out followed by the frenzied baaing and crying of her sheep. She leaped up and rushed out from behind the rocks to see a group of five men on horses riding down on the flock and shooting the scrambling sheep that fell twitching and kicking until all thirty of them lay dead, their blood staining their wool and absorbed by the desert sand.

When the resounding echo of gunfire died away, Tasker's men rode their sweating frothing mounts sidestepping through the carnage over to the Navajo girl. The leader spit a stream of red tobacco at her feet. Fearing they would do her harm, she cowered away back toward the spring.

"Think she knows English?"

"Doubt it."

"Hey, you know English?"

Raven did not move or nod or shake her head. She did not understand the sounds coming from the reddish mouth of the leader. Her eyes stared horror struck.

"She don't know. Probably shit her dress," said a second Anglo cowboy.

"She don't have to know. She'll go back and tell her Navvie relatives."

"She stinks. Kin smell her from here."

"All injun whores stink. They don't take off them damn skirts but once't a year."

"You don't want to lift 'em up and take a peek?"

"Hell no!"

"Let's go back," the leader turned his horse. "Shouldn't have any more trouble, now they see what'll happen to 'em."

Flooded with relief and despair, Raven watched the men ride off into the desert. She walked out among the carcases of her sheep and saw the wounds encrusted with flies. With a cry of anguish, she ran to her horse and retrieved the halter rope. Pulled taut by the animal attempting to get away from the rampage, it had become tangled and ensnared in the brush. She untied the knot at the halter, left the rope on the ground, and pulled her trembling body up onto the saddle. Her moccasined heels drummed the horse into an unaccustomed trot. Hot tears flashed from her eyes as she faced into the wind.

Late that night, as one of Tasker's men on guard duty paused to light a cigarette, an arrow passed cleanly between his shoulder blades, penetrated his heart and breast bone and came out the other side. He fell without uttering a sound.

Fifteen minutes later, the new drilling rig went the way of its predecessor.

***

The killing of the guard and sabotage of Lee Stark's oil wells prompted one of the biggest manhunts in the state of New Mexico. The story filled the pages of *The Mesa Independent* and was picked up by the *Albuquerque Journal*.

Stark wanted to strike back conclusively against the Navajos who grazed their sheep on what he now considered his land and who plagued his oil drilling operations and had killed one of his men.

An itinerant Mexican family of four came across Carmody's son, Bobby, unconscious in the back seat of the car belonging to the Reverend Sims of the local Methodist Church of Mesa. At first, they nudged him to see if he were alive and noticed he was barely breathing. He was unconscious and dehydrated, but they could not coax water into his mouth. They carefully lifted him from the car onto their wagon. The two children, a boy and a girl, and their mother shielded him from the direct afternoon sun. The father walked along beside their burro, urging the animal to quicken its pace toward town.

Not knowing where to take the young man, they wandered down the main street until they came to the sheriff's office. The father went inside and came out a few moments later with Carmody. Shocked to see his son beaten about the face and unconscious, he choked down his rush of emotion and asked the Mexican man in Spanish to help move Bobby from the wagon into the back seat of his car. He lunged behind the wheel, started the engine, and roared away down the street to Dr. McAffrey's house which doubled as a clinic at the edge of town.

When he arrived, he rushed inside and returned with Dr. McAffrey, who assisted him carrying Bobby's limp body into the clinic. They gently placed him on the examining table.

"What the hell happened, Ev?"

"Don't know. A Mexican family brought him into town on their cart."

"What about Erin? Where is she?"

"Don't have an answer."

"They were just going on their honeymoon. Must have had an accident on the road."

"They would have brought her in with Bobby."

"From the cuts and bruises, looks like he was beaten."

"I'm afraid of what might have happened to Erin."

"He took a severe blow to the side of his head." McAffrey lifted Bobby's left eyelid. "Concussion. He's dehydrated. I'll start him on an IV."

"I'll send Sheila over, then go out on the road and see if I can find their car. Do whatever you have to. Just keep him alive."

McAffrey nodded quickly and turned back to his patient as Carmody raced out the door.

***

The phones at *The Mesa Independent* rang into the night with calls from people in Albuquerque and Santa Fe wanting the latest information about "the Indian uprising."

Some offered their assistance to join the vigilante force, described in the news story, being organized at the Stark-Degrood Ranch.

Logan found Carmody with his wife, Sheila, at their son's bedside at Dr. McAffrey's. He hesitated to interrupt the sheriff, but Carmody noticed him waiting outside under the porch light.

"What do you want, Logan?"

"Dr. McAffrey told me. I'm sorry to hear about Bobby. The doc said you don't have any news on Erin."

"Not yet."

"Do you know about Stark forming a posse. One of his guards was killed and another well blown up. He wants blood."

"Stark will break the law if he crosses onto reservation land and mounts a raid against the Navajos. I'm more concerned now about my son and Erin. Only Bobby can tell who did this. As for Stark, he and his politicians violated a Federal treaty by claiming reservation land where he's drilling for oil and putting up fences and running cattle. He doesn't own mineral rights or any other rights on the reservation."

Shreve had sent Tom Bell, the other reporter, out to the Stark-Degrood Ranch to follow the vigilante posse. Logan decided to stick close to Carmody.

"As soon as I learn what I need to know from my son, I'll go after the men who did this. Vigilante justice will only cause more violence and drive the Navajo to fight back. Stark can't just order his gang to ride onto the reservation and attack."

"I heard that Halen Braun is going to help them. He said that an uprising has brought the U.S. Government into it."

"He's covering for Stark and the politicians. He's in bed with them."

Around ten o'clock that night, Logan received a call from Bell at the Stark-Degrood Ranch informing him, "A mounted force of fifty armed men will be riding into the disputed region with the intention of destroying every Hogan and sheep camp they come across. They didn't say anything about killing Navajos, but you know it's going to happen."

Logan wasted no time conveying the news to Carmody. Carmody didn't wait any longer. He left Dr. McAffrey's, and to Logan's surprise, asked Logan to accompany him.

"I need you for a witness," he said.

They drove into Mesa to the livery stable. Carmody loaded two saddled and bridled horses into a double trailer. He hitched it to his Buick, then he and Logan headed toward the boundary between the reservation and the scattered rangelands of the Stark-Degrood Ranch.

After twenty miles, they turned off onto a narrow dirt road that curved away into the desert. Ten spine jolting miles later, the track ended abruptly in a dry wash. They quickly unloaded the horses.

Leaving the car and trailer, they crossed the arroyo and headed due east with the benefit of a full moon. They rode for about two miles at a walk when they heard distant gunfire off to their right. Carmody swerved and put his horse into a hard gallop. Logan's horse followed without any urging as he hung on to the saddle horn. It amazed Logan that the two animals were so sure-footed in the dark. The terrain afforded many gradual hills and level open spaces.

The sounds of battle continued unabated, giving the impression of a small war up ahead. They topped a rise and there below saw a Navajo sheep camp in flames. The burning brush illuminated the entire arena of battle.

Riding in a circle, filling the night air with gunfire and war cries, Red Tasker and his fifty vigilantes had a small number of Navajo men, women, and children pinned down among a cluster of large boulders at the center. Logan did not understand how they could endure the heat of the fire closing in on them. If the flames finally drove them away from cover, they would be easily picked off by Tasker's men.

As Logan followed Carmody clattering down the hillside, he prayed that fate would spare them from a stray bullet. The air buzzed with flying lead like attacking bees.

Carmody singled out Red Tasker and went right for him. Logan had not seen him pull out his rifle, but suddenly it was there ready in hand. When the other riders saw Carmody, they ceased fire. The rifles of the trapped Navajo families immediately fell silent. All eyes were on Tasker facing off with Carmody to see what would happen.

Logan noticed some of the men swigging whiskey as they sat there on their horses. To them, the incident was nothing more than sport, like a wild roundup, only with an excuse to kill.

Logan couldn't hear what was being said between Tasker and Carmody because of the distance and the brush crackling with flames. He realized that Carmody must have placed him under arrest. Tasker handed over his rifle and unbuckled his holster and cartridge belt. Logan could not clearly discern what happened next.

A sudden scuffle broke out between the two men still on their horses as they fought for possession of Carmody's rifle. Their horses half-reared and plunged back and forth. Tasker's guns fell to the ground between the stomping fidgeting animals. As they momentarily parted, the shot from Carmody's rifle lifted Tasker clear of his saddle. He slammed to the ground with a gaping hole in his stomach spouting founts of blood.

Not another man there challenged Carmody's authority. Several dismounted. They lashed Tasker's dead body to his horse, who shied and plunged at the blood smell. The posse remounted, and led him away. The crackle of flames filled the night.

Four Navajo men stepped away from the boulders followed by three women and four young children. Logan joined Carmody as he rode over to them. Carmody spoke in Navajo. They kept referring to another Navajo man who was badly wounded.

Carmody dismounted and talked briefly with the young man, a barely conscious Duncan Zaragoza. He had lost a great amount of blood. Pain wreathed his face.

Twisted charred metal remained from an old pickup truck parked nearby that had exploded from the fire. The Navajo men brought horses from a corral untouched by the flames. Two of the men rode back with Logan and Carmody at a slow walk. One rode double supporting Duncan in the saddle before him.

When they came to the arroyo, they transferred Duncan to the back seat of Carmody's car, then loaded Carmody's and Logan's horses into the trailer. Not one of the Navajo men rode in the car in the backseat with Duncan to the Fort Defiance Hospital. They feared being next to him if he should die on the way. They did not want death to touch them.

They arrived at two o'clock in the morning. Duncan had fainted from a loss of blood. Dr. Shumway, who lived at the hospital, took him immediately to the emergency ward. He administered drugs and a transfusion before surgically extracting the slug.

At six o'clock the next morning, the nurse woke Logan where he had fallen asleep on a couch in the hospital lobby and told him that Duncan would survive. Logan asked her about Carmody. He had gone home two hours before. His son, Bobby, had not regained consciousness and whatever had happened to Erin Carmody was still unknown.

Chapter 32
ESCAPE

Lee Stark raged at Carmody and raged for his own personal justice.

"I want Carmody dead," he shouted stomping about his office and waving a revolver in one hand and an unsmoked cigar in the other. "I'll pay any man a thousand dollars who kills him. If that doesn't happen, I'll have that son-of-a-bitch removed from office. I'll get a Federal judge to do it." Stark believed he had the power and the political connections to issue such an order.

Late that night, the informer, Wesley Zuber, was brought from Coal Town to speak with Stark.

"I heard you was lookin' fer a man to kill that sheriff, Carmody. How much you willin' to pay. I tol' you I have an assassin. He'll do the job if the money's right."

"One thousand dollars! Two thousand dollars! What's his name?" asked Stark. "Clayton Byrne. All he needs is a gun."

Stark reached into his desk drawer and pulled out a Colt 45. "Well, goddam it, give 'im this. And he better not miss."

"He wants half the money up front."

Stark counted out the bills and shoved them across the desktop.

***

Logan first got wind of what was happening when he received a United Press bulletin that Stark had demanded Federal intervention to put down an uprising by a militant band of Navajos.

Halen Braun received orders from Clyde Tolson in Washington to go to Mesa and oversee Howard Gimbel in putting down "the uprising on Federal property. Capture and arrest them and see to it that they are incarcerated. Kill them, if you must."

"I'll kill them all right," said Braun. "When I find them, they're dead."

Halen arrived in Mesa with a "staff" of ten agents from Texas. Six of them were marksmen with both handguns and rifles. He also had commandeered a contingent of personnel from the state militia, three convoy trucks, five jeeps, small field artillery, and a Navajo interpreter assigned to the mission by the United States Army.

With all the preliminary fanfare on the radio and in the press about Halen Braun and Gimbel and that they were going to fight an "Indian War, " Carmody went immediately to the Fort Defiance Hospital and assisted Duncan Zaragoza in making an escape.

Relying on moonlight and the weak cast of yellow light from the hospital windows, Carmody, Gimbel, Logan, and the nurse, Sara Sims, carried Duncan wrapped in a blanket on a stretcher from his bed to the sheriff's car parked at the entrance to the adobe building.

Others from Duncan's small fugitive band with their wives and children accompanied him with their horses and wagons. Amid the flurry of an intense exchange of orders among the men, Sara Sims told Carmody she would travel with Duncan and take care of him.

Jim Picker from the local BIA picked up the phone and called Halen Braun at his office in Santa Fe.

"Agent Braun, I heard you're coming to Mesa."

"We're leaving in an hour."

"I thought you'd like to know that the entire population of the reservation will be advised that it is in their best interest to cooperate in assisting the Law & Order in its search. Cash rewards for information leading to the capture of the militants are expected to promote such cooperation."

"I sure as hell am glad to hear that, Picker. Do you have any idea who they are?"

"Could be any one of 'em or all of 'em. They stick together. That's the way they are. They do things by tribal consensus."

"Fuck that! We're goin' after 'em and kill anything that moves."

"Do you need me to come along?"

"No, Picker, I don't need you to come along. You're Stark's boy and you did your job for him."

Braun's condescending tone and insulting comment stung Picker.

"We're grateful," said Braun. "He's grateful. I'm grateful. We're in a different game now. The BIA needs to stay out of it."

"I know who their leader is."

"What did you say?"

"I know who their leader is." As news of the battle between the Navajos and Stark's vigilante posse filtered into the BIA offices, Picker had overheard the name of Duncan Zaragoza mentioned by elders of the tribal council in a quickly assembled meeting to discuss the protest. The tribal chief had told John Collier that his Civilian Conservation Corp program had caused the violence to happen. "You are destroying the Navajo way of life." Red-faced and fuming, Collier had walked out of the meeting. Picker had remained at the back of the room and heard more.

Gimbel was not surprised when Halen Braun showed up at the Bureau of Indian Affairs at Fort Defiance. Flanked by three Texas agents, Halen swept into his office and left the door standing open behind him. Gimbel noticed he was wearing his usual cowboy boots and a Stetson hat. The thought occurred to Howard that J. Edgar Hoover would disapprove of Halen's outfit. It was clear that Halen was geared for action. He was the Special Agent In Charge.

Without any greeting or explanation, he ordered, "We're going after the Navajo insurgents. I have ten men with me, six marksmen. We want Carmody. He's committed an act of conspiracy and treason against the United States Government. He killed Lee Stark's foreman at a drilling site on land owned by Stark. We learned from a BIA informer that Carmody went to the agency hospital and assisted the ringleader, Duncan Zaragoza, in making an escape. Zaragoza is wounded. It will slow them down. I have a gun for you. Get your hat. Carmody's gone. We checked at his home and the jail on our way into town."

"He's most likely somewhere out in the desert then with the Navajo."

"Don't matter. We'll find the son-of-a-bitch and put his ass in a Federal pen."

"What is it you want me to do?"

"Since you fucked things up with Yelena Ivanov and it appears she's gone over the border, you're gonna take Carmody down when we find him and the rest of us are gonna back you up."

Howard stared at him and reluctantly accepted the gun and holster that Halen Braun held out to him. "I have an idea where they're headed." Howard never mentioned that he had met and talked with the young Navajo man who had come to his office. He would lead the vigilante posse in a chase that would give Duncan and his followers time to disappear into the deep canyons and backlands of the reservation.

"Good. You can tell that to the army interpreter."

"You won't be able to get there with vehicles."

"What the fuck you talkin' about? These are military. They can go anywhere."

"I would recommend you bring horses. At some point, you'll have to leave the road. It's rough terrain, almost impenetrable."

Braun's accusing stare bore down on him. "How is it you know where he's going?"

"I spent a lot of time out there on the law and order program. Carmody showed me where fugitives go to hide when they don't want to be found."

"Then our scout should know that. You tell him."

"I will."

Four truckloads of horses brought up the rear of the convoy of three military trucks, and a jeep towing a mounted 155mm howitzer.

Gimbel overheard the soldiers bragging about their firepower.

"You ever see the damage this baby can do. Cut a man in half like he was tree sap."

"Fuckin' redskins don't stand a chance in hell of winning against us."

Listening to their posturing and racial slurs, Gimbel interpreted their vociferous comments as a way of unintentionally letting the Federal agents know they were compensating for being nervous and lacking confidence. They were raw recruits not long out of boot camp.

"So, you think we're ridin' into an ambush, pardner?"

"That General Custer's goin' to take us into the valley of death and damnation sure."

"Don't look like Custer to me. Looks more like Wild Bill Hickcock. You see them handlebar mustaches he's wearin'. Reminds me of pictures of my granddad in the Civil War."

"Phew, have to take a piss."

"Don't go too far out there in the dark, pussy. Injun could be waitin' to cut off your balls. Probably worth more than your scalp these days. They can fry 'em and eat em like buffalo nuts."

Nervous laughter trembled in the air, then quickly subsided.

"That's enough talk like that," barked their sergeant. "This is serious business. You're working with professionals here, from Washington. So have a little fuckin' pride in yourselves. You're soldiers. You're in the U.S. Army."

"Oh, Sarge, thanks for remindin' us. I thought we was goin' overseas to fight Germans, not howl with the coyotes."

"A remark like that can get you court martialed, private."

"Not bloody likely, mate. I'm supposed to train to be a fly boy with the Brits."

"Let me remind you what happened to white men at the hands of these savages."

"We know they ain't our enemies, Sarge. This is just a little diversion, a training exercise to hone our skills and to keep us from gettin' fuckin' bored."

"You're fighting for your country here and now by putting down this insurrection."

Another soldier pantomimed masturbating. "It's an erection all right," and raised a laugh.

The FBI marksmen kept to themselves and spoke in low murmurs to each other to exclude the soldiers and make it clear that grunts in uniform were beneath them in importance, lower than dirt. During rest breaks, Halen Braun joined them and offered them drinks of whiskey from his flask and handed out cigars.

"It's okay," he said. "Hoover ain't hidin' behind every goddamn rock out here. He's a fuckin' lush himself anyway and a pansy. Loosen up. This ain't no different than huntin' coons and possums in Tennessee."

Two purists declined his offerings. The others, who had never received or been acknowledged by any respect from Hoover, accepted the gut warming alcohol and cigars. The glowing tips congregated in a tight circle that reminded Howard of the proboscae of hulking ogres from which shared guttural laughter floated out into the cold night air like escaped farts.

Gimbel told the Navajo interpreter, Shon-ge, where he wanted to lead the posse. It was the same location where the Zaragoza brothers had escaped. Duncan could hide for the rest of his life in the endless canyons.

The sergeant expressed his vast disappointment when the road finally disappeared into impenetrable hills of rocks, cactus, and sand. "Why the fuck would someone build a road out here and just stop?" He shouted. "Jesus fuckin' Christ. We can't just leave the trucks and howitzer sittin' here."

"You can thank that asshole John Collier for this and his fuckin' Navajo program," Braun shouted.

"We can go forward from here only on foot or horseback," said Gimbel. "There's no other way."

"I'm responsible for the vehicles and artillery. The FBI brought us into this. If this is where the road ends, then it's where me and my troops end."

The soldiers raised a war whoop.

"Shut the fuck up," the sergeant ordered. "Two of you are gonna babysit these fuckin' trucks and the howitzer while the rest of us go on with the goonies."

Braun strode across the twenty feet that separated them. "You say anything like that again about the FBI and I'll lay you out, Sergeant. You may be in the army, but for now, you're under my command. I'm your fuckin' general. You got that?"

Thinking he was about to be struck, the intimidated sergeant, who was physically much shorter and wider than Braun, stepped back and floundered. "Yes, sir. Yes, sir. My apologies, sir. My words were unthinking, sir."

"Unthinking words are worse than no words at all," said Braun.

"Of course, it won't happened again–sir."

"That's more fuckin' like it, sergeant."

"Yes, sir." The sergeant inwardly cursed himself for acting like such a mouse before this bully. He blamed the fact that he had a recessive chin while Braun had a jutting chin, incinerating eyes and an imposing handlebar mustache. The sergeant, whose name was Eagleton, had never been able to live up to that symbolic image of avian power until he had enlisted in the U.S. Army. He had redeemed himself in the eyes of his family, with the exception of moments when he was confronted by truly powerful men like Halen Braun.

Braun did not have any difficulty riding a horse and sleeping out on the cold desert ground. He had often done the same on hunting trips for quail and deer and elk. For the marksmen from Texas, the experience was quite a different story. To a man, they developed diarrhea with the covert assistance of one of the enlisted troops who slipped chocolate Exlax into their morning coffee as he obsequiously served them upon their stiff awakening.

The hunt lasted for only two days. The Navajo scout said there was no way to track the fugitives. They had disappeared into the rocks and cliffs and had left no trail.

Braun was incensed, but was forced by circumstances to admit defeat. He wondered why only he and the agents had contracted the runs and the soldiers had not. He determined he would take revenge of another kind in another way.

Chapter 33
PASSAGE

Carmody returned late at night from helping Duncan Zaragoza make his escape into the back country where he and his relatives vanished into the landscape.

He avoided the jail and went to Dr. McAffrey's at the other end of town.

McAffrey poured another bourbon and noticed that the two of them had consumed half the bottle in less than an hour. McAffrey thought this was not a good sign. But he considered their reasons for drinking. He wasn't certain if they were in mourning or in celebration or both. He decided it was both.

They celebrated the recovery of Carmody's son, Bobby, who McAffrey had moved to the Fort Defiance hospital. He would live. McAffrey knew that Carmody felt a sense of relief, but shared equally the sorrow of his son's loss. Erin was still missing.

Carmody couldn't sit still. He paced the room and stared out the window into the night. Like a hovering bat, a flutter of hate kept him moving, hate for his apparent meaningless life. He saw only a void in society. He saw nothing that he could truly grasp that was not created out of his own mind or out of the minds of others. Where were the absolutes of integrity and honor? Were they gone forever or had they only been an illusion. Where was serenity? Where could he become whole again? His final evaluation of himself, of his life, left him in despair. He was an ordinary man without feeling and not heroic.

He poured another drink. He could never drown the doubt and despair. He felt himself sinking in spite of holding on to tradition. There were forces working against him.

"We kill everything we touch," thought Carmody. "We've been on this poor planet for thousands of years and we've still barely crawled out of the slime."

***

During a phone call from Halen Braun, Gimbel told him that it was a fact that Yelena Ivanov had fled across the border into Mexico. Although Braun did not say so at the time, he suspected that Gimbel had assisted her. "I have orders for your return to Washington," said Braun. "I'll bring them to you at your house tonight."

Remembering Braun's threat, Gimbel was immediately on guard.

"What time?"

"About midnight. It's a long drive from Santa Fe. If you're asleep, I'll knock on the door."

"I tend to be a heavy sleeper, so knock loudly."

"You'll know I'm there."

Howard heard the click at the other end of the line and hung up his phone. Braun was coming to kill him.

***

Braun turned off his headlights as he brought his car to a stop a quarter mile from Gimbel's small house located a short distance out in the sagebrush. A pale sliver of moon hung just above the mesa and did not catch his figure moving at a fast walk along the narrow dark road. At the turn-off, he paused in puzzlement. Gimbel's car was gone.

Son-of-a-bitch, He knows, thought Braun. *He's on the run.*

Wary that he might be walking into an ambush himself, Braun headed off into the brush and approached the small adobe from the side. He suddenly stopped and crouched low upon catching the glare of headlights from a truck approaching along the road. To his chagrin, it turned in at the dirt driveway and ground to a halt at the front of the adobe. He could not believe what he was seeing. Yelena Ivanov stepped down from the cab and walked to the front door. Braun's prayers had been answered. He could deliver to Stark both the dead bodies of Yelena Ivanov and Howard Gimbel. But then he noticed something strange that gave him pause.

The front door had been left ajar. A lantern glowed dimly on the kitchen table. Sweat poured from his brow. He sensed he was being stalked and that the tables had turned. He was the hunted. Gimbel could be out there in the brush at that moment sighting down on him.

Yelena entered the adobe and called out, "Howard, it's me, Yelena. I need your help."

When he didn't appear, she quickly searched the adobe and discovered he was gone. She thought he might be out in the privy, but he would have heard her truck. Nevertheless she stepped out into the back yard and walked toward the privy. "Howard, it's Yelena. You in there?"

She heard a slight rustle and saw his barely illuminated figure crouched in the sagebrush.

"Yelena," he whispered. "Get down. Get down now."

Sensing some eminent danger, she dropped to her knees.

"What are you doing here?"

"Something terrible has happened. I need your help."

"Halen Braun is out there. He came to kill me and now he has us both. Stay out here out of the light. Move away from the house. Stay low to the ground."

"If I don't go back inside, he'll know you're out here waiting for him. We have to make him think you're inside. I'll go back."

"No, the risk is too great."

"I'll make it seem like we're talking for a minute, then come back out again."

"Yelena, you don't have to do this. It's not worth it."

Without another word, Yelena rose and walked quickly to the adobe and entered at the back door. She simulated a brief one-sided conversation with a non-present Howard, then slipped out again into the darkness.

Convinced that now both Yelena and Howard were in the adobe, Braun crouched along through the brush to the entrance and slowly pushed open the door with the barrel of his shotgun. Nothing happened. Neither of them were in the room.

"Gimbel, you in there? I've got your paperwork from Washington."

He kicked the door open wide. Still nothing.

"Shit."

He entered and swung the barrel to rapidly cover every corner of the main room, then moved toward the bedroom. He saw that the bed had not been slept in. A shirt, coat, and trousers lay neatly over the back of a wooden chair. As he slowly turned, he saw Gimbel barefoot wearing trousers and a strapped undershirt. His service revolver was trained on Braun, who scatter shot blasting away at the spot where Gimbel had been standing a moment before. Gimbel fired off three quick rounds as he rolled across the wooden floor. The first penetrated Braun's left lung near the heart. The second shattered the cartilage of his throat, and the third entered his brain. He pitched backward into the bedroom and lay still. Howard waited, then avoiding the blood pooling around Braun's body, crawled over to him on his hands and knees.

He stared down at the florid depraved flesh of his face collapsing in death as though weighed down by Braun's dark handle bar mustaches, the tips pressing into the blue whiskered accordion folds of his throat.

"Yelena," he called out. "Yelena! He's dead." His voice dropped to a whisper. "He's dead."

Yelena heard his voice, muffled by the adobe wall and the wind that snatched away sound like a thief and left her guessing as to what had happened inside the house. Afraid to move, she waited concealed in the brush with a clear view of the back door. What seemed to be a long time passed before pale yellow light sliced into the desert night. Yelena held her breath until she saw Howard's tall figure appear.

She scrambled up out of the sand and crashed through the brush in a mad run to reach him. Clutching his arm, they walked back into the room.

"What are we going to do?"

"Coyotes."

"What do you mean?"

"He'll disappear. Maybe they'll find his bones someday."

"Howard." Yelena pulled him forward out through the front door to the truck bed.

***

Yelena's description left no doubt in Carmody's mind that Thompson and Leuentky had murdered Erin. He didn't even want to bring them in. He wanted them to resist or try to run so he could gun them down.

He stared at Erin's small crumpled body stinking of exposure and decay in the bed of the truck that had brought her to his door.

***

Red dust rose in a plume behind his car, as Carmody, Gimbel, Yelena, and Logan drove out to Coal Town the next morning. They went directly to the mine foreman's shack and Carmody told him he had come to arrest Thompson and Leuentky for the murder of his daughter-in-law, Erin Carmody.

The foreman explained that the men had three more hours until their shift ended, when they would return to the surface. Carmody said, "I'll wait."

He brought a canteen and sat in the shack with the foreman, who was uncomfortable at having the sheriff in such close proximity. Carmody did not want to risk any advanced warning being relayed to the two killers.

Even with their helmeted heads and coal blackened faces, Yelena identified them as they came off the lift. Upon seeing the sheriff, the cluster of miners hesitated, shuffling about, then warily split and scattered as Carmody's deep voice filled the shaft landing area.

"Thompson and Leuentky, you're under arrest for the murder of Erin Carmody."

With a savage grunt, Thompson raised his pick and charged like a quivering lumbering bear. Carmody drew his Colt .45. Taking deliberate aim, he shattered Thompson's right knee, spewing bone fragments. The huge man crashed to the ground. Moaning and whimpering with pain, Thompson grasped at his blood-soaked pants leg and clawed the air.

In a flash of panic, Leuentky turned and ran. Carmody's second bullet smashed the vertebrae and penetrated the base of the flailing man's brain.

Carmody then stood over Thompson and fired a shot into his groin as the heavy man writhed in the dust to get away. His screams caused the other miner's to stop and watch dumbfounded as Carmody pumped three more shots into Thompson's groin which erupted in a bloody mass of pulpy flesh. He holstered his gun and walked away, leaving Thompson to hemorrhage to death.

The act of violence did not intimidate Clayton Byrne, who witnessed the killings with fascination. Thinking himself concealed by the anonymity of the crowd, he drew the hidden gun that had been given to him by Halen Braun. He carefully sighted down on Carmody and fired three shots. But Carmody was no longer there. Howard Gimbel had seen the flash of the revolver and knocked the marshal to the ground. The FBI agent was now running straight toward him and shouting at those within range, "Get down! Get Down!".

Those standing near Clayton fell and leaped aside. Three slugs drove into the assassin's heart, spinning him to the ground with blood leaking in sudden gouts from his chest.

As he lay sprawled in the dust, the last sound that he heard came from far across the desert. The long haunting whistle of a passing train whispered by on the wind.

Chapter 34
INVESTIGATION

They had not planned to drive over to Mesa from Santa Fe. Halen Braun's absence from the office was not unusual. They figured he might be on another one of his junkets into Mexico or shacked up with a woman somewhere or sleeping off a drunk. During the past five years under his jurisdiction, he had often excluded them from what he was thinking and doing with a case, except to give them a direct order. They knew little or nothing as to why he had made repeated trips to Mesa and what was even going on there until the call from Clyde Tolson in Washington. Ken Ferguson had been the one to answer the phone.

"FBI Santa Fe, Agent Ferguson speaking. How can I help you?"

"This is Assistant Director Clyde Tolson speaking. Put Agent Braun on the line," ordered Tolson.

"Ah, sir, Agent Braun is not in the office this morning."

"If he's not in the office, what is Agent Braun doing?"

"Well, sir, we don't really know. He went over to Mesa on a case and we haven't seen or heard from him in a week."

Ferguson listened to the audible silence at the other end of the line. For a few moments, he thought Tolson had hung up on him or the connection had been broken when Tolson's ominous voice invaded his ear.

"How many of you are there in Santa Fe?"

Ken Ferguson understood that Clyde Tolson knew very well who was assigned to Santa Fe and that now he was exerting his authority in a backhanded way.

"There are three of us, sir–Agents Braun, Stuart, and myself."

"Since you comprise such a small group, I would imagine you keep each other informed as to your whereabouts."

Ken knew he needed to tread carefully in offering his next statement to avoid the wrathful backlash of Halen Braun, who would surely be reprimanded by Tolson. In the privacy of the Santa Fe office, Braun withheld nothing in his vituperative disgust and disrespect for Hoover's assistant.

"Well, sir, to be quite honest, Agent Braun informed us that he's working on a highly classified case for the Washington Bureau and has not shared that information. Of course, we, Agent Stuart and I, have not questioned his authority."

"It is imperative that I speak to him."

"I suppose we can drive over to Mesa and try to find him, with your permission, of course, no questions asked."

Again, dead silence, only longer.

"Sir, are we still connected?"

"It would be wise of you to find him."

"Yes, sir, Agent Stuart and I will leave immediately."

"And one more thing."

"Sir."

"A news article in the Washington Post has come to my attention through the United Press. I'm looking at it on my desk as we speak. Director Hoover is so outraged he's about to take a train to New Mexico and make the arrests himself. But that's your job. That's why you are there. It's your duty to protect the interests of the Federal Government."

"Yes, sir, we are well aware of that, sir."

"From what I see here, you're not fulfilling that duty. Do I make myself clear?"

"Yes, sir. We need more information, sir."

"And here it is. It was first published in the Albuquerque Tribune. I want you to find and question the journalist who wrote the article. Apparently there have been a series of what I will loosely term 'exposes' regarding a Government program in the region of Mesa."

"Do you mean the Civilian Conservation Corps?"

"That and the illegal activity of a communist union organizer with coal miners in your region."

"Agent Braun didn't really bring us in on that, sir. We did know about an uprising on the Navajo reservation. But Agent Braun brought in sharpshooters from Texas for that."

"This is the first I've heard of such a problem. We have a special agent placed inside the Bureau of Indian Affairs who should have reported that."

"Agent Braun never told us about a special agent."

"He was following orders, which is what you and Agent Stuart are now going to do."

"Yes, sir, of course, sir."

"I want to know how the news reporter came by what is supposed to be classified information and who provided it to him."

"We'll look right into it. What is his name, sir?"

"Randolph Logan."

"The same guy as last time?"

"Yes, Agent Ferguson, the same suspect."

Ken quickly jotted the name on an empty note pad. "Got it, sir. Anything else, sir?"

"I want you to report to me what you find out–about Agent Braun and about the reporter. If you haven't seen the latest article, I strongly suggest you buy a copy of the newspaper and read it."

"We'll go right out and do that, sir."

"So you are not completely in the dark, Agent Ferguson, the name of Agent Braun appears more than once in the incriminating article. From the nature and tone of the article, Director Hoover suspects the reporter is a communist and has ordered him dealt with accordingly."

"Do you want Logan arrested?"

"Not yet. We need more evidence. That is your job, to get us the evidence. When you see Agent Braun, tell him I have given you a direct order to proceed with your investigation. Tell him also to read the article and to then call me."

"Yes, sir, we'll follow through, sir."

There was another silence at the end of the line followed by a distant, but distinct click. Ferguson moved the receiver away from his ear and stared at it a moment. He returned it to his ear. The silence remained. He slowly hung up. Melbourne responded to the tension in the man's wide face.

"What is it? What did he say? What's going on?"

"We're in the middle of something hot."

"Something?"

"Not good." Braun was supposed to report back to Tolson a week ago–something about a case over in Mesa that made the papers. United Press spread it everywhere. Even Tolson has the piece. That's why he called looking for Braun. Told us to go find him, but to read about it first."

"Braun in trouble?"

"We're all in trouble."

"Shit! What'd we do? More like what'd he do?"

"They sell the Journal somewhere around here?"

"I can get one free at the barber shop."

"Then go get it. We're up to our ass in alligators and we don't know how we got there."

While Melbourne ran off to get a newspaper, Ken wondered what his wife might have concocted for lunch.

When Melbourne returned rattling a Journal opened to an inside page continuing the embarrassing expose', Ken said, "We need to have lunch before we go."

"I'm not thinkin' about lunch and you won't be either once you read this. There ain't no names called out, but the Bureau's mentioned more than once and it's enough to make us culpable. No wonder we got a phone call. Our ass is on fire and we're stuck in the mud. Braun made the Bureau look bad. Don't know how he can get out of this one."

Ferguson grabbed the paper and riffled the pages. "Where the fuck does it start."

"Page one headline news. It's a big story. Goes on for two more pages inside."

As he read, Melbourne watched for his partner's reaction. Halfway into the article, Ferguson gasped, "This is unbelievable. How could someone get away with writing this about us."

"Us? It's not about us, you and me. Our ass ain't on the line. Braun did us a favor keepin' us out of it."

"We're in it, Mel, right along with Braun. The whole Bureau was made to look bad all the way up to Hoover hisself. Who do you think I was talkin' to on the goddam phone? We're in the line of fire."

"If we're goin' to get over to Mesa before the end of the day, we'd better move."

Ferguson threw the paper into a wrinkled pile on his desk. "This has caused me more grief than I need. When I feel grief, I need food. I'm goin' home for lunch." He stood up from his desk and clumped heavily to the door. "I'll meet you back here in one hour. In the meantime, you can do whatever you want. I'd suggest you eat. We have a long drive ahead of us." He slammed out.

Melbourne searched for a toothpick in his desk drawer and thoughtfully chewed on it.

Their progress was slow due to the increased number of ruts and pot holes from a thunderstorm that had lashed the landscape the night before. The two men were grateful they did not have to often travel the narrow dirt road wending its way far into the western desert.

Clyde Tolson's phone call from the Bureau Headquarters in Washington was Ferguson's and Stuart's first indoctrination into a high profile case. Melbourne, who was pretty good at reading human motives, voiced his opinion to Ferguson that "Braun excluded us because he wanted to grandstand and take credit for the whole thing." Now, the corruption underlying the Bureau and its collusion with the Wooten Mining Company to suppress union activity was blown wide open by what the journalist had written and the newspapers had published. The two agents had been given the unsavory task of smoothing over the damage and helping the Bureau save face. What Clyde Tolson wanted from them was grist for Hoover's propaganda mill, to brand Randolph Logan as a communist traitor brought to justice by covert agents of the FBI.

"I hear what you're sayin'," said Ferguson at the wheel of the Ford Coup. "But we ain't undercover by a long shot."

"Hoover will make it look like we are."

"That agent in the BIA was undercover."

"Not no more."

"What do you suppose 'll happen to him?"

"Nothing. He was exposed through no fault of his own. He'll probably get a promotion and assigned back in D.C." Ferguson swerved to avoid a large rock in the road as it dipped into an arroyo. He wondered how a rock could end up in the road in the first place on this flat desert plain. The force of the water no doubt. There must have been a flash flood.

"And what'll we get?"

"We get to keep our jobs."

Two hours later, they spotted Braun's abandoned car a short distance from the road. "There," said Melbourne. "It's his car. Over there."

The doors stood wide open. Several broken bottles of whiskey lay scattered about. The constant wind and shifting sand left no sign of Braun or of where he might have gone.

"What the hell!" Ferguson stopped the car with a jolt. Leaving the motor running , they stepped out of the vehicle and waded through the sand and sagebrush to the wreck. Lizards vacated the interior as they approached and a desert rat that had taken up residence in the chewed seat padding scuttled off into a pile of nearby rocks.

"What you suppose happened here?" Ferguson mused. "How long you suppose this has been here?"

"At least a week, maybe two. Bruan left Santa Fe two weeks ago."

"What do you make of the broken glass?"

"He was drinkin'. Could of fell asleep, lost control and crashed. Bottle got smashed. That's how I read it."

"But where did he go? That's the question."

"Could be how did he go?" said Melbourne. "If he walked away, he would've gone back to the road."

"Unless he was disoriented. Could've hit his head. Lost a sense of where he was."

"Strange, don't see any sign of blood. If there'd been an impact, there'd be blood somewhere in the car." Melbourne looked inside. "Nothin', not even a spot."

"Must have been a blow to the head."

Melbourne straightened up from leaning over the dashboard and the driver's seat. "Another thought occurred to me."

"What's that?"

"I remember seein' a suitcase in the backseat when he left Santa Fe. So he would've been stayin' somewhere."

"The key still in the ignition?"

Melbourne reached in, "Yeah, right here," and pulled out the key.

"Check the trunk."

Melbourne walked around to the rear of the vehicle and opened the trunk. "Look at this."

Ferguson stared at the suitcase next to a rifle, a shotgun, boxes of ammunition, blankets, a shovel, and a coil of rope. "Never opened the suitcase."

"Which means he didn't get to where he was goin'."

"So this had to happen two weeks ago, when he was on the road."

"The suitcase was just part of my thought," said Melbourne.

"What's the other part?"

"We're standin' on the reservation out here. Navajo could have taken him somewheres."

"It's a possibility, but do you think it's likely?"

"You read the story in the paper. There's bad blood 'tween the Injuns and the U.S. Government."

"But why? What the hell would they do with 'im?"

"Revenge. Take revenge. In the story, you saw what they think of us, the FBI. We're the enemy."

"Now that you put it that way. What're you doin' now?" He watched Melbourne walking in a wide circle studying the ground away from the stranded vehicle.

"Lookin' for signs."

"Of what?"

"Anything I can find. Tracks, blood, piece of clothing. I used to track animals when I was a boy huntin' in the Carolina woods."

"Bear, deer, bobcat, panther, coons and possums. I could read sign that no one else could. 'Course, we used dogs most of the time. Followed their nose."

"I grew up in the city, downtown Chicago. My dad never took me huntin', or fishin'. He just worked and came home and drank. Slapped my mother around once in a while. Brothers and sisters too. Hit me once for the last time and I cold cocked the bastard. Left home and never went back. See anything?"

"Nothin'. If there was sign, it's wiped clean or likely the wind and rain washed it away. Not even a print, 'cept for animals. Coyote's been around recent. Pack rat. Quail. Nothin' else."

"Better take these." Ferguson lifted the rifle and shotgun and coil of rope from the trunk.

"It wasn't Injuns," said Melbourne.

"How can you be sure?"

"They'd have taken what you're holdin'."

"We need to get on on over to Mesa. Tell the sheriff about this. Let him have a look. Mainly we need to question that news reporter."

"Yeah, still a ways to go." Melbourne pulled out his penis and sent a steady stream of urine rattling into the dry brush.

"Good idea." Ferguson dropped the weapons into the trunk of his car, then followed Melbourne's example.

A small number of low-lying adobe structures appeared like dried warts growing in the desert scrub as Melbourne and Ferguson approached and entered the town.

Melbourne tipped his hat back on his head. "Don't look like much. Same as when we was here before."

"How long's it been since we were here?" asked Ferguson.

"About a year," said Melbourne. "The Federal Marshal, Carmody's his name. He takes care of things, runs the show."

"Hasn't changed."

"What's there to change? More like it's a wonder the place is still here."

"It's the mine. That's what keeps it alive. The mine and the rail-road."

"And the Injuns."

"And the Injuns."

The main street was deserted in the heat of the day, the only visible movement being small whorls of dust kicked up by the hot blowing wind.

"There it is," said Ferguson. "Must be there. Patrol car's out front." He pulled his own vehicle to a stop before the jail and sheriff's office, a stand-alone adobe distinguished from the sparse few other buildings only by the black iron bars on the windows. The two men got out and looked up and down the street. Ferguson yawned from the heat. Perspiration fell from his jowls in a steady drip.

Upon entering, they found Carmody writing a report of a recent arrest. A ranch hand was sleeping off a drunk in one of the three cells. Carmody looked up. He recognized the two agents from a visit they'd made a year ago.

"Agent Ferguson, Agent Stuart, what brings you from Santa Fe?"

"At least it's cool in here," said Ferguson. "Sheriff."

Melbourne nodded a silent greeting.

"We're looking for the Special Agent in Charge, Halen Braun. He's been missing for a week. Have you seen him?"

"Not for some time."

"Did he talk to you? Give you some indication what he was here for?"

"I saw his car a few times parked over at the newspaper office, *The Mesa Indpenedent*. A while ago, we talked once about a union or-ganizer. We haven't talked since."

"Well," said Melbourne, "the real reason we stopped by is to tell you we found Agent Braun's car abandoned between here and Santa Fe. No sign of foul play, but he might have wandered off into the des-ert. Broken glass and such like he lost control and crashed. He'd been drinkin'. Broken bottle of hooch."

Carmody remained silent.

"We thought maybe he came to see the agent on the reserva-tion. Never met him ourselves. You know him."

Carmody nodded. "Howard Gimbel."

"Agent Braun only spoke his name once. He still out there?"

"As far as I know."

"How do we find him?"

"Take the road east that you passed just before coming to Mesa. Follow it for five miles. You'll come to the Bureau of Indian Affairs office."

"Thank you, Sheriff. We appreciate your assistance."

Carmody nodded and they walked out.

As they approached the office of *The Mesa Independent*, Ferguson grunted, "They actually publish a newspaper here?"

"Don't look like much to cause us so much trouble."

"What's the name of the reporter again?"

"Logan, Randolph Logan."

"Hope he's inside."

"Where the hell else would be be. Can't be any news around here. Too damn quiet."

A bell tinkled over the door as they walked in. Junius Shreve looked up into the polished brass of two badges.

"FBI," said Ferguson.

"Well, obviously. Gentlemen, my name is Junius Shreve, editor and publisher of *The Mesa Independent*. To what do I owe the honor of being visited by two of the FBI's finest?"

"We're looking for Randolph Logan," growled Ferguson.

"What's young Logan done now to bring the FBI to my door?"

"We'll ask the questions," said Ferguson.

"Of course, that's your job. Mine is to give answers. But first you might like to know that Randolph has gone to Alburquque and will return in three days."

"We need to know where he lives," said Melbourne.

Shreve suddenly became wary. "He lives with his dear old mother."

"We need an address."

"Number three Pinion Road. Side street goes straight out from the train station. Tell me fellas, what is it you're after. Maybe I can be of help."

"Randolph Logan has written and your paper and others have published news articles considered seditious and dangerous to the United States Government. J. Edgar Hoover, the Director of the FBI suspects Randolph Logan is a communist agitator and a traitor to his country."

Shreve laughed.

"What's so damn funny," Ferguson bellowed.

"Excuse me. I'm not laughing at you. Now I know why we've been getting these letters from Washington, D.C." He scrambled the stack on his desk and held one up to the light. "They use words like traitor. You know Agent Stuart and Agent Ferguson, I've been in the news business for a long long time, forty years. When I smell a rat, I can smell a rat. These were ginned up by Hoover's publicity mill and you damn well know it. The writing is terrible. God awful. It would never make it across my desk."

"You're entitled to think what you want, Mr. Shreve, but we mean business. This is no laughing matter."

"Yes, I know. The FBI never laughs."

"You could be held culpable for publishing the articles."

"Culpable? I would certainly hope so. Otherwise, I wouldn't be doing my job."

"You're proud of what you printed?"

"Absolutely right, gentlemen. I am most proud. Be sure to tell that to Hoover. If I'm not already in his files, I should be. I would consider it an honor."

"Maybe you been out here in the sticks too long. That talk is crazy."

"It's the best kind of talk. It's necessary talk."

Ferguson restrained himself from venting his frustration with a stream of verbal epithets. He glanced at Melbourne and motioned with his head toward the door. As they turned and walked out, Shreve shouted after them, "If there's anything further I can do to help, please don't hesitate to ask."

"Just an old coot," he heard Melbourne say before the door slammed shut leaving the bell tinkling violently.

Upon reaching the Logan house, they found Randolph's mother sitting on a rocking chair on her front veranda. The closing of two car doors snapped her out of her afternoon doze. She watched the two men approach, boots crunching on the gravel walk. She visibly stiffened when she saw them bring out their badges.

"Afternoon, Ma'am. I'm Agent Ferguson and this is Agent Stuart. We've come to speak with your son."

"My son isn't here. What business do you have with him?"

"He's under investigation."

"Investigation? For what? He's done nothing wrong."

"The FBI believes he has. We intend to find out."

"What do you mean by that?"

"Does your son live with you?"

"Yes, he lives here with me."

"We need to search his room. Would you please let us in."

"Of course I'm not letting you in my house. You don't have a warrant. I believe the Constitution still protects me from your unlawful entry."

"Ma'am, the Director of the FBI, J. Edgar Hoover himself has identified your son as a communist sympathizer."

"The last I heard there wasn't a law against holding a political viewpoint."

"There's a law against conspiracy to undermine the Federal Government."

"My son is not involved in any sort of conspiracy. He is involved in exposing highly placed corrupt people in business and a few in the Government who are in violation of its laws in their pursuit of greed at the cost of the human well-being of others. You're talking to an old school teacher, gentlemen. There isn't any law against doing what he does. Read the Constitution. In fact, my son is doing your job for you."

"I beg your pardon, ma'am. We are conducting a criminal investigation under the jurisdiction of the Federal Government."

"That's exactly what my son does, gentlemen. He investigates."

His face enflamed with rising anger and frustration, Ferguson took a step toward the front door."

"If you force your way into my house, Agent Ferguson, I will summon the Federal Marshal to come and stop you."

"You do realize that when Mr. Hoover hears about this, there will be consequences."

"I'm sure there will be–for the two of you. Mr. Hoover is nothing more than a fascist bureaucrat who drags our Government down to wallow in his pig sty. He's a sick man, paranoid, corrupt, and cruel, and has done more to ruin people's lives than to help them according to your creed or code or whatever you call it. He's no better than Hitler's secret police in our own country."

Ken hesitated. "Ma'am, you don't know what the hell you're talkin' about." Purple with rage, he turned abruptly and went back down the steps.

Melbourne touched the brim of his hat. "Ma'am., You don't know who you're dealing with. You have a lot to learn."

"At my age, I've learned what is worth learning." She watched them return to their car and climb inside. Talking animatedly between themselves, they cast a final glance in her direction and drove away.

"Didn't expect that," said Ferguson. "Didn't expect that at all."

"She's right about the Constitution."

"Yeah, unfortunately."

***

"Still can't get over bein' stuck with this." Ferguson hunched over the wheel as they followed the dirt track onto the reservation. "Never been out here since I came to New Mexico. Never had a reason to."

"Know anything about the BIA?"

"No, we don't work with 'em."

"Maybe we're gettin' in over our heads."

"This Gimbel must know somethin'. Under cover."

"Why you suppose Hoover stuck 'im in the BIA?" Melbourne pointed out the window. "There it is."

"Not much of a place to work."

"What do you expect. Look where we are–the middle of no-where."

Howard's desk and chair were positioned so that he could see anyone approaching along the road. He didn't recognize the car, but suspected who was inside. He didn't know their names, but that their appearance was just a matter of time. He was ready for them. He left his door open so they could enter without having to knock. They did so in a hesitating manner.

"Agent Gimbel," said Ferguson.

"Yes, I'm Agent Gimbel. What can I do for you?"

"We're Agents Ferguson and Stuart. You need to see our badg-es?"

"No, please sit down."

Ferguson and Stuart scuffed and scrapped the two available wooden chairs across the hard earthen floor and sat directly in front of Howard's desk.

"You've driven a long way."

"We have," said Ferguson. "Our reason for coming is Agent Halen Braun has been missing for a week. We found his abandoned car out in the desert along the road from Santa Fe. There was no sign of him or what happened to him. We were hoping you could shed some light."

"Agent Braun and I were part of an assignment that is now over. I'm returning to Washington, D.C. to report to Clyde Tolson for my next assignment."

"You spoke with Clyde Tolson?"

"We've talked on the phone and I received written orders, as well."

"Tolson called us this morning. That's how we know about Braun. Gave us orders to find 'im."

"I don't know that I can help you with that. The last time I saw Agent Braun was over two months ago. He came here to my office. I haven't seen him since."

"Can you tell us what you talked about?"

"I'm afraid not. We were sworn to secrecy. He said he was the only agent from the Santa Fe office I could talk to."

Ferguson and Stuart glanced at each other. "Since he's disappeared, it would be helpful if we knew. We've got orders to find him," said Ferguson.

"Well, I've told you what I know."

"Mind if we look around?"

"Not at all. You're on Government property."

"Thanks," Ferguson and Stuart rose as one.

"We're likely to have more questions."

"I'll be here."

Ferguson removed his hat to fan his perspiring face. He and Stuart went slowly and thoughtfully out the door.

When they were out of earshot, Melbourne said, "Not sure I believe his story. Don't have any reason to suspect him, but somethin' strange about this whole thing."

"What worries me is what're we gonna tell Tolson.

"Everything we've seen and everything we've heard."

"We haven't seen and heard enough to report," said Mel. "We don't have anything conclusive. Tolson and Hoover aren't gonna like it."

"I think Gimbel is hiding something. He's holding out on us. What about the union woman. What the hell happened to her?" Ferguson removed his hat and rubbed his sweaty scalp.

"We should watch Gimbel, see what he does."

"He can't go anywhere without us knowin', not in this town." Ferguson replaced his hat. "We better find out where he lives."

"He'll know we're tailin' 'im." Mel spit into the dust.

"Don't really matter."

"How's that?"

"Braun disappears. The woman is nowhere. Gimbel's the only connection. It'll do him good to know he's under suspicion."

"For what?"

"Conspiracy."

"Don't you think we should've told him that?" Mel eyed his partner.

"No, let 'im think about why we're out here. Let the son-of-a-bitch sweat."

"We aren't ready for a stakeout," said Mel. "We need provisions."

"Once we know where he lives, we can take care of that."

"So, I guess we follow him home."

"Too obvious," said Ferguson. "We'll check at the post office."

***

Howard had waited until he saw the receding tail dust of the Santa Fe agents' car. He knew they weren't done with him, didn't believe him. But they had no evidence and nothing to go on. He was running out of time. The evidence was still at his house.

There was only one road from the BIA headquarters that intersected with the main road one mile south of Mesa. Howard left the reservation road and drove cautiously to the main street past a few adjoining dirt tracks to adobe houses beyond the center of town. Not seeing any sign of the agents' car, he turned off onto the track that led to his. To his relief, Yelena came to the door at the sound of his approach, but did not step outside. Her smile vanished at seeing the tension on his face.

"I have to get you across the border into Mexico tonight," he said ushering her back inside. "Two agents came over from Santa Fe. They're sniffing around trying to find out what happened to Braun. We can't let them see you."

"How much do you think they know?"

"Nothing, at least about Braun. They must know about you."

"Can they arrest me?"

"They can try."

"On what charge? I haven't broken the law."

"They work for Hoover. It's his law."

"Should we go now?"

"We'll wait 'til dark. It'll be harder for them to follow us."

"Do you think they'll come here to the house?"

"They already talked to me at the reservation office. There isn't any reason for them to come here, but they're suspicious. My guess is they want to see what my next move is."

Toward midnight, Mel nudged his snoring partner awake. They had located on the main street a short distance from the dirt track that led out to Howard's adobe.

"There's a car comin'."

They stared out into the desert blackness at the dim yellow glow of approaching headlights.

"He's up to something," said Ferguson. "This hour."

Howard's car passed within fifty feet of where they were parked and turned west.

"He alone?"

"Hard to tell. Couldn't see but him. But I swear there was two people."

"We better follow him?" Ferguson started the engine.

Howard and Yelena had turned south at the west end of town.

"How far is the border?" she asked.

"About four hundred miles."

"You have enough gas to get back?"

"Three cans in the trunk. You might as well get some sleep."

"I'll doze off."

A distant spot light flashed in the sideview mirror, then was instantly gone.

"We're being followed. Those two agents from Santa Fe. Just saw their lights."

Yelena twisted around in her seat to look through the rear window. The dark shapes of the desert landscape revealed only the moving shadow of their own car wending along the single dirt road through cactus and mesquite and sharp boulders. "I don't see anything."

"Must have been on a curve, but they're back there."

"Can they do anything?"

"They can make trouble, if they catch us. They're Hoover's men."

"Will you have to fight them?"

"Have to outrun them or outsmart them. We don't want a confrontation."

"Not much of a road."

"It's the same for them. They can't go any faster than we can."

After twenty miles, Ferguson lost sight of the pinpoints of red tail lights leading them deeper into the desert terrain. "What happened? I don't see their lights."

"Lot of rocks and boulders. We know they're out there."

"They're movin' fast. Road's bad. Hard to close the distance."

After ten more miles, Ferguson said, "They're gone. I can't see any sign of 'em. Did you notice if we passed a fork or a side road somewhere?"

"Curvy as all hell," said Stuart. "If there was a turn off, I missed it."

"There's another thing."

"What's that?"

"If we keep goin' and don't find 'em, we could be stranded out here."

"How's that?"

"Run out of fuel is how. Didn't plan to drive all the way to the border, which it seems that's where they're headed." Ferguson slowed and stopped, allowing the engine to idle.

"So what do we do now?" asked Stuart. "We go back empty-handed, what're we gonna tell Tolson?"

"That they went to Mexico and we couldn't follow 'em."

"Don't look good for us."

"Don't look good for Agent Gimbel, if he comes back."

"He's not our concern."

"Nope, not anymore. Let's go back to Mesa. We'll put up at the Harvey. Go back to Santa Fe tomorrow."

Howard and Yelena waited for an hour until they saw the returning headlights of the Santa Fe agents' car pass headed north. Howard maneuvered his vehicle from where it was hidden among scrub brush and a jumbled pile of boulders and continued southward.

At four in the morning, he and Yelena crossed the border at Juarez. The train to Mexico City did not stop long at the windswept adobe town where they waited at the siding.

"I guess we won't be seeing each other again," said Howard.

"You never know," said Yelena. "Life has a way of giving us what we least expect."

Howard suddenly took her in his arms and they exchanged a gentle kiss.

"I love you, Yelena. I always have."

"I love you too, in a special sort of way."

"Take care of yourself. I'll be thinking of you. Goodbye, Yelena."

"Only for now."

He wondered what she meant as he watched her board the passenger car.

The engine belched a cloud of black smoke and the whistle blew.

She reappeared at an open window and leaned out slightly to wave. He raised his hand in farewell and remained at the siding until the train vanished into the desert.

Chapter 35
TIME AND DISTANCE

"Sit down, Agent Gimbel."

Clyde Tolson's unwavering stare followed Howard slowly lowering himself into the chair facing the assistant director's desk.

"We didn't expect to see you back here in Washington. The last we heard from the Santa Fe office you had escorted Yelena Ivanov into Mexico."

"That's true. I did take her to Mexico, according to an order from Agent Halen Braun."

"Agent Braun ordered you?"

"That's correct, sir."

"Do you have any information as to the disappearance of Agent Braun."

"As I told Agent Ferguson and Agent Stuart from the Santa Fe office, I don't know anything about his disappearance."

"Why didn't you arrest Yelena Ivanov?"

"She didn't break the law."

"You know why you should have arrested her."

"My assignment was to stop her from continuing her union activity. That is exactly what I did. She's not returning from Mexico."

Tolson shoved a copy of the Washington Post across his desk. "Did you ever talk to the man who wrote this?"

Howard picked up the newspaper and read the headline:

FBI Behind U.S. Government Corruption
In New Mexico.

"I've never seen this. I wasn't aware of it."

"It contains information that was highly confidential."

"I met the journalist a few times. He visited the BIA office and interviewed Collier."

"There are comments there that have made Director Hoover extremely angry."

Howard scanned the front page column. "Obviously the writer took some liberties being inventive with his information. This is sensationalism designed to sell newspapers and probably help his career along. He did talk extensively with Agent Braun."

"Are you saying this is Agent Braun's doing?"

"From my brief acquaintance with Agent Braun, he impressed me as being quite a story teller."

Tolson let a long silence pass between them.

"I don't know quite what we're going to do about you, Agent Gimbel. The Director and I will be discussing your future. Until you hear further from us, you may go."

Howard rose, nodded, and silently departed.

***

Howard waited until the lights went out in the house located in the next block from where he was parked on a tree-lined street. The German family lived in an older established neighborhood. They were the first on the list of 92 American citizens who had been identified as German spies. Night was the best time to conduct a raid. Suspects were not focused and could more easily be caught off guard. The element of surprise was compounded by the night. Throughout the city, Federal agents were poised to forcibly break into targeted homes and apartments and arrest husbands, wives, their children, and single men and women who had been identified. Even without evidence of treasonous acts of espionage, they were to be incarcerated in a Federal jail and turned over to immigration authorities until investigations were undertaken to prove their guilt.

The American people were outraged. The attack on Pearl Harbor had prompted the need for a gesture of immediate retribution. Since his return from New Mexico three years ago, Howard had been plunged into general intelligence work. With the outbreak of war in Europe, the major focus of the FBI had turned to the investigation of subversion, sabotage, and espionage. Agents were quickly trained in general intelligence work. European Fascists had their counterparts and supporters in the United States in the German-American Bund. A 1939 Presidential Directive strengthened the FBI's authority to investigate subversives in the United States, and Congress reinforced it by passing the Smith Act in 1940, outlawing advocacy of violent overthrow of the government.

Gimbel had been instrumental in developing informational sources, using members of fraternal and veterans' organizations. With leads developed by these intelligence networks and through their own surveillance work, Special Agents investigated potential threats to national security.

The FBI Headquarters and all 54 field offices operated around the clock and the arrests of identified aliens who threatened national security began. Internal security efforts sought potentially dangerous German, Italian, and Japanese nationals as well as native-born Americans whose beliefs and activities aided the Axis powers.

Howard waited slightly to the rear of four agents who pried the lock and broke through the front door of the house with a splintering crash that woke the unsuspecting family. One of his men turned on the lights and, with guns drawn, the other three raced up the stairs.

Howard saw an ebony black grand piano in the living room. On a nearby table next to a French horn, a violin lay cradled in its open case. A cello stood resting against its stand. Howard's memory flashed back to when he had been a boy. His father had broken into the home of the Ivanov family in this same manner and ruined their lives. He saw the agent about to topple the cello and reaching for the violin.

"Don't touch anything," Howard's voice ordered flat and hard.

The agent glanced back at him. Howard firmly shook his head. The agent backed away as the other three agents dragged a man and his wife and two daughters down the stairs. The man protested in clearly spoken English with a slight German accent. His wife and the two girls of ten and twelve years were sobbing in fear. Howard watched them being led out of the house and loaded into a waiting paddy wagon. He felt sick and saddened at what he was doing but

America could no longer reason that time and distance from German and Japanese and Italian aggression would not reach its shores and infiltrate its society. The news headlines proved this fact.

Changes in the Bureau were happening rapidly as the countries of the world reeled from the forces and magnanimity of war that decimated cities and towns and destroyed villages and farms. Thrown into the cauldron of chaos, people's lives ruptured and bled like diseased bodies.

Howard became aware of a unique contingent of agents. In South America, assisted by legal attaches, the Special Intelligence Service (SIS) established by President Roosevelt in 1940 collected and reported on information on Axis activities and worked to destroy its intelligence and propaganda networks. Several hundred thousand Germans or German descendants and numerous Japanese lived in South America. FBI agents exerted pressure against Axis communications facilities.

Yelena Ivanov had passed through Nazis organizations in Mexico and Brazil. Howard did not believe he would ever hear from her or see her again until one night he was paid a surprise visit at his home by two agents of the recently formed Office of Special Investigation.

"We're from the OSI," they briefly introduced themselves. "Name's Holmes and Seltzer."

"Come in. What can I do for you gentlemen?"

"How strong are you in staying with the Bureau? If you had a chance, would you get out?"

"I don't know what you're asking."

"The OSI broke from Hoover. You know that."

"I heard that it happened."

"We understand you know a Russian woman by the name of Yelena Ivanov."

"I know her name. She was a union organizer."

"She contacted us from Brazil. She has offered to work with us as a double agent on one condition."

Howard waited.

"She will work only with you."

***

"Why are you doing this?" Clyde Tolson queried Gimbel. "With one exception, you have a good record with the Bureau. We don't want to lose men like you. We now employ nearly 14,000 people. Four-thousand of them are agents like yourself. Why throw away your career?"

"In a way, you're not really losing me. I'm just offering my services in a different sector."

"You're not going over to the OSI!"

Howard avoided answering the question directly. "I'm loyal to the Bureau. But for personal reasons, I've made the decision to leave."

"You still haven't explained why and to what."

"I feel I've done all I can for the Bureau. Now it's time to do something for my country."

"You're joining the armed services?"

"Yes, that is where I'm going, in a manner of speaking."

"Combat?"

"Legal services. I may be in combat areas."

"Intelligence."

Howard shrugged. "I have some training in that field."

Tolson smiled, rose, and extended his hand. "On behalf of the Director and myself, I wish you a healthy and safe return."

"Thank you. Your support is appreciated."

"If you change your mind, we will always have a place for you."

"Thank you. Give my regards to the Director."

"I will certainly do that, Agent Gimbel. I certainly will."

"Goodbye." Howard turned on his heel and walked away out through the foyer and paused briefly at the desk of Helen Gandy, J. Edgar Hoover's secretary. "Goodbye, Helen." No one ever dared to call her by her first name. "It's been nice knowing you."

She stared up at him as though he were some deranged cretin.

"I'm leaving," he said, "for good."

She returned to her typing without any further acknowledgment of his existence.

He walked out the door and never looked back.

American Landscape

He walked outside and down Pennsylvania Avenue past the White House. Several minutes later, he was running along a footpath to a low bluff overlooking the Potomac. Yelena Ivanov rose from a bench where she had been waiting for him. They briefly embraced, then, holding hands like young lovers with the hope that one day they would have a normal life together, they returned to the city that had disowned them.

Bibliographical References

Evans, Harold, *The American Century*, New York, Alfred Knopf, 1998

Brown, Dee, *Bury My Heart at Wounded Knee: An Indian History of the American West,* New York, Henry Holt & Co., 1970.

Waters, Frank, *Book of The Hopi*, New York, Ballantine Books, 1974.

Gentry, Curt, *J. Edgar Hoover, The Man and His Secrets*, New York, W. W. Norton & Co., 2001.

Flower, Desmond, Reeves James, *The War 1939–1945*, New York, Harper & Row Publishers, 1988.

Kahn, David, *Hitler's Spies, German Military Intelligence in World War II*, New York, Da Capo Press, 1978.

J. Edgar Hoover, Wikipedia.

J. Edgar Hoover 1895–1972, PBS Documentary Film.

Steinbeck, John, *The Grapes of Wrath*, Penguin Classics, 2006

Nichols, K. L., *Native American Oral Poetry/Songs*, Website.

Capelin, Emily Fay, *Source of the Sacred: Navajo Corn Pollen*, A Thesis Presented to The Faculty of the Southwest Studies Program The Colorado College, May 2009.

American Landscape

The Navajo Nation, Website.

Navajo Education (History), Wikipedia.

Dunn, Roy, *Navajo Customs, Southwest Crossroads*, Website

Emma Goldman, Wikipedia.

Franklin D. Roosevelt, Wikipedia.

Eleanor Roosevelt, Wikipedia.

John Collier (Reformer), Wikipedia.

Santa Fe 5000 (2-10-4 Steam Locomotive), Wikipedia.

Dover Harbor, Pullman History, Website.

Pullman Company, Wikipedia.

Fred Harvey Company, Wikipedia.

Gray, Lauren, *Navajo Reservation Trading Posts*, New Mexico Office of The State Historian.

Chatauqua, Wikipedia.

Appalachian Mountains, Wikipedia.

.